Thirty-two year old Olivia Darling was born and raised in Cornwall. At the age of eighteen she met an Italian art student in St Ives and ran away to Tuscany in hot pursuit of him. The love affair didn't last but Olivia's sojourn in Montepulciano inspired a much more enduring passion for Vino Nobile. She lives in London.

Priceless

OLIVIA DARLING

HODDER

First published in Great Britain in 2009 by Hodder & Stoughton
An Hachette Livre UK company

1

A CIP catalogue record for this title is available from the British Library

ISBN 978 0 340 95081 4

Typeset in Jenson by Hewer Text UK Ltd, Edinburgh
Printed and bound by Clays Ltd, St Ives plc

Hodder & Stoughton policy is to use papers that are natural, renewable
and recyclable products and made from wood grown in sustainable forests.
The logging and manufacturing processes are expected to conform to
the environmental regulations of the country of origin.

Hodder & Stoughton Ltd
338 Euston Road
London NW1 3BH

www.hodder.co.uk

For Nat Wilde

Prologue

I N a small village on the south-east Mediterranean coast of Italy, in a room with windows that opened out right on to the sea, an artist was painting a portrait of a young girl. The girl was positioned at a table by the open window with a fig in her hand. The sunlight fell on her hair, turning it from plain yellow to a sheet of glittering gold. Her face was smooth and flawless, pink-cheeked and red-lipped without any need for artifice. Her expression was as sweet and calm as an angel's as she looked out on to the waves. Her name was Maria and she was modelling for a portrait of her namesake, the Virgin Mary herself, captured in a moment of quiet reflection before the annunciation.

But the thoughts that were running through the mind of the lovely Maria were more than a little at odds with the subject of the painting. Maria was thinking about the man behind the canvas, Giancarlo Ricasoli, the artist who was recording this moment for posterity. They hadn't spoken much; he had told her he preferred to work in silence. But she had heard quite a bit about him and what she knew of his reputation made her shy.

'How much longer will I have to sit like this?' she chanced to disturb him as she saw her father's boat come into the harbour.

'Are you uncomfortable?' Ricasoli asked.

'No,' she said. 'But I will have to go to mass. It isn't long now.'

'Ah, church,' said the artist. 'Of course.'

Maria had heard that Giancarlo Ricasoli didn't go to mass. Apparently the priest had given him a special dispensation on the grounds that he'd already spent as much time in the church as an ordinary member of the flock might spend there in a lifetime while he was painting the fresco on the ceiling. Having promised that he would provide a beautiful Madonna and Child for the priest's private residence as soon as he had finished this annunciation for which Maria now posed, Ricasoli had been assured that no more would be said about the matter. At least not officially.

Maria wished she had a talent that could allow her to be excused another hour in that dark old church. But dodging mass was the least of it. She'd heard other things about the artist too. She'd heard that in Florence he had been responsible for the ruination of not one but *five* young women. All had been models for his interpretation of the meeting of Christ and Mary Magdalene. All of them were virgins when they were first summoned to his studio and fallen women by the time they left.

And so Maria was horrified when it was first suggested that she sit for this painting of the Virgin Mary before the Annunciation, as were her parents. They too knew of the artist's reputation. Wasn't it true that five angry fathers had chased Ricasoli out of Florence? But then the artist told Maria's father how much he would be willing to pay for the privilege of painting his daughter. It was more than her father could hope to make in a year. And the priest had vouched for the artist, saying that he was a changed man since he'd come to their little village by the sea. 'I believe he is a good and proper man at heart,' the priest said, after beating Ricasoli at cards. So it was agreed that Maria would sit for the painting that was destined for the walls of a church near Naples. Her aunt Stefania, her father's sister, would chaperone.

Right then, however, Maria's aunt was doing a pretty bad job. Ricasoli had offered the older woman a glass of wine with their simple lunch and she had taken it. And another. Now Stefania was snoring lightly on a couch at the other end of the studio, in a most undignified position, shoes off, bare legs akimbo and her skirts hiked up to her thighs.

'I should make a sketch,' Ricasoli joked. 'I need someone posed like that for my depiction of the fallen in purgatory.'

'Don't you dare,' said Maria. 'She would be so upset.'

'Ah, sweet Maria,' Ricasoli sighed. 'Always thinking of other people. I hope that I can capture your good pure heart in this painting of mine.'

The way he said 'good pure heart' made Maria wonder if Ricasoli really thought such a thing was an asset.

While he dabbed away at something on the canvas; a crooked line or a smudge of colour gone awry, Maria regarded him closely, grabbing the chance to stare as closely as he had stared at her.

He was handsome. And he had a sophistication rarely seen in the local men folk of her little fishing town. When he wasn't dressed in his artist's smock, grubbily colourful where he'd wiped his brushes clean, he was adorned in the finest silks. He wore the latest fashions from Florence and Rome. Maria had often spied on him from her bedroom window, which had a good view of the road down to the harbour where he took his evening promenade. Of course, it hadn't occurred to her that was how he had first noticed her with her shining blonde hair and chosen her for his innocent Mary.

What was it like to be ruined? Maria wondered. How did it happen? As Ricasoli turned his back to her while he mixed some more pigment, Maria regarded the artist again. He was a surprisingly big man. He had a way of carrying himself that made him seem lithe and slim, but as he bent over the pot of ground lapis with which he was to paint her robes she could see that his shoulders were wide and strong. His buttocks, in their tight buckskin trousers, were square and powerful. Utterly masculine. Maria had a sudden flashing vision of what they might look like naked. Pumping. She had seen two people making love once, in a field behind the village. The woman's small heels pressed into the man's buttocks as he thrust into her. Suddenly Maria found herself imagining her own feet against the artist's flesh.

He had finished mixing his paints. On the couch, her aunt was still fast asleep.

'Are you ready to continue?' he asked.

Maria nodded as she gave one last stretch to get the blood back into her limbs. Ricasoli's eyes travelled the length of her body as she did so and Maria luxuriated in his look for as long as it took her to remember that such vanity was almost certainly a sin. She sat back down at the table and picked up the fig she had held in her hand for the last three days. The fruit was warm and sticky; its ripe skin was stretched tight and ready to burst. Maria assumed the position as closely as she remembered it.

'Not quite,' said Ricasoli. He stepped up onto the podium on which the table had been placed to make the best of the light coming through the window and the shadows and shards of brilliance it cast upon Maria's face. 'A little more to your left,' he told her. Maria shifted in her seat. 'No. Too far. Wait. You were here. More like this.'

Very gently, he took her chin in his hand and tilted her face towards him. But when he had her where he thought she should be, he did not immediately take his hand away. Maria looked at him with huge unblinking eyes. He had never before laid a hand on her to help her into her pose. Ordinarily, her aunt Stefania would be standing right beside him, ensuring that such a thing didn't happen. From the back of the studio, the sleeping chaperone let out an enormous snort.

Maria and the artist jumped apart. Was that snore enough to have woken her up? It seemed not.

'You moved,' Ricasoli said to Maria. 'Now I will have to put you into position all over again.' Once more he took her chin in his hand and tilted her face towards the light. But this time he did not stop when she was in the perfect position for the painting. He kept on tilting her face until they were almost nose-to-nose. She let out a small gasp of surprise as he said, 'I'm going to do it.'

'Do what?' she asked in a squeak.

'This.'

He kissed her.

Maria had never been kissed by a man before. Not like that. She had wondered if she ever would be and, if she was, whether she would be good at it. It turned out that her older sister was right. It came to her as though she had always been kissing. Maria let herself fall into the tender trap.

The artist's lips were so warm and gentle. As he kissed her, his fingers explored her long, fine neck, her bare shoulders, her soft décolletage. Never touched before.

Maria felt a blush rise on her skin. Her heart beat faster. Her head and stomach felt light. As Ricasoli continued to touch her, she realised she wanted to throw her clothes off and feel his hands on every part of her. She trembled as she felt her body begin to unfurl for love. At the same time she squeezed the fig so hard it split open in her palm.

On the couch in the corner, her aunt slept on. Ricasoli held out his hand and invited Maria to step behind the screen where she changed out of her own clothes and into the Virgin's robes each morning.

'What if she wakes up?'

'We'll say you were washing your hands,' said Ricasoli, as he sucked fig juice from her forefinger.

'I'm going to be ruined,' thought Maria.

And it was wonderful.

Chapter One

$\mathcal{I}$T was the moment he sucked whipped cream from her fingers that Lizzy Duffy realised her relationship with her boss had changed irrevocably. Subsequently, losing her virginity to him was either the best – or the worst – career move she could possibly have made. As she lay on her back in Nat Wilde's bed, worrying at a cuticle and examining a cobweb in the corner of his bedroom ceiling, Lizzy decided that it was probably her worst move. And staying the night had compounded it. She remembered something she'd read in some magazine: don't act clingy after the first time you have sex. It was clingy, wasn't it, staying the night in the hope of a reassuring cuddle? Nat had fallen asleep right after he'd come. Lizzy knew she should have got straight up and caught a taxi home right then to prove she wasn't bothered. Beside her, Nat slumbered on, seemingly unmoved by the same dilemma.

What on earth had possessed her? Fact was, Lizzy knew exactly what had possessed her. Nat Wilde had possessed her the moment she first laid eyes on him at her interview for a position in the Old Masters and Nineteenth-Century department at Ludbrook's, the auction house on New Bond Street. Fresh from her master's degree in art history at the Courtauld, Lizzy had prepared a pretty speech about her passion for nineteenth-century British watercolourists. But she didn't have an opportunity to deliver it. Nat Wilde was running late. He breezed into the Ludbrook's office fifteen minutes after the interview had been due to start. He was slightly inebriated, having lunched with his best friend Harry Brown, head of Ludbrook's' department of fine wines, at their gentleman's club on St. James's. Nat picked Lizzy's CV up from the desk and seemed unable to focus on it. Then he looked at her, focused very well on the hem of her skirt, and said, 'You've got the right degree, you're passably pretty and you wear short skirts. You're hired.'

The right thing at that moment would have been for Lizzy to take offence but before she could open her mouth to protest at such a superficial and sexist dismissal of her proper talents, Nat Wilde smiled at her. And it was the kind of smile that made her feel he had been joking about her being 'passably pretty'. That was an understatement, of course. He found her far more attractive than that. Lizzy couldn't help but smile back. She was smitten.

'Your first assignment,' said Nat. 'Tell me about this little painting right here.'

Her heart still fluttering like a hummingbird with the hiccups, Lizzy followed Nat Wilde across the room. Balanced on a shelf was a small watercolour of a farmer bringing cows in from the field at the end of the day.

'Artist?'

'Easy,' Lizzy trotted out the name.

'Real?'

Lizzy peered closely. 'I think so. The only way to know is to see the signature. But he wouldn't have signed a piece this small on the front. You'd need to turn it over and . . .'

'Already done that,' said Nat. 'Put a reserve on it of ten to twelve grand. What do you think?'

'I think that's just about right,' said Lizzy. 'How about you?'

'I think you and I are going to work together very well.' And they did.

Never before had Lizzy found getting up for work to be such a pleasure. She was thrilled to be working with the art that she loved surrounded by fellow enthusiasts. She had long been determined to have a great career in an auction house but now she had an added incentive to sparkle. Each morning she veritably sprang out of bed at the sound of her alarm. She spent at least an hour getting ready, blow-drying her fine blonde hair into something resembling a do. And oh how her efforts were rewarded. Nat Wilde could make her day with a wink and the winks were plentiful. Nat and Lizzy had flirted like crazy for the past six months. And now here she was. In his bed.

That afternoon's sale at Ludbrook's had been a barnstormer. Lot after lot bust through the ceiling prices Nat had predicted. And finally, Nat achieved a price of seven figures for an early nineteenth-century oil. It went to a Russian collector. All the good papers would cover the news.

After such a successful day, Nat announced that the entire team deserved a treat. He utilised his direct line to the maitre d' at The Ivy and booked a table for eight o'clock.

'Sit here,' said Nat to Lizzy, patting the seat beside him. 'You're my right-hand girl and I want you on my right hand.'

Lizzy settled into the seat, catching the envious glances from the other girls in her department – Olivia and Sarah Jane – as they found themselves at the other end of the table, between the two bespectacled boys, Marcus and James.

'Champagne!' Nat announced. He ordered a bottle of Champagne Arsenault's Clos De Larmes, which Lizzy understood was the good stuff. It certainly went down easily. They polished off six bottles between them, the restaurant's entire stock.

'It's on old John Ludbrook's account,' Nat reminded them. 'And you deserve it!'

He toasted the team, as one and individually.

'Olivia,' he said. 'You are the goddess of typing. Sarah Jane, without you, my mailing list would be nothing.'

Lizzy felt herself colour crimson when Nat praised her pretty blue eyes. 'Which are so good at spotting a masterpiece!'

Dessert arrived. Lizzy chose sticky toffee pudding with cream, getting some on her finger as she pulled the dish towards her. Quick as a flash Nat grabbed her hand and stuck his finger in her mouth.

'Don't want to waste any,' he said.

Lizzy almost crawled under the table for shame. She was hugely relieved no one else seemed to have noticed.

'How are you getting home?' Nat asked Lizzy as they were collecting their coats.

'I'll get a cab,' she said.

'Where to? Hammersmith, isn't it? My place is on the way there. We'll share a ride.'

They started kissing as the cab sailed past the roundabout at Hyde Park Corner. By the time they got to Nat's flat in South Kensington, Lizzy knew she wouldn't be taking the taxi on.

'Do you have any cash?' Nat asked. 'I left my last tenner as a tip.'

Lizzy duly dug out her last twenty and handed it to the driver.

'Thank you. You're a poppet. I'll pay you back tomorrow.'

Nat took her by the hand and led her into the shared lobby of the mansion block in which he lived. They continued to kiss in the mirrored lift. Nat's tongue flickered inside her mouth like an eel in a bucket. Lizzy smiled at her reflection over Nat's shoulder as he nibbled at her neck. She sighed with delight as Nat slipped his hand up her cashmere sweater and started to fumble with the clasp at the back of her bra.

Once inside the flat they went straight to the bedroom. Lizzy's nerves were as taut as violin strings as her clothes fell to the floor. Would Nat still want her when he saw her naked body? Nat's growl soon told her that he did.

'Oh. Yes,' Lizzy sighed as Nat cupped his hands around her bare breasts and fiddled with her nipples. As he sucked each one of them in turn, he somehow managed to slide her little white cotton knickers down as far as her knees. While Nat turned his attention to Lizzy's buttocks, the knickers dropped to her ankles and Lizzy kicked them off. Now she was completely in the raw but Nat was still fully clothed. He soon remedied that.

While Lizzy arranged herself on the sheets in what she hoped was an alluring manner, Nat divested himself of his tie, his shirt, his trousers and underpants as though the clothes were on fire. There was a brief and awful moment when Lizzy thought Nat might actually be intending to ravage her with his socks still on, but he remembered just in time and pulled them off as well. They went flying across the room. One ended up dangling from the standard lamp.

Nat dived onto the bed, narrowly avoiding head-butting Lizzy in the nose as he did so. Lizzy hadn't really thought about what would happen next. More kissing, she hoped. She wanted to be covered in kisses from head to toe. Top to bottom. Indeed, it seemed that Nat was already very fond of her bottom. It wasn't long before he flipped her over onto her tummy and was bestowing naughty little love-bites to her shapely pink buttocks. So far, so silly. Lizzy giggled as Nat jiggled the spare flesh on her bum. But then things turned rather more serious. He stuck his hand between her legs. She felt his fingers groping for a way inside. And then, suddenly, he lay fully on top of her, squashing her face into the mattress. She felt his erection – which she hadn't really seen yet or got to know – pressing hard against the place where his fingers had been moments before.

'Nat, I . . .'

She meant to tell him but before she knew it, the inevitable was already happening. Lizzy drew breath sharply at the first thrust. Fortunately, there were only five more of those before Nat came with a terrifying bellow that made Lizzy respond with a cry of her own.

'Good for you?' he asked as he pulled out.

Good? Well, it hadn't hurt as much as she expected. And there was no blood. If she was honest, most of Lizzy's enjoyment of the moment had been stymied at the thought that she might leave a dirty red stain on Nat's pure white sheets. But she didn't. She checked. There was no evidence whatsoever that anything monumental had taken place.

Fact was, Nat didn't even know she was a virgin. Lizzy thought he might have guessed, but, if he had, he didn't say anything. He just rolled off her and fell asleep. His face as he lay dreaming was youthful and perfectly untroubled. Unlike Lizzy's.

She lay awake all night, staring at the bare, plain walls of Nat's bedroom (utterly typical for the home of a forty-something divorced guy), replaying the event over and over, wondering and worrying if she had done what was expected. And then, of course, there was the question of contraception. They hadn't used any. Would her local chemist stock the morning-after pill? What were the rules about taking it? How had she got to twenty-six without actually knowing this stuff? How had she got to twenty-six without losing her virginity anyway? She shook her head in disbelief as the disapproving face of her only serious boyfriend came to mind. He had been president of the Christian Union at university and had flat out refused to have sex outside marriage. They broke up when Lizzie was twenty-five. There had been opportunities since but by then Lizzie had decided that getting to your mid-twenties without having done it was just plain weird and she didn't want to have to explain so she avoided the issue. And after all that she lost it to her boss. In just eleven minutes from taxi to finish. Was that it?

Finally, at seven in the morning, Lizzy decided it was time to go.

'See you in the office at nine,' she said brightly. Nat nodded groggily. Lizzy bounced out of bed and headed for the tube and a change of clothes in her grotty flat in Hammersmith. She was borne all the way there on a tide of regret. And so preoccupied was she with her big faux pas that it wasn't until she got to the office that she remembered it was a Saturday.

Chapter Two

 P.'

Carrie Klein issued her first order of the day.

'Wha . . . ?'

The young man in her bed sat up against the pillows and rubbed his eyes.

'What time is it?' he asked.

'Seven thirty,' she said.

'Seven thirty? But it's a Sunday.'

'Makes no difference to me. I have things to do today and I need you out of the apartment while I'm doing them.'

'Carrie,' Jed opened his arms. 'There is nothing that really needs to be done at seven thirty on a Sunday morning. You need to chill out more, babe. Let me help you. Come back to bed.'

Carrie eyed Jed's firm chest dispassionately. He was a male model. There was no doubt that he was beautiful but lately Carrie had been wondering if this relationship was working for her. It was a funny thing. A female model was the Holy Grail as a partner for a high-flying guy but what high-flying woman should be with a man who pouted for a living?

'Jed, I have a position of responsibility,' she reminded him as he tried to slip a hand inside the folds of her dressing gown.

'I can think of several irresponsible positions I'd like to see you in . . .'

'Not now,' she insisted. Jed never seemed to understand when she was being serious.

Carrie Klein was second in command in the Old Masters department at Ehrenpreis. Of all the auction houses in New York, Ehrenpreis was the newest. Founded in the 1960s, it didn't have centuries of history like Christie's, Sotheby's or Ludbrook's but it had already had a reputation for excellence. Recently, the house had held some very high-profile sales that had set tongues wagging. The older houses at last admitted they had something to worry about.

Carrie had begun her career in Christie's. When she moved to Ehrenpreis aged thirty-one, leap-frogging many of her peers, some of her former colleagues had tried to belittle the appointment, saying that there was no way Carrie would have got such a senior position in any 'proper house'. She was determined to prove them wrong. And that meant working hard. Working on the weekends if she had to. And she did have to.

'Jed, please don't make this difficult for me,' she said. 'I have a big auction coming up next week. There are people I need to talk to. People in different time zones. You do realise that they're already halfway through Monday in Asia?'

'Then call them on their Tuesday. They can wait.'

'They won't wait.' Her mobile phone vibrated to let her know she had voicemail. 'See?' she said. 'I've got to get going.' She tugged on a turtleneck sweater.

Carrie sat down on the edge of the bed and began to roll her stockings up over her long slim legs. Jed moved so that he was right behind her. He started to knead her shoulders and much as she didn't want to, Carrie found herself responding to his expert touch. To supplement his income as a model-cum-actor, Jed had learned the art of Swedish massage. He made home visits to society ladies all over Manhattan and was very much in demand. He had a real talent for touch.

'Jed . . .' Carrie began to protest but now he had moved on from massaging her shoulders to kissing what small part of her neck he could reach. Before she knew what was happening, Carrie lifted her arms and let Jed pull her turtleneck sweater off over her head.

'Oh. All right . . . I guess it *is* the weekend. But just thirty minutes, OK?'

'I can do a lot in thirty minutes,' Jed grinned at her. She knew it.

Carrie let Jed unpin her long blonde hair. She shivered as the silky soft tresses settled on the bare skin of her back above her dove-grey slip.

'Arms up again,' Jed instructed.

Soon her slip was on the floor, too.

'Lie down,' he said.

Carrie lay back on the pillows and tried to look a little more relaxed even if she wasn't exactly feeling it. Jed, who had often told her that he worshipped every inch of her, seemed determined to prove it that morning. He started at her feet.

'You have the most beautiful feet,' he told her as he kissed the arch of each perfectly pedicured foot in turn. Then he placed another kiss on each ankle. He laid a little path of kisses up her shins to her knees.

'Great knees,' he said with a smile.

'Behave,' Carrie warned him. 'You know I'm self-conscious about my knees.'

'They are my favourite part of you,' Jed responded.

'Just keep kissing me.'

Jed moved on to her thighs. He traced a line from her left knee to her hip with his tongue, and then repeated the move on the other side. With gentle hands he parted her legs. He dipped his head and nuzzled the soft triangle of her pubic hair.

'Feeling better yet?' he asked.

'Much,' she said, as she felt his warm breath on her clitoris. 'I might have to let you have forty-five minutes instead.'

'I'll make the most of it,' Jed promised.

But then the telephone in the hall started ringing. Carrie immediately tensed up.

'Ignore it,' said Jed. 'Just ignore it.'

Carrie tried. She lay back in the pillows again and closed her eyes and tried to concentrate on nothing else but the feeling of Jed's tongue on her clitoris, but it was no good. It wasn't working. Soon she was biting her lip with anxiety. She had turned the ringer on the phone beside the bed to silent, but the set in the hall rang out loud enough to keep her from all thoughts of the erotic. And then her cell phone joined in, vibrating urgently on the nightstand.

'Stop!' she pushed Jed away.

'For fuck's sake.'

'I'm sorry,' she said. 'But whoever it is has been trying every way they can to get hold of me. It must be important.'

'What?' Jed snapped. 'What on earth can be more important than letting me pleasure you?'

'Jed, I will make it up to you,' she said as she simultaneously pulled on her dressing gown and checked the messages on her cell phone.

'I don't know if you'll have the chance,' said Jed, hopping out of bed and searching the floor around it for his own clothes.

Carrie nodded vaguely. Already absorbed in her voicemail messages, she didn't hear Jed's threat. She waved him in the direction of the kitchen.

'There's juice in the refrigerator,' she said.

'I'll get some on my way home.'

He left, slamming the door as he went.

Carrie hardly noticed. She was already calling her boss.

'I'm sorry. I would have picked up but I was on a call to Asia,' she lied.

'Don't worry about that,' said her boss Andrew Carter. 'But I need you in the office right away. There's an emergency. You know that small Constable in next week's sale?'

'The one with the sheep in the stream?'

'Exactly. I just got a call from a guy in England, tells me he's looking at the *exact* same painting hanging on the wall in the study of a stately home where he's on a shooting weekend.'

'F—.' Carrie swallowed a swear word. 'And he thinks it's real?'

'He does. And as long as I've known him, he's never been wrong. Where did ours come from?'

Carrie sat down heavily on her sofa as though she were receiving bad news about her health while Andrew ran through the nightmarish details. His informant was one of the UK's most respected experts on the artist in question. If anyone knew the real thing, it was he.

'Shit.' This time Carrie couldn't keep the expletive in.

'Exactly,' said her boss.

Jed's attempt to get Carrie's morning off to a good start was all but forgotten now. She closed her eyes and let the horror wash over her. She had consigned a fake.

Chapter Three

SERENA Macdonald could only dream about waking up next to some hot young guy who wanted to give her a shoulder massage. That morning, as had been the case most mornings for the past few months, she awoke to the sound of a small pink puppet making farting noises. She opened one eye to see her five-year-old daughter Katie sitting on the end of the bed, absorbed in *CeeBeebies* on the television Serena had inherited from her kindly brother.

'Morning, Mummy,' said Katie, without turning round.

'Morning, sweetheart.'

'Breakfast?' Katie suggested.

Serena glanced at the clock. It was half past six in the morning. 'Jeez,' she sighed. As an artist, Serena had always considered people who got up before ten deliberately to have lost the plot. But it was Monday. And a school day. And now she was one of those people.

Serena snaked one bare arm out from beneath the duvet and felt around on the floor for the jeans and jumper she had been wearing for the past four days. There was no way she was getting out of bed without dressing first. It was icy cold in that farmhouse. Cornwall? It may as well have been Siberia.

Serena had grown up in Cornwall. She'd had what anyone would describe as an idyllic childhood but, all the same, she'd been only too eager to leave the county and head for London at the first possible opportunity. She went to the Chelsea College of Art and Design and after that worked in the art departments of a few private schools. And London was where she met Tom, her soon-to-be-ex-husband. Serena often thought about that moment when Tom walked into her life. The second she laid eyes on him, she had a feeling that he was going to play a big part in proceedings from that day forward. How had she failed to foresee that ten years after Tom asked her to marry him (on their first passionate date), he would be shacked up with someone else?

The day on which Tom asked for a divorce was as clear in her mind as the day they met. She'd sensed that something was wrong as he walked into the kitchen. His tie was askew. He looked as though he had been wrestling a tiger rather than pushing paper at his banking job in the City.

'I'll fallen in love,' he said. 'With someone else . . .'

It was the last thing any wife wants to hear.

It got worse. It transpired that the woman Tom had fallen in love with was his boss's wife. Serena was stunned when she discovered her rival's identity. They'd met a few times, as corporate functions and Tom had always been quite scathing about the woman: a social X-ray transplanted from New York who spent her days shopping and meeting her superannuated 'girlfriends' for lunch. Donna Harvey was always immaculately groomed. Hair, nails, whiter than white teeth . . . She dressed in that way only American women of a certain social status do. It seemed she had exchanged her jeans for a Chanel suit and pearls the moment she left grad school and would not change out of them again until they were fitting her up for her shroud.

'She makes me feel so unkempt!' said Serena, after one particularly tortuous dinner party. 'You must be so ashamed of me.'

'Nonsense,' Tom had said that night. 'You are a thousand times sexier than she will ever be. I bet she's the kind of woman who takes a shower before and after she shags.'

Well, now he would know for sure, thought Serena bitterly.

Naturally, Tom's boss didn't take the news all that well either. Though technically he couldn't sack Tom for shagging his wife, he made it practically impossible for Tom to stay. Tom leapt at the chance to take redundancy. But there was no fabulous redundancy package. Tom's boss moved back to New York as soon as he could, leaving Donna in the house in South Kensington. Tom moved in.

'We can't afford to keep the house in Fulham, Serena. I'm sorry. I've got no money coming in. We've got to put it on the market. Start looking for something else for you and Katie. You should be able to get two bedrooms in Stockwell.'

Serena quailed at the thought of such a rough neighbourhood. 'You want me to live in *Stockwell* while you're living it up in your love pad in South Ken? For fuck's sake, Tom, ask *her* for the mortgage money.'

'I can't. I'm sorry. It could prejudice her settlement. I'm doing my best.'

'Well, if this is your best . . . I hope you can hold your head up when you explain to your daughter that she had to move into some flea-infested pit because you couldn't keep your dick in your pants.'

There was no way that Serena was going to move into some two-bedroom flat on an estate she was afraid to walk through in the daylight but she couldn't afford anything big enough somewhere nice. After viewing a couple of shoeboxes in SW6, Serena bowed to the inevitable. The only option was to move out of London altogether. She started looking around Guildford, thinking she should try to stay within an hour's distance of Tom so that he could see Katie whenever he wanted. But the sad truth was that, even though he lived just a couple of tube stops away and, in theory, had nothing to do all day in his state of unemployment, Tom wasn't making much effort to see Katie at all.

The final straw came when Serena needed Tom to look after Katie one Wednesday evening while she attended a meeting at the local college where she was hoping to teach a figure-drawing course to help cover the rising cost of groceries.

'I can't baby-sit,' he said. 'Donna's giving a dinner.'

'I'm not asking you to *baby-sit*, Tom. I'm asking you to look after your own daughter. To be a dad, for once.'

'I'm sorry,' he said hopelessly. 'She's invited someone who might be a good contact for me. I can't take Katie. It's just not going to work.'

'Too right,' said Serena. This arrangement wasn't working out at all. There and then Serena decided she would no longer run her life for Tom's convenience. The following day she started browsing the Internet for property in Cornwall.

And then – finally – she had a stroke of luck. Her brother Joe called. His high-flying wife Helena's company were sending her to Hong Kong for a couple of years and he was going too, meaning they would have no time at all to use their house in the country.

'It's all yours, sis,' he said.

Serena and Katie moved to Cornwall just before Christmas. Sure, Tom protested at the thought that his daughter would be so far away but he didn't come up with an alternative. And when the day came for Serena and Katie to hand over the Fulham house to the nice young couple who had bought it, Tom was nowhere to be seen. Donna's concierge service arranged for a removal van to pick up what remained of Tom's chattels and take them to her sterile South Kensington mansion, where even the books on the shelves had been chosen by an interior designer for their covers rather than their content. Tom had told Serena she could keep all the furniture. He even left behind his favourite leather chair. The one he'd bought with his first pay packet. She knew it had nothing to do with being fair however. As she thanked him, Serena could hear Donna's voice in her head.

'You think I'm going to have that filthy chair in my salon?'

That Christmas was not the usual festive occasion. Serena forced herself to go out and buy a tree for Katie's sake. She bought a little chicken rather than a turkey for lunch. Serena had worried that Katie would be miserable spending Christmas day without her father but the ridiculously extravagant gifts he sent seemed to make up for his absence. Katie spent New Year in London with Tom and Donna. Having spent the evening absolutely alone, Serena toasted herself with a cup of tea as the old year turned into the new. Alcohol seemed too risky while she was feeling so very down.

It seemed too much to hope that the New Year would be better but she prayed for it all the same.

About a week into January, one of Serena's new neighbours dropped by to introduce herself. Serena liked Louisa Trebarwen at once. Not least because she brought with her home-made chocolate cookies.

'I'm from next door,' said Louisa.

She didn't have to introduce herself. Serena knew of her already. The house next door was called Trebarwen and Serena had heard plenty about its chatelaine. Louisa lived in the enormous house on her own. She was in her late seventies but still slim, sprightly and very elegant indeed. That afternoon she wore a neat skirt and a Hermès scarf around her neck. Serena glanced down at her own jeans and felt ashamed.

'Is this a good time?' Louisa asked.

'I . . . er . . . Of course.' Might as well let the woman in now, Serena thought. The house was a tip but it was unlikely to get better. At least she could realistically claim unfinished unpacking as an excuse for the disarray.

But Louisa Trebarwen seemed oblivious to the mess around her. She perched on one of the high stools next to the breakfast bar and chatted about the weather while Serena made tea in the pot she never used.

'What a lovely painting of your daughter!' Louisa admired the little picture on the sitting-room wall. 'Where did you find the artist? I've been looking for someone to paint my two for the past five years. This is the first portrait I've seen that doesn't look as though you had it done by one of those caricature chaps in Leicester Square.'

'Thank you.'

'So, are you going to tell me who painted it?'

'Actually,' Serena looked down at her shoes a little shyly. 'It was me.'

'You painted that picture?'

'I did.'

'Wow. I mean, Helena told me that you had been to art school but . . . gosh. It's like an old master.'

'That was the idea,' said Serena. 'I spent a bit of time in Florence after I graduated, getting to learn the traditional techniques.'

'Well, it was certainly time well spent,' said Louisa with real admiration. 'I'm in awe.'

'Oh, please . . . It's not so good. I knocked it out in a couple of hours.'

'No, Serena. You must not belittle your talent. You really have something. Will you paint my babies for me?'

Serena started to shake her head. It was one thing painting her own daughter for herself but she couldn't imagine painting Louisa's children. She hadn't painted properly in a long while. When she left work to go on maternity leave, Serena told herself that she would soon pick up her paintbrushes again, but the reality was that she simply didn't have time. Before the baby was born, she spent all her time getting ready for the new arrival. And after the baby was born . . . well, finding a moment to sleep became a far greater priority.

Later, Serena had wanted to go back to work but Tom insisted there was no need. He'd had a promotion. He was earning enough to support them both. Besides, if Serena went back to work they would have to get proper childcare, which would all but wipe out the money she earned anyway.

'And I don't like the idea of my daughter being looked after by strangers,' he added. 'That's not going to happen to you.' He kissed Katie on the head.

He seemed to have forgotten about that little promise. How could Serena be expected to support herself without going back to work and leaving Katie in the care of a stranger now?

'I would pay you,' Louisa interrupted Serena's thoughts.

'I really couldn't accept any money,' Serena said, fearing that she would only have to give it back when Louisa saw the result.

'But you must. Serena, I hate to be presumptuous but Helena has told me all about your situation. That terrible feckless husband of yours going off with another woman.'

Serena blushed.

'I know it hurts, my dear.' Louisa placed a hand on Serena's arm. 'It happened to me. And because it happened to me, I know there is no place for moping around. You have to pick yourself up as quickly as you can. And that means earning some money of your own. I am willing to pay you a thousand pounds for your trouble. Please don't turn me down.'

Serena opened her mouth to protest.

Louisa misread her hesitation. 'Was that insultingly low? How about one thousand five hundred? Two?'

'Mrs Trebarwen . . .'

'Call me Louisa.'

'Louisa, I can't take your money. Heaven knows I would love to. I can't deny I need it. But this little painting of my daughter. It was a fluke. I don't know how I managed to get such a good likeness. I'm out of practice. This was my first attempt having not picked up a paintbrush for years. It was lucky. I suppose it helped that I know the subject's face better than I know my own. I promise you would be disappointed if I tried to do portraits of your sons.'

'My sons?' Louisa Trebarwen gave a little giggle. 'Who said anything about my sons? Darling, I don't want portraits of those great ugly lummoxes. They both grew out of their looks a very long time ago. Serena, you'll have to get used to me. When I refer to my "babies", I am talking about my dogs.'

Dogs were an altogether different matter. Serena could easily paint dogs. Later that same afternoon, when she had picked up Katie from school, Serena dropped by Trebarwen House to meet her new subjects. Louisa was delighted to meet Katie and Katie was instantly smitten with Louisa's beloved pets. They were two rather regal-looking greyhounds, called Berkeley and Blackwater Bess.

'I got them from a greyhound rescue charity,' Louisa explained. 'They both raced when they were young but now they've retired they're actually the ideal companions for older people like me. They don't need half so much exercise as you would imagine.'

As if on cue, Berkeley opened his mouth and curled his tongue in an extravagant yawn.

'How would you like to paint them?' Louisa asked. 'You're the artist so I'm giving you free rein.'

Serena thought for a moment. 'How about I paint them together, standing at the top of the steps leading down to the garden with a stormy sky in the background. A cloudy sky would be the perfect way to highlight the sheeny grey of their coats.'

'That sounds wonderful,' said Louisa.

Serena set to work that very day. While Louisa took Katie all over the house and even let her ride the delicate old rocking horse that had carried Trebarwen children since the nineteenth century, Serena got out her somewhat out-dated digital camera and took a few snaps of the dogs. Then she headed outside and took some more snaps of the garden to help her make a start on the portrait's composition. There was little hope that the dogs would stand still on the step for real. It was hard enough to get them to stand at all. They really were the most amazingly lazy creatures.

A week later, Serena had completed a number of preliminary sketches and let Louisa choose the composition she liked best. Then it was time to transfer the sketches on to canvas. Serena asked Louisa how big the painting should be. She would order the canvas online.

'Hmmm. Actually I was wondering if you could paint over this?' Louisa asked as she produced a Victorian portrait of a rather dour-looking man.

'But that . . . I can't . . .'

'It's not a family portrait,' Louisa explained. 'I think I found him at a fete in 1973.'

Louisa quickly became a friend. Serena set up her easel in the drawing room of the big house so that she could look out on the garden as she filled in the background. Louisa was always happy to have Katie around. Katie was delighted to have so many dusty old rooms to roam in.

'I rarely see my grandchildren,' she sighed. 'My eldest son's wife doesn't like me. God knows if the youngest will ever breed. He doesn't seem to be able to commit to any one woman for more than a month. He takes after his father. Couldn't keep his pecker in his pants for a minute, that one . . .'

It was odd but listening to Louisa's stories about her feckless ex-husband was strangely comforting. Serena liked

Louisa very much and the knowledge that she too had been a victim of infidelity reassured Serena that it happened to the best of people. It didn't mean that she was a loser.

And so Serena began to feel better. For the first time since Tom walked into the kitchen and announced that he wanted out of their marriage, Serena felt as though she had reason to smile. Katie was happy. Serena had a great new friend in Louisa. And then there was her work. She had forgotten the most important reward of painting: a sense of flow that pushed all other concerns to the back of her mind if only for a little while.

The portrait of the dogs turned out very well. Though she was usually her own harshest critic, Serena allowed herself to be pleased with the result of her hard work. She had been right with her initial thoughts for the piece. The stormy sky was a perfect backdrop for the regally silky grey of the dogs' glossy coats. Serena thought perhaps that even the dogs' faces had turned out better than she hoped. There was individuality to them. Louisa could tell at once which was which.

'I love it,' said Louisa. 'You are an absolute marvel.'

She enveloped Serena in an extravagantly perfumed hug. 'I will hang it above the fireplace right here in the drawing room.'

'Really?' Serena was stunned. That would mean moving a painting of Louisa's two sons as small children. 'But that's such a wonderful picture. Are you sure?'

'Absolutely. I'm bored to death of that old thing. And my beautiful babies need a truly regal setting.'

'Well, OK,' said Serena.

'Help me hang it now,' Louisa asked.

*   *   *

The following weekend, Louisa's elder son Mark dropped by.

'What happened to the painting of me and Julian?' he asked the moment he stepped into the drawing room. 'Where did you get that bloody awful dog picture? How much did it cost you? Tell me it isn't . . .'

'It's Berkeley and Blackwater Bess,' Louisa told him proudly. 'Since my real children only visit when they want something, I decided to have my new babies on the wall instead.'

'Mother. For heaven's sake.'

'It's rather wonderful, don't you think? The girl who moved into the cottage painted it. She trained in London and Florence.'

'I don't care where she trained. I can't believe you would take down a portrait of your own children and put a picture of your bloody rescue greyhounds in its place!'

'Well, you will be able to put yourself and your brother back up there when I'm gone,' said Louisa. 'And don't worry,' she added. 'The dogs may have replaced you above the fireplace but they haven't replaced you in my last will and testament. Yet. You'll have to keep visiting for a few more months, at least.'

'Years, more like,' said Mark, barely disguising his annoyance. 'I have no doubt that you will outlive us all.'

Chapter Four

I T turned out that Mark Trebarwen was wrong. Just over a month after that exchange, Louisa passed away in her sleep. It was Serena who found the body. She and Louisa had been planning to drive down to St Ives together, to see a new exhibition at the Cornish outpost of the Tate. Thank goodness Katie was safely in a holiday let in Newquay with her father, who had actually bothered to turn up to do his share of the half-term 'baby-sitting'.

Serena was devastated. Like Louisa's sons, she had assumed that she had years yet in which to get to know her lovely neighbour. It was just too sad to lose her so soon.

The doctor called Louisa's sons and told them the bad news. They arrived the following day and arranged the funeral with great alacrity. It was well attended. Louisa had been well loved. She would be much missed.

* * *

Serena met Julian Trebarwen, Louisa's youngest son, for the first time at his mother's wake. She had noticed him as soon as he walked into the church, but it seemed the wrong moment to make his acquaintance. Though Louisa had often said that Julian took after his father, there was plenty of his mother in his face. His eyes were the same, grey-blue and intelligent. Despite what she had heard of his fecklessness, Serena couldn't help but feel instantly warm towards this man whose smile reminded her so much of her friend. When she happened upon him along in the kitchen, she introduced herself and offered her condolences.

'Drink?' he asked, topping up her glass without waiting for her answer.

'I don't know if I ought to. I mean . . .' she was thinking: this is a wake. I shouldn't get tipsy.

Julian drained his own glass and poured himself another. Serena put it down to grief.

'Mark told me it was you who found her,' said Julian. 'What a terrible thing for a neighbour to have to go through. I'm sorry.'

'It's OK,' said Serena. 'She wasn't just a neighbour. She was a friend. I feel honoured to have known her.'

Julian Trebarwen gave Serena an appraising sort of look. 'I'm sure she was very glad to know you too.'

Inappropriate as it seemed to be thinking such a thing at a funeral, Serena wondered if he hadn't just given her the glad eye.

Alongside her sadness at losing a friend, Serena felt a great deal of curiosity about the future of Trebarwen House.

Everyone in the village wanted to know what was going to happen to the place. It was the only topic of conversation in the grocery store, the post office and at the school gates. There were so many beautiful things at Trebarwen. Louisa had spent a lifetime building up a collection of wonderful art and ornaments. Serena wondered if Louisa's sons understood the significance of some of those pieces. Would they appreciate their worth?

She needn't have worried. Mark Trebarwen had every intention of knowing the value of every last stick in that house.

'Do you want any of it?' Mark asked his younger brother as they sat together in the grand drawing room after the wake.

'I'd love some of it, but I don't have room for knick-knacks in my two-bedroom house.' Julian laid great emphasis on 'two bedroom', to remind his older brother of the difference in their circumstances. 'I don't need more stuff. I need the money.'

'Me too,' Mark admitted. 'Eldest looks like he's going to fail his A levels which means I'll have to pay for a crammer. In any case, the inheritance tax is going to be crippling. I don't see how we'll be able to meet it without selling something. I'll call Nat Wilde at Ludbrook's. Get him to come down and take a look over the house. But I've got to go back to Singapore this weekend. Can you be here to let him in so he can tell us what's worth putting up for sale? Sooner the better.'

Julian nodded. Though he had the feeling that Mark's reasons for wanting cash had very little to do with inheritance tax or his son's education. More likely, he wanted to fund a divorce from his hideous horse-faced wife. In any case, it wouldn't be such a hardship for Julian to stay down in Cornwall for a few more days. It would mean at least that he wouldn't have to deal with Mia, his most recent ex. She was taking the end of their relationship very badly, turning up in the middle of the night to try to persuade him to take her back. He had to admit he had been tempted. Mia may have been high maintenance but she was very good in the sack and Julian missed that. It was very hard to maintain a sensible distance when Mia turned up in some low-cut top, specifically designed to showcase her fabulous tits. But she was mad as a box of frogs and there was a very real danger that if he took her to bed again she would stab him to death as he slept. Julian needed to find a replacement shag as soon as possible to prevent him from slipping back into that crazy situation. As that thought crossed his mind, so too did a picture of the girl from the house down the lane. Serena. She wasn't at all bad-looking and there had been no bloke in tow. Was she single? Divorced? Perhaps he should give her a call. Take her to the pub on the pretext of recompensing her for having had to deal with the corpse of his mother. See what happened next.

Chapter Five

NAT Wilde was delighted to hear from his old prep-school chum Mark Trebarwen.

'Chubby!' he exclaimed, using a nickname that had been hard lost. 'How the devil are you? How's your dear old mother?'

'She's dead,' said Mark shortly.

'Whoops. Sorry about that, old chap. Can't believe I missed the announcement in the *Telegraph*.'

Nat had his staff scan the death notices and obits every day. He had a file full of extremely tasteful condolence cards ready to be sent out to newly bereaved relatives at the drop of a hat.

'We didn't put an announcement in,' said Mark, aware it was bad form to have forgotten. Still, his mother wasn't such a stickler for form in her latter years, as that bloody painting of the dogs had proved.

'Oh, well. In that case I don't feel quite such a chump,' said Nat. 'So, to what do I owe the pleasure? Want to arrange some work experience for one of your children?' he suggested disingenuously. They both knew why Mark was calling.

'No. Not yet. I was wondering if you wouldn't mind coming down to Cornwall and having a look over the house. There are a few things that might be worth something. I really don't know. I haven't been able to look that closely. Mother's death is still too, too fresh.'

'I understand,' said Nat, voice dripping with concern. 'Well, don't trouble yourself about it. You've come to exactly the right man. I'll take care of everything. When would you like me to come?'

Nat was unusually accommodating. He and Chubby Trebarwen hadn't been the best of chums at school, but Nat had sensed from very early on that the Trebarwen family had a bob or two. Mark Trebarwen senior sent his driver and a Bentley to pick his two sons up at the end of each term. And when Louisa Trebarwen graced her boys with her presence on speech and sports days, she was usually wearing fur and dripping in diamonds. Nat was almost salivating at the thought of what her house might contain.

'I can come down tomorrow,' he said. 'I've always been of the opinion that when you suffer the loss of a beloved parent, you should deal with the grief by keeping on the move. It's once you stop that the unhappiness hits you. But if they get straight on with sorting out their affairs, people usually find that by the time they've stopped moving the pain has lessened a good deal.'

Nat didn't mention that he'd also found that the more quickly you pushed bereaved families into putting up their loved one's estates for auction the more likely they were to agree with whatever you told them. Grief. Befuddlement. Despair. They all worked in Nat's favour. Of the three 'Ds' that kept the auction business going – divorce, debt and death – death was definitely Nat's favourite. And by far the easiest since the deceased couldn't quibble about the sale of their treasured possessions. The pressure of inheritance tax was also a great joy to the auctioneer.

'I will drive straight there. I know it's a terrible thing that has brought us back into contact, Mark, but I'm very much looking forward to seeing you and catching up.'

'I won't be there,' said Mark. 'I've got to go back to Singapore. You'll be dealing with my little brother.'

'Wonderful,' he said through gritted teeth. Mark Trebarwen was a known quantity but Julian Trebarwen Nat didn't know, except by reputation. Hadn't he been expelled from Radley for knocking another boy's teeth out? 'I'll look forward to meeting him,' Nat lied.

Nat Wilde needn't have worried about Julian Trebarwen foiling his plans to get Louisa Trebarwen's estate in the saleroom at Ludbrook's. When he talked to him on the phone, Julian Trebarwen was much friendlier than his brother had been. And he was obviously skint, Nat surmised, as when the very next day he pulled his Range Rover into the grand drive of Trebarwen House and clocked the ancient BMW estate that was parked there.

This was to be a perfunctory visit. As well as making sure that he was in the running to sell the contents of the house, Nat wanted to be equally sure it was worth bothering with. As he followed Julian from room to room, ostensibly making small talk about their memories of prep school and friends in common, Nat was ruthlessly totting up the potential worth of the house's contents. He may have appeared blasé but in his head he was making a detailed valuation worthy of an insurance broker. There was much to salivate over but like an estate agent, Nat knew that it was important not to raise his potential client's hopes too high. That way you could more easily exceed them. That was how reputations were built.

'I think we'll be able to do something for you,' said Nat. He handed Julian a glossy brochure detailing Ludbrook's' terms and conditions. 'If you and your brother think that Ludbrook's is the house for you, I'll send somebody down to make a proper inventory at your earliest convenience.'

'Thank you,' said Julian. They shook hands cordially on the steps to the house but Julian had felt an instant distrust of Nat Wilde upon meeting him and the feeling was absolutely mutual.

The next afternoon – Sunday – as he lay in bed in the green room, as the main guest suite at Trebarwen was called, Julian guiltily recalled the last time he had seen his mother and how, having failed to extract any cash from the old girl that time, he had wished that the day when she finally shuffled off the mortal coil might come quickly.

Julian knew he had been his mother's favourite, but for the past couple of years even she had refused to fund any more of his get-rich-quick schemes. General opinion was that everything Julian touched went belly up. That wasn't entirely fair. He had made a paper fortune before the dot.com crash. Likewise, his decision to open an estate agency just before the credit crunch took hold had been based on very sound accounting. And if his mother had shown more faith in him, perhaps Julian wouldn't have felt compelled to commit the insurance fraud that landed him in prison for three months.

No, Julian would not stand in the way of any sale of his mother's stuff. He needed the money.

A twenty-minute nap turned into a three-hour snooze. It was hunger that eventually forced Julian to get up. He wandered down to the vast kitchen where once upon a time three cooks had turned out dinners for a hundred but there was absolutely nothing in the fridge and nothing in his mother's cocktail cabinet either. It was a Sunday, it was Cornwall and it was after four o'clock. There was scant chance he would find anywhere open and serving lunch. Perhaps it was time to pay his mother's neighbour a visit.

'Oh, hello,' said Serena when she opened the door to Julian Trebarwen. 'I wasn't expecting anyone,' she added by way of excusing the shabbiness of her dress. Not that she would have looked much smarter had she been expecting visitors. Serena's wardrobe contained clothes she could no longer fit into and jeans. She'd not had the money or time to shop for anything since Tom walked out.

'Oh, don't worry about that,' said Julian. 'We're in the country. Here, I brought you these.' He thrust a fistful of flowers, pulled together from the floral tributes that had been left for his mother, towards her.

'Oh, thank you. That's very kind.' Still Serena remained on the doorstep, blocking Julian's entrance. 'What can I do for you?' she asked eventually. 'Oh, God. I can't believe I said that. I mean, I'm sure you just popped round to be neighbourly.'

'Actually,' said Julian. 'I did have an ulterior motive. I'm afraid you'll think me a rather hopeless bachelor, but I find myself without a thing in the house. I drove down to the village but . . .'

'Everything is shut. I know. You can't get anything after midday unless you want to drive to Truro. Takes some getting used to after London.'

'I wonder if I could possibly borrow a little milk and a few slices of bread to tide me over?'

Serena smiled.

'I think we can do a little better than that. Katie and I were just about to have a little supper. Why don't you join us?'

Bingo.

'Really,' said Julian. 'I don't want to disturb you.'

'Oh no,' said Serena. 'Please do. I haven't had an adult conversation since your mother died.'

Serena Macdonald was not quite who Julian expected her to be. He had thought she would be like all the other women in the village, dull and slightly desperate. But she was much more interesting than that.

Julian guessed that the shabby clothes concealed a not too shabby figure. Her hair was untidy but it was a nice colour and she had a pretty face. Even prettier when she smiled, which was often.

The supper she'd prepared was delicious. Possibly all the more so because Julian had fully expected to spend the next twenty-four hours subsisting on toast and Marmite. Serena had cooked lamb with rosemary. Her roast potatoes rivalled those Julian's nanny used to make.

'This is really wonderful,' he said, meaning every word.

'I prefer chicken,' said Katie.

Over supper, Julian did a bit of digging about Serena's marital status.

'A husband!' she laughed. 'Barely. He's on his way out. What about you?'

'Confirmed bachelor,' he said, puffing out his chest in comedy pride. 'Much to my mother's annoyance.'

'I know,' Serena smiled.

'Ah well,' said Julian. 'Just haven't found the right girl.'

Serena nodded. 'Your mother said that too.'

It was one of those lovely Sunday suppers that just doesn't seem to want to end. Katie, of course, got down from the table as soon as Serena said she could and went to play with the Trebarwen dolls' house that Louisa had given her for her sixth birthday. Serena and Julian remained at the table – Serena only getting up to put a tired Katie to bed – until they'd finished almost two bottles of red wine between them. They were starting to feel as though they had known each other for years.

Still, Serena was a little surprised when Julian made his move, slipping his arm around her waist while she was running water over the roasting tin in the kitchen sink. He lifted her ponytail out of the way and she knew at once he was about to kiss the back of her neck.

'I can't,' said Serena, gently pushing him off. 'It's been, you know. It's been a long time.'

Julian dutifully stepped back.

'I understand,' he said.

'But thank you. I suppose . . .'

'I'd better go?'

'It is almost one in the morning.'

'And I only dropped by to cadge a few slices of toast. Thank you. You've looked after me very well.'

'It's what your mum would have wanted, I'm sure.'

'Well, I'll be able to return the favour,' said Julian. 'I'm going to be around for a bit longer. Getting the estate sorted out. It would be nice to see you again.'

Serena nodded. 'I'd like that too.'

Serena closed the door behind him and leaned heavily against it, her heart beating fast. A silly grin spread across her face. Julian Trebarwen had made a pass at her. It was the first time anyone had made a pass at her since the day she got pregnant with Katie (and that included her own husband). The knowledge that someone had found her worthy of a quick feel, even if it was largely driven by alcohol, had a better effect on Serena's face than a shot of botox. She sneaked a look at herself as she passed the mirror in the hallway and, for once, was quite pleased with what she saw.

'You've still got it, Serena Macdonald,' she winked at her reflection.

Chapter Six

C ARRIE Klein was fighting hard to hang on to her assets. She was just thirty-nine years old. There was no danger that her chin was going to slide into her neck like melting ice cream the moment she hit forty, but Carrie was still putting in the work. Prevention being better than any cure and all that. She had been having botox for years. Just a little to ward off the frown lines she'd seen appearing on the faces of most of her peers. It had the added bonus of seeming to stop the migraines that had bugged her since graduate school.

But it wasn't just the face that needed maintenance. Every morning Carrie could be found running around Central Park. Not just jogging but *running*, like her life depended on it. Forty-five minutes every day without fail, before she got into the office and put in a ten-hour day (if her work load wasn't too heavy – more usually she pulled twelve or thirteen).

* * *

Carrie's heart had only just recovered from that morning's run when she got a call that set it thumping again. It was her boss.

'Carrie, I need to see you in my office right away,' he said.

It sounded serious. It had been months, but ever since the debacle over the fake Constable, Carrie had been waiting to receive her marching orders. The painting had been withdrawn from the sale with little fuss but still Carrie felt humiliated. She'd been such an idiot. It wasn't as though she had been so certain that the painting was real in the first place. Since then she had been even more assiduous, even more driven, spurred on by the fear that her colleagues – her competitors – saw this chink in her armour as a way of bringing her down. This was it, she decided. Her colleagues had finally decided to make an example of her. She prepared her best argument as to why she should be allowed to stay on. Andrew would take her seriously, she was sure. But when she walked into his office and saw that the chairman of the house, eighty-six year old Frank Ehrenpreis, was sitting in the third chair, Carrie's composure deserted her. She was finished, for sure. Why else would Andrew have called Frank in?

'Gentlemen, I feel that I need to explain once more how that painting came to be in my sale,' she jumped the gun.

'Carrie, hold it right there. You think you're getting the sack, right?'

What could Carrie do except nod?

'This isn't about the Constable. That's dealt with. You're not getting the sack. You're much too valuable for that.'

Then what, Carrie wondered.

'We want you to go to London.'

'What?'

'What I'm about to tell you is highly confidential. For some time the board have been discussing the expansion of Ehrenpreis overseas. The world has shifted on its axis. New York is no longer the centre of the world. For the past decade, the power and the money have been moving steadily east. Russia, China, India. The new money isn't coming to the States right now. They want to do their business closer to home. London is where it's at. And Ehrenpreis needs to be there too. We've made an offer on the lease to a premises in New Bond Street.'

Carrie's mouth dropped open.

'Right across the street from our old friends at Sotheby's. We want you to fly there tonight and check the place out tomorrow morning. You are going to head up Ehrenpreis London. Assuming that you want to.'

'I . . . I . . .' Carrie was flabbergasted. 'Why me?'

'Because we know that we'll get our money's worth. Sure, you made a mistake with the Constable, but if Ehrenpreis gave out a star for employee of the month it wouldn't have left your shirt since the first month you got here. You've got what it takes. You're brilliant, professional and ambitious. You're prepared to live your work, which is what would be required of you if you took this offer up. So whaddya think? Do you want a while to consider what I've told you? Ask your significant others?'

Carrie shook her head. She didn't need any time to think. And there weren't any significant others she needed to ask. The thought of what Jed would say flashed through her mind but she put it to one side. 'I would be delighted to accept your offer.'

'Great. I already had your assistant book the flight, knowing that's exactly what you would say.'

Chapter Seven

CARRIE was booked into first class on the red-eye flight from JFK to London. She left a message for Jed, cancelling their date for that evening, saying that she had to go to London on business but without elaborating. When she got back to New York, she would take him out to dinner in compensation. They would, she hoped, be drinking champagne.

London. How Carrie loved that city. It was so exciting. She loved the history. The pace. The manners. As she settled into her seat for the flight, an English guy in his forties was being shown to his place. The sound of his accent as he thanked the stewardess for her help filled Carrie with delicious expectation. Such class. At least, he sounded like he had class. Carrie was well aware that such things could be deceptive but still it gave her a thrill.

Her assistant Jessica had, as usual, made an excellent job of arranging the trip. A limousine was waiting at the airport to whisk her straight to her hotel, Claridge's, the most convenient for the proposed offices of the new Ehrenpreis endeavour and for easy visits to Christie's, Sotheby's and Ludbrook's. She was especially excited to visit Ludbrook's. There was an old friend she wanted to see there.

Carrie's excitement was only slightly dimmed by the angry message from Jed that greeted her when she turned her phone on upon landing at Heathrow.

'Is there nothing more important in your life than work?' he asked.

Right then, the answer was 'no'.

Having slept a little on the flight (thanks to a couple of Ambien, which Jessica had also sourced), Carrie was ready to start work right away. She went straight to Sotheby's. The place buzzed as they prepared for their famous modern art sale. That year, the sale was expected to break all records. Carrie was filled with envy and awe as she looked at the works on display. There were some seriously good pieces: paintings by Francis Bacon and Lucien Freud and sculptures from Giacometti, which had been fetching increasingly high prices since Russian oligarch Roman Abramovich had come out as a fan. Well, give me a couple of years, she thought, and Ehrenpreis will be the house to watch.

After her visit to Sotheby's, Carrie met with the real estate agent from Savills who was hoping to lease the London premises to Ehrenpreis. He let her into the empty building and guided her around. Carrie was relieved to see that the premises had so much potential. There were fabulous high ceilings in the ground-floor rooms. Perfect for hanging art. She chose her office – with windows that overlooked the front door of Ludbrook's – and marked it as such on the floor plan. She put in a call to Andrew, her boss, as she stood in the lobby.

'It's perfect,' she said. 'We've found our London home.'

After her meeting with the estate agent, Carrie decided to take her lunch break in the café at Ludbrook's. Like Sotheby's, Ludbrook's had realised that if they couldn't sting every person who walked through the door for the price of a Picasso, they could at least be able to get them to part with the price of a panini. The café was nice. Basic. Carrie chose a club sandwich that was delicious, despite being roughly twice the price and half the size of the same thing in the USA.

As she sipped a cup of mint tea, she tuned in to the conversation of the two guys who were settling themselves at the table beside her.

'You won't believe what's going on in that place across the road,' said the shorter of the two, a ruddy-faced chap that Carrie recognised as Ludbrook's wine expert Harry Brown. She'd seen his picture on their website. 'They're only opening a branch of bloody Ehrenpreis. I heard it from my estate agent cousin at Savills.'

The other guy had his back to Carrie but his beautiful upper-class voice was oddly familiar as he asked, 'Really? Is that worrying you, Harry?'

'Of course it's worrying me. And I don't know why you're taking the news so calmly. They're more bloody competition.'

The other guy gave a little chuckle. 'Harry, Nat Wilde doesn't have any competition.'

Nat Wilde! Carrie started at the name. She turned as subtly as she could to get a look at the man. Could it really be him?

'Besides,' Nat continued. 'That's a terrible location. Too small. The whole thing will go tits up in six weeks. Mark my words. I'm not going to lose any sleep.'

It definitely was him. The arrogant sod.

Carrie Klein smiled into her fresh mint tea. There was nothing she liked more than a challenge. This was going to be sweet.

Having finished her lunch, Carrie presented herself at the front desk at Ludbrook's and asked the girl there about the upcoming Old Masters auction. The fresh-faced young thing was extremely enthusiastic and explained that there would be a private view that very evening. A couple of calls later and Carrie had an invitation to the exclusive black tie event. Then it was back to Claridge's to answer emails and take a very short nap. Carrie didn't want to miss a moment of that evening's entertainment.

She took especially great care with her appearance. She had brought with her a couple of dresses. One of them, a black satin number from Lanvin, would do for a cocktail event. Especially when it was accessorised with a pair of enormous diamond clip earrings, borrowed that afternoon from one of Ehrenpreis's favoured London dealers. Carrie piled her hair up in a neat chignon. The effect was perfect. Classy. Nothing to distract from the impressive diamonds that said 'high-roller'. Or, at the very least, 'high-roller's wife'.

Carrie knew this would be her last chance to move around Ludbrook's incognito. The moment Ehrenpreis opened its doors and the Ludbrook's staff found out who she was, she knew she could not expect any more cocktail party invitations.

The intention was to see how Ludbrook's operated at first hand. What kind of care and attention they lavished on their clients and consignees. Carrie was particularly interested in getting close to the legendary Nat Wilde. He was a man who could sell snow to the Eskimos, sand to Saudi Arabi. He was a man who had, only recently, sold a picture of a potato for close on thirty-five million pounds. Admittedly, it was a potato by Van Gogh . . .

Carrie couldn't wait to see him in action.

Chapter Eight

$\mathcal{L}$IZZY Duffy had approximately three and a half minutes to dress for that evening's Old Masters cocktail reception. She was running late. She had spent far longer than she wanted to on the telephone to one of Nat's old biddies: the elderly gentle-ladies whose friendship he cultivated in the hope that if they didn't actually leave him all their worldly goods in their wills, he would at least get to sell them on behalf of their rightful heirs. Mrs Kingly was not one of Nat's favourites. She was a decidedly acidic old bag, who had nothing but complaints to impart whenever she telephoned, which was often. But she lived alone in a vast Queen Anne house filled with immaculate contemporaneous furniture and paintings. And she was on her very last legs. Honestly, this time she *really* was.

Nat rolled his eyes every time Mrs Kingly talked of having so little time left to go before she met her maker. She had been saying that since 1998. Still, any day now she would be right, so when she called and wanted to gripe, at great length, about the difficulty of finding a good gardener or butler or doctor, someone in the office had to listen. That afternoon it was Lizzy's turn.

'Tell young Mr Wilde I want to speak to him as soon as he comes back into the office,' said Mrs Kingly. 'I have some very important paintings that will need to be sold on behalf of the cats' home the minute I die and I don't appreciate being palmed off on a junior.'

'Yes, Mrs Kingly. I'll tell him. Just as soon as he comes back from Hamburg.'

Nat was always pretending to be in Hamburg.

Like Carrie, Lizzy chose to wear black that evening. Well, it wasn't a choice, exactly. It wasn't as though she had a whole wardrobe of designer gear to pick from. This particular dress was from Karen Millen. Her flatmate Jools, with whom she had been shopping at the time, told her it looked a little bit Prada. And Lizzy felt a little bit Prada when she wore it. For the first couple of times in any case, until she found herself standing next to a woman dressed in the real thing and suddenly felt extremely chain store again.

Her diamonds at least were real; though they were mere chips compared to the rocks many of the guests would be sporting that night. She pulled a comb through her hair. There was no time to wash it and it looked a bit greasy. She did her best to disguise the fact by scraping her hair back into a ponytail and sticking a velvet Alice band over the top.

'Very Christie's 1984,' joked Sarah Jane as she joined Lizzy at the ladies' room mirror.

It was important to Lizzy that she look especially good that night, not just because she was on duty, but also because she had something big to ask Nat. They had been romantically involved for almost six months now. Lizzy's sister would be getting married in June and Lizzy wanted to ask Nat to be her 'plus one' at the wedding.

Lizzy was convinced that things were moving forward with her boss. Though he had said that there was no way he could officially announce that they were together without causing problems in the office, Lizzy was spending at least three nights a week at Nat's apartment.

The sex was greatly improved. Since that first time, it just got better and better. Lizzy had been enjoying herself so much she was almost regretful that she had waited so long to lose her virginity. But most of the time she was just thrilled that she had lost her virginity to Nat. How wonderful it would be if they did get married and Lizzy was able to avoid the misery of casual sex and its repercussions. Yes. That was what she wanted. To marry Nat Wilde and be faithful to him and him alone for the rest of her life. She was certain she wouldn't miss out if she never kissed another man.

Sarah Jane caught her daydreaming. 'Come on, dozy,' she said. 'Doors open in five. Apparently there are people down there already. Anything for a free glass of champagne.'

'Coming,' said Lizzy. She adjusted her headband and followed Sarah Jane down into the gallery.

Chapter Nine

As Carrie walked into the lobby at Ludbrook's, she was immediately relieved of her coat by a girl in a neat white shirt, black skirt and black waistcoat. A similarly uniformed waiter offered her the choice of juice, water or champagne. She took champagne. Not because she intended to get drunk but because she wanted to know how much Ludbrook's were spending on this do and the quality of the champagne would be a good indicator. She took a sniff. Not bad, she decided. Later in the evening, she would get the name of the maker on the pretence of wanting some for her own cellar.

She moved on into the main room. It was already thronged with guests who all appeared to be much more interested in each other than in the lots adorning the walls. Carrie was familiar with that scenario. In one corner, in front of a couple of what Carrie correctly judged to be the smaller, cheaper paintings, a string quartet provided perfectly inoffensive and unobtrusive background music. The canapés were plentiful and of pleasingly high quality.

Carrie spotted Nat Wilde as soon as she walked into the room. He was holding court, surrounded by a little gaggle of women who seemed to be finding him hilarious. It could have been a disaster, but Wilde was obviously handling the situation well, bringing husbands in whenever he could, perpetuating the myth that while he might be flirtatious, he was perfectly harmless too.

So, he was busy but Carrie knew how to draw him over. She took up a position near a portrait of a young woman in a fabulous blue dress. She opened the catalogue to the page that displayed the picture and let the end of her pencil rest on her bottom lip as she gazed at the picture as though trying to imagine it above her fireplace of her enormous apartment on Central Park West. Nat Wilde was by her side within a minute.

'Beautiful painting, isn't it?'

'Yes,' said Carrie turning to face him. 'It is rather lovely.'

As, she thought with a little thrill of surprise, was Nat Wilde. The elegance of her rival was only enhanced upon a closer view. His dark hair was shot through with silver and his skin was lightly tanned, the perfect foil for mischievous bright blue eyes and the straight white teeth of a movie star. Very good teeth for an Englishman, noted Carrie. And they did seem to be all his own, even though he must be nearer fifty than forty by now.

'Nat Wilde,' he offered her his hand. 'I don't believe we've met.'

'I'm just in from the States. I'm Carrie Barclay.'

She used her mother's maiden name – she'd practised trotting it out for occasions just like this – and watched with amusement as Nat flicked through his mental Rolodex in an attempt to place her.

'Ah, yes,' he said. 'That name is familiar. Didn't we sell your husband a small painting by . . .'

'No husband,' said Carrie, wiggling her empty left hand. 'Divorced.'

Nat's eyes lit up. Carrie knew exactly what he was thinking. Freshly minted divorcees were often bigger spenders than wives incumbent, filling the new gap in their lives with pretty pictures.

'Well, I'm sorry. He must be kicking himself,' Nat added.

Carrie gave a mock frown. Nat Wilde had all the patter.

'So,' he continued. 'Now that you can decorate the house exactly as you want it, which I don't doubt is with a great deal more taste than your ex-husband ever had, perhaps you'd like to tell me if anything has caught your eye.'

'Well, this one, of course,' said Carrie, gesturing shyly towards the portrait. 'The moment I saw her, I was drawn to her.'

'I know exactly what you mean,' said Nat. 'The first time I saw her was like falling in love. It's something about her eyes. There's a sadness there, but you can't help but feel that if she smiled it would be the most beautiful smile in the world, and if she turned it on a guy like me, well, I would be jelly.'

Nat put his hand on his breast pocket. Where his heart should be.

'You know,' he said, turning to face Carrie. 'If I may be so bold, I'd have to say she looks a little like you. Now, if only I could persuade you to smile, I think I might just die and go to heaven.'

'Oh please.' Carrie flicked her catalogue in Nat's direction as though to swat him away. She hammed up her accent, making it pure South Carolina and said, 'I heard that English men were full of false flattery.'

'You'll never hear a lie pass these lips, Ms Barclay.'

Carrie was tempted to disagree but she remembered just in time that she was suppose to be an ingénue in the world of art who knew nothing more of Nat Wilde than he chose to tell her.

'Well,' she said instead, 'in that case, I will allow myself to feel faintly flattered. Now, perhaps you could tell me a little more about the history of this painting. Who was the sitter? What was her relationship with the artist? It's quite unusual for someone to allow themselves to be painted looking so sad.'

'I agree. Unless there was something going on between the artist and his muse. My research tells me that the sitter was the daughter of a wealthy landowner. At the time this portrait was made, she had just become engaged to a distant cousin who decided to emigrate to America to make his own fortune there. Naturally, his young wife would be expected to go with him. Unfortunately, she was madly in love with the artist and wanted to stay in England to be closer to him. That, I imagine, is the reason why she looks so very sad. This is the last portrait he painted of her. In fact, it is the very last portrait anyone ever painted of her. She was married that autumn and travelled to the States with her husband the following spring. Alas, she went into labour during the voyage and died of complications, two hundred miles from New York.'

'That's terrible,' said Carrie.

'Her baby survived. Perhaps you're a descendant.'

Carrie smiled coyly. 'Nat Wilde,' she said. 'You are too much.'

Nat grinned at her like a fox making eyes at a chicken.

*   *   *

On the other side of the room, Lizzy was having a slightly less enjoyable time. The moment she walked in to the reception, she was pounced upon by Charlie Taylor and he had not let her go. Unfortunately, Charlie Taylor, an old-school investment banker with halitosis, was not someone Lizzy much felt like flirting with. Not that he seemed to think the fact that he was thirty years her senior and had a face the same rich red as the gallery walls was any impediment to chatting her up. And he kept her hanging in there by insisting that he was interested in spending a 'great deal of money' at the upcoming sale. Though, as far as she knew, Charlie Taylor hadn't bought a painting through Ludbrook's since 1993, Lizzy couldn't risk calling his bluff. So she allowed herself to be backed into a corner. Charles boxed her in by leaning one arm against the wall and blasted her with breath that could strip paint. The only consolation was that Lizzy had a direct line of sight beneath Charles's arm towards Nat and the woman he was talking to.

Who was she? The woman was beautiful. Lizzy saw that at once. On anybody's scale of attractiveness, that girl had it. She looked so poised. Her hair was perfect. Her face had the elegant planes and proportions of a Hollywood star from the forties. Her dress was obviously expensive. And her jewels. Lizzy could tell from the way they sent out glittering sparks each time the woman moved her head, that those enormous diamonds were real.

Lizzy couldn't help hating her. She almost certainly had a rich husband who doted on her and now Nat seemed to be falling under her spell too.

'Don't you think?' asked Charlie.

Lizzy realised that while she had been checking out the competition, Charlie had asked her a question.

'I'm sorry,' she said. 'I didn't catch that. It's terribly noisy in here.'

'We could go outside?' Charlie suggested hopefully.

'I'm at work,' Lizzy reminded him.

Nat too was working very hard. He squired Carrie Barclay about the gallery, drawing to her attention paintings that he thought might be of interest. Nat was very skilled at working people out. With great subtlety he guided the conversation on to subjects that would give him an idea of her net worth. He talked about New York. She soon revealed she had an apartment with a lovely view of Central Park. Now that was prime real estate. And Carrie didn't seem in the least bit phased as he took her to see paintings with reserve prices in the multiple millions. He soon decided that she was a big fish and a jolly attractive one too, which helped. It made Nat's work so much more pleasurable.

Carrie glanced at her watch. Cartier, Nat clocked at once.

'It's getting late,' she said.

'Have you eaten?' Nat asked, suddenly.

'No,' said Carrie. 'I have a little work to do so I thought I might just get room service back at my hotel.'

'You most certainly will not,' said Nat. 'You cannot come all the way to London to sit in your hotel room and eat an overpriced sandwich in front of CNN. Will you allow me to take you for an overpriced sandwich at my club instead?'

'I don't think so,' said Carrie.

'I know. You're absolutely right to refuse. I'm a strange man in a strange town. It'd be madness. But just about anyone in this room will vouch for me and I promise that if you agree to have dinner with me, I will not give you preferential treatment when you come to the auction tomorrow.'

Carrie laughed. 'In that case . . . you're on.'

'Good girl. If you'll excuse me for a moment,' said Nat. 'There are just a couple of people I should say goodnight to. Wait for me in the lobby. I'll be out in less than a minute.'

In the ladies' cloakroom, Carrie grinned at herself in the mirror over the basins. Fifty per cent of her thought that this was a stupid idea but the rest of her was more optimistic. Plus, this would be the last chance she ever had to spend time with Nat Wilde incognito. Her last chance to get a close-up view of the man she would be in competition with the following month. And, if she was honest, she was rather enjoying herself.

Seeing her chance as the blonde headed for the ladies' room, Lizzy crossed the room to catch up with Nat.

'How's it going?'

'A good night, I think,' said Nat. 'Busy.'

'I was wondering whether you wanted to go and get something to eat when this is finished?'

'Didn't you get any canapés?' asked Nat.

'Missed the lot. I was stuck in the corner with Charlie Taylor.' She rolled her eyes. 'I thought I might get a Chinese when this lot go home. Want to come?'

'Can't,' said Nat. 'There's an important client in from the States. I said I'd take her out to dinner.'

'Oh,' Lizzy tried to hang on to her smile. 'The dark-haired one?' she asked, hoping that he would say yes. She had seen Nat talking to a dumpy brunette before he got caught up with the goddess.

'No. The blonde.' He confirmed her worst fears.

'She's American?'

'Yep.' Nat nodded. 'She just flew in from New York for the sale. Interested in the blue lady.'

Lizzy's heart sank. The blue lady was the most valuable work in the sale. There was no way that Nat could be persuaded not to have dinner with someone who wanted that picture. 'Got to keep her in the game. Work, work, work,' he said as he wandered towards the door.

Lizzy tried hard to hide her disappointment. Though Nat had slipped away with that American woman, the evening was far from over for the rest of his team. There were still a few guests hanging on, drinking the last of the champagne, and trying to stretch the reception into a whole night's worth of entertainment.

'Good evening, Lizzy.'

Lizzy put on a smile for the man at her shoulder. 'You look very lovely this evening,' said Yasha Suscenko.

'Thank you,' she replied, though she didn't feel it. It was as though Nat had taken her sparkle with him when he walked through the door. Her dress seemed droopy. Her earrings so obviously worthless.

'It's been a busy party,' said Yasha. 'So much for the recession.'

'Yes,' Lizzy nodded. 'But then I think that paintings like these always do well in times of recession. People like to put their money into something that has already proved itself over generations. It's the more contemporary stuff that suffers first.'

Yasha nodded.

'But you know that,' said Lizzy, feeling suddenly shy. Her companion was one of London's most successful dealers, assembling collections for people who would think nothing of having a Rembrandt hanging in the loo. On their yacht.

Yasha Suscenko was the owner of The Atalantan Gallery in Mayfair. Born in Moscow, Yasha had left the USSR for the United States in the early 1990s, together with his parents. His father was an academic. His mother was an artist. It was she who had encouraged Yasha to make art his passion too. Those early years in the USA had been rough. Yasha could barely speak English when he entered the American high school system at sixteen and there was very little money to spare for extra lessons at home. There was little money to spare for anything, except the essentials. Still, Yasha had graduated and went on to study art history. He worked for several galleries in New York before setting up on his own, working out of his apartment. When the privatisation of Russia's industry began in earnest under Putin and the oligarchs emerged, Yasha was well positioned to make a killing, being one of the few international dealers who truly understood Russian art at that time. His older brother, who had remained in Moscow and become a successful nightclub owner, sent many customers in Yasha's direction.

When he opened his space in Mayfair with an exhibition of Russian art that drew praise from the most grudging of critics, Yasha felt that he had finally made it. Now he had a client list that read like the Forbes rich list. For that reason alone, Lizzy Duffy knew she should be more attentive to him.

'Seen anything interesting?' Lizzy asked.

'A couple of things,' he said.

'So you'll be at the sale?'

'Of course. Wouldn't miss it. Your boss always turns these things into quite the party.'

A cloud passed over Lizzy's face as she thought about Nat and his plans for the evening again. She couldn't help feeling jealous. She tried to tell herself that Nat was just schmoozing. He might be taking Carrie Barclay to dinner but it wasn't a date. He was thinking about Ludbrook's bottom line. Really, he was.

Yasha Suscenko noticed Lizzy's frown. 'You look much prettier when you smile,' he said as he left.

Chapter Ten

$\mathcal{N}$ AT had a feeling that his club would not especially impress Carrie Barclay. Her Manhattan-style elegance would be out of place amongst the crusty old codgers who seemed to live in the leather chairs. He decided that schmoozing Carrie Barclay required something altogether more chic.

'I've got us a table at Gordon Ramsay at Claridge's,' Nat announced as he caught up with Carrie in the lobby.

'You're kidding?' she was impressed. 'I'm staying there and they couldn't find me a slot.'

Nat tapped the side of his nose. He could get a table just about anywhere. Keeping concierges sweet was all part of his job.

'Let's get there before they give it away.'

He hailed a taxi to Bond Street and helped her inside.

Carrie had slipped into the role of rich young divorcee quite easily, giving in to all her most princess-like tendencies. She resisted the urge to open her taxi door for herself as they pulled up outside the hotel. She happily accepted Nat's help with her chair in the restaurant itself and when the menu arrived, she simply handed it over to him.

'You choose for me,' she said.

'Well,' said Nat. 'That's a tricky one. I hardly know you. Would you say you're a red-blooded kind of girl?'

'Oh yes,' she said, holding his gaze.

'In that case, you're having the venison. It's very good.'

'Lovely,' she said with something approaching a growl.

The venison was terrific and Nat did not skimp on the wine to accompany it. Though Carrie knew that he would doubtless expense this particular outing – she was a potential client, after all – she was still impressed at his extravagance.

After a while, Carrie took off her jacket. The satin shift dress beneath showed her body at its very best. Her slender arms were one of her favourite features. She wore her Cartier watch and tennis bracelet slightly loose to enhance the delicacy of her wrists. She could sense Nat's eyes travelling over her body, lingering on her bare shoulders, her well-turned biceps. She knew that he was extrapolating from what he could see, wondering if her stomach muscles and buttocks were just as well toned. Carrie gave a small secret smile, knowing as she did that they were. And then she returned the favour, letting her own eyes drift down the front of Nat's crisp white shirt to where his belt encircled an impressively slim waist for an English man of his age.

Despite his trim figure, Nat insisted that they ate dessert. Nat suggested that they might share but Carrie shook her head and ordered her own tiramisu, though she knew she would eat less than half of it. When she offered Nat a bite, he leaned forward, as though expecting her to spoon-feed him.

She made it clear that he should take the spoon himself. But her little gesture of distance only made Nat try harder. He covered her in compliments as though shooting them at her from a scattergun.

'A digestif?' he suggested.

Carrie shook her head, but while Nat visited the mens' room, she took the opportunity to check her phone and found another message from Jed, telling her she was selfish and rude. It turned out she had forgotten that night was the anniversary of their first date. He'd planned something special and she'd ruined it. When Nat came back, she told him she had changed her mind. She would have that drink after all.

'Well, Mr Wilde,' she said as they drank their fine brandies. 'It's been a real pleasure.'

'The pleasure,' he assured her, 'was all mine.' He looked deep into her eyes across the top of his brandy glass.

Carrie lifted her own brandy glass to her mouth automatically, not sure whether she was shielding herself from his charms by echoing his own move or sending a mating signal. Nat Wilde clearly assumed the latter. He put down his glass and moved so that his arm was along the back of the chair. His fingers were within millimetres of her bare shoulder. Carrie licked her lips and moved ever so slightly closer herself. His fingers brushed her skin. She felt, much to her guilty delight, a distinct shiver of pleasure at the contact.

'You are a very beautiful woman,' said Nat, for the fiftieth time that evening. He really had been laying it on thick. 'And intelligent and funny, too.'

Carrie looked into her glass. 'Thank you.'

'I'm just saying what I see.'

There was no ambiguity about it now. He really was stroking her shoulder.

'I must be going,' Carrie said. 'I'm very tired. Jet-lag.'

But still she lingered.

The darkness of the bar at Claridge's lent itself to moments like this. At the table to Nat and Carrie's right, a couple were already engaged in a bit of tonsil hockey. Nat moved his hand from Carrie's shoulder to cup her chin. She knew what came next. Her treacherous body leaned in towards his in readiness.

Oh God. It would be so good to take Nat Wilde up to bed and make love with him. Just to know for sure that he wanted her.

'I've got to go.'

'Can I see you tomorrow?' Nat asked, almost forlornly. 'After the sale?'

'I don't have time,' said Carrie. 'I'm sorry. Next time I'm back in London perhaps.'

She felt a twinge of guilt as she said that. Next time she was back in London she would definitely not be going out for dinner with Nat Wilde. Carrie almost felt sorry for him.

'That's no good for me,' said Nat. 'I'm afraid I can't let this evening end. Not yet.' He circled her wrists with his fingers, making handcuffs.

'One more brandy?' he implored. His eyes implored 'bed'.

Carrie demurred.

Did it really matter? she thought. As long as Carrie didn't talk business, then this could hardly be seen as the kind of unorthodox business practice that got Christie's and Sotheby's into trouble back in 2001.

'Have you ever stayed here at Claridge's?' she asked.

'Never.'

'Then perhaps you might like to see one of the rooms?'

'Yes,' he said. 'I'd like that very much.'

She could tell from his expression that Nat thought he had died and gone to heaven.

There were a great many reasons why Carrie shouldn't have gone to bed with Nat Wilde. First and foremost there was the potential for awful repercussions in the professional world. Then there was Jed. Though he and Carrie had never had 'the talk' about being exclusive, Carrie would have had to be an idiot not to know that was what Jed wanted and expected from her. His face haunted her as she kissed Nat Wilde in the elevator to her hotel room. But right then Carrie was better able to ignore it than usual. Carrie was angry with Jed, thanks to the nasty message he'd left on her voicemail.

Then there was lust. Pure and simple. The champagne, the wine at dinner, the brandy. All had served to soften her resolve, so that sleeping with Nat Wilde seemed like another harmless indulgence. It would be the sexual equivalent of an after-dinner cigarette. A substitute for an after-dinner cigarette, in fact, since you could no longer have one of those, even in Claridge's cigar bar.

Nat followed Carrie into her room, placing a guiding hand on her bottom as he did so. Carrie had a brief moment of panic when she spotted her diary – black leather embossed with Ehrenpreis in big gold letters – lying on the floor beside her briefcase. A swift kick from her Manolos hid that beneath the bed. It didn't really matter. Nat was too focused on getting Carrie out of her clothes to notice anything else in the room.

Carrie wriggled out of the Lanvin sheath to reveal her fantastic underwear. Nat murmured appreciatively when he saw the black silk brassiere and matching knickers that set off Carrie's caramel tan so perfectly. He took them off but requested that she left her shoes and stockings on, as Carrie had known he would. Men of Nat's vintage were fairly predictable when it came to their 'kinky' tastes. She didn't mind. She knew that her legs looked great in the lace-edged hold-ups.

Carrie sat down upon the bed and pulled Nat towards her by his tie. He shrugged his jacket off. Carrie admired the flash of kingfisher blue lining that gave the well-cut grey suit a certain dandy edge. She helped him with the buttons of his shirt – Hilditch and Key bespoke, perfectly pressed. Nat released himself from his trousers and underpants, revealing an impressive erection that brought an instant smile to Carrie's lips.

'Ready for me?' Nat asked as he prepared to climb on board without any further preamble.

Carrie bit her lip and nodded. 'Though you'll have to put this on,' she said, taking out the square packet of foil that contained a condom that she had in her handbag.

Nat grumbled but did as he was told, soon realising that he wasn't going to get laid without protection. After that the sex was brief and messy if enthusiastic and energetic. Carrie knew that she wasn't going to get within a mile of an orgasm herself, it was all over too quickly for that.

It was only afterwards, as Nat lay beside her panting like he had just run a marathon dressed as a rhino, that Carrie realised he had made love to her without first removing his socks.

Carrie was glad when Nat announced that he had to leave just half an hour later.

'Got to get into the office early,' Nat said.

'Of course,' said Carrie. She glanced at her watch. 'The sale.'

Had Carrie been overseeing a sale of her own, she would have been in her office all night.

Nat dressed though he didn't bother to put his tie back on.

'Here's my card,' he said. 'I hope that you and I will see each other again very soon'.

'I'm sure we will,' said Carrie.

'Make sure you wave to me from the back of the sale, won't you? Though only if you want to buy the painting I'm taking bids on.'

'Ha ha,' Carrie gave an impression of a laugh. 'I'll see you around.'

Chapter Eleven

'WHAT'S the matter with Wildey?' Sarah Jane asked Lizzy later the following day. 'There's something weird about him. That was a fantastic sale but he seems positively subdued.'

Nat came out of his office moments later. His forehead was creased with irritation. Carrie Barclay had not been at the sale. He had been so sure she would be there and he had intended to ask for her number afterwards. But she didn't turn up. Nat was frankly astonished that she didn't want to see his performance in the saleroom after such an impressive performance in bed.

'Sarah Jane,' he barked. 'You're supposed to update the database. Why can't I find the details for Carrie Barclay?'

'Who?' Sarah Jane replied.

'Carrie Barclay. New York divorcee from the Old Masters launch. Black dress, blonde hair.'

Sarah Jane was non-plussed but Lizzy knew exactly who he was talking about.

'The one you took to dinner?' she said. 'The really important client?'

'Yes. Where are her contact details? I can't find them on the database.'

'Perhaps they haven't been inputted yet,' Lizzy suggested.

'For God's sake,' said Nat. 'Why do I have to deal with such incompetence?'

Sarah Jane and Lizzy shared a look. 'He definitely didn't get laid,' Sarah Jane mouthed once Nat went back into his office.

Lizzy couldn't keep the relief off her face.

Nat had recovered his equilibrium by the Monday of the following week. The Trebarwen sale was his. Though, as he explained to Lizzy there had never really been any danger that the Trebarwen estate would go to Sotheby's or Christie's. 'This should serve as an example to you of how important it is to keep up with those old-school ties . . .' Lizzy nodded, hanging on his every word as usual. 'Which school was it you went to? Cheltenham Ladies?'

'No. I was at the High School for Girls in Gloucester,' she reminded him. 'State grammar.'

'Ah well,' said Nat with a subtle frown. He didn't need to know any more details. 'Anyway, since you've been such a star of late, I've decided to give you the all-important job of making sure this sale runs smoothly.'

Lizzy's heart leapt.

'You'll need to go back down to Cornwall and make a proper inventory.'

'Will you be coming?' she asked.

'I don't think there's any need. You know what you're doing.'

'It's quite a responsibility. Your old schoolfriend . . . Perhaps Sarah Jane could come with me.'

'No,' said Nat. 'I need Sarah Jane here in London. Don't know what I'd do if I didn't have at least one of you looking after me.'

Lizzy found that thought much less amusing than Nat did. 'Right. Have we got a date for the sale?'

'Mid-April,' said Lizzy. 'We can fit it in on a Wednesday.'

'That's good. But it means that you'll need to get cracking right away. The catalogue deadline is . . .'

'In five days,' Lizzy told him.

'Then you better book yourself on to a train for tomorrow.'

'Where should I stay?'

'Oh, you can stay in the house. But watch out for Julian Trebarwen. He may be good-looking but he's a terrible shit. Can't be trusted. Understand?'

Lizzy nodded. She was at least slightly mollified that Nat cared enough to warn her off another man.

'I got the Trebarwen job,' Lizzy told Sarah Jane. 'And I've got to take Marcus with me.' She nodded at the bespectacled junior.

Sarah Jane patted her hand in sympathy. 'It'll be great. I would kill for a few days out of London. Fresh air. Country-side.'

'I'll swap,' said Lizzy hopefully.

'No chance,' said Sarah Jane.

Chapter Twelve

$\mathcal{L}$IFE in Cornwall was much the poorer for Louisa's death. Katie had sulked about it for weeks, though Serena suspected that her daughter was pining more for the right to ride on the Trebarwen boys' old rocking horse rather than for her dear auntie Louisa.

Serena still wondered what would happen to the place. Since Julian had gone back to London 'on business', the house had remained empty. Three months had passed. The shutters were closed, like sleeping eyelids. It was eerily silent. The dogs had been packed off to 'a relative'. Serena suspected that relative might actually be a dogs' home. The lone peacock that had roamed the grounds had also disappeared, leading Serena to conclude that perhaps she really had heard a shot one night while she lay in bed rereading *Pride and Prejudice*.

It being early in the year, the garden remained pretty much under control. Everything was dormant. But it wouldn't stay like that. If the Trebarwen boys decided to put the house on the market, they would need to make sure it looked tidy. Would they put it on the market? Serena definitely didn't fancy the idea of having Mark Trebarwen, his brittle wife and their whey-faced teenagers as neighbours. Just as she was sure that the brittle wife and teenagers would not want to be so far south of Exeter. But would Julian's work allow him to live in Cornwall? What did Julian actually do for a living? And if neither brother took the house, would the alternative be any better? Serena had a horrible vision of Donna Harvey buying the house with her divorce settlement so that Tom could be closer to his daughter. She imagined all Louisa's beautiful furniture and paintings gone and replaced by an interior designer's version of country chic – all of it straight from the furniture department at Harrods.

Bloody Donna. Tom had called that morning to make arrangements for the Easter holidays. Easter was late that year. Donna wanted to take Katie to Majorca, where she had a villa, so that they could 'bond'. Serena took it as another sign that the cow that had stolen her husband was staying on the scene. She feared for her little girl, growing up with a woman like Donna Harvey in her life. Someone so controlled and controlling. Someone who might eventually convince Katie that her mother was the loser Serena so often felt herself to be.

It was almost time to pick Katie up from school. Feeling somewhat flabby and frumpy after her conversation with Tom, which seemed to have been nothing more than a list of places where he would be shagging his hard-faced new love, Serena decided to walk rather than take the car. Katie would groan, as she always did when she had to walk back, but it would be good for her, too. It was one of those unusually beautiful early spring days. The sky was clear. Those birds that hadn't flown south for the winter were stretching their wings and their lungs. Serena relished the sound of the skylark. You wouldn't hear that in London, she reminded herself.

The quickest way to the school took Serena straight across Trebarwen land. Louisa had insisted that Serena should consider the path that went behind Louisa's house as her personal right of way. And Serena was half over the gate before she remembered that Louisa wasn't around anymore and Trebarwen's new owners might feel differently.

'Hey!'

Rats. Julian Trebarwen had caught her in the act.

'Sorry,' Serena climbed down on her side of the fence. 'Was just walking to pick Katie up from school. I used to take a shortcut through here when your mother was alive but . . . I'll take the car.'

'It's OK. You can walk through here if you want to,' said Julian. 'I was just coming over to give you a hand. Thought you might get stuck on the gate and rip your jeans or something.'

Serena blushed as she pushed her hair out of her face. Of course she was wearing her very worst jeans again. The ones that had been 'decorating jeans' back when she and Tom were still playing happy families and experimenting with National Trust tester pots in what would become Katie's room. The jeans were covered in paint splodges. And worse. Why was it you never noticed you'd got egg yolk on yourself until you were in company?

'Need a hand?' Julian asked, reaching out for her.

Serena nodded. 'Thank you.' He helped her over the gate. 'Which way is school?' he asked.

'Over there.' Serena waved towards the village, thinking it odd that Julian didn't know where the village school was before she remembered that he and his brother had been sent to boarding school at the age of five.

'Mind if I walk with you?'

Serena tried not to think about the egg yolk as she and Julian skirted the edge of the garden.

'I suppose I should think about getting someone in to deal with all this,' said Julian, waving his hand at the flowerbeds.

'I don't imagine you've had much time to think about anything,' said Serena kindly. 'It must be so hard for you to take in. I know what it's like when one of your parents dies.'

Julian agreed. 'Yes. I have been rather shocked by how much I miss the old bag. When she was alive, I could just about manage three hours in her company without incurring her wrath in some way or other. I couldn't wait to be back on the motorway to London. But now . . . what was that old song? You don't know what you've got till it's gone?'

'Families are difficult,' said Serena. 'I'm sure she knew that you loved her in her own way and I know she loved you very much in return.' That much had come through, even when Louisa was expressing her disappointment.

'Well, it's certainly strange to be here in the house without her.'

'How long are you here for?' Serena asked.

'At least a week,' he said.

Serena found she was pleased to hear that.

'Got a couple of people from Ludbrook's the auctioneers coming down tomorrow to take a look at the stuff in the house. See if there's anything worth putting up for sale.'

Serena was surprised he was going ahead with it.

'It's quite early to be making a decision like that, isn't it? I mean, you might inadvertently sell something that you might regret losing in years to come.'

'I don't think so,' said Julian quite firmly. 'It's not as though we're talking about family heirlooms. It's all crap. My mother got most of it at car boot sales.'

'You're joking.'

'It doesn't matter anyway. Neither my brother nor I want any of it. You've got to keep moving forward, don't you think? If you don't move forward you die. Like a shark.'

They'd come to the other side of the surrounding wall. Serena didn't know if Julian intended to come any further. She stopped and studied his profile as he looked into the next field with an expression of contemplation. She had the sense that all that talk about boot sales and moving forward was just bravado. Here was a man who had lost his mother. In his face she could see the little boy he had once been. He was charmingly vulnerable.

'It's twenty-five past three,' said Serena. 'I should get a move on. Katie will give me hell if I'm not there when the bell goes.'

'OK.'

Julian gave her some help getting over the next wall.

'Perhaps you'd like to come to dinner again one night this week,' Serena suggested. 'I mean, if you're not busy.'

'Tonight?' Julian suggested at once.

'Well, OK. But it'll have to be spag bol.'

'My favourite.'

Serena walked the rest of the way to school with a slight skip in her step. Had she just made a date?

*   *   *

The food may have been basic (no time to go to the supermarket) but supper was great fun. Julian garnered many brownie points with Katie by bringing across the rocking horse she had missed so much. He got brownie points from Serena with a nice bottle of red.

The next day Serena found herself back inside Trebarwen for the first time since the funeral. Julian had asked her, very nicely indeed and with the promise of a fish supper at the village's one and only restaurant, if she might be kind enough to sort through his mother's most personal effects. Serena agreed happily. And though it wasn't exactly a happy task to go through Louisa's dusty wardrobe and pick out those items that should be binned and those that should go to a charity shop, Serena was glad to be in the company of adults for a while.

The team from Ludbrook's arrived at lunchtime. Serena was surprised to see that the venerable auction house had sent such a young woman down but Lizzy Duffy, as she was called, seemed to know what she was talking about. When Julian introduced Serena and explained that she was sorting through the wardrobe, Lizzy's response was instant.

'If you don't mind,' she said. 'I'd like to look at anything with a big label on it. We have a designer vintage clothing sale every three months at Ludbrook's.'

'My mother dressed like a hobo,' said Julian. Serena shot Julian a glance.

'Mrs Trebarwen was very elegant. I have found a couple of dresses by Chanel,' she confirmed. 'Could be 1960s.'

'Wonderful,' said Lizzy.

Along with Lizzy Duffy and her squinting assistant Marcus came a photographer with his own assistant. Lizzy explained that some of the larger items of furniture were to be photographed in situ. It had become a popular way to display items to their best effect.

Over the course of the next two days, the catalogue shoot was executed with as much precision as a cover shoot for a glossy magazine. The photographer and his assistant dressed each 'set' with incredible care. Meanwhile, Lizzy studied the Polaroids to be certain that all the detail she required for the catalogue was easily visible.

Serena found herself envying Lizzy Duffy. She had her entire life before her. She was young and beautiful and obviously intelligent. She had a responsible, interesting job. Lizzy reminded Serena of the way she herself had once been, before marriage and Katie and divorce.

'I studied art too,' Serena felt she had to tell her. She wanted to make clear that she wasn't just some local yokel stay-at-home mum but an equal. 'Painting. At Chelsea. I did a year in Florence studying the techniques of Old Masters after I graduated.'

'Lucky you. I would love to have studied art. My parents were dead set against that. Thought it would just leave me unemployable. Closest I got was art history.'

'It's never too late to pick up a paintbrush,' said Serena, echoing the encouragement that Louisa had given her.

'I think I'll just stick to selling art,' said Lizzy with a shrug.

Lizzy was very pleased indeed with the way the photographs for the catalogue had turned out. She felt sure that Nat would be impressed. She was feeling much more relaxed about having left him alone with Sarah Jane since hearing that Sarah Jane had gone home sick that afternoon. She in turn let Nat know that Julian Trebarwen wasn't the dangerous cad that Nat had described at all. Far from it. There had been no midnight creeping along the corridors to the guest rooms. He hadn't addressed a single inappropriate comment in Lizzy's direction. She guessed that was because he was trying to impress his mother's neighbour; Julian only had eyes for Serena. By the time Lizzy and Marcus had finished in the house, the sexual tension between Julian and Serena was palpable.

'Do you think he'll get laid?' Marcus asked Lizzy as the cab pulled out of Trebarwen's grand driveway to take them to the station. Neither of them were looking forward to the train ride.

'What kind of question is that?' Lizzy asked, pausing for hardly any time at all before she added, 'Yes, I think he will.'

'Serena, I'm so grateful for what you've done for me these past few days,' said Julian. 'I don't know what I would have done without you.'

They hadn't gone out to dinner. Serena had reckoned without the difficulty of finding a baby-sitter in deepest, darkest Cornwall. And so Julian had fetched the fish and chips and brought them with him to Serena's house, where they ate them at the kitchen table by the light of a candle in an empty wine bottle.

Katie had been persuaded to go to bed early. Serena had allowed her to have the portable DVD player (a bribe from Tom to make up for another weekend missed) in her room. Katie was delighted. The prospect of snuggling beneath the duvet with a pile of Disney films was infinitely preferable to joining her mother and her guest downstairs.

Julian brought with him a bottle of St Emilion. Cheval Blanc.

'Oh my goodness,' said Serena. 'Are you sure? With fish and chips?'

'If you don't think it's a good match, I can run back out to the Spar and get a bottle of Lambrusco.'

'No,' said Serena. 'I mean, this is fantastic. Thank you.'

'Lots more where it came from. My mother had crates of the stuff. Not keeping it properly, of course.'

And indeed, that particular bottle was horribly oxidised.

'Damn,' said Julian. 'I'll just have to sell the rest,' he added with a wink. 'Or shall we try one more?'

'No. There's no need.' Serena brought out a bottle of Chianti. Which was perfect.

Julian Trebarwen was turning out to be such an interesting guy. He was amusing company and passably good-looking. Better looking with every sip of wine Serena took. Halfway through dessert – tiramisu – Serena decided that if he tried to kiss her again that night, she would let him. In fact, she told herself, it might well be time for her first post-separation shag.

She'd been thinking about sex a great deal lately. Its resurgence in her thoughts was as surprising yet inevitable as the first shoots of spring breaking through the frozen ground. When Tom left her, Serena's libido went into hibernation. Her whole energy became focused on her daughter: keeping her happy, finding somewhere new to live and ensuring that Katie got through the separation and subsequent divorce without being scarred for life. Serena's mental state had been reflected in her outward appearance: her daily costume of jeans and T-shirt and the fact that she hadn't bothered to have her hair cut for months. Her make-up bag gathered dust. Everything about her screamed 'leave me alone'. She hadn't dared let her thoughts wander towards the carnal. Until Julian Trebarwen walked into her life.

And now, almost four months after their first meeting after the funeral, she allowed herself to think that perhaps Julian returned her interest in a real way. The first time he had tried it on could have been put down to grief and confusion after Louisa's death, but he had come back. Could it really be that he just enjoyed her cooking? Over the past few days, she'd caught him looking at her a couple of times when he thought she hadn't noticed. Back in the old days, before Tom smashed her confidence, she would have interpreted looks like those as lust at the very least.

While Julian was drinking coffee, Serena slipped upstairs to tell Katie that it was time for bed. She found her daughter already asleep, *Cinderella* still playing on the tiny screen. Serena turned off the DVD player and pulled up the duvet to cover Katie's shoulders. It was chilly that evening. Halfway down the stairs, Serena paused and ran back up again. This time she went into her own room. At the bottom of her knicker drawer was a set of lingerie she had never worn. She'd bought it the day after Tom announced that he had fallen in love with Donna, hoping and praying that the two tiny strips of silk might bring him back to her. It didn't work. In fact, she didn't even get a chance to try. The knickers and bra had remained in her lingerie drawer ever since, a pretty reminder of a very ugly new reality.

But maybe Serena's luck was about to change. Maybe fate didn't ever have Tom in mind when Serena stood in the changing room at La Perla, her eyes red from crying and her stomach flat, for once, from throwing up. Maybe these knickers were always meant to be seen by someone else.

Serena quickly pulled off her jeans and her sweater and replaced her rather more quotidian underwear with the

Italian scanties. To her delight, a glance in the mirror showed a reflection that looked far better than the sad girl she'd been in the store changing room. All those months in Cornwall, all the walking to and from school and along the beach at weekends had really paid off. Serena looked fit. She was pale, sure, but Julian wouldn't be expecting a supermodel.

With her jeans and jumper back in place, keeping for now Serena's secret, she wandered back downstairs. She felt naughty and wondered if it showed.

'What took you so long?' asked Julian, patting the empty space on the sofa beside him.

'Oh, you know what it's like. Katie asked me to read a story and then she wanted another one . . .'

'Of course,' Julian nodded. 'I shouldn't be jealous of a six-year-old girl, but I am. She deprived me of your company.'

Serena felt a flutter of delight in her chest. This was all so utterly wonderful. For once, for just a moment, bitter angry thoughts of Tom and his horrible new woman were the furthest thing from her mind. Serena found she was trembling as she brought her coffee cup to her mouth.

'Something a little stronger, perhaps?' she suggested. She thought she might have some cooking brandy somewhere.

'Not for me,' said Julian. He was gazing – that was the word for it, gazing – at Serena's face now and he reached out one big hand to push a strand of hair from her face. 'I don't want anything to cloud my vision.'

'OK,' said Serena.

'You are quite exquisitely beautiful,' he said.

Serena could hardly speak. She nodded her thanks.

'I have wanted to kiss you since I first saw you,' Julian continued. 'But you know that and . . . of course,' he let his hand drop. 'I understand that it still might not be the right time for you.'

'Oh. No no no,' Serena protested. 'I mean. It's fine. I'd like that now. I think.'

Julian smiled. 'I'm very glad to hear it.'

He didn't give her time to change her mind.

As he leaned forward to kiss her, he simultaneously pushed Serena back into the cushions. It was, thank goodness, a great kiss. He tasted so marvellous. The wine they'd been drinking that evening couldn't disguise that fact that he tasted right to Serena on a more fundamental level. This was chemistry at its best. Soon Serena let her lips open and felt his tongue inside her mouth. Meanwhile, Julian's hands sought out her bare skin beneath her sweater. The warmth of his palms against her flesh sent Serena giddy with desire.

Later, in the bedroom, when he uncovered the pretty lilac knickers and the matching balconette bra, Julian gave a low whistle of approval.

'My God,' he said. 'Those are fabulous knickers.'

Serena shrugged as though she wore such exotic scanties every day.

'And that bra. Seems a shame to take it off. Though I can't wait to see what's beneath.'

Lying beside her on the bed, Julian propped himself up on one elbow. 'I just want to look at you,' he said. 'I want to drink in your beauty with my eyes and treasure the memory for ever.'

The nerves Serena had expected to feel when unveiling her body for someone new for the first time in a decade had soon dissipated. Julian's obvious and very vocal appreciation of her gave Serena the confidence to relax into his embrace. He was exactly the kind of lover she needed after so long alone. He was gentle and attentive. He catalogued every part of her body with praise. He ran his fingers across her shoulders and pushed the bra straps out of the way.

'Such lovely breasts . . . Your shoulders are so fine . . . I want to kiss your neck all night long.'

Serena felt worshipped and appreciated in a way that had become all too unfamiliar. It gave her the courage to be herself once more.

'How about a little less conversation, a little more action?' she asked as she pulled Julian so that he was on top of her. Her arms encircled his back and she kissed him deeply.

She felt the hard length of his penis against her pubic bone. She parted her legs and tipped her pelvis upwards towards him, to let him know that it was OK. She was ready for this. She wanted it.

Without taking his eyes off hers, Julian slid his hand between their bodies and guided his penis into her. Serena gasped at the almost forgotten delight of penetration; that moment when two become one. As Julian slowly began to move inside her, she closed her eyes to better relish the pleasure. The warmth of his body against hers and the joy of feeling taken flooded her body and mind. As Julian rocked, Serena wrapped her legs around his waist. It had been so long. So long. She was as surprised as Julian by the speed and intensity with which she came.

The next morning, Serena was on cloud nine. It must have shown because, over breakfast, Katie narrowed her eyes and asked suspiciously what she was so happy about. And at the school gate, one of the other mums asked Serena if she'd had 'something done'.

'I don't mean botox or anything,' the fellow mum added swiftly. 'It's just that . . . well, you look really fresh this morning. Have you had something done to your hair?'

'That'll be it,' Serena joked. 'I actually combed it.'

Considering the amount she had drunk the night before, Serena knew she should have had a hangover, but instead she was feeling the best she had in years. It was a feeling that persisted even when she called Tom later that morning and got Donna instead. Serena hoped that her newly found bliss echoed in her voice, as she asked Donna to tell Tom to ring. 'See Donna,' she wanted to say. 'You're not the only one who's getting laid.'

Serena felt better still when Julian called her around lunchtime.

'Come over to the big house and have some beans on toast?' he suggested.

Putting on her second best set of lingerie for the occasion, Serena skipped on over. The idea of beans on toast was soon forgotten. Instead, Serena joined Julian in a big four-poster bed in what had been his mother's room. They made love until it was time to pick Katie up from school. For the rest of the week, they met every day to do the same thing again and again and again.

By the time Julian had to go back to London the following Sunday night, Serena looked and felt ten years younger. What's more, she had an awful feeling she might be falling in love.

Chapter Thirteen

EASTER arrived at last. It was near the end of April, the latest it had been in centuries. Lizzy spent her Easter weekend walking on air. Nat had asked her to spend the two bank holidays with him. Four blissful days in bed. He'd even changed the sheets. It almost took Lizzy's mind off what she would be going back to: the Trebarwen sale on the very last day of the month. It was to be Lizzy's first auction as actual auctioneer.

She'd had the in-house training, which had been awful to begin with but later became good fun. By the end of that week, she could hold her own with the boys who had started out louder and so much more confident than she. They'd been a pretty tough audience to practise in front of. Always trying to trip her up, heckling and forcing her to stumble. Nat assured her that the real punters would not be half so difficult. They were there to buy art, not to make a fool of the auctioneer. They had no reason to want her to fail.

'Just take your time,' said Nat. 'Remember everything I've told you and you will do brilliantly.'

'Of course I will,' said Lizzy. 'You're my Yoda.'

'Yoda? You're going to have to make up for that comment,' said Nat as he unzipped his trousers and motioned that Lizzy should get under his desk. 'Come on,' he indicated his hardening penis. 'We've got ten minutes.'

As sales went, the Trebarwen sale was relatively unimportant. It was to be held on a Wednesday afternoon. Though there were plenty of interesting lots, there was nothing that had drawn the attention of the media. Fact was, no matter how rare a piece of china or chest of drawers might have been for its type, such things just didn't have the glamour of Old Masters, expensive contemporary art (which had the added benefit of the 'is it really worth it' factor when it came to getting a mention in the *Daily Mail*) and jewellery that had been owned by someone glamorous.

Nat expected that the turn out for the Trebarwen Sale would largely comprise dealers who specialised in what he called 'chocolate box' pictures. There were plenty of those in the sale. These dealers were pretty straightforward people to deal with. That made it the ideal sale for Lizzy to cut her teeth on. That didn't mean to say that she wouldn't be taking it very, very seriously indeed.

She had Sarah Jane help her put her hair up in a bun and eschewed her contact lenses for a pair of glasses, giving the impression of gravitas, professionalism and experience even if it only lasted the afternoon.

The sale started reasonably well. Lizzy was pleased to see that while the room wasn't full, it was far from empty. There were enough people there to create the kind of buzz she wanted. Lizzy's voice wobbled a little as she welcomed everyone into the room and there was some feedback that had to be corrected by a technician. But then she was off.

Really, it was simple. Lizzy read out the description of each lot as her white-gloved colleagues carried it onto the stage. Then it was a matter of spotting the interest in the room. With interest from two it was easy. Take a bid from the one to first catch her eye and then ask the other to go higher. Back and forth, back and forth until one of them dropped out. It was always a relief to get two bidders. Lizzy wasn't entirely sure she had the chutzpah to take a 'bid from the chandelier' – as a bid on behalf of the house was called – and convince a genuine buyer they had competition in the room when they were actually the only one bidding.

But by the time she got to the twenty-third lot, Lizzy was beginning to hit her stride. She glanced over at Nat who gave her the thumbs up. She began to be filled with a sense of exhilaration as strong as she had ever had before. She was presiding over her first auction and everything was going well. She had reached another milestone in her life. Like passing exams, a driving test or getting her first job. Taking an auction would never seem so daunting again.

She came to lot forty-four. By now Lizzy felt confident enough to deviate a little from the script and emulate Nat by adding embellishments to the item descriptions to whet her audience's appetite. 'This is a charming oil painting of two greyhounds standing on the steps of Trebarwen house itself. I think you'll agree that the quality of this oil is so wonderful and of such vibrancy, it might have been painted just yesterday. Who will start the bidding at five thousand pounds?'

Three hands shot into the air and Lizzy faltered for the first time that afternoon. What was she supposed to do? Could she take bids from all three? It wasn't an ideal situation but Lizzy decided to give it a shot.

She tried to keep calm as she tracked the bids from each of the three audience members. But every time she asked for a higher bid, two paddles went up and it was impossible to know whose was first. The room was confused as to who was leading. Lizzy was confused as to who was leading, though she seemed to have got to eleven grand.

From the side of the stage, Nat gestured wildly, slashing his flattened hand across his throat in the gesture that could only mean 'cut'. Lizzy ignored him for a while. The three people in the room were all bidding wildly and the price was rising higher and higher. But then a fourth joined in and Lizzy panicked. Not knowing how to bring the room back to order, she brought down the hammer.

'I need to start again,' she said.

'For fuck's sake,' said the dealer who had been leading.

'I'm sorry,' she said. 'But I've lost track. I think that he bid the same as you and . . .'

'No, he bloody didn't,' said the second dealer. 'The picture was with me at twenty-five grand and you brought the hammer down. I think you'll find that's a sale.'

Lizzy didn't know what to do. Had she just inadvertently entered into a binding contract by bringing down the gavel? There was a deafening chorus of disapproval and jeering and Lizzy just couldn't recover herself though she begged the crowd's indulgence. They just weren't going to cut her any slack. There was nothing for it. Nat strode onto the stage.

'I'm sorry, ladies and gentlemen. It seems that Lizzy's beginner's luck has run out.'

He gave her a pat on the back. Lizzy ran from the stage in tears.

Lizzy spent the rest of the day in the office, replaying the horror of her first time on the podium and shuddering at the memory.

'It's OK,' said Nat. 'We can't all be great auctioneers. Some people have it and some people . . .'

'Don't. I know. I don't,' said Lizzy.

'Dry your tears,' he said. 'It doesn't matter. The sale brought in way more than we expected for such a bunch of old tat. You're not going to get fired.'

Lizzy was worried about far more than that. Had seeing her make such a spectacular hash of her first auction made Nat fancy her less?

Well, it may have done, but the corresponding spike in testosterone that Nat got whenever he pulled off a great sale had more than made up for any diminishment Lizzy had suffered in his eyes. Nothing made him feel more like fucking than the applause of his audience – especially an audience of his peers – when he blasted through a high estimate. The last thing he wanted to do when he was on such a high was go home alone. And so Lizzy was thrilled to be invited to share some supper and a taxi. And even more delighted when, as usual, Nat suggested that she got out at his place.

As it turned out, it was a great way to end a terrible day. The sex that night was simply fabulous. Lizzy laughed with delight as Nat picked her up and carried her through to the bedroom without stopping to complain about his knee. He threw her onto the counterpane and jumped on top of her, kissing her wildly until she stopped giggling and responded with the proper passion he required.

Lizzy felt borne to the top of a wave by her desire and Nat's all too obvious lust for her. Her body sang for Nat Wilde. In his arms she felt like the beautiful woman she'd always wanted to be. His kiss had the power to transform her from the dumpy girl who never quite felt at home in her skin into a siren. Lizzy had always found the thought of someone crying out as they came embarrassing but when Nat Wilde made love to her, Lizzy wanted to shout.

As he thrust into her, she took hold of his buttocks, pulling him further and further in. She wanted every inch of him. Every bit of him she could get. Feeling him stiffen in the moment before he orgasmed, Lizzy felt quite incredibly powerful. She loved that he lost control before she did. It meant that she was irresistible to him, didn't it? He couldn't hold back because he wanted her so much. As he shuddered on top of her, the Trebarwen sale was all but forgotten.

That night he was so kind to her. As she lay in his arms in the delicious afterglow, she felt so protected, so secure. Nat had soothed away the pain of making such a hash of her first auction. He had restored her confidence with his desire for her, so that she felt sure that one day soon she would get up on that podium again. Nestling with her head on his chest, Lizzy felt so close to him. It was time to tell him the truth, she decided. That she had been a virgin when he first made love to her.

'Nat,' she murmured close to his ear.

'Mmmmm?' he responded dreamily.

'There's something I've got to tell you,' she continued in a whisper. 'About the first time that you and I made love. The thing is, Nat. I know you're going to think this is silly. You may not even believe me. But the first time that you and I. Well . . .'

She paused. Seconds away from revealing the truth. But the dramatic silence was interrupted by a snore. Nat Wilde was asleep.

Chapter Fourteen

THAT same day, Julian Trebarwen was in Cornwall. He received the detailed results of the Ludbrook's sale via email.

'Well,' said Julian when he called his brother Mark, who was in Singapore again. 'I hope you've got the champagne on ice. Nat Wilde sold everything.'

'Everything?'

'Yep, absolutely everything from that hideous credenza to our mother's fake pearl earrings.'

'Fantastic.'

'I think you'll be pleased with the figure.' Julian recited the digits.

'What? That's incredible?' It was far more than either of them had expected.

'I know. But there were obviously some good lots in there. Apparently those nasty gold earrings in the shape of frogs were actually Cartier, which made a big difference. And can you believe that old painting of the greyhounds made twenty-five grand?'

'Old painting?' said Mark.

'Yeah. Can't say I'd even noticed it before the funeral. It was hanging over the fireplace where that awful daub of you and I used to be. I think mother must have brought it down from some room in the west wing to piss you off last time you were there for dinner.'

'Oh, it pissed me off all right,' said Mark. 'But are you sure it went for twenty-five grand?'

'I'm quite sure. Incredible, eh?'

'Yes,' said Mark. 'Because it wasn't an old picture at all. It was painted just last year.'

Julian was confused.

'I don't get it.'

'It's true. Mother had her next door neighbour paint her bloody rescue greyhounds.'

'What? Which neighbour?' Julian couldn't believe what he was hearing.

'The one with the tits and the hair.'

'You mean Serena?'

'She the brunette?'

'Yes.'

'That's the one.'

'But . . . but. She didn't tell me.'

'Mother told me the last time I saw her. Shortly before she told me that she wanted to skip a generation in her will and leave Dad's Patek Philippe to my youngest. I assumed you knew.'

'I had no idea. And neither did Nat Wilde's team. They attributed it to some Victorian. Follower of Stubbs.'

'Should we tell Wilde?' Mark asked.

'Mark, are you insane?'

'He'll want to know.'

'Sure. But it's too late. We're talking about a painting that sold for twenty-five grand. It was one of the biggest lots in the sale.'

'But it was a fake . . . it's less than two years old.'

'And we didn't say otherwise. We didn't say anything about it at all. Nat Wilde's the one who made the mistake. And the girl he sent down afterwards should have spotted it was new. The way I see it, we're in the clear. We've done nothing wrong. I say we treat this as a little windfall and keep quiet.'

'Are you serious?'

'I need the cash.'

'Oh, sod it. You're right,' said Mark, giving in quickly. 'So do I. We'll keep quiet. I've got school fees to pay. But bloody hell . . . twenty-five grand. Mother gave nearly that much of our inheritance to the dogs' home anyway.'

'Fuck, yes. It's our right to claw some back.'

'I've got to go,' said Mark. 'Give the missus the good news.'

'Don't tell her about the dogs. The fewer people who hear about this the better.'

'She's only interested in the money. Though she'll probably blow the lot on some more bloody designer orthopaedic shoes. I'll call you tomorrow to talk about the house. I was thinking we could try to rent it while the market's so flat.'

'Good for me,' said Julian.

'Twenty-five grand for those dogs. Un-bloody-believable.' Mark whistled through his teeth.

*   *   *

Unbelievable indeed. When the conversation ended, Julian paced the empty room, an unlit cigarette between his lips. He'd been trying to give up for a long time but found that having a fag in his mouth helped him to think and right then he was having some particularly interesting thoughts.

He grabbed his coat and went next door.

Chapter Fifteen

JULIAN hadn't told Serena he was going to be in Cornwall that week, so she was a little shocked but pleased, he fancied, to see him, when he rang on her doorbell at ten to ten.

'I've got something really important to talk to you about.'

Serena put her hand to her throat in surprise.

'It's ten o'clock at night!' She wasn't sure she should accept a booty call. 'You might have phoned.'

'I'm sorry but I won't be able to sleep if I don't tell you about this now.'

Serena's face fell. Julian looked anxious. Had he come to break up with her already?

'Can I come in?' he asked again.

Might as well get it over with, Serena thought. 'Of course,' she said. She led him into the sitting room. The atmosphere between them was heavy, as though he were a debt collector turned up to take what he was owed, rather than her lover.

'Can I have a drink?' he asked.

'Sure.' Serena poured out the last of her whisky. Julian had finished off most of the bottle on his last visit.

He took a sip and seemed to relax a little.

'So, tell me what this is about,' said Serena. Having agonised while she rinsed out a glass for the whisky which chair she should sit in when she brought it to him, Serena chose to sit down next to Julian on the sofa. She pondered putting her hand on his but decided against it. Hopefully her decision to sit next to him would make it easier to come out with what it was he wanted to say.

'I know it's a bit much coming round here so late at night. You've got to get up early to take Katie to school. But this thought popped into my head earlier today and I've just got to put it out there.'

'You've met someone else,' Serena jumped in.

'What?' Julian was taken aback by Serena's assumption.

'I understand,' she continued. 'I'm a single mum. I'm pushing forty.'

Julian took her face in his hands. 'Serena, I don't want to stop seeing you, if that's what you're thinking. Far from it.'

Then what did he want?

'It could be that what I'm about to say to you is pure madness, in which case, I'd be grateful if you could promise me before I put my proposal to you, that if you're not interested, you will never, ever tell anyone we had this conversation.'

'Of course not,' said Serena. What was going on? Julian had on his face a look that Serena had seen on a man's face only once before. When Tom proposed. 'Go ahead,' she said. 'It's just me here. Katie's asleep.'

'OK,' he took a deep breath. 'I want you to go into partnership with me.'

Well, that was a very formal way to put it but a smile still spread across Serena's face.

'I'm not yet divorced,' Serena reminded him.

'What's that got to do with anything?'

'Well, if it doesn't bother you, my still being married. If you're happy to wait. Tom is certainly keen to untangle himself as soon as possible and I . . . well, I thought I would never want to look at another man so long as I lived but then you arrived next door and . . .'

Julian cocked his head to one side. Confused.

'Oh. Er . . . Ha! You thought I meant . . . Oh God. No. No no no. Business partnership, Serena. I want to go into *business partnership* with you.'

'Right,' she said. 'That's what I thought.'

She got up on the pretence of stoking the fire. When she sat back down again it was in the seat opposite Julian rather than on the sofa with him.

'Carry on,' she said. Though she couldn't possibly imagine what kind of business he thought they would go into. Open Trebarwen as a B & B perhaps, with Serena doing all the donkeywork, changing the beds and cooking the breakfasts no doubt. She might have known that Julian Trebarwen only saw her as a skivvy.

'What is it you want?'

'You remember that painting you did for my mother?'

'The dogs? Yes.'

'I've got a confession to make. I didn't know you were the artist behind that painting. I assumed it was something that had been in the family for years. And so, when Nat Wilde sent those kids from Ludbrook's down to value Mother's estate, I had them value that painting along with all the others. And they attributed it to Richard Delapole, which is how it ended up in the auction along with Mother's genuinely valuable paintings and eventually sold for twenty-five thousand pounds.'

'What?' Serena blinked at the mention of one of the region's most famous early nineteenth-century artists. 'They thought my painting was by Delapole? That's ridiculous.'

'Apparently not. It was bought by an American collector. He paid another thirty thousand for a painting of my mother's rather stern-looking maiden aunt. There is no accounting for taste. Which is not to say that your painting wasn't good. Obviously, it was excellent. It fooled Nat Wilde, who has, so I was always led to believe, the best eye on New Bond Street.'

'So, you told him he was fooled . . .'

'Of course not! No. I mean, what good would that do anybody? Wilde's reputation would be ruined. The American buyer would feel embarrassed. Who would benefit? As it stands, Nat's reputation is intact and the buyer is probably very pleased with his new purchase. I bet he loves it.'

'Where is this going?'

'I want you to paint another picture of Mother's dogs,' said Julian, coming to the point at last.

'For you?'

'No. I want to sell it.'

'Ha! This is all a joke, right?'

'I'm deadly serious. Nat Wilde fell for it. Other people will too. I'll make it worth your while. Look,' Julian reached into his inside pocket and pulled out a wedge of fifties. 'Here's an advance on half my share of the dog picture proceeds, minus the seller's premium. We can cut the same deal on everything else. I know you need the money.'

Serena recoiled from the cash.

'What kind of person do you think I am? What you're proposing is illegal. You could end up in a lot of trouble.'

'I won't try to pass your stuff off as antique, I'll just take it along to a few dealers or auction houses and say I found it in my mother's attic and have no idea who it belongs to. The way I see it, if they spot that it's a new painting the minute they see it, I just look like someone who doesn't know anything about art. If it's not spotted until after the painting goes to auction, then it falls on the auction house's head, as far as I can see. And it'll never be traced back to you.'

'How can you be sure?'

'If you don't tell anyone, I certainly won't. You'll paint the pictures in your attic and I'll find them in mine. What do you say? If we could sell even two paintings a year for as much as the one you did for Mother, that'd make an enormous difference to you and Katie, right?'

Serena looked down at the coffee table, where Julian had put the cash she refused. He was right. It would make a big difference to her life but she couldn't take it. She shook her head.

'Just think about it, OK?' he said. 'You don't need to give me an answer now. And you can keep that cash regardless. Because it was your talent that earned it. And because I wish I could give you and Katie more.'

That last sentence surprised her. Serena looked up and into Julian's eyes. His expression was serious and sincere. Serena felt herself melting.

'OK. I'll think about it,' she said.

After Julian had gone, Serena went up to her studio. She took the cash with her and hid it inside a paint-box along with the engagement and wedding rings she no longer wore. She still had the sketches of Louisa's dogs pinned to her wall. Serena looked at them closely. She knew that the dog painting had been one of her better efforts but the idea that it had fooled an expert in Old Masters was quite incredible. She would never have believed it. Though in fact, as an art student, she had been stung by a tutor's assessment that she could copy *anything*. The implication being that she would never find a style of her own.

But did that matter? Albeit inadvertently, Serena's talent for pastiche was worth twenty-five grand.

Closing the door on her studio, Serena looked in on Katie, who had slept all the way through her mother's dodgy business meeting. Serena smoothed a strand of hair away from her daughter's forehead. Katie deserved so much more than she was getting from life. Now that Tom had abandoned them, it was up to Serena to be two parents' worth of mother. And that meant, she decided, showing Katie that there were possibilities. Setting an example. Serena wanted to show Katie it was possible for a woman to be a creative force outside the kitchen. Julian's proposition would enable her to pick up the plans she had abandoned the moment she married Tom.

If Serena was to be honest with herself, she already knew that she was going to say yes. She'd have been a fool not to. The possibility of twenty grand a year for doing two paintings was just too enticing. It would be enough to fund some childcare so she could take some time away from motherhood and do some new, more adventurous work of her own.

It wasn't long before Serena's doubts had been all but vanquished and she was thinking bigger. If two pictures a year would net her twenty grand then three meant thirty. She could use that extra money to take some fantastic holidays.

She would show Katie France and Italy and the United States. She would show her the world. Katie would have the best of everything again. Suddenly, it would have seemed foolish not to get involved in Julian's plans.

The following morning Serena picked up the phone to tell Julian she was on board.

'So,' she said. 'Let's get on with it. What do you want me to paint first?'

'I think another painting of those two noble greyhounds, the beloved pets of the seventh earl of Trebarwen . . .'

Serena grinned. 'I think I can manage that.'

Chapter Sixteen

CARRIE Klein's leaving party was not a raucous affair. At least, not for her. Carrie drank nothing but mineral water in the chi-chi new bar on top of the Gloria Hotel on Central Park. She made a brief speech of farewell at six forty-five and was out the door by seven. The colleagues Carrie was leaving behind would be partying until late (and possibly singing 'ding dong the witch is dead' as soon as she was out of earshot) but she had to get to the airport. She was flying from JFK to London that very night, intending to be settled in to her new flat over the weekend and at the office bright and early on Monday morning.

She had suggested to Jed that he might like to come with her. Ehrenpreis would be more than happy to pay for his ticket. They'd even stretch to business class for the *de facto* partner of the new London boss. Wouldn't he enjoy spending a weekend in London with her? Jed confirmed that he would love to spend a weekend in London with her, but not that one, or any weekend when her body might be next to him but her mind would be one hundred per cent focused on work.

'Though that doesn't really leave us a lot of scope, does it?' Jed added sadly. 'Your mind is always focused on work.'

Carrie frowned as she remembered the conversation. Why did that have to be such a bad thing? Why shouldn't she be ambitious? And this was the chance of a lifetime. Fuck Jed if he couldn't understand just how important this London posting was to her.

If he really cared, she told herself, he would have come with her if only to see her safely installed in her new home. As it was, she decided that he was just like all the other guys she'd dated. If he wasn't the star of the show, he wasn't interested in taking part. Men were all the same. So egotistical. They could not be trusted to be there for you when it really mattered.

And so, Carrie flew to London alone. Though she was flying first class, this time she didn't sleep at all. Instead, she spent the entire night awake, tap-tapping away on her laptop, fitting figures into spreadsheets and writing endless lists of tasks that would have to be implemented the moment the plane touched down.

It was early morning in the UK when the plane landed. London could not have been greyer. The cloud was low. Though it wasn't actually raining, the air was so damp that Carrie soon felt soaked through. The chap sent to fetch her in a 'limo' turned out to be driving some ancient sedan and he didn't even help Carrie haul her luggage into the trunk. She didn't tip him at the end of the drive into Chelsea and made a mental note never to use his company again.

The apartment where Carrie would be staying until she had time to look for something better was fairly typical for a rental. It was on the third floor. There was a lift but that morning it wasn't working and, because it was a Saturday, there was no hope of getting someone to come out and fix it. The walls of the apartment itself were painted magnolia. The furniture was all blond wood and oatmeal upholstery. Most of it Ikea, she could tell. The floors throughout were covered in a badly fitted laminate that bounced when you walked. It was all so offensively inoffensive. You didn't have to be in there for long to see that a developer had spent the least amount of money possible in turning the place into a corporate crash pad.

Still, Carrie knew she wouldn't be spending much time there. Ehrenpreis had sent her to London to set up an entire outpost of the auction house. Carrie expected to be working round the clock to get things off the ground. On Monday morning she would meet the few British people she had already recruited. Her own personal assistant would not be flying in to London until the following week. Carrie was a little miffed at that. She had wanted Jessica to be with her from day one. There would certainly be plenty for her to do. But Jessica had never been out of the country for more than a week before, and then only to Canada. Unlike her boss, she was quite unnerved by the prospect of spending at least six months in the United Kingdom and had begged Carrie for an extra week so that she could say goodbye to her family properly. It was as though she were leaving for war rather than a new job.

Jessica was only young, on her first job since college, and so Carrie tried to be understanding. But it was still frustrating. Carrie hadn't seen her own family in nine months, even though they had been living just a couple of hundred miles away from her home in New York. They would have to continue to content themselves with emails and the odd conversation on Skype.

There was to be no slow start for Carrie. Having dumped her cases in the apartment, Carrie got on the Tube and went straight to her new office. Once there she saw that her first job would be to rearrange the furniture that had been delivered the previous week and dumped in the middle of the room. With no one to help her, Carrie simply rolled up her sleeves and dragged her desk into place by herself. Then she passed a jolly hour cleaning the small bathroom that led off her office, making a mental note to sack the team who were supposed to have got the building into shape in readiness for her arrival. She spent the rest of her Saturday day firing off emails that would remain unanswered until Monday.

At eight o'clock she got back to the apartment. She picked up one of the leaflets that littered the hallway table and called for a Chinese takeaway. She fell asleep on the inoffensive cream sofa before the takeaway even arrived.

Chapter Seventeen

CARRIE'S first few weeks in London were a whirlwind. She was hardly ever in her little corporate flat. The boxes from Manhattan, that arrived the day after she did, were still waiting to be unpacked after a month. Her house did not look like a home. On the other hand, the office was soon looking very well established.

Jessica arrived exactly on time. Carrie had been worried, during her first week alone in London, that Jessica would change her mind about coming to the UK after all. Jessica had recently met a guy from New Jersey and Carrie was struck by the horrible idea that this new boyfriend would be the type of idiot who proposed after three weeks of dating. She'd read that something like this – a posting overseas – could bring out the romantic in a guy.

But Jessica's boyfriend didn't propose. The closest he got to making a commitment was saying that he might 'swing by' London on his way to some football match in Barcelona. Not great news for Jessica, who was devastated by his lack of interest, but a huge relief for Carrie, who promised her much-valued assistant that there would be consolation aplenty in the form of English boys with their lovely accents and fabulous manners.

Alas for poor Jessica, there wasn't much time for flirtation. Carrie grudgingly allowed her three days to settle in to her own new place and get over her jet lag. After that, she expected one hundred and ten per cent. The two women began work at eight every morning and finished twelve hours later.

The official launch of Ehrenpreis London was set for six weeks after Carrie first opened the doors to her new staff. Jessica responded to the challenge with her usual skill and alacrity. She had begun researching caterers and staff agencies via the Internet even before she left New York. On arriving in London, she chased up references and tasted a hundred different canapés before settling on a company called 'Elegant Eatz'.

'That name is far from elegant,' Carrie pointed out.

'I know. But they do a great mini-burger,' Jessica explained. The theme of the party was to be the 'special relationship' between the US and the UK. Elegant Eatz would be providing mini-burgers and bagels for the USA and tiny Yorkshire puddings with a sushi-like sliver of beef on top to represent the UK. A little tacky, Carrie worried. But fun, Jessica persuaded her. And when Frank Ehrenpreis saw the menu Jessica faxed to his office, he pronounced himself delighted with the idea. Carrie had to admit that Jessica understood the older American male and his sentimentalities far better than she did.

*   *   *

Carrie had hosted plenty of parties before but this one was really important. The entire board of Ehrenpreis would be flying in to London for the official opening. Though the real proof of her abilities would come with the house's first sales, it was vital to make a good impression from the get go.

The RSVP list looked pretty good. Almost eighty per cent of the people Carrie had invited to the opening night party had responded in the affirmative. During the week running up to the party, Carrie drove Jessica nuts, constantly checking that no one important had suddenly sent their apologies. She was particularly anxious that the high-rollers she had been courting so assiduously all showed up to be schmoozed.

The day itself ran like a military operation. Armed with a clipboard, Jessica proved that she was worth every dollar of her much-increased salary as she checked in the caterers and the sound system people and made sure that the grand gallery of Ehrenpreis looked exquisite. That had been a headache, involving the re-hanging of a whole two walls' full of wallpaper to ensure that the subtle red on red pattern was even. There was another brief moment of panic when the sound guy managed to blow a fuse but that was soon dealt with.

However at five o'clock, Carrie was still in her office, checking her emails for last-minute RSVPs.

'Carrie,' Jessica interrupted her. 'People will be arriving in an hour and a half. You've got to go and get ready. Now.'

'But I need to stay here. Call Jo Hansford and cancel my blow dry.'

'No way. Everything is under control. I promise you.'

'You have to get dressed too.'

'I'm just going to fling on my Diane von Furstenberg,' Jessica told her. 'No one is going to be looking at me. You, on the other hand, are going to be the centre of attention. You've got to make a speech.'

Carrie felt a momentary wobble as she thought about her first speech as London boss of Ehrenpreis.

'You can practice while you're getting your hair blown out,' Jessica suggested.

Carrie sat under the dryer at Jo Hansford running through her speech. Meanwhile, another aesthetician attended to her nails. That done she returned to the office. Jessica had made sure that her dress was perfectly pressed. It was a black silk jersey number by Azzaro, simple yet sexy, with a plunging neckline that was accented by a diamante clip. Carrie applied her own make-up with the expertise that came from years of covering up her acne scars. She put a little heavier make-up on her eyes than usual. Like a ballerina preparing for her stage debut, she wanted to be sure that the people at the back would be able to see and understand her expression. On her feet she wore a pair of Louboutin's highest heels – his Altadama platform pumps in grey water-snake leather. They gave her almost another six inches in height.

The result was pretty impressive, even if Carrie thought so herself.

'You look amazing,' said Jessica.

'Thank you. Good enough for the new head of Ehrenpreis London?'

'Definitely.'

Jessica gave Carrie a little squeeze, though she was careful not to crease her dress. 'I know you're the boss, but I'm so proud of you,' she said. 'This is your night.'

It really is, thought Carrie.

Chapter Eighteen

Nat Wilde put rather less preparation into his look for the Ehrenrpreis launch that night. To be honest, he was surprised to have been invited. But the invitation on his desk had his name and a 'plus one' neatly written on it in calligraphic hand. He hadn't had to blag his way in at all, which was a little disappointing in some ways since Nat considered himself to be a very good blagger and liked to exercise his skills from time to time.

At six thirty, Nat showed up at the fine wines department in search of his partner in crime.

'Come on then, Harry. Let's go and find out what Ehrenpreis think they're made of.'

'I don't know if we ought to go,' said Harry, who didn't quite have Nat's brass neck.

'Nonsense,' said Nat. 'I had an invitation and you're my chosen guest. Plus, I need you there to let me know how much they've spent on the wine. Half an hour? They won't have time to lynch us.'

Still, while Nat strode into Ehrenpreis as though he were on their board of directors, Harry slinked into the showroom like a burglar casing a joint.

'Will you try not to look so shifty, Harry? We are here at their invitation after all.'

'I don't know why they invited us. They just want to gloat.'

'Of course they do. It's all about showing off. But the last thing we want to do is give them the impression that we are in any way impressed by all this . . .' Nat waved his hand around the room. 'This gaudy frippery. Would you look at that terrible wallpaper? I don't know what they expect to look good against a red like that. Much too bright. Nouveau.' He ran his finger along the top of a mantelpiece as though inspecting for dust. 'Someone needs to tell them they're not in the colonies now.'

'That's their wine guy,' said Harry. 'I recognise him from the trade press.'

Nat glanced at the man Harry pointed out. He looked every inch the wine expert from his red nose to his gaudy silk cravat. But then Nat's attention was drawn to someone altogether more interesting.

'Well, I never,' he said, subconsciously straightening his tie. 'What is *she* doing here?'

'Who is it?' Harry asked anxiously.

'Remember that bird I told you about? The one from the Old Masters' party?'

'The athletic American divorcee?'

'The very same. There she is. Chatting to old Frank Ehrenpreis. I think I should go and re-introduce myself.'

Nat swiped a couple of fresh glasses of champagne from a passing waiter.

'Stay here, Harry. Don't say anything stupid.'

Nat weaved through the crowd towards his target, practising his opening lines as he moved. He was a little disappointed that Carrie Barclay hadn't called him to let him know she was going to be in town – not least because she was obviously still looking for artwork and he had plenty to sell – but he felt confident that he could charm her into spending the evening with him again. There was no need to fear rejection. His resolve stiffened as he remembered that night at Claridge's when she'd been so hot and wild. Carrie Barclay may have been a tiger but Nat Wilde could tame any pussy . . .

As he got within six feet of her, Carrie turned in Nat's direction. He fixed her with his best smile and raised both champagne glasses. Carrie smiled back at him. Her big blue eyes flashed in recognition. It seemed like quite a warm smile. Excited. She obviously remembered their night at Claridge's as well and as fondly as he did.

'Game on,' thought Nat. He ran his eyes appreciatively over her curves in that little black dress and gave an involuntary shudder of pleasure as he thought about being underneath those incredible shoes.

Then Carrie turned back to old Ehrenpreis who muttered something before giving her a firm handshake and a clap on the shoulder that seemed an odd sort of gesture to make to a potential client.

Ehrenpreis walked off in the direction of the auctioneer's stand. Carrie remained, talking to a younger woman with a clipboard.

'Carrie,' Nat called, waving her glass.

But she was following Ehrenpreis.

'Carrie!'

She didn't turn around.

Now old Ehrenpreis was up at the microphone. He tapped the side of his champagne glass with a pen in an attempt to draw everyone's attention. It didn't work, so instead he picked up the heavy wooden gavel and brought it down on the pad with a resounding thwack.

'Ladies and gentlemen, your attention please.'

That worked. The crowd was silenced. Nat, frustrated in his pursuit for a moment, leaned against a wall. Damn, he hoped the speeches would be short.

'You all know who I am and most of you have been bored witless listening to my speeches before, so I'm not going to say anything much today except thank you for turning out on this rainy night when you could have stayed home watching – what is it you Brits watch? – *Coronation Street.*'

There was a polite ripple of laughter.

'I am very proud to be able to welcome you to the first London office of Ehrenpreis the Auctioneers. I think you'll agree that we have a wonderful place here,' he waved his arms to take in the room. 'But I can't take any of the praise for that. It all has to go to this wonderful woman standing at my side . . .'

Bloody hell, thought Nat. Is Carrie Barclay screwing that old bastard? He was torn between feeling disgusted that she would even consider such an old codger and impressed that she'd bagged herself one of Manhattan's wealthiest bachelors. Perhaps his proximity to the grave was exactly what had attracted Carrie to him.

Ehrenpreis continued. 'You may already know her as head of fine art sales at Ehrenpreis New York. Well, now I'm

exceptionally happy to be introducing her as head of Ehrenpreis London. Ladies and gentleman, I give you the fabulous
Ms Carrie Klein . . .'

'Good God,' said Nat out loud in shock. 'Carrie Klein?'

Glowing from Ehrenpreis's praise, Carrie took the microphone from him and launched into her own speech of
welcome. She'd gone over her speech while sitting under
the blow-dryer but instead she gave a very successful off-the-
cuff vote of thanks to the team she had brought from New
York and their new London counterparts. She made extra-
special effort to ensure that the room gave Jessica a little
round of applause.

Nat Wilde wasn't listening. As Carrie thanked her new
team, he was already slinking back through the crowd towards
Harry. He necked the glass of champagne he had pinched for
Carrie en route. 'My God,' said Harry. 'You screwed the new
head girl at Ehrenpreis. Didn't you recognise her?'

'Of course I bloody didn't.'

'But she must have recognised you. Bloody hell, Nat. Did
she ask you anything about Ludbrook's? You better get on to
compliance.'

'The hell I will. The news that I shagged that monster is
going no further than this room. Understand me?'

'I can't believe you didn't recognise her. Don't you ever
read the trade press?'

'Of course I read the bloody trade press. She doesn't look
like that in her corporate picture. She used to have a
moustache.'

'Looks pretty hot right now.'

'For fuck's sake, Harry. Don't make it worse. Let's go. This
party isn't turning out to be half as much fun as I hoped.'

From her place on the podium, Carrie spotted Nat and Harry making for the door.

'Finally,' she purred into her microphone as she gestured to her fleeing rivals. 'I'd like to thank the good people of Ludbrook's for crossing Bond Street to be with us tonight. And wish them the very best of British luck.' She paused. 'They're going to need it.'

In that moment, Carrie Klein declared war.

Chapter Nineteen

Nat was in a terrible mood when he got into the office the following morning. His colleagues assumed it must be a hangover, but it wasn't long before the truth about Nat's mood spread via the gossips in the fine wine department.

'No wonder we couldn't find Carrie Barclay in our records,' said Olivia.

'How could he not have known who she was?' Sarah Jane asked. 'I mean, doesn't he read the trades?'

But when Lizzy and Sarah Jane googled the new boss of Ehrenpreis London they had to admit that they too would not have recognised the glossy blonde now installed across the street. All the official pictures of Carrie Klein showed her with brown hair scraped back in a bun and big round glasses. They were completely out of date. Somewhere a transformation had occurred.

As it happened, Nat Wilde had an even less flattering memory of the woman who had set up shop across the road.

It was such an unflattering memory that Nat wondered whether there were in fact two women called Carrie Klein in the auction business. The thought that this vixen at Ehren-preis might be the one and the same girl as he had met so many years ago made him shake his head in bewilderment.

It was 1990. Nat had just joined Ludbrook's from Bonhams. He was the rising star, tipped to be the best auctioneer of his generation. His early sales had been shockingly good. He had the patter. He could hold a room in the palm of his hand and squeeze it until the punters left with nothing in their pockets but chewing-gum wrappers. Nat Wilde could sell anything.

Every couple of months, a crop of new interns would arrive at the auction house. Most of them were students on the house's fine art course. An internship was their chance to get their hands on some of the world's best paintings. Quite literally. Most of the work of an intern involved physically shifting paintings and other *objets d'art* from one end of the house to the other, while wearing those white gloves and overalls that Nat had come to find strangely erotic.

Carrie Klein's internship started fairly inauspiciously. As was usual on the first Monday of the month, Nat and Harry Brown watched the arrival of the new boys and girls from the window of Harry's office, which had a good view of the building's entrance. They counted the interns in, making comments, appreciative or otherwise.

'She just has to be mine,' said Nat, watching a pretty redhead wriggle across the pavement in a pair of impractical shoes.

'So unfair,' said Harry. 'I get all the boys.'

'He's definitely yours,' said Nat, pointing out a zitty youth in an ill-fitting two-piece. 'And she's mine.' Nat bagged a ditzy-looking blonde.

'Which one of us is going to get that one?' Harry pulled a face.

'That one' was Carrie Klein, fresh in from the East Coast of the United States. She resembled early pictures of Hilary Clinton. Her hair was arranged in the most unflattering of styles. Half of it was pulled back into a hair-band, keeping it out of her eyes. The rest hung limply to her shoulders. Her glasses covered most of her face. Angry red spots covered that part of her face that wasn't covered by her glasses. She was wearing a Princess Diana pussy-bow blouse of the kind long since abandoned by anyone but Sloaney spinsters over the age of thirty-five.

'Surely some mistake,' said Nat. 'She must be meant for Christie's.'

But no. She was for Ludbrook's. Even worse, Carrie Klein was meant for Nat's very own department. Cruel fate had decreed that the wriggly redhead was the first ever attractive female intern in the fine wine department. In celebration of that fact Harry Brown declared it the right day to open a '47 Petrus.

Nat was not best pleased to have been saddled with the least attractive of the interns (he thought the girl he'd shagged in human resources might have had something to do with it) but he couldn't deny that Carrie knew her stuff. She may not have been up for a little frolicking around the office but she was ready to work and work hard, which was some consolation. And lucky too. Nat's most prized junior had gone and got herself married and was off on a two-week honeymoon in Tuscany. It wasn't long before Nat had delegated all Clara's workload to Carrie.

'It's perfect,' he said. 'Your names are almost interchangeable.'

'But not,' said Carrie. She was terribly serious.

Meanwhile, Harry Brown was having terrible trouble with Erica, his redhead. At the end of her first day, she had copped off with one of his juniors after a few too many post-work drinks. Harry had to endure a week of watching them moon around after each other and another week of tears when the junior's full-time girlfriend came back from staying with her parents in Barbados and normal service was resumed. Red turned up every morning, eyes brimming with tears. She couldn't concentrate. She dropped a bottle of '61 Chateau Mouton Rothschild in the marble lobby. Not good at all.

Nat soon came to realise that he had got the better end of the bargain. It was quite a change to have a female in the office who didn't fire up his testosterone. It was, Nat considered, actually somewhat relaxing. Because he didn't feel he needed to put on a show, he was able to get some paperwork done. And there was something rather nice about being able to discuss business with someone who was actually interested in that side of things. It was clear that, unlike most of her contemporaries on the art history course, Carrie did not view a career in an auction house as a brief interlude before marriage, babies and Labradors. Fine art was Carrie's life.

At the end of Carrie's two-week stint in his office, Nat decided Carrie deserved some kind of reward. Ordinarily, he would take the intern out to lunch, since he was still married at the time. But his wife was away and Harry was not available for dinner. So, Carrie got upgraded as it were.

'Dinner?' Carrie put her hand on her heart as she repeated the word.

Nat nodded. He was faintly pleased with her reaction. Even though he didn't fancy Carrie Klein, it was good to see that she was as excited at the prospect of dinner with him as any other girl.

'Wiltons,' he told her. 'Eight o'clock. Wear a skirt.'

Carrie had been in a trouser suit most days that week.

'I don't have a skirt,' she said. 'Though I do have a pair of culottes.'

'Anything,' said Nat. 'Anything but those bloody slacks.' They were a total abomination.

Nat felt quite pleased with himself as he got ready to go out that night. He was doing a nice thing for sweet little Carrie Klein. A charitable thing, almost, making her feel appreciated. It would be good to have half a bottle of wine and be in bed early. Nat could very nearly see the attraction of a quiet life.

But at seven fifteen, just as he was about to walk out the door, the telephone rang. It was his wife, Miranda. *Much-Admired Miranda*, as he had called her when they were courting. He didn't call her that very often now. She sounded in a bad mood. She so often was these days. Her father and grandfather had been very big in investment banking and Miranda had settled into a permanent state of disgruntlement when she realised that Nat wasn't going to be pulling down anything like the same money.

The conversation began badly.

'What are you doing?' Miranda asked.

'Nothing,' said Nat automatically.

'Nothing? What do you mean nothing? You can't be doing nothing,' Miranda parried. And a row ensued. As he thought back on that fateful evening, almost twenty years later, Nat couldn't remember what he and Miranda had argued about. It had probably, like all their arguments, ranged far and wide and brought in transgressions that he thought had been forgiven months earlier. He had a vague recollection of Miranda saying she should have followed her mother's advice and married Piers Mackesy, the tosser wine merchant Nat had seen off with a punch on the nose outside Brooks'.

Whatever they argued about, the result was that Nat left the house in a very different mood to the one he had been luxuriating in before Miranda's call. Gone was the sense of calm benevolence. Now he was angry with his wife and wanted to make her pay for having called him all those names. By the time Nat got to Wilton's, Carrie's fate was sealed. It no longer mattered that she wore glasses as thick as the bottom of a champagne bottle and was dressed in a shirt with a piecrust collar that kept everything to the imagination.

Nat ordered two glasses of champagne.

'I don't normally have an aperitif,' Carrie began. 'I find that a glass of wine over dinner is enough for me.'

'Well, it's not enough for me,' said Nat grimly.

Carrie sipped in quiet astonishment as Nat necked his glass of champers down in one. Mood and charm restored by the bubbles, he became much more the Nat Carrie had nursed a small crush on. A whole bottle of burgundy later, he had his hand on her knee.

Poor Carrie. The last thing she intended to do on her trip to London was sleep with a married man, but she had been working so hard at impressing Nat with her expertise in art, she hadn't listened to enough in-house gossip to even know that he was married. And so she was unduly flattered when Nat removed her glasses and told her that she had nice eyes (even though she couldn't stop blinking with her specs off).

Nat kissed her before they left the restaurant. As he put his hand up the left leg of her culottes, Carrie felt incredibly naughty, though the waiters didn't bat an eyelid. They saw this kind of thing every night.

'Where are you staying?' Nat asked, as he scanned St James's for a cab.

Carrie told him the name of her hotel in Earls Court. Nat didn't know it, but he knew from its location that it wouldn't be great. The Earls Court Road was lined with fleapits. For a moment he considered inviting Carrie back to his place but that was always a risky proposition. It was unlikely his wife would come back in the middle of the night but she was friendly with half the fishwives on the street and, inevitably, one of them would be peeping out from behind her net curtains when Nat ushered Carrie into or out of the house. The possible fall-out was unthinkable. And then there was the potential horror of undressing Carrie, discovering that he didn't want her after all and being unable to do a runner . . . But a hotel in Earls Court? Was a shag with Carrie really going to be worth the risk of catching scabies? Nat weighed up the pros and cons and decided that it might be.

And it wasn't bad. Beneath her terrible clothes, Carrie had a reasonable body. She was carrying a few extra pounds, but from the neck down her skin was so young and smooth and springy that the overall effect was rather nice. In any case, Nat had always secretly wanted to go to bed with a big girl. His wife seemed to get bonier by the day and there was nothing sexy about bones no matter what the fashion mags said.

And Carrie was enthusiastic. God that made a nice change. Sex with Miranda had become so bloody perfunctory, offered and performed as though it were some great favour that cost Miranda dearly. As Carrie shrieked and sighed each time he touched her, Nat soon became reassured of his own greatness as a lover and the thought of his own greatness made him very hard indeed.

Carrie was tight. Perhaps, the thought passed through Nat's mind briefly, it was because she was overweight. He'd heard that was the case. Fat girls had tighter snatches. Harry Brown swore that it was true, though Nat always thought Harry was trying to pretend that he went after the big ones because he wanted them, rather than because they were the only ones who would have him.

Carrie let out a sound of slight surprise as Nat pushed into her. A sound of slight protest, perhaps, but she didn't make it again so Nat carried on shoving. In out in out. In and out. He was grateful that his right knee seemed to be behaving itself for once. Ever since he tore the meniscus in a skiing accident it had been bloody agony for him to go on top but since he hadn't had sex with his wife for the past three months, it seemed his knee had had time to recover somewhat. It felt all right. And if it stopped feeling all right, he would just flip Carrie over and have her go on top instead. The thought of her breasts dangling in his face popped into his mind. It was swiftly replaced by the thought of his wife's breasts dangling in his face. Miranda's tits were tiny. But those big nipples! Where had they come from? Had they always looked like a couple of cigar butts? He couldn't think why he had ever found that attractive.

In danger of losing his hard-on at the thought of his wife's chest, Nat swiftly brought his attention back to the matter in hand. Sort of. He closed his eyes. Carrie's tight pussy on his cock felt magnificent but in his mind's eye he attached her genitalia to another girl's body. There was a rather pretty girl who worked in the contemporary art gallery across the street from Ludbrook's. She had long brown hair and a neat little arse, which she showed off in a pair of obscenely tight black trousers. Nat hated to see a girl in trousers but he made an exception for that pair. She'd smiled at him once. He'd immediately pictured her naked and had been doing so periodically ever since. Now, in his imagination, she was smiling up at him from the pillows while he pounded into her superbly exciting fresh little vagina.

It worked like a charm.

'Oh God,' Nat cried out. 'I'm coming!' It all happened much more quickly than he expected but it was an impressive orgasm that seemed to last longer than it ordinarily would. As he fell onto Carrie's pillowy breasts, Nat felt as though he had been hit on the back of the head with a plank of wood. It hadn't been his best performance ever, he decided. But it had been great fun for him and that was what mattered. He was soon fast asleep, leaving Carrie looking up at the ceiling, wondering if that was what it was always like.

The following morning, Nat's charm had completely deserted him. His head thumped. His mouth was as dry as a camel's armpit. His eyes were pink and framed by impressive pouches. He was formulating his excuses for a swift exit even as he woke. But there was no need.

'I've got to go,' said Carrie. 'My flight leaves Heathrow at eleven. I ought to leave now. To be sure.'

'Yeah, yeah,' Nat waved his hand at her. 'Just leave me here. I'll show myself out.'

'I think you'll have to check out of the room when I do,' said Carrie.

'What? Oh fuck.' For a moment he'd forgotten they were in a hotel.

Nat sat up. Two small men with anvils clanged in unison on the inside of his skull.

'Thank you,' said Carrie. 'Thank you for everything. I mean, not just for last night but for the whole fortnight. I feel like I've learned so much. You've been really kind to me. And, well, last night.' She blushed and looked down at her feet. Big feet for a girl, thought Nat. 'I have to say that I didn't expect what happened to happen. In fact, can you believe that I was saving myself . . .'

Nat looked confused.

'For marriage,' said Carrie shyly. 'I signed a pledge with the other girls in my sorority. But, well . . . I'm not sure how many of them have kept the promise. And it just felt so right.'

Nat was aghast as he realised what she was trying to tell him. Carrie read his expression as something else.

'This is my number and address,' she said, handing him a piece of paper covered in her neat rounded script. 'I have another six weeks at school before my next break but then I could come and see you again. Or maybe you could come and see me.'

'No, no, no.' Nat put his head in his hands. 'Noooooo.'

'What's the matter?' asked Carrie. 'It's OK. Really. I'm glad it happened the way it did. It was just right. You know.'

'It wasn't right,' said Nat.

'Why not?' Carrie asked.

'Because I'm married.'

The rest of that morning in Earls Court was just terrible. He got dressed quickly and carried Carrie's bags downstairs. He paid her bill. It was the least he could do, though it meant he would have to hide his credit card statement from

Miranda. Nat's wife had an eagle eye for any possible infidelity-related expenditure. Nat did try to give Carrie a little consolatory kiss goodbye but she wouldn't have it. By the time he bundled her into a taxi fifteen minutes later (why can you never find one when you really, *really* need one) she was sobbing uncontrollably.

'It'll be OK,' he said. 'We only did it once. Your future husband need never know. I'm sure you're still largely, er, what's the word . . . Intact?'

Carrie whacked Nat in the solar plexus with her handbag leaving him doubled-over in pain.

Miranda was already at home when Nat got back. She didn't want to hear his excuses.

'I've had a long talk with Daddy,' she said. 'And we've decided that I want a divorce.'

That was the last time Nat had seen Carrie Klein before she walked into his Old Masters reception. The early nineties had been a bad time in Nat's life in so many ways. But oh God, hadn't Carrie Klein grown since he saw her into a taxi on the Earls Court Road? Angry as he was that he hadn't recognised her (and that she must have taken such pleasure in deceiving him, the silly bitch), Nat couldn't help but be impressed by the transformation of the frumpy little brunette into the ice-cold killer blonde she was now. An ice-cold killer blonde who probably had her heart set on ruining him . . .

Chapter Twenty

CARRIE wasn't actually spending half as much time thinking about Nat Wilde as he liked to think she might be. Sure, it had been fun to see his face when he finally put two and two together, but there had been other, better moments at that party. A week after the Ehrenpreis launch, Carrie was still on a high. The coverage of the event had been fantastic. There had been enough famous faces at the party – old Frank Ehrenpreis was a very popular guy – to ensure that the launch made the party pages of all the best magazines. It was all over the *Evening Standard* and the diary pages of the *Telegraph* and *Times*. Looking at the photographs, Carrie was very pleased that Jessica had persuaded her not to cancel that appointment at Jo Hansford.

The mousy little Carrie who had been an intern at Ludbrook's would never have guessed that one day she would be mentioned in a glossy UK magazine as a 'woman to watch'. But Carrie knew she could not rest on her laurels quite yet. The fantastic opening party had to be followed up with real results. Her bosses had given her a helping hand for the first few sales, shipping over jewellery that would ordinarily have been sold through the office in New York. There were some magnificent pieces that Carrie hoped would generate even more publicity.

Ehrenpreis didn't have the history of Christie's or Sotheby's or Ludbrook's. That was something Carrie could never emulate. Instead she had decided to work on making it the fashionable place to go. Like Nat, Carrie knew that death, divorce and debt were the most common reasons that people brought their property to auction. Ludbrook's concentrated on 'death', courting the elderly. Carrie concentrated on divorce. She had Jessica put together a luncheon for some of London's most fashionable ladies. They dressed it up as a charity event in support of a women's refuge. Carrie's team of bright young women circulated professionally, forging friendly new relationships. The divorce rate being what it was, some of them would pay off.

Carrie also cultivated her own relationships with the big London dealers. She knew that they were important clients, buying speculatively or for collectors who were too nervous to buy at auction themselves. She made it her mission to get to know every middleman in town.

Every mealtime was an opportunity to schmooze a potential new client or work on her professional connections. Carrie never took a coffee break without wondering if she could use the time to get to know one of her staff better. She was very pleased with the way her team seemed to be gelling.

Carrie certainly didn't have time to get lonely. Night after night she got home from the office far too late to call anyone in Europe and too tired to catch up with friends in the States. That included Jed. At first he had called her religiously every two days. But a month later, the calls were coming every four nights. And two months after Carrie arrived in London, Jed stopped calling at all.

In fact, he sent an email telling her that he would not be coming to London as promised. He said it was clear to him that Carrie was not invested in keeping anything going at all. A long-distance relationship was impossible if she couldn't even return a phone call. Carrie felt a mixture of regret and relief. But far more relief than regret.

'I don't have time for this,' she told herself.

Carrie's career was the most important thing in her life. Though these days she was considered a beauty by anyone's standards, as a young girl she had quickly learned that she wasn't going to get anywhere on looks alone. Her older sister Bella was the beauty of the family, born with all the best elements of her mother and her father arranged in perfect harmony. When she looked at herself in the mirror, Carrie decided she must have been fashioned out of the leftovers. Bella was the archetypal blonde bombshell; Carrie was a mouse. As the girls were growing up, their parents reinforced the differences, referring to Bella as 'the beautiful one' and Carrie as the 'clever one'.

So Carrie had done the only thing she could do. She played up to her stereotype. She spent long hours in the library, signing up for anything that would keep her from having to be out on the playing fields. She excelled in all her academic subjects. She was the first person in her family to go to college and she aced that, getting scholarship offers from the very best schools. She chose Princeton.

Years later, Bella admitted to her younger sister that she had spent her entire childhood envying her. Bella had struggled at school and worried, since it was drummed into her every day that her face was her fortune, what would happen when she started to age.

At the time, Carrie looked at Bella's life and couldn't see why she was worried. She had a great husband, a successful wealthy man who seemed to adore her. She had two beautiful children who had inherited Bella's looks and would inherit the earth when their father passed on. Bella seemed set for life. But perhaps, as she had told Carrie that she envied her ability to provide for herself, Bella already knew what was around the corner. Of course the perfect husband was fucking one of her friends.

Bella's divorce was bad enough, but the family was dealt another blow less than a year later when Carrie's father walked out on their mother after forty-five years of marriage, leaving her for the housekeeper. Her mother was an emotional wreck and discovered soon afterwards that she was poverty stricken too. Ed Klein had taken out a secret mortgage on the family home to fund his affair. After that, Carrie vowed she would never allow herself to rely on a man.

However, while Carrie knew that looks weren't everything and certainly couldn't protect you from heartache, she soon came to realise that appearances were important. As a single woman, it was vital she take care of her health. That was a given. The side-effect of working hard to take care of her body was that she started to look better in her clothes. Looking better in her clothes gave her more confidence. It was a virtuous circle. She soon became more adventurous with the way she looked, swapping glasses for contacts, brown hair for blonde. Just over two years before she left for London the transformation was complete. Carrie was virtually unrecognisable.

The day she went blonde she walked into a bar to meet a girlfriend for cocktails and met Jed while she was waiting for her friend to arrive.

'Can I buy you a drink?' he asked.

Carrie did a double take. She had never been offered a drink by a stranger before. Her immediate reaction was to refuse his kind offer.

'I shouldn't,' she said.

'Shouldn't?' said the guy. 'Well, at least it's not a "won't". Please, let me buy you a cocktail. You are an exceptionally beautiful woman and such beauty must be appreciated.'

Carrie rolled her eyes. She had never been called beautiful in her life. The old Carrie, buried deep inside, expected to find out that this was some kind of joke. This man had been dared to approach her by one of his friends. Some of the guys Carrie had known at college had made a game of bedding ugly chicks. They even had a scoreboard in their fraternity house. Carrie had heard that her name was on the board, though thankfully she had never given any of the assholes a reason to score any points out of her.

And so, faced with a guy who was so good-looking he could have had any woman in that bar, if not any woman in Manhattan, Carrie was immediately suspicious.

'Hey, Jed!' Both Carrie and Jed turned to see who was calling him and, to Carrie's surprise, she discovered it was the friend she was due to be meeting.

'I see you guys have already met,' said Laney as she kissed first Carrie and then Jed hello. 'I met Jed in my yoga class,' Laney explained.

'I'm very bendy,' Jed elaborated.

Carrie granted him a smile. All at once he had become much less threatening. He knew Laney. He did yoga.

Laney was obviously enamoured of Jed. She insisted that he join them for dinner. But unfortunately for Laney, it was clear that Jed's interests lay elsewhere. He only had eyes for Carrie. He peppered her with questions about her work. Many of them stupid, she thought. Her low opinion of his intelligence was compounded by the news that he was a model and a part-time masseuse. Carrie's attention began to drift. She was used to men who spent their days in offices or laboratories, finding cures for cancer or solutions for world peace.

'I'm going to Paris in a couple of days,' said Jed. 'Fashion week.'

Before Carrie could stop her, Laney jumped in. 'Carrie is going to Paris next week too. You guys should meet up.'

Carrie shot Laney a look but Jed didn't notice and was already making plans. He picked up Carrie's cell phone from where it lay on the table and used it to call his own, so that he had her number.

'I'm going to be working,' said Carrie. 'I'm attending a conference on techniques for dating Renaissance work at the Louvre.'

'I'm going to be working too,' said Jed. 'But if I just keep calling you, there's bound to be a moment when we're both free to play.'

To play? Carrie winced at his choice of words. She wasn't the kind of girl who 'played' even when she did have downtime, which wasn't often since she'd been promoted to head of her department.

'Well, I hope you won't be disappointed if we don't manage to find that time,' she said.

Laney rolled her eyes this time. 'Carrie,' she said later. 'Go for it. If only so you can report back to me.'

Carrie flew to Paris two days later and, sure enough, Jed began bombarding her with phone calls as soon as her plane touched down in Europe. He was persistent. And in the end it worked. Carrie had just one night off and somehow, much as she resisted, Jed claimed it.

They met at her hotel, the Hyatt Vendome. They drank champagne in the incredibly dark bar. It being the fashion show season, the bar was full of beautiful people who might otherwise have made Carrie feel dowdy, but Jed kept laying on the compliments until she had to believe that he meant them.

Jed had booked a table in a small restaurant in the Fifth called Itineraires. The minimalist bistro was buzzing with locals. Carrie was impressed that Jed had researched the restaurant scene rather than take her somewhere obvious, like a brasserie on the Champs-Elysées. She'd spent all week eating croque monsieur.

Dinner over, Jed told Carrie that he would take her back to her hotel. They intended to take a taxi but there were none to be seen. After a while they gave up looking and simply wandered in the direction they thought they should be taking, crossing over the Pont des Arts, pausing in the middle to admire the Seine in the moonlight.

'The perfect place for a first kiss,' Jed suggested. Carrie didn't bite.

But as they got closer to her hotel, Carrie's opinion of Jed began to mellow. Or perhaps it was just that his puppyish adoration of her was beginning to wear her down.

Because she didn't take Jed seriously from the start, Carrie didn't have to bother with all the usual manoeuvring she employed to make sure that a man didn't get the wrong idea. Ordinarily, she would wait as long as possible before going to bed with a new guy. But since she didn't expect to ever see Jed again, the rulebook could be thrown away. Why shouldn't she just go for it? What happened in Paris could stay in Paris, right?

Jed was like a dog with two tails when Carrie invited him up to her room for a nightcap.

Once inside her room, 417, Carrie asked Jed to find something for them to drink in the mini-bar. He brought out a bottle of champagne. Carrie balked momentarily, imagining the champagne appearing on the receipt she would have to submit to the Ehrenpreis accounts department. But Jed had already peeled off the foil and was unwinding the muselet. Soon he was popping the cork, sending it flying across the room. Carrie held out two glasses to catch what remained in the bottle after most of it landed frothing and fizzing on the carpet. It was still fizzing wildly and escaped the glass to coat one of Carrie's hands. Taking the glasses from her and setting them down on a little table by the window, Jed took Carrie's hand and licked it clean.

'Oh God,' she said as she felt that telltale pull deep in her abdomen. Jed licking her hand like that was the sexiest thing that had ever happened to Carrie Klein. But that was just the start of it.

Without saying anything, Jed started to take off his clothes. He pulled his T-shirt off over his head, revealing the kind of body that Carrie had only ever seen in magazines and movies. Before Jed, her boyfriends had been nerdy types. She had never fucked a man with a six-pack. A man with a selection of hard degrees, yes, but a hard body? Never. Having spent years telling herself that personality was the most important thing in a man, she was surprised at just how excited the sight of Jed's body made her feel, as he stood there in his underpants like he'd just stepped off a Calvin Klein shoot.

Fully naked, Jed knelt on the ground and slipped Carrie's feet out of her shoes. With gentle care he ran his hands up her legs to find the tops of her stockings and rolled them down. It wasn't long before he was helping her out of her dress, an easy-access number by Vanessa Bruno. He murmured his approval as he got his first look at the body beneath.

He couldn't seem to get enough of her. Her kissed her harder than she had ever been kissed. There was no timidity there. He was not ashamed of how much he wanted her. His enthusiasm was infectious. Far from feeling more self-conscious about her physical flaws in the presence of such a beautiful body, Carrie felt released by Jed's obvious delight in her.

Parting Carrie's thighs, Jed moved so that he was lying between them, his head hovering over her pelvis and the neat landing strip of her pubic hair. Murmuring his appreciation of her form, Jed carefully spread Carrie's labia and dipped his head towards her clitoris.

'Oh, please!'

She felt a shudder of delight before his tongue even touched her. She reached out and held his head in her hands as though trying to delay the moment because she knew the sensation would be just too much. But she couldn't hold him off. He was determined to pleasure her. Nothing would stop him.

With his smooth, long tongue he flicked at her clitoris until the tiny bud became swollen and each movement of his tongue made Carrie cry out in delight. She tried to stop him a couple of times, as if she feared a loss of control, but he wouldn't let her escape his attentions. He continued to caress her with his warm wet mouth. Sucking and licking and driving her wild. At the same time he slipped a finger into her in search of the elusive G-spot. His flickering tongue and his finger stroking deep inside made her feel so aroused she thought she would faint.

Carrie gasped as Jed worked faster. She begged him to stop but he overrode all her objections. He was going to take her to the edge. And at last she stopped protesting. She lay back on the bed, her body arching towards Jed's mouth. Like a hang-glider walking to the edge of the cliff, one more step and she was airborne.

'Oh, oh, oh!'

Carrie had her first orgasm at the age of thirty-seven.

'You are awesome,' Jed said afterwards. 'I hope you are going to let me do that again. And again and again.'

Carrie's conclusion that evening was that blondes definitely have more fun.

Chapter Twenty-One

Serena's disappointment that Julian's late night visit had not brought a wildly romantic proposal had soon abated. After all, Julian was still very much in her life, spending lots of time in Cornwall while the big house remained unlet, and she hoped that the more time they spent together, the closer they would inevitably become. They'd been seeing each other for six months. She knew that was a record for Julian. She decided to hang in there. See how things developed.

Julian certainly seemed to get along well with Katie. She would bound out to meet his car. It was cupboard love for the most part. Julian never forgot to bring some trinket that Katie would appreciate: a book, a bracelet, a magazine. All the same, Serena was gratified to hear Katie say that she definitely preferred Julian to Donna.

And god it was good to be having sex again. Her libido,

which had once been so low she thought it might have died and gone forever, was back with a vengeance.

Meanwhile, Serena and Julian's little business venture was soon up and running. Serena explained to Julian that the best way to make a painting look old was to use old materials. On his trips to London she had him source authentically old paper and canvases from junk shops and antiquarian booksellers. Worthless old paintings could be overlaid with something more interesting. The end papers of old books could be ripped out to create contemporaneous drawings.

Serena was versatile. She would study the haul that Julian brought to her on a Friday night and decide what it might become according to what she had to work with. Sometimes Julian was frustrated that Serena wouldn't bang out a Raphael on a piece of MDF, but he bowed to her greater knowledge of such things. Better to sell a few little 'early Victorian' paintings than blow their cover with something less authentic right at the start.

It was Julian's job to get Serena's paintings out on to the market. The smaller ones were easy to get rid of. Julian would take them into antique shops up and down the A-road to Cornwall. He would choose a new shop on each occasion, claim that his mother had just died, and that he'd found whatever he happened to be carrying at the time in her attic.

He had his patter down perfectly. Julian had a natural melancholy to his expression and thus he was able to convince most people he met for the first time that his bereavement was still fresh. Often he found he could summon up tears by thinking of his childhood pet, a Cavalier King Charles spaniel called Bucket, who had been run over by a Land Rover, while running to fetch a stick he had thrown.

Julian's ruse worked particularly well with female antique dealers, especially of a certain age. They would be so busy finding cups of tea and ginger biscuits to console this poor middle-aged orphan that they wouldn't ask too much about the provenance of the picture. Julian would explain that he had to be rid of it as soon as possible. The sight of it made him so unhappy. And then he would ask for a sum of money that he knew to be well below the going rate for a decent Victorian watercolour. And the dealer, spotting the opportunity to take the pretty painting and sell it on at a much higher price, would usually hand over a couple of hundred in cash there and then. No questions asked.

But Julian knew this method was far too labour-intensive. And there was a strong possibility that one day soon a few of the antique dealers would find themselves at the same antiques fair with some very similar-looking pictures on their stalls. Plus, he had not forgotten the serious wedge of cash that painting of his mother's dogs had achieved at auction. In short, Julian was greedy for more. Tens of thousands per painting. That had been the original plan. He had no intention of spending the rest of his life making a couple of hundred here and there like some bloody Lovejoy.

'But I can't make a silk purse out of a sow's ear,' Serena explained to him. 'If you only ever bring me Victorian paper, then you can't expect me to paint a Renaissance Madonna.'

'I know,' said Julian. 'It's just that I'm sick of this fannying around. These silly little daubs.'

Serena bristled slightly. Despite her initial misgivings about Julian's scheme, she had come to enjoy being back in the studio. And whatever he thought about the speed and efficiency with which she executed the pieces, Serena always did her best to ensure that the final result was something she was proud of.

Julian must have sensed that she was unhappy with his comment. He tried to recover his position. 'I only mean "silly little daubs" in that it must be very boring for you, painting more or less the same thing over and over. I can see from the old stuff you have upstairs that you're capable of really great things.'

Serena frowned.

'Then bring me some great materials,' she said.

'I'll do my best.' Julian wrapped his arms around her waist and nuzzled at her neck. And, despite wanting to be angrier with him for whining about having to deal with all those middle-of-the-road antique shops, she found herself melting. And before too long she had turned to kiss him back and was very grateful that Katie was already in bed.

They made love in the kitchen that night. It was quite warm and Serena was wearing a long white skirt with nothing underneath. Turning her so that she was leaning over the kitchen sink and he was standing behind her, Julian simply lifted her skirt up and entered her from behind. Serena clung to the edge of the sink as Julian thrust hard into her, filling her with his manhood.

Serena loved this impromptu, urgent sex. It made her feel so desirable in a pure, almost animal way. She loved the idea that Julian was so attracted to her that he simply had to have her right then, no matter what she was doing, with no preamble. It was hot and hurried, but oh so fantastic. As he pushed into her, she pushed back against him with equal force, inviting him deeper and deeper inside. She could not get enough of him. She moved his warm hands from her waist to her breasts and moaned with lust as he played with her nipples and nibbled gently at the back of her neck.

'I'm coming,' Julian's voice was ragged with lust as he discovered he could hold back no longer. Serena didn't try to slow him down. The best part was when he lost control. His hands tightened upon her. He lost his rhythm and gave in to his orgasm with a cry of surprise.

Afterwards he rearranged her skirt for her and said, as he tucked his penis back into his underpants, 'You can finish washing up now.'

'Cheeky swine!'

He was lucky it had been a good shag. Otherwise Serena might have taken his head off with a low-flying plate.

The following morning, Julian went back to London promising that when he returned it would be with something that would lend Serena some real inspiration. He was back just three days later, clutching a very inauspicious looking parcel, wrapped in a dirty brown cloth.

'What is that?' Katie asked as she opened the door to him.

'It's something very special for your mother.'

'Doesn't look very special to me,' said Katie.

But when Serena saw what Julian had brought for her, she was almost as happy and surprised as if he had given her a diamond. Katie watched with great interest and incomprehension as Serena went into raptures over the ancient piece of wood the dirty rags had concealed.

'What is it?' Katie asked again.

It was a tiny fragment of a piece of work from the sixteenth century. Back in those days, everyone who was anyone would have had a little altar in his or her home and this was part of a domestic altarpiece. Serena marvelled at the fragments of paint that still clung to the wood. She thought she could make out the sleeve of a garment. A hand with finely tapered fingers.

'Where did you find this?' she asked Julian.

'Bloke down the pub was doing a house clearance. History teacher. Died of a stroke. Had lived in the same house for forty-seven years. This was just sitting on a bookshelf. His daughter thought he might have picked it up in Italy but she assumed it was just junk.'

'It's amazing,' said Serena.

'I don't think it looks amazing,' interrupted Katie.

'Ah, but it will,' said Julian. 'By the time your mother has finished with it.'

Julian was right. Here was something that Serena could really get excited about. As it was, the piece of wood was practically worthless. A nice thing to have, sure. But unless you really knew what you were looking at, it was just a piece of wood with a few flakes of pigment on it. Even if you did know what you were looking it, the painting wasn't so exciting. The fragment contained no real features of note. Even being able to see a bit more of the hand would have made a difference. And it had not been painted particularly professionally. As it was, the picture was too abstract and too naive. If it contained part of the Madonna's face, however, by an artist who might have learned at the feet of one of the greats . . .

'You have to understand that this is going to be an experiment,' she warned Julian. 'I've never attempted something from this period before and it's unlikely that I'll be able to pull it off. It's easy to fake something from the nineteenth century, but paintings in the Renaissance were produced in an entirely different way. The materials were different. Techniques were different.'

'Spare me the art lesson,' said Julian, kissing her wrist. 'Just work your magic.'

A few days later, Julian had the chance to work some magic of his own. At a dreadful Fulham drinks party, he had met a young girl called Annabel. He'd been drawn across the room by her country-fresh prettiness and her long, bouncy hair, redolent of a freshly groomed pony's tail. Once he got closer he realised that to go with her horsey hair, Annabel also had the laugh of a donkey. For the first time ever, he found himself making a conscious effort not to be amusing, in order to avoid having to hear it. But what looked as though it would be a very short conversation ended up stretching until the end of the evening because just as Julian was ready to excuse himself to the loo and hide out in the kitchen, Annabel revealed that she worked at a small private art museum in Kent.

'Really?' said Julian, perking up. 'Tell me about it.'

'Oh, it's just too unspeakably dull,' she said.

Not to Julian. Back when he first thought of the forgery racket, the one thing that had bugged him was how to fake provenance. That, more than anything, could convince a doubting dealer or auctioneer that what they were seeing was the real McCoy. He had come across the answer when reading about John Myatt and John Drewe, the most successful forgers of the twentieth century. Their deception had been so difficult to uncover because they were able to produce museum records for their work. Museum records that they themselves had introduced into museum libraries.

Upon hearing that she worked at a museum, Julian suddenly saw Annabel as less of an annoyance and more as a potentially useful accomplice. Of course, he would first have to gain her trust and loyalty. And, unfortunately, that would probably mean taking her to bed.

'I want to know everything about your job,' said Julian. 'In fact, I want to know everything about you.'

Annabel blushed at his intensity.

'Can I get you another drink first?' he asked.

Two more glasses of Chardonnay and Annabel was done for. She invited Julian back to her flat where she played him a Robbie Williams CD.

'I just love "Angels", don't you?'

Julian nodded, though he didn't love 'Angels' at all.

Annabel got to her feet and swayed from side to side, singing along with her hero. Not quite in time. Not quite in tune. Julian got up and kissed her, in part to stop the singing, but also because he wanted to cut to the chase.

If he was going to have to sleep with Annabel on a regular basis for any length of time in order to make use of her position at the museum, then he wanted to know how pleasurable the assignment was likely to be.

An hour after the first kiss, he had his answer. It was a mission he could happily throw himself into for a short while. In the sack, Annabel was as bouncy as a cocker spaniel on a trampoline. She kissed a bit like a cocker spaniel, too. And practically howled when she came. But overall the experience was not a bad one and thus Julian decided that he would take one for the team. Or several, because that was what it would take.

After all, it would be a while before he could innocently ask Annabel if she might just be able to organise a private and unsupervised visit to the museum archives.

Chapter Twenty-Two

ʙᴀᴄᴋ in Cornwall, Serena had no idea how hard Julian was trying to help their scheme succeed. As the seasons turned and summer became autumn, Serena was busy working on her part of the deal. But for months the little piece of panel that Julian had found for her remained untouched. It was too valuable for Serena to risk making a mistake. Instead, she spent hours experimenting on bits of broken fencing or old cupboard doors as she tried to recreate authentic sixteenth-century pigments. Whenever she had a spare moment she pored over books on the subject, learning how the Renaissance artists had made their paints and the tools with which they applied them. Katie was banned from her mother's studio while Serena worked with toxic ingredients: lead oxide to make white, mercury oxide for cinnabar and burnt sienna. Other ingredients were too precious and rare to risk having them end up in one of Katie's own creative spectaculars. It took Serena seven weeks to obtain a tiny piece of lapis with which to recreate the luxurious blue so precious it was only ever used for the Madonna's cloth.

Creating authentic pigments was expensive and time-consuming but Serena knew that there was no point cutting corners. Modern techniques made short work of analysing the tiniest slivers of paint for elements that were out of place or out of time. The legitimate ingredients to be found in a genuine Renaissance work were well documented. Discrepancies in the make-up of pigments were the first thing an investigator would look for.

But the work wasn't over when Serena got the paints right or even after she'd applied them using the right techniques. She had to make them look suitably aged. Working on a piece of board from the correct period would go a long way to achieving that aim, as anything added over the top of the original paint would eventually crack along the same fissures. There were ways of hurrying the process of craquelure along. The painting could be baked in a low oven for days at a time. Another book recommended the addition of human urine to the paints. Serena wasn't sure how that would work but she gave the technique a try all the same.

Eventually, Serena had in her possession the equipment and knowledge she felt she needed to start the real work. Her subject was a simple one. A small Madonna. Probably not unlike the one that had originally graced the panel. In fact, she worked out a way to incorporate some of the folds of fabric that could still be seen on the board.

By November, Julian was getting anxious to know what Serena would produce. He'd been seeing Annabel twice a week for three months by the time Serena told him she was ready to start the painting. The cocker spaniel routine was definitely starting to wear thin. It was nearing Christmas and, assuming that Julian was her bona fide boyfriend, Annabel was starting to make demands. She wanted him to accompany her to her museum's Christmas party. That Julian would do, since it might be a good way to make an even more useful contact at the museum. But Annabel also wanted him to spend Christmas with her and her family in Dorset. That would not do at all.

'I've told you before,' said Serena, when he begged her to hurry with her work. 'We can't rush this. Why are you in such a hurry?'

Julian couldn't tell Serena the truth: that he had been sleeping with some random girl to get access to her archives and had somehow got himself into a position where the girl in question thought they were going to get engaged and he knew he needed to press eject. Instead he said, 'My museum contact is looking for a new job, that's all.'

'In museums, presumably.'

'Actually, he's thinking of going into insurance,' Julian lied. 'More money.'

Serena didn't question it.

'So,' she said later. 'I've talked to Katie and she's told me that she would really, really like it if you joined us for Christmas dinner. And,' she added with a wry smile, 'here is her Christmas list. Will you come?'

Julian nodded. 'Of course.' What else could he say? He would have to sort the logistics out afterwards. Perhaps if he spent Christmas Eve with Annabel in Dorset he could drive on down to Trebarwen first thing Christmas morning. How long would it take? Three hours?

'And what do you want for Christmas?' Julian asked Serena when he had finished reading Katie's list.

'I'm sure you'll think of something,' said Serena. She stepped up to him and straddled his lap. As she leaned forward to kiss him, her shirt fell open, revealing a sexy red bra that lifted her breasts and presented them to him like a pair of freshly baked donuts. Julian felt a distinct stirring in his trousers.

'Would you like to have your present now?' he asked.

Serena looked up at the ceiling. Katie's room was right above them. She cocked her head as though to listen for a sign that Katie might still be awake.

'Come on then,' she took Julian by the hand.

Julian's plan for the holidays went without a hitch, He spent Christmas Eve with Annabel, telling Serena that he was visiting an elderly aunt in Weymouth. He left Annabel first thing after breakfast on Christmas morning, telling her he had to spent the day with an ancient aunt down in Cornwall. She was on her last legs. This might be her final Christmas.

'I'll come with you,' Annabel had told him, but Julian put her off, saying that his old aunt Serena suffered from advanced dementia and rarely recognised her own favourite nephew. The presence of a complete stranger might send her into a serious decline.

'And she could be violent,' Julian added. 'It's best that you go to your parents. I'll miss you terribly but . . .'

Annabel accepted his excuses and the delicate silk scarf he had picked up from Hermès on his way over to her flat. Annabel wrapped the scarf around her neck like the Home Counties girl that she was.

'I will keep this next to my skin until you are with me again,' she assured him.

*　　*　　*

Serena and Katie accepted Julian's excuse for his absence on Christmas Eve, which was that he had to spend it with his ancient auntie Annabel. They gave him a warm welcome when he showed up on the doorstep in time for Christmas lunch, arms laden with presents. Serena tied her gift of an Hermès scarf around her head, like Carmen Miranda. Christmas in the Macdonald household was a far happier affair than it had been the previous year. Katie was delighted with the gifts that Julian brought for her. She'd decided, with all the pragmatism of childhood, that getting twice the amount of presents more than made up for her father's absence.

'I've got something for you too,' said Serena. 'But you'll have to come upstairs to see it.'

Julian opened his eyes wide. Serena was usually pretty careful about not making double entendres in front of her daughter.

'To my studio,' Serena elaborated.

And there it was, on an easel. Serena's first Renaissance masterpiece. A sad-eyed Madonna holding a world-weary baby Jesus on her lap. The child's expression was exquisite. The infant Jesus seemed to hold in his eyes a complete and painful knowledge of all that would befall him before he could sit at God's right hand.

For a moment, Julian could say nothing. He stared at the painting as though Serena had just unveiled a Polaroid picture of the actual nativity. Eventually, smiling and shaking his head at the wonder of it, he stepped closer and peered beyond the fabulous composition to the technique.

'I wouldn't get too close,' Serena warned him. 'I had to pee on it to get that authentic patina.'

Julian took an automatic step back.

'I'm joking,' Serena lied.

'It's incredible,' Julian told her. 'The painting is beautiful. But the ageing is amazing. How did you get it to look so real?'

Serena swallowed her disappointment that Julian was more interested in the technique than her artistic flair but she told him all the same. 'I just put it in the Aga for seven days. And it's not quite done yet. But I had to take it out of the oven to put the turkey in.'

'You are a genius,' Julian told her. Then he kissed her and kissed her then paused and listened for noise from downstairs.

'It sounds like Katie is watching *The Wizard of Oz*,' said Serena.

Julian responded with a sly smile, then he put his hand up her skirt.

'Have you been a good boy this year?' Serena asked.

'Oh yes,' said Julian. 'I've been very good indeed.'

'In that case, perhaps you can have one more present.'

Serena quietly closed the studio door.

Chapter Twenty-Three

Carrie's first year at Ehrenpreis London had been a great one. When she flew to New York to meet with her bosses she found for the first time ever she was excited about her upcoming appraisal. There was no doubt about it. Her results were far more impressive than she had hoped for or, she suspected, than old Frank Ehrenpreis and the rest of the board had expected.

So, it was with delight that she joined Ehrenpreis for dinner at his very own home. Frank Ehrenpreis lived alone in a vast apartment overlooking Central Park that contained as much fine art as many small European museums. Carrie could not hide her admiration when she was shown the tiny Raphael in the library.

'When I go,' he said. 'I want you to put this under the hammer.'

'You could just leave it to me,' Carrie flirted. Frank squeezed her arm but they both knew it was harmless. Since the death of his wife seven years earlier, Frank hadn't so much as looked at another woman.

Business over, Carrie took a couple of days holiday to extend her stay in New York. There were a few things she needed to do. Now that she was sure she was going to be in London for the next few years, she needed to move everything out of her apartment so that it could be rented out.

It was strange to be back there. Though the concierge of the building had promised to keep an eye on the place and her cleaner had continued to stop by once a week to keep things tidy, the place felt musty and unloved. Once she had packed up the boxes that need to go into storage Carrie opened the windows and looked out on the familiar view. As she did so, she had a flashback to a Friday night, more than twelve months earlier, when she stood at that window with Jed, his arms around her waist, as they watched a summer thunderstorm breaking over the Hudson river. She couldn't help but remember what happened next too. How Jed kissing the back of he neck led to a bout of deliciously slow love-making with all the windows open and the lightning playing outside. Closing her eyes for a moment, Carrie could see Jed's back, slick with sweat, reflected in the mirrored door of her wardrobe. She felt her arms wrapped around his neck, her thighs clamped tight around his waist. Carrie shook the thought off and went back to her packing.

But later that afternoon, as she walked back to her hotel, Carrie saw him. Right there on Fifth Avenue.

'Jed.'

As soon as the word came out of her mouth, Carrie regretted having drawn attention to herself. There was no reason on earth why Jed should be pleased to see her. They hadn't spoken in more than six months. But he turned towards her voice with a smile and the smile remained even when he realised who was calling him.

They joined each other in the middle of the pavement and exchanged an awkward kiss with his hands holding the tops of her arms as if to keep her at a distance.

'I didn't know you were in town,' he said. Carrie wondered if there was a tone of accusation in his voice.

'I would have let you know but I wasn't sure how much time I was going to have here,' she explained. 'I just came in for some meetings. I'm going back tomorrow.'

Jed's eyes betrayed disappointment.

'And I'm sure you're busy tonight?' he said.

'Actually,' said Carrie. 'I'm not. But . . .'

'No buts. Let's go out to dinner. I'll collect you. Where are you staying?'

'The Trump Tower,' she said. 'I had the rest of my apartment packed up.'

'So, you're doing well in London. Obviously. Planning to stay for a while.'

She nodded, not sure why she felt so bad about it. It wasn't as if she and Jed were still trying to make it work.

'Well,' he plastered on a smile. 'Good for you. I can't wait to hear all about it. I'll pick you up at seven. Trump Tower?'

She nodded.

'Nice. I'll see you then.'

He continued on his way and Carrie watched him go as though he were a figure from a dream.

Carrie dressed carefully that evening. She didn't want Jed to get the wrong idea. Not only that. Where was he likely to take her? She hadn't dare ask. The answer wasn't likely to be a good one. It wasn't as if Jed had got himself a job on Wall

Street since she left. That afternoon he had looked as he always did. Like a male model with new age tendencies. Baggy jeans, tight vintage T-shirt, open-toed shoes, even though it was only April. They would almost certainly be going for a pizza in the village . . .

But Carrie didn't have 'pizza in the village' clothes in her suitcase. She'd come expecting to divide her evenings between fine dining with her bosses or ordering room service while she went over emails. She had the kind of dresses that could get you in anywhere or she had pyjamas. Carrie put on a DVF wrap, the least dressy thing she had brought with her. If she wore it with her hair down and knee-high boots rather than patent court shoes, she'd probably pass for casual.

At seven on the dot, Jed called up for her. She kept him waiting a little longer while she took a call from a client in Singapore, who was planning to fly into London for Ehrenpreis's next furniture sale. When she got to the lobby, she apologised profusely, fully expecting Jed to comment on her tardiness. But he simply smiled and told her she looked great.

He looked wonderful too. He was wearing a suit with the grace and elegance that had helped him to a pretty good career on the catwalk.

'Where are we going?' she asked.

'It's a surprise.'

It certainly was. No pizza in the village that night. Jed took Carrie to one of the hottest new addresses in town: the new refurbished Montrachet restaurant at the top of the Gloria Hotel.

'How did you get a reservation?'

'I know the maitre d',' said Jed. 'He used to be a model. We worked together on a spread for *Men's Health*.'

As Jed mentioned the connection, the maitre d' walked over to greet them.

'Hey, Jed!' the maitre d' clapped him on the back. He was clearly pleased to see him. Jed seemed to have that effect on everybody. New York was full of the friends he'd made on photo shoots or commercial sets or while standing in line at Starbucks. Everybody wanted him in his or her life. He made people feel special. Right then he was enquiring about the maitre d's daughter, who was starting school that fall.

'You got her into the place you wanted, right?'

'We did, thank you for remembering. She's very excited. Now, I've saved a very special table for the pair of you. Follow me.'

It was the best table in the room, right against the windows with an uninterrupted view of downtown Manhattan, magical in that moment before nightfall, when the buildings glowed like a fairy city.

'This is why I live here,' said Jed.

Certainly, Carrie had to agree there was nowhere else on earth like Manhattan at dusk. Or at any time.

'Champagne,' the maitre d' had brought them a couple of glasses. 'On me,' he added.

Jed raised a toast to Carrie. 'I am so glad to have you here,' he said. 'However briefly. I have missed you.'

'I've missed you too,' she said.

'Have you?' Jed asked.

Don't start, Carrie begged him silently. He didn't get a chance to. A waiter interrupted the conversation before it had a chance to begin in order to recite the specials. Spring lamb. Some kind of fish on the bone. Carrie and Jed both had the lamb.

*　　*　　*

It was a far better evening than Carrie had hoped for. Apart from the tricky start, the conversation flowed easily. She had expected Jed to be angry with her and for the entire evening to be taken up with going over what went wrong and why. But it wasn't like that at all. Jed regaled her with some funny stories about his massage clients, the social X-rays. One of them had asked him to accompany her on a month-long ski-trip as her personal masseuse, so addictive was his touch. The money would have been good, he admitted, but he'd refused because it would have meant a month out of the class he was taking. He was studying film at night school and putting together a show reel with a view to becoming a commercials director.

Jed also seemed genuinely interested in hearing about Carrie's time in London.

'How's Jessica?' he asked.

Carrie was impressed that he remembered her assistant's name.

'She's doing well. I thought she would insist on being allowed to return to New York after six months but she got herself an English boyfriend and that seems to have changed everything.'

'And how about you?'

Carrie raised her eyebrows quizzically.

'English boyfriend?' Jed spelled it out.

'I don't have time,' she said.

Jed gave a little smile. '*Plus ça change*. I do understand,' he said then.

'What?' she asked.

'That you had to leave. I don't think I was supportive enough at the time. I could only see your promotion as losing a playmate,' he sighed. 'But I understand now that you had to go. It was what you'd been working towards since you were a girl. And it was the right choice. Look at you.'

He lifted his hands and traced the shape of her face in the air. 'When you talk about your life in London, there is so much animation in your face. So much excitement and anticipation. You've found your place. I don't think I've ever seen you look so radiant and beautiful as you do tonight.'

Carrie looked into her coffee cup. 'Thank you,' she said quietly, feeling inwardly guilty that she had actually dressed down for this outing.

'To you,' Jed raised what was left of his wine. 'I hope we'll always be friends,' he added.

Carrie found the word 'friends' strangely stinging.

After dinner they walked back to the hotel. It was something Carrie missed about Manhattan. The ease with which you could get around. London was on a more spread-out scale. And whatever you thought about Manhattan traffic, it didn't move as quickly or erratically as that in London.

It was a beautiful evening. The cherry blossom was out. In fact, the restaurant had been decorated in it.

Jed offered her his arm. She took it willingly. It was so easy to be with him. She found herself leaning into his body. There were few men who could make her feel so feminine. So petite.

When they reached the hotel lobby, Carrie knew she should end the night there. But Jed lingered, finding more questions to ask about London. About anything. Until eventually, she asked him to come up for a nightcap. 'Since we've still got so much to tell each other,' as he said.

Carrie had not made love since she and Jed were last together. She wondered if it had been the same for him. She doubted it. A heterosexual male model with massage skills in a town like New York, Jed was the ultimate catch. She didn't want to think about it, how many offers he must have had. There was probably someone waiting for him right then. And that thought was partly why Carrie said 'yes' when Jed asked if he could stay.

They both understood what 'stay' really meant. As soon as he had Carrie's agreement, Jed kicked off his shoes and moved from the armchair to the bed. He smoothed the counterpane beside him, wordlessly inviting Carrie to join him. She took off her own shoes, placing them neatly beside her half-packed case with the precision that had always made Jed smile and tease her. She sat down on the bed. Not quite right next to him though she knew that soon she would be. They both knew.

'This reminds me of that hotel room in Paris,' said Jed. 'What number was it?'

'417,' Carrie responded. On their return to New York after their Paris interlude, Jed had sent flowers with nothing but '417' written on the card.

'There I was, thinking that you were going to give me a coffee and send me on my way but you jumped me. I was quite taken aback.'

'Were you, hell,' said Carrie, shuffling back so that they were properly side-by-side against the pillows.

'It's a memory that I will treasure for the rest of my life. It isn't everyday a guy gets ravaged in a hotel room.'

Carrie went to give Jed a playful cuff. He caught her wrist and used the leverage it gave him to pull her into his arms. She fell willingly and soon they were kissing. It was as hot and heavy as the first time they kissed and yet as intimate and relaxed at the last. Still, after a minute or so, Carrie pulled away. She looked deep into Jed's eyes. They shouldn't be doing this. And yet . . .

It was so easy. So natural. They fell back into each other's arms like two dancers repeating steps they'd learned and practised years before. If they didn't think too hard about it, everything would be fine. They'd go through the old routine and then part. Back to the real world.

And Carrie had spent so long without this kind of contact. She wanted to be held and kissed and, she admitted it, fucked. She wanted to feel desired.

When they were both naked, their skin slick with the heat of their passion, Carrie moved so that she was on top of Jed, her legs about his waist. She edged backwards so that she could feel the tip of his cock against her. Her body cried out to be penetrated. She felt a moment of supreme release as Jed took matters into his hands and pushed up into her.

The fit was so good. Carrie had never had a lover like Jed. His cock seemed to have been made for her. As she rocked her way to an orgasm, he grew and stretched inside her until she felt that she had never been touched so absolutely before. Their bodies were completely joined.

With her hands on Jed's wide, flat chest, Carrie eased herself up and down. Jed held her by the waist, helping her, speeding her up or slowing her down. As her arousal grew and she felt her orgasm creeping up on her, Carrie let her head tip backwards. Jed's hands moved to her breasts, magnificent above him. Carrie was in a world of her own now, rocking, rocking. Faster and faster. Her thighs tightened against Jed's waist. She began to dissolve around him. The only thing she could hear was the pumping of her own heart as the blood raced around her body, taking her pleasure to every part of her being.

Carrie didn't have to worry about Jed. The moment she started to come, he was coming too. The feeling of her pulsing around his shaft was too much to resist. Each time she moved downwards, he thrust upwards to meet her. Their sighs echoed each other. Jed cried out Carrie's name.

'Can I stay the night?' he asked.

Carrie nodded mutely. She shouldn't have done it, she knew. She shouldn't have made love to him. But it felt so good to be back in his arms. She felt so connected to him right then. Almost connected enough to tell him the truth about her feelings. Almost connected enough to admit them to herself.

If only it could always be like this. If only she could trust that Jed would always want to be this close to her. Then she might have been able to give their relationship a proper shot. But the shiver of unhappiness she had felt earlier, when he called her his friend, was nothing compared to the pain she would feel if she totally invested her heart and found herself rejected.

So Carrie said nothing. It was far better to do without these moments than find herself like her mother or sister. Loved and then abandoned and unable to get over it.

Next day, Carrie was taking the first flight back to London out of Kennedy. She left Jed sleeping, putting a note on hotel paper on the side of the bed where she had lain.

'I hope you'll come to London sometime soon,' she wrote. But before she left the room, she crept back and stole the note away again. Jed would never know how close she came to admitting her vulnerability.

Chapter Twenty-Four

As she waited for her flight back to London, Carrie picked up a copy of *Vanity Fair* in the BA first-class lounge. Flicking through it, her attention was drawn to a name she hadn't heard in a while: Mathieu Randon.

Carrie knew all about Mathieu Randon. When she began her career in the auction houses, he was a client for whom everyone rolled out the red carpet. Head of Domaine Randon, a multi-national luxury goods conglomerate based in Paris, he was high on the list of invitees to any big event at Ehrenpreis in New York. He rarely showed up himself, though he had bought certain items through the house. Most notably a painting by Andrew Wyeth, who was the artist of Carrie's own favourite painting: *Christina's World*.

The last Carrie heard of Mathieu Randon was that he had recently come out of an eighteen-month-long coma. He'd fallen into the coma after being struck on the head by a falling wine barrel when an earthquake hit his company's Napa

Valley vineyard. Photographs taken at the time of his recovery showed him leaving hospital in a wheelchair, his head lolling to one side, his eyes unfocused and glazed. It was widely assumed that would be the last anyone heard of him. He was facing a long time in rehabilitation. According to reports, he was hardly able to speak. Nobody could be sure that his laser-sharp business brain was what it once had been.

But here he was. Back from the dead and back in his office, giving an interview to *Vanity Fair*.

'People ask if I have changed,' said Randon. 'Of course I've changed. How could anyone spend eighteen months in a coma, away from the stimulation of the outside world and remain unchanged? But I do not believe that my life has been diminished for that time away. Rather it has been enriched.

'It sounds like a cliché to say that right now I understand the value of things far better than I once did. Whereas once I was only content to spend my waking hours generating money and thought contemplation was for the simple-minded, now I am just as happy to look out of my window and see a butterfly or a flower in bloom.'

'He's losing it,' thought Carrie.

'I have found new meaning in my life. And, most importantly, I have found God.'

Lost it, Carrie confirmed to herself.

The interviewer expressed the cynicism of much of his readership when he asked Randon how he could possibly square his billionaire lifestyle with the ethics of Christianity.

'Indeed it is easier for a camel to pass through the eye of the needle than for a rich man to enter the Kingdom of God,' Randon quoted. 'That's why I'm formulating a strategy for disposing of some of my assets with a view to establishing a place where people of a like mind can find peace and contemplation. That is my mission now. That is the real reason I was put on this earth. That is clearly why I spent the first fifty years of my life so focused, to the point of blindness, on amassing material wealth. It was all part of God's plan. To enable me to one day establish a haven for pilgrims and students of the word of Christ, our Lord.'

'Like a monastery?' the interviewer suggested.

The question drew a smile from the lips of Mathieu Randon, one-time fixture on the European party circuit. He was rumoured to have bedded more than a thousand women. Allegedly he had the books of several model agencies on his bedside table. The photos of those models he had slept with were marked with a cross and rated out of ten. Married men all over the world had cursed his wife-stealing name. And now . . .

'A monastery. Yes. A bit like that,' he said.

Carrie Klein couldn't care less about Mathieu Randon's new-found faith in Jesus, but all at once her own mission was very clear. If Randon wanted help in disposing of his assets then she was the girl to help him.

'All mobile phones must be switched off . . .' came the cabin announcement.

'Rats,' said Carrie, as a flight attendant politely reiterated the message to her personally. Carrie grudgingly switched off her phone and made a note to ask Jessica to find out how she could get to Mathieu Randon the moment the plane touched down.

Reading the six-page article about himself and his miraculous recovery from the coma, Randon couldn't help but wonder if he'd unwittingly committed the sin of pride. Was it true, as the interviewer had suggested, that he sounded smug when he spoke of the community of believers he hoped to create? He was merely a conduit for God's work. There was no room for smugness.

The best way to dispel that kind of ugly aspersion was for Randon to get on with building his Utopia as soon as he possibly could. He must begin to liquidise his assets, as he had promised he would. Sitting at his desk in his office on the Champs-Elysées, Randon surveyed the paintings that graced the room. In that single room hung art worth many millions of Euros. There were yet more riches in the headquarters of Maison Randon Champagne in Epernay. And then there was Randon's private collection, scattered between his apartment in Paris, his homes in New York, Napa Valley, and Tuscany and on the Cote D'Azur, and on his eighty-five metre yacht, the Grand Cru, which was currently moored outside Monaco.

Randon buzzed through to his assistant.

'Bellette,' he said. 'Would you be so kind as to come into my office for a moment.'

Bellette closed down her Internet connection – which was open to Net-A-Porter – and responded to his call. She stood in front of his desk, notebook at the ready. She was dressed in a plain grey shift that hit her legs at mid-calf. It was the most unflattering garment she had ever worn but it had become the unofficial 'uniform' of the women who worked at Domaine Randon since their boss came back from hospital. Lots of things had changed since Mathieu Randon got caught in that earthquake.

Randon smiled at her beneficently and motioned that she should sit down. Bellette decided that she had preferred the old days, when Randon leered at her breasts as they strained the buttons of a tight blouse, as though he were a wolf watching a three-legged lamb stumble away from the flock.

'I have a very special project for you,' he said. 'But I want you to think very carefully about whether you're willing to take it on.'

Bellette perked up a little. She was getting rather bored of typing up letters to the Pope.

'I need to prepare some of my art collection for auction.'

'I'd be happy to do that,' said Bellette.

'I want you to be sure,' said Randon. 'Because, as you know, I have great respect for you and your personal integrity and I must warn you that some of the paintings concerned are nudes. If you think that it would compromise your morality in any way, then you must feel free to refuse.'

Morality? Bellette looked at the man who had once bent her over his desk and fucked her hard while dictating a letter. Bellette had to bite down on the end of her pencil to stop a laugh bursting out.

Chapter Twenty-Five

Back at his apartment that evening, Randon felt much better for having taken steps to put the plan for his new community of believers into action. Bellette had been very mature about the whole thing, assuring him that she would be honoured to catalogue the more risqué of Randon's artworks, knowing that it was all in a good cause. Jesus would have understood, she assured him. After all, didn't he associate with ladies of the night? Randon was glad that Bellette had been paying attention to his sermons.

Alone in his bedroom, where once he had entertained supermodels and Oscar-winning actresses, Randon poured himself a glass of water from the jug on the coffee table. He no longer drank alcohol, though his family's empire had been built on the foundation of one of the world's finest champagne houses.

Sipping the water contemplatively, with one hand resting lightly on his late mother's well-thumbed Bible, he gazed on the small Madonna and Child that stood on the mantelpiece. Around that small painting was an enormous patch of faded wallpaper that betrayed the fact that a larger painting, of a voluptuous nude with a lotus between her legs, had hung there for many years before.

As Randon gazed at the Madonna, the feeling started to come again. It seemed to happen every time he looked at that painting. The harder he stared, the faster it came. His field of vision narrowed. There was a glitter of lights at its periphery, as if a sparkler were being held just out of view. Then came the headache. The searing pain that preceded every visitation. Oh God. The pain was so intense. Each time Randon thought he might die.

'Mother Mary preserve me,' Randon cried out before he lost consciousness and slid to the floor.

Coming round five minutes later, Randon scrambled for his pen and pad of paper. It was as important to write down as much as he could remember as quickly as possible. These were, after all, messages direct from God.

Still sitting on the floor, Mathieu Randon began to scribble. This time he'd seen a riverbed. Tall reeds. Was it in Europe? Or in Egypt? Was God showing him the Nile? Then he saw the face of a woman. Beautiful as an angel. Her clear white face was framed by soft black hair. She had brown eyes edged by long dark lashes. Full pink lips. Her eyebrows were arched in surprise. Or was it concentration? She was leaning forwards towards him. Her smile looked uncertain. Who was she? She was wearing white. Her arms were bare. She held them out for him. Beckoning? Beseeching?

After filling two pages with his fractured recollections, Randon could drag no more clues to the surface of his mind. As the light faded, he read through once more all the notes he had written over the past two years whenever the vision came to him. The river had featured often. And the woman. And sometimes a house. Almost a château in size and scale. It had to mean something significant. Was the woman a saint guiding him towards the perfect setting for his community? That made sense.

Randon called Bellette, who knew that she should always be ready to receive his call. No matter what time of day.

'Where are you?' he asked, when he got through to her mobile. 'It sounds noisy.'

'At the station,' she lied. She was sitting in a bar.

'Tomorrow morning I want you to call someone at Sotheby's real estate. I'm looking for a house next to a river. First thing. It's very important. There must be a river.'

Bellette switched off her mobile phone. Her boyfriend Olivier leaned over and nibbled her neck.

'Got to get you into my room and out of this sack,' he said, regarding her horrible dress. 'Was that Randon again?'

'Yes,' Bellette sighed.

'More work for the mission?'

Bellette nodded. 'He wants me to start looking for a property.'

'Do you think if I got my head shaved and pretended to be a monk he might bung me a few hundred grand?' Olivier asked.

Bellette ran her hands through Olivier's wavy dark hair. 'Well, if you shave your head, you'll definitely have one thing in common with a monk,' she said. 'You won't get laid.'

Chapter Twenty-Six

$\mathcal{L}$IKE Bellette, Lizzy had an early start the following day. That week Ludbrook's would be hosting a sale of important eighteenth- and nineteenth-century paintings. There had been a lot of interest. Like the Old Masters, the Victorians seemed to be riding out the recession rather well. Their inoffensive subject matter and pretty execution made them the artistic equivalent of a two-bedroom flat in Chelsea. Blue chip. Nat was expecting great things.

'May even put you up on the block if I get tired,' he said.

Lizzy paled, remembering her humiliation at the Trebarwen sale.

'Only joking,' said Nat. 'Though if you are going to be an auctioneer, you're going to have to get back up there at some point.'

'I know that,' said Lizzy. 'It's just . . . give me time.'

'Whatever you want,' said Nat, dismissing her with a pat on the bum.

The team at Ludbrook's were not the only people looking forward to the Victorians' sale with eager anticipation. From passing Serena's work through small antique shops up and down the country, Julian had decided that it was time to make the leap to selling through a proper auction house in preparation for off-loading her little Madonna. He took one of Serena's larger works, a painting of the Clifton Suspension Bridge, up to London and requested a meeting with Nat Wilde.

Nat was only too pleased to meet Julian for lunch. The Trebarwen sale, although low key, had been a highlight of the previous year's calendar. Not only that, of late Nat had learned the importance of keeping your client relationships up to date. Nat didn't think he would ever stop feeling bitter at the fact that, just before she finally got round to popping her clogs, Mrs Kingly changed her will so that it instructed that her estate be sold through Ehrenpreis. It was just too much. Carrie Klein had put up with just a few months of the old dear's moaning. That bloody American woman had been siphoning off Nat's clients left, right and centre.

Nat and Julian passed the lunch in small talk. Mostly slagging off Julian's older brother Mark, whom they both agreed was a terrible prig, who hadn't changed a bit since prep school.

'All right,' said Nat. 'I'm sure this isn't just about catching up with an old friend. I assume you've got something to show me?'

'It's in the back of the car,' Julian confirmed.

*   *   *

'Hmmm,' said Nat when Julian unwrapped the painting in his office. 'Very nice. Who is it?'

Julian gave Nat the name of the relatively sought after early Victorian artist, Richard Delapole, to whom Nat's assistant Lizzy Duffy had attributed Serena's painting of the greyhounds. Delapole was the perfect artist for her to fake since he had Cornish connections and had died not fifteen miles from Trebarwen House.

'Another Delapole. Really?' Nat raised an eyebrow.

'Really.' Julian reminded himself that he had to stay cool. Nat was only trying it on. He didn't really think the picture was a fake. Why should he? After all, everything in the Trebarwen sale, with the exception of Serena's painting of the dogs, had been absolutely kosher. If Julian had form, it was as a source of real and important antiques, not as a faker.

'Where did you find it?' Nat asked.

'In the attic at the house,' Julian told him steadily.

'I thought my team went through the attic. Obviously didn't do such a thorough job.'

'It was well hidden.'

Nat got out his spectacles and peered closely.

'Bit of foxing there.'

'I noticed that,' said Julian, thankful that the conversation was already moving on from 'provenance' to 'condition'. It was unlikely that a Victorian watercolour kept in an attic for any length of time would have escaped the experience unscathed so damage was to be expected. Though of course the foxing was as fake as the painting itself. Serena had added the little brown mould marks as an authenticating touch, using a diluted solution of HP sauce.

'Beautifully executed. In fact, I would say it's unusually fine handiwork for this artist. His strokes are normally a bit more . . .' Nat pulled a face. 'Naïve.'

He had a magnifying glass – a loupe – out now. Julian began to feel a little hot. And not just because it was warm outside.

'So,' he said, eager to get some kind of agreement to sell out of Nat before he spent too much more time looking at the bloody thing.

'I think it could be just the thing for our nineteenth-century sale,' Nat told him. 'I'm glad you brought it to me.'

Julian exhaled. He hoped his relief wasn't as noticeable as it felt. Nat took off his glasses and put the loupe back in its velveteen pouch.

'And if you find any more of these unexpected treasures then I hope that I will be the first to know . . .'

'Well, actually . . .' said Julian. He was prepared. Another painting resided in the boot of his car.

That afternoon, when Julian drove back to his Fulham flat, the painting remained in Nat's office at Ludbrook's, waiting to be photographed for the catalogue. Julian had achieved his aim. Serena's painting of the Clifton Suspension Bridge was in the sale, attributed to Richard Delapole.

Safely inside his house, Julian poured himself a large whisky. Serena called a few minutes later.

'Is it in the sale?' she asked without preamble.

'It's in the sale,' Julian confirmed.

'Oh my God! You're kidding. You mean Nat Wilde actually thought it was real?'

'He did. In fact, he's taken two.'

'What?' Serena shrieked. 'Which one?'

'I let him see the little milkmaid too.'

'I hated that picture,' said Serena.

'It was rather sentimental,' Julian agreed. 'But Nat Wilde loved it.'

'I'm going into shock,' Serena laughed. 'I can't believe he thought it was genuine.'

'He said it was an "unexpected treasure",' said Julian, using Nat's own words.

Chapter Twenty-Seven

Two months later, both Serena's paintings were hanging on the wall in the main gallery at Ludbrook's. Potential buyers and interested onlookers milled around the room, admiring or disparaging the paintings on offer.

Meanwhile, in his office, Nat changed his old-school tie for his 'lucky' one, the tie he always wore for auctions. It was a Hermès tie. His first-ever tie from the legendary Parisian fashion house. It was dark blue and had a pattern of tiny pink rabbits bouncing across it. The tie had been a present from his ex-wife Miranda, back when she considered that Nat's propensity to go at it like a rabbit was an asset and not a liability. Fortunately the divorce didn't seem to have diminished the tie's ability to turn Nat into a silver-tongued salesman but it was starting to shows signs of wear and tear. The ends were ever so slightly frayed. It wouldn't go on for ever, Nat thought.

'How's the audience tonight?' Nat asked Lizzy.

'They seem pretty buoyant.'

'Excellent. Going to be a big night, I think,' said Nat.

And it was. Lot after lot went for more than the high estimate. Nat squeezed more money out of his audience than they even knew they had. Even the lots that Lizzy had thought might go unsold achieved very respectable prices. Lizzy could only watch in awe. Nat had the knack of making everything seem worth having.

Lizzy certainly felt that Nat was worth having. That week marked the passage of eighteen months since she had lost her virginity to him. During those eighteen months, Lizzy had not so much as looked at another guy. As far as she was concerned, Nat was her man, even if he still wouldn't come out and say so officially.

'It just wouldn't look good,' he said every time Lizzy raised the subject. 'Even if I don't give you any preferential treatment, people will assume that I am. It could bring us all sorts of trouble.'

'Then perhaps I should start looking for a job at a different house,' said Lizzy. 'So that it isn't an issue. We could have a normal relationship, then.'

'No,' Nat insisted. 'You mustn't do anything on my account. You've got a good position here. Besides, I value your presence in the office too much. Especially under my desk.'

That was where Lizzy found herself after the nineteenth-century sale, when everyone else in the fine art department had gone home. Nat buzzed Lizzy through into his private office, with its enormous eighteenth-century desk, of the kind that generals once planned campaigns on. Nat was sitting behind it, in his reproduction chair. He could have had the real thing but he liked a chair that swivelled and had casters so that he could scoot across the parquet floor. It was the culmination of all his childhood fantasies to have an office big enough to scoot about in. And there he was in the chair, with his jacket off and his tie already loosened, about to have another fantasy come true.

Lizzy knew the drill by now. She entered, carrying the pristine white gloves she had been wearing to handle the paintings at the auction. A bit of small talk first.

'Who did the painting of the milkmaid go to?' Nat asked.

'Yasha Suscenko,' said Lizzy.

'Ah,' Nat shook his head. 'Bastard. It pisses me off so much that some dim Russian oligarch's wife will pay over the odds to let that shyster be the middleman rather than buy straight from me. When will they ever learn?'

'But he has an eye,' said Lizzy. 'His collections are always very interesting.'

'Hmmm. Whatever you say, sweetheart.' Nat straightened up in his chair. 'Ms Duffy,' he said then. 'I seem to have dropped a pen beneath my desk.'

'Let me get that for you,' said Lizzy, pulling on the white gloves in preparation. She made a meal of it. The opposite of a strip tease but, to Nat's mind, just as seductive. Lizzy adjusted the fit of the gloves finger by finger, until they were as perfectly moulded to the contours of her hands as a second skin.

By the time she was under the desk in search of Nat's Mont Blanc rollerball, his hard-on was already straining at the front of his trousers. Lizzy unzipped Nat's trousers with great efficiency and released his tumescent cock. She held it in her white-gloved fingers as carefully as though she were about to demonstrate the finer points of a valuable antique. Dipping her head so that her tongue flickered across the tip while she moved Nat's foreskin with one hand, Lizzy had barely administered two strokes when there was a knock at the door. Nat didn't have time to say 'just a minute'. His visitor walked straight in.

'Hope I'm not interrupting anything, Nat,' said John Ludbrook, the company chairman.

'Not at all, John,' said Nat. 'Not at all.'

Lizzy froze beneath the desk. It was unlikely that John Ludbrook could see her. Nat's desk was surrounded on three sides by a long mahogany skirt. Still, Lizzy was filled with something approaching terror as John Ludbrook drew out the chair opposite Nat's and sat down so that the toes of his highly polished Lobbs were practically touching her bottom.

'Good sale?' asked Ludbrook.

'Yes,' said Nat. 'I was pleased.'

Slowly, oh so slowly, Lizzy tucked Nat back into his trousers and inched his zipper shut just in case he had to stand up.

Nat and Ludbrook discussed that afternoon's results for a while.

'How about a brandy?' Ludbrook asked.

Damn, thought Lizzy as Nat got up to fetch the decanter on his sideboard. Ludbrook was clearly settling in for a while.

'Cheers.'

Lizzy heard the clink of glasses.

'Now, Nat,' said Ludbrook after a moment's silence. 'This is a tricky subject but I have to bring it up.'

He paused.

'Go on,' said Nat.

'There has been talk around the house about your relation-ship with a certain junior member of your staff.'

'Really?' Nat sounded surprised.

'Yes. The gossip says that you have been seeing Lizzy Duffy after hours. Someone saw the pair of you walking out of Wiltons . . .'

'Oh,' said Nat. 'Well, I can't deny that I did take her there. But it was all above board. We were just talking about her plans for the future.'

'You're sure about that?'

'Of course I'm sure. You know me, John. I won't deny that I like the ladies but Lizzy Duffy? She's not my type.'

'That's what I thought,' said Ludbrook. 'As soon as I heard the rumour, I knew it had to be idle gossip. I mean, she's rather flat chested. What was it we used to call tits like that,' he mused. 'Ah yes. Fried eggs. That's what we used to say. That's exactly what Lizzy Duffy's got in her blouse.'

'Which isn't to say that she isn't an attractive girl,' said Nat.

'But there are definitely better lookers in the building,' said John. 'That Sarah Jane Kirby, for example. She's one of yours?'

'Yes,' said Nat.

'Quite the little vixen,' John sighed wistfully.

'Quite.'

'Much bigger breasts . . . even so, it's a terrible mistake to dip your pen in the company inkwell, if you know what I mean. It can only lead to trouble. But I trust you, Nat. I trust you to know what you're doing.'

'Thank you, John.'

'Care to join me at my club for a spot of supper?' Ludbrook asked.

Nat glanced down between his knees to where Lizzy's face looked up at him.

'Not tonight, John. Paperwork to get done.'

'Good lad,' said John. 'Enjoy the rest of your evening.'
John left.

The moment she heard the door close behind her, Lizzy
scrambled out from beneath the desk.

'Not your type!' she wailed, pushing Nat out of the way.
'Flat chested!'

'Well,' said Nat. 'You have to admit . . .'

Lizzy looked as though she might be about to cry.

'Darling, I only went along with it to put him off the scent.
If I had leapt to your defence he would have been immediately suspicious. You know that I think you are by far the
most beautiful woman in Ludbrook's. Now, where were you?'

'You think I'm going to get back under your desk?'

They heard the sound of footsteps approaching along the
polished wooden corridor. Thinking that it might be John
Ludbrook again, Lizzy had no choice but to get back where
she had been. There were no decent-sized cupboards in Nat's
office and the curtains didn't fall to the floor. With a string of
heartfelt expletives, Lizzy resumed her position.

'While you're down there,' said Nat.

Chapter Twenty-Eight

Yasha Suscenko collected his purchase right after the sale and carried it under his arm across the street to his gallery with little regard to how much he had paid for it.

The painting was beautiful. No doubt about that. It wasn't exactly to his taste but he knew he would be able to flip it easily enough. There were plenty of people out there who liked a good sentimental servant girl. His clients may be über-rich but their tastes had been formed in straitened circumstances.

Yasha hung the painting on the wall opposite his desk. He often did that. Put a painting right where he could see it every time he looked up from his papers or was taking a phone call. It helped him to absorb the best qualities of the work and figure out how to sing its praises most effectively.

Yasha poured himself a drink and sat down at his desk. He had emails from several clients already, asking whether he'd found anything good at the sale.

*　　*　　*

Yasha had a large clientele among his fellow countrymen. He was particularly amused and frustrated by some of their requests. They would call up and demand that he find them a Caravaggio, as though they were commissioning a new Lear Jet. When Yasha explained that it could take years to track down the painting they so desperately wanted at that moment, they were surprised. Sometimes enraged.

'It's not quite like the days of Catherine the Great,' he would say. 'You can't just invade another nation and loot its museums like they used to.'

Yasha had one client in particular who didn't find that amusing. He didn't want to wait. Not for anything. And he wanted a Ricasoli.

'You want a Ricasoli?'

Yasha's first instinct was to laugh out loud.

A painting by Giancarlo Ricasoli was as rare and precious as a Raphael. Ricasoli was an Italian artist of the early seventeenth century, a follower of Caravaggio who had taken the skills of his mentor and used them to create a body of work that some believed to be even more outstanding. In his lifetime, Ricasoli was more notorious than famous, having been chased from one end of Italy to the other for gambling debts and other misdemeanours. He was rumoured to have fathered thirty-seven children. His most recent catalogue raisonné estimated that he had produced just thirty-six works of art during the same period.

'There aren't many Ricasoli paintings in existence,' Yasha told his client. 'And very few indeed in private hands. It may take decades before one becomes available for sale.'

'I think perhaps you are not so good an art dealer as I was led to believe,' said Evgeny Belanov.

Yasha didn't like that at all. He tried not to rise to it.

'I will pay a great deal of money for the picture I want. A great deal. And I don't care where you find it.'

The implication was clear.

'I'll keep my eyes and ears open,' said Yasha.

Yasha didn't like to have to deal with men like Evgeny Belanov. Belanov was no art lover. He was a small-time gangster who had become a big-time 'businessman' in Putin's Russia. This was a man who didn't know anything about Ricasoli other than having such a rare painting would mark him out as truly wealthy. Paintings were just another commodity. What he wanted so desperately one week would be back on the market the next if there were the slightest hint of a drop in its monetary worth. Yasha would rather have torn a Ricasoli canvas in two than pass it to someone he knew would not appreciate it. He had no choice but to try to find one however.

Lay down with dogs and you're going to get fleas. Yasha knew that. But the problem was, once you had lain down with the dogs, they weren't always happy to let you get back up again. And Yasha had accepted too many favours back when he was starting out. He understood much better now how some debts could never be repaid and written off.

Indeed, right then the screen on Yasha's mobile phone lit up to announce an incoming call. Yasha had turned the ringer off, but this was the one caller he couldn't ignore. For Belanov he was always at home.

Fifteen minutes later, Yasha was in a car on his way to deepest darkest Surrey. All the lights were burning in one of the county's biggest houses, a building that had once been a school but which had recently been converted back into a private home with room for one man, his second wife, their eleven-month-old baby and sixteen body guards.

'Thank you for making the effort to see me so late in the evening,' said Evgeny Belanov when he finally received Yasha a full hour after he arrived.

Yasha nodded, though they both knew that it wasn't as though he had a choice.

Yasha had met Belanov through his brother. Yasha's brother Pavel had once pimped Oksana, the astonishingly beautiful woman who became Belanov's second wife. To compensate Pavel for the loss of revenue following Oksana's engagement, Belanov had put some other business Pavel's way. Drug business. In turn, when Belanov decided that he wanted to leave Russia and make his mark overseas, Pavel had pointed him towards his little brother Yasha, as someone who might help him acquire the culture his education had not provided.

At first, Yasha was pleased. Belanov was the first of his truly rich clients. The commission Yasha earned on providing art for Belanov's apartment in New York was enough to fund the move to London and the opening of The Atalantan. Yasha was more than happy to source the art for the fortress in Surrey too, sitting on the principles that objected to the fact Belanov had robbed his fellow Russians to get so rich. Yasha consoled himself with the business of creating a truly wonderful collection. But then the trouble started. It wasn't long before Pavel owed Belanov money. Belanov made it clear that he considered it a family debt.

'Come through into my office.'

Yasha followed Belanov into the basement of the house, where an office had been built in the former cold-store. The walls were thick and sound-proof. This was a safe place to conduct any dangerous business.

Taking his seat on the opposite side of the desk to his host, Yasha sighed inwardly as he noticed a painting by celebrated Russian seascape artist Ivan Konstantinovich Aivazovsky – a painting bought for several million dollars – propped up against a wall, vulnerable to clumsy bodyguards in big boots. Belanov followed Yasha's eyes.

'It doesn't look so good in here,' he said. 'I think it will go in the pool house.'

Yasha nodded. No point arguing that it might be better kept somewhere less damp.

'Have you heard from your brother lately?' Belanov asked conversationally.

Yasha shook his head slowly, knowing at once that something was awry.

'Well, I'm not surprised,' said Belanov. 'Having lost all his teeth like that, he probably doesn't feel much like talking.'

Yasha felt a wave of fear but managed to stay calm as a mill pond on the surface.

'Silly boy,' said Belanov. 'I told him he needed to manage his money more effectively. You have to service your debts first, isn't that right, little Yasha? I mean, Pavel can't keep expecting my wife's enduring affection for him to excuse him from his obligations. In fact,' said Belanov, looking at the framed photograph of his wife on his desk. 'It's starting to count against him.' He turned the photograph over so that his wife was face down on the blotter. 'You look worried,' he said, focusing his gaze on Yasha.

'What do you want me to do?' Yasha asked, getting straight to the point.

'I want you to take a trip to Russia for me. To see a painting. A dear friend of mine wants to sell something that I am interested in. But I'm only interested if it's the real thing.'

'What is it?'

Belanov slid a Polaroid across the table to Yasha. Picking the photograph up, Yasha's eyes widened.

'That has to be a fake,' he said.

'Well, you're going to find out.'

'And if it's not a fake? If it is the genuine picture?'

'You're going to bring it back for me.'

'You're asking me to move a painting that, if it's real, is stolen and could be worth over a hundred million dollars, across international borders? It can't be done.'

'You'll find a way. Leonid will go with you.' Belanov nodded at one of his men, who had entered the room quite noiselessly. 'Now, if you'll excuse me. It's getting very late.'

Chapter Twenty-Nine

In Cornwall, Serena and Julian were celebrating a pretty decent windfall. Good old Nat Wilde. He really could sell anything. Arriving with Serena's share of the loot from the sale of the Clifton Suspension Bridge and the Milkmaid in cash, Julian also brought with him a bottle of vintage Bollinger. Feeling like she had just won the lottery, Serena held a fan of fifties in each hand and laughed at her amazing good fortune while Julian poured the champagne into two flutes – a wedding present from Tom's sister. Serena was glad she hadn't smashed them over Tom's head after all.

'I've got some more good news,' he told her. 'We have our provenance for your little Madonna.'

'What? How?'

Julian had at last found a way to slip a note regarding the painting into the archives at Annabel's museum. He'd told Annabel that he'd always wanted to make love among the stacks and she had granted his wish for his birthday. Not his real birthday. That was months away. But Julian was desperate to get out of his arrangement with Annabel. The situation was becoming more and more complicated. It was clear she thought they were headed for the altar and Julian really didn't want to have to go so far as to jilt the silly cow.

So they made love in the stacks and afterwards, when Annabel scampered upstairs to answer her phone (which Julian was actually ringing from his mobile), he found just enough time to do what he really needed to do, which was place a copy of a letter purporting to be from the museum to his mother, thanking her for agreeing to the loan of the Madonna, in amongst the exhibition archive for 1973.

Serena was impressed, though of course Julian didn't tell her exactly how he had come to achieve such a coup. She was still under the impression that his museum contact was a man.

'So you think we should go for it?' she asked him.

'Now or never,' said Julian. 'I have to be honest. I've already let slip to Nat Wilde that I might have a Renaissance altarpiece in my possession. He's very keen to know more.'

Serena put her hands to her cheeks, suddenly overcome with a mixture of excitement and panic. 'What exactly did you say?' she had to ask.

'I described your painting. I said it looked Renaissance to me but because I'm not an expert, I couldn't be sure it was real. I said that I found it when I went to collect the contents of a strongbox from Mother's old bank in Exeter. I told him I had no idea what it was but that when I thought about it for a little while I vaguely recalled having seen it in a museum. Then it dawned on me that Ma and Pa must have lent the painting to a museum for a while. If only I could remember which one . . .'

'And of course,' said Serena, warming to the theme. 'You're going to remember the museum where you have your contact!'

'Exactly. And when Nat Wilde researches the provenance, he will find a record of the loan right where it should be.'

'God, you're clever.'

'We'll leave it to Wilde to make the final decision. If he decides the painting isn't real, no problem. I never claimed that it was. But I don't think he'll come to that conclusion.'

Serena chewed her lip.

'I wonder what sort of price he'll put on it.'

'It's unattributed so it won't be millions, but in the tens of thousands, I should think. It's very rare to find works from that period in such good condition, after all.'

Julian picked up his champagne flute to toast her.

'To a formidable team,' he said.

Julian had no idea how much it meant to Serena when he referred to them as being a team. It was wonderful to feel part of a partnership again, especially since every day seemed to bring a new reminder of how she had failed in her partnership with Tom.

Divorce proceedings were well underway. From time to time, the idea that it was actually happening, that she and Tom were legally parting ways, still took her by surprise. But he had been living with Donna for well over eighteen months now. Tom's mother, who still called a couple of times a week to talk to Serena and her granddaughter, had given up telling her favourite daughter-in-law that Tom would realise his mistake and crawl back. Instead, Joyce started to tentatively mention Donna in her conversations with Serena about Katie's weekends in London, which was when Joyce got to see her. It was clear that Joyce was preparing herself for Donna to become Tom's second wife.

'She's actually really very nice,' Joyce muttered one day.

Well, that was more than could be said for Donna's lawyer, who was now Tom's lawyer too. Serena's own solicitor was utterly cowed by the vile woman, who seemed to have made it her personal mission to ensure that Serena limped away from her marriage with less than she had brought into it. Serena noticed from the headed notepaper that Tom's lawyer, Beverly Grange, was a 'Mrs' and wondered how it was possible to remain married when you spent all day stripping people of any illusions they might have about the enduring nature of love and romance. Did Beverly Grange go home at night and tell her husband that she had just billed her client a year's worth of school fees to settle an argument over a silver serving platter worth five hundred quid?

While the lawyers' letters were flying back and forth, it suited Serena very well to have Julian turn up with a case full of cash. Mrs Beverly Grange need never know.

But it was more than the money. Julian's presence inoculated Serena from the worst of the divorce. As time went on and Tom refused to come to a reasonable agreement as to how to split their assets, she knew that they were heading for court. And if they got to court, the gloves would be off. Tom had already warned her, in the heat of an argument about his wanting to take Katie out of school so that she could accompany him and Donna to the Hamptons, that if it came to it, he would be more than willing to tell a judge how 'mentally unstable' Serena was. As far as she could tell, this diagnosis of mental instability was based solely on the fact that she didn't always agree with him, but ridiculous and groundless as she knew it was, Serena worried that a judge would think otherwise.

On the other hand, Julian made her feel human. He made her feel beautiful. He made her feel talented. He made her feel loved. She trusted him. When they made love, Serena felt fully herself again. She was no longer the downtrodden wife who had sent her husband running into the arms of another woman with her dowdiness. She was the free spirit Tom had fallen for. Serena sensed that the painting of the Little Madonna had given her part of herself back too.

When he went back to London the next morning, Julian took Serena's little Madonna with him, wrapped in the scruffy old cloth in which he had delivered the original piece of board for extra authenticity. As she waved him off, Serena said a little prayer. *Please let my work be good enough to fool Nat Wilde.* Julian muttered a similar prayer. Not least because he wanted – no, *needed* – to break up with Annabel before the next weekend, when he had promised to go with her to her parents' house. The prospect of sitting across a dinner table from Annabel's father made him more nervous than his upcoming appointment to show the Madonna to Nat Wilde.

After a night with Serena and with a night of Annabel ahead of him, Julian wondered why so many men thought it would be good to have more than one wife. Personally, he was exhausted by the very thought. He understood why alpha male lions seemed to spend so much of their time asleep.

Julian called Nat Wilde from the service station at Membury. Wilde took his call at once.

'Julian Trebarwen. How the devil are you?'

'Good, good,' said Julian. 'I've got the Madonna I was telling you about. I could be in London in two hours or so. Shall I bring it straight to your office?'

Wilde paused.

'No,' he said eventually. 'Don't bring it here. Not to the office. Bring it over to my place later. I'll be home from six thirty. You know where I live.'

Julian agreed the rendezvous. Leaving the 'priceless' Madonna wrapped in her rags on the back seat of the car he scuttled across the rain-swept car park into the service station itself. He had a pee, then bought a coffee and a sausage roll, which he ate sitting next to a window, watching the rain.

'God,' he thought to himself as he looked out on the grey, grey landscape. 'How on earth did my life get so bloody complicated?'

Chapter Thirty

MATHIEU Randon's plan to sell his art collection to fund his good works was swinging into action. His assistant Bellette issued invitations to the world's best auction houses to pitch for Randon's business. He had met with and decided against most of the big names and thus invitations were sent out to a second tier of smaller houses, including, in London, Ludbrook's and Ehrenpreis.

'Fuck me,' said Nat Wilde when he heard Randon had summoned him. 'I thought the old bugger was dead.'

Carrie was rather less surprised when she received the call from Bellette. Since reading that article in *Vanity Fair*, she had been waiting for this moment.

'Where would Monsieur Randon like to meet me?' Carrie asked in immaculate French.

Bellette replied in perfect English. 'He has requested that you join him on the Cote d'Azur. On his yacht. *The Grand Cru.*'

'That will be fine.' Carrie betrayed no hint of excitement. She wanted Bellette to be clear that she was used to dealing with people who had yachts. She wanted Mathieu Randon to be sure that she was a professional who could handle the wealthy without getting flustered. Inside, however, she was very excited indeed. *The Grand Cru* may not have been the biggest yacht in the world, but it was definitely one of the most beautiful boats plying the Med right then.

'You are to fly to Nice next Thursday,' Bellette continued. 'And stay overnight at the Hotel Du Cap in Antibes. Monsieur Randon will send a tender to fetch you from the hotel jetty the following morning at eleven thirty sharp.'

'Of course,' said Carrie, flicking to the correct page in her diary and seeing that, thank goodness, she had a very light couple of days. Mostly in-house stuff. Meetings that could easily be set back or brought forward. She would be in France whenever Randon wanted her.

'I'll email you with the travel arrangements.'

'I wonder,' Carrie asked Bellette. 'If it would be possible for me to see an inventory of the work Monsieur Randon is hoping to consign.'

'That's not possible,' said Bellette. 'He would rather talk you through the collection himself.'

Damn it, thought Carrie as she put down the phone. That was not helpful. Like most of her peers in the auction world, Carrie was a generalist. She knew a little about a lot of things. When visiting a client such as Mathieu Randon, she would generally swot up on their collection before she arrived, cramming her head with facts that would remain just long enough to convince the potential client that she knew more about Rembrandt or Picasso or Giacometti than anyone else in the business. She wondered if Randon was being deliberately difficult, in order to suss out what she really knew. Well, she would do her best to short-circuit that ruse. She called Jessica into her office.

'I need you to track down every piece of information you can about Mathieu Randon. I want you to find out which dealers he's brought from before. I need to know as much as you can possibly find out about his taste.'

Nat Wilde tasked Lizzy Duffy with exactly the same mission.

Randon's arrogance – getting his assistant to call up to *tell*, rather than ask, Nat when they would be meeting – suggested that he knew he had something special. Possibly enough to build an individual sale around. Nat salivated at the thought.

Having been asked to produce a report on the type of artwork Randon was likely to have in his collection so that Nat could pitch his presentation just so, Lizzy naturally assumed she would be accompanying him on the jolly to the Cote d'Azur. As soon as she heard about the trip she started to plan her holiday wardrobe in her head. How hot would it be? Back home that evening she studied her winter white body in the bathroom mirror. First thing the next day she made an appointment to have a spray tan. She'd never done it before but the girl at the salon, who was the same colour as a fish-finger, assured Lizzy that it would look 'Really natural. Because it's formulated with natural oils and stuff.'

Lizzy wasn't entirely convinced but she went ahead anyway. The alternative, to have to wear ankle-length kaftans the whole time, was not an option. If Nat was going to take her to the Hotel Du Cap, one of the world's most romantic hideaways, she wanted her body to look its very best.

* * *

Lizzy had her first spray tan session two days after Nat got the call from Randon's office. She timed it for the end of the day so that she could sleep in the gloop for maximum effect.

'Lizzy,' said Sarah Jane, the next morning. 'Are you OK? You look a bit yellow.'

Yellow was not the colour for Lizzy later that day when Nat thanked her for the report she had written about Mathieu Randon's art habits.

'I'm extremely grateful. You're such a star, Lizzy darling. So diligent. It's great to know that the office will be in good hands while Sarah Jane and I are in the Cap D'Antibes.'

'What?' Lizzy spat the word out. 'You and Sarah Jane? You're taking *Sarah Jane*?'

'Well, I need to take somebody but I can't take you, can I? Not after that lecture I got from old Ludbrook the other week. It'll make him suspicious.'

'But,' Lizzy tried, 'surely he'll be just as suspicious if you leave me behind? I'm the natural choice for the job. He might think you're trying to double bluff him if you don't take me. I'm your number two.'

'Exactly,' said Nat. 'Thus you're next in line when it comes to control of the office.'

'Olivia could go to France,' Lizzy tried. 'She hasn't been on many trips.'

It got worse.

'Now, darling,' said Nat. 'You didn't hear this from me, but Mathieu Randon is an infamous ladies' man and, alas, our sweet Olivia is no real beauty. We're going to need every advantage we can get to bring this baby back to Ludbrook's and my suspicion is that Randon will find Sarah Jane slightly more enticing than Olivia and her terrible glasses.'

Lizzy didn't know what to be most offended about. Nat's bloody awful sexism, which he seemed to find such a joke, or the implication that Sarah Jane was more attractive than Lizzy too.

'Fine,' said Lizzy. 'I'm sure I'll be able to manage the office on my own in your absence. After all, you're only going to be away for one night.'

'Three nights. It's a long way to go for twenty-four hours. But two of those nights will be over the weekend so you won't have to worry about that.'

On the contrary, Lizzy worried very much indeed.

Lizzy's mood did not improve when Sarah Jane came by her desk and announced that she had mislaid the paperwork relating to one of the paintings in that evening's Old Masters' sale.

'The little Madonna,' she clarified.

'What was in the file?'

'Just a copy of an entry in a museum inventory from the seventies.'

Lizzy spent two hours chasing down the museum's curator and persuading her to go down into the dusty archive and pull the inventory out again. The photocopied entry regarding the Madonna was faxed over just in time.

'Thanks,' Sarah Jane said. 'You really saved my butt. Look, I'm sorry about the Randon job. I was really surprised when Nat asked me to go with him. I mean, you're the obvious choice,' she added, echoing Lizzy's thoughts. 'Seeing as how you know so much more about just about everything.'

'It's OK,' Lizzy shrugged. 'I have plenty to do here. And in some ways, Nat has paid me the ultimate compliment, by saying that I'm too important to leave the office if he's not here in charge.'

Sarah Jane frowned. She knew that this was a dig at her but couldn't quite understand it.

Lizzy knew she had to sit on her annoyance. Her department was a small department in a small firm and Sarah Jane was popular with everybody. But Lizzy couldn't help measuring herself up against the other girl. Sarah Jane was taller than her and thinner and had bigger breasts. Did Nat prefer bigger breasts? He'd always been very complimentary about Lizzy's A-cups. He'd called them 'delicious' on more than one occasion and frequently sent text messages enquiring as to their well-being. Still Lizzy couldn't help thinking back to that awful conversation she'd overheard while stuck under Nat's desk. What was it Ludbrook had called them? Fried eggs? The truly galling thing was that Lizzy could have sued John Ludbrook from here till Christmas for sexual harassment had she not been in such a compromising position when she overheard the slur.

The thought was preoccupying Lizzy as she and Olivia manned the phones at that evening's auction.

'Are you still there?' her client asked her as it neared his time to bid. Lizzy was miles away. 'Er, hello?' said the voice at the other end of the line. 'You've gone all quiet. I really don't want to lose this picture.'

The picture in question was the Renaissance Madonna whose provenance documents Lizzy had spent the afternoon tracking down. Right at that moment, Sarah Jane, wearing pure white gloves, was carrying the little painting onto the stage. She turned from left to right, slowly, showing everyone in the room exactly what they were bidding on. Nat gave the description and opened the bidding. There was a bid from the floor right away, and then Olivia jumped in with her phone bidder. Lizzy would have to wait.

She waited in vain. By the time Olivia's phone bidder dropped out, the price of the painting had exceeded Lizzy's bidder's limit. He was not happy. Lizzy apologised, though what she really wanted to do was point out that he wouldn't have got the painting even if he had had a chance to bid. It had been bid beyond his price. Simple as that. Still, she murmured a few words of condolence before she called her next phone bidder and put them on alert.

The little Madonna was sold to Yasha Suscenko.

'Who's it for?' Sarah Jane asked him when the sale was over.

'She's so beautiful,' said Yasha. 'I may have to keep her for myself.'

His dark brown eyes moved from the painting to Sarah Jane's face. She blushed.

Chapter Thirty-One

Yasha Suscenko should have been pleased. He took his latest purchase straight back to his office. Though the painting had been unattributed, Yasha had a feeling that there was a very talented hand behind it. A student of Ricasoli's studio if not the man himself. Yasha knew that several of his rival dealers had had the same idea, which was why it had bust through its high estimate within seconds. To have secured it was a result, but Yasha had other things on his mind. Not least the black Bentley Continental Flying Spur that had been parked outside his building since his meeting with Belanov in Surrey. As surveillance vehicles went, it was far from discreet, but Yasha knew that was the point. Belanov wanted Yasha to know that he was being watched.

In just a couple of days, he would be flying out to Moscow, to the palatial Rublevka Avenue home of Yuri Vasilyev, the man who currently owned the portrait Belanov wanted so badly. In the top drawer of Yasha's desk was the Polaroid that Belanov had shown him. Yasha had studied it closely for anything that might enable him to tell Belanov that the trip would be a waste of time, but the damn thing looked real and that meant that Yasha would have to bring it back to London for his master. If Belanov didn't take the painting, someone else would, and if it ever reappeared on the market at twice what Vasilyev was asking for it now, Yasha's head would roll.

Yasha took the Polaroid out again as he sat at his desk, a glass of red wine before him. He studied the little photograph until he could hardly focus. Then he looked up. The Madonna he had bought that evening gazed down on him. In the soft light of his desk lamp, the painting glittered. The gentle glow of the bulb lent the gold leaf of the Virgin's halo a truly heavenly aspect.

In the cold light of day, however . . .

It was the middle of the next morning when Yasha started to have his doubts.

He saw something that Nat Wilde had missed. This painting was not genuine.

'Fuck,' Yasha leaned back in his chair. It wasn't possible. The painting had a low estimate of fifty grand. Surely to God Nat Wilde would have done his homework on something that expensive.

Focusing the lamp on the little Madonna once more, Yasha confirmed his suspicions by dipping a rag in alcohol and holding it close to the paint. At once the surface began to shimmer and dissolve. This painting was definitely not four hundred years old.

What to do? Yasha knew that Ludbrook's would be insured for this kind of eventuality. A clause in their contract specified that a buyer had up to four years to return a painting that had been mis-sold. And this painting had definitely been mis-sold.

But it was easy to see why. The forgery was so good. Whoever had executed this painting had put a great deal of time and effort into creating something that would have fooled most people. It was the detailing in the face that gave it away to Yasha. There was a hint of modernity in the Madonna's expression that made Yasha sure this wasn't even a nineteenth-century fake. It was more recent that that.

Something – an instinct – made Yasha go into his gallery and fetch down the Victorian milkmaid he had purchased a few weeks earlier. He hung it next to the Madonna. There shouldn't have been anything to compare and yet there was. Though in theory the paintings had been completed by different men who lived centuries apart and in different countries, there was a curious similarity of technique. If an artist's brushstrokes were his or her DNA then Yasha, with his well-trained eye, could see that the artist who had painted the watercolour and the painter who had finished the Madonna were closely related at the very least.

Yasha picked up his mobile and began to scroll through the numbers for Ludbrook's. But then he changed his mind. There was a much better way to deal with this.

Chapter Thirty-Two

'AFTERNOON, Lizzy.'

Lizzy grunted a greeting at Yasha Suscenko. She had been grunting all day. Sarah Jane had tried to make a joke of the fact that Nat was taking her to the Côte D'Azur but it had not lightened Lizzy's mood one bit.

'You look a little stressed out,' Yasha observed. 'Perhaps a little tired.' He peered at her closely. 'In fact, your skin is yellow. Have you seen a doctor? Could be your kidneys.'

'It is not my kidneys,' said Lizzy. There was something about Yasha that made her feel confessional. Maybe it was his kind eyes. 'It's a fake tan gone wrong,' she admitted.

'Ah. Thank goodness for that. You'll soon be your beautiful self again'

Lizzy accepted the compliment with a wan smile.

'Was Nat able to tell you everything you needed to know?' she asked, switching back into professional mode.

'Not quite everything. No.' In fact, Nat Wilde had not been forthcoming at all, refusing to tell Yasha exactly where the Madonna had come from. Client confidentiality and all that. Did Yasha really need more than the documentation he already had? Nat had asked. The painting was unattributed, after all. There was nothing to be disproved.

Yasha was about to leave but changed his mind. 'Would you like to grab a bite to eat?'

Lizzy did a double take. Was Yasha Suscenko asking her out? Was she allowed to go? On the other side of the open-plan office, Sarah Jane, who had heard the whole exchange, raised her eyebrows in surprise. Lizzy looked to her for some kind of clue as to how she should handle it. Sarah Jane, who had often extolled the virtues of the young Russian with his extraordinarily masculine good looks, gave her a covert thumbs up. And Lizzy suddenly felt as though she should go for it. If it gave Nat pause for thought, then good. She wanted him to know that he wasn't the only man who found her desirable – assuming he still did.

'That would be nice,' she said.

'Now?'

'Why not?'

It was already half past six in the evening. A good hour after the official end of Lizzy's working day. Ordinarily, she would have hung around the office until Nat left, but that night there was no point. He was taking bloody Sarah Jane to the Cap D'Antibes at the end of the week. The last thing Lizzy felt like doing was staying late to finish working on the presentation that he and Sarah Jane would give Randon.

'You lucky girl,' Sarah Jane whispered as Lizzy passed by her desk to get to the coat rack. 'I have been flirting with that man for years. Never a sniff of interest. Thought he might be gay. Report back, won't you?'

'Will you let Nat know that I've left?' Lizzy asked.

'But not who with, right?' Sarah Jane tapped the side of her nose.

Yasha took Lizzy to Scott's. It was another small triumph for Lizzy who walked past the restaurant on her way to and from the office every day but had never been inside its hallowed walls. A small clutch of paparazzi was hanging around on the opposite side of the street, suggesting that Lizzy would be dining among the stars that night.

The maitre d' greeted Yasha warmly.

'How did you get a table in here at such short notice?' Lizzy was impressed.

'I have a standing arrangement,' Yasha explained. 'It's practically my office.'

Lizzy tried to keep her poise as she entered the room. A very famous film star was handing over her coat to the cloakroom attendant just ahead of them. When Lizzy handed over her own coat, she folded it so that the label – Mango – was carefully hidden inside.

Yasha guided her in front of him for the walk to their table. Lizzy thrilled to the touch of his hand on her elbow. His was a good table with a view of the whole room. Lizzy slid onto the banquette. Yasha ordered a couple of glasses of champagne.

'You do like champagne, I assume.'

Lizzy assured him that she would like nothing better.

'So, tell me,' he said. 'What did you think of that little daub I picked up at your nineteenth-century auction?'

'I liked it,' said Lizzy. 'It's very pretty.'

'Yes. It is. I'd be very interested in more paintings along the same line. Do you know if the person who consigned it might have others hidden away in the attic? Is it some old lady who might be pleased of a few more quid to spend in her twilight years?'

'Well,' said Lizzy. 'It's someone who would be happy to have a few more quid, I should think.'

'Can you tell me his name?'

'I don't know if I'm supposed to. The sale was done anonymously.'

'You can tell me. I promise not to go over your head.'

'OK. It was another painting from Trebarwen. I can't believe I didn't see it when I was down at the house last year, cataloguing things for the main sale. Louisa Trebarwen's youngest son brought the picture in. He claimed that it was in the attic.' Lizzy frowned as she recounted the tale. 'I really don't know how I missed it. But his mother obviously had art hidden all over the place. I couldn't believe it when he turned up with such a beautiful Renaissance altarpiece.'

Bingo, thought Yasha. The fact that the same person had consigned both paintings added considerable weight to his theory.

'It was in a safety deposit box at a bank in Exeter. Been there for decades. Julian Trebarwen found it when he was tracking down some premium bonds. Talk about a windfall.'

Yasha quickly put two and two together. This Julian Trebarwen must know someone who was faking art. And with some considerable skill.

'So what do you think the Trebarwen guy is going to do with that big house?'

'I don't know. It's such a beautiful place. I would want to live there. But there's another brother so I think they'll probably sell it eventually and split the proceeds. Julian Trebarwen seems like the kind of guy who likes to be in the city.'

'He's in London?'

'Yes,' said Lizzy. 'Fulham, I think. Why do you ask?'

Concerned that it might start to seem odd if he continued with the line of questioning 'just out of interest', Yasha said, 'I don't know. Just making conversation. And I'm sure there are more interesting things to talk about than a middle-aged Englishman who just inherited a fortune.' He fixed his brown eyes on Lizzy's. She blushed. 'Tell me about you,' he said.

Lizzy instantly found herself tongue-tied. She found it hard to imagine that Yasha really wanted to know about her. Her path to this table at Scott's on a Tuesday night had been utterly unremarkable. A middle-class childhood – a very happy one – in Gloucester. Good grades at school. A place at Bristol University to read art history with a whole load of very nice gels. Then an MA at the Courtauld. A few years interning at Christie's and now Ludbrook's.

Yasha's story was undoubtedly a better one. Where had he come from? His looks were straight out of a romantic novel. There was melancholy in his eyes. What had they seen? Lizzy had heard that Yasha drew his clients from the very top levels of Russia's new elite. While walking through Mayfair, Lizzy had seen the huge black cars stop outside Yasha's gallery, disgorging hard-faced men she recognised from the business pages flanked by even bigger, harder-looking men paid to protect them from new enemies and old friends.

Nat had denounced Yasha as a small-time gangster. He claimed the Russian's clients weren't interested in art except as a way to clean their dirty money. Nat pointed to the sudden rise of Russian art. 'It's shit,' he said, with his trademark subtlety. 'It's been shit for centuries. It always will be shit. It's just a way for cash to change hands.'

But Yasha didn't look like a gangster to Lizzy right then and even if his clients were philistines as Nat claimed, he knew what he was talking about when it came to paintings.

Had Lizzy asked him his opinion on the man, Yasha might have been as disparaging about Nat Wilde as the auctioneer had been about him. A lazy generalist. As far as Yasha was concerned, Nat might just as well have been selling second-hand cars as fine art. But Lizzy didn't ask and in any case, Yasha wanted to wind up the conversation.

'Shall we share a taxi?'

Lizzy hesitated for a moment but just a moment. Why not? She asked herself. Nat had never promised her anything. She had no doubt that he would even deny they had a relationship if asked. And so it didn't matter if she went to bed with Yasha.

But Yasha had other ideas.

'Where do you live?' he asked.

Lizzy gave her address.

Yasha relayed the details to the driver and explained that he would be taking the taxi back to his own home in Chelsea straight afterwards. He took Lizzy home, getting out of the taxi to walk her to her door. But that was it. A kiss on the cheek. Nothing more.

Yasha had everything he wanted from Lizzy Duffy.

Outside the building that housed Yasha's office and his apartment, Belanov's goon had fallen asleep in the front seat of the Bentley. Yasha tapped on the window and spoke to the man in Russian.

'No snoozing on the job. I could have killed you.'

The goon, Leonid, struggled upright while Yasha walked around to the passenger door and let himself into the car.

'It's OK,' he said. 'I won't tell your boss.'

Leonid shook his head.

'I told him you need two guys for a twenty-four-hour operation. I can't be expected to stay awake all night.'

'You had anything to eat?'

Leonid shook his head.

'I'm going inside to make a few phonecalls. After that, we'll swing by McDonalds,' said Yasha. 'I need you to drive me somewhere. Got some errands to do before we leave for Moscow.'

Chapter Thirty-Three

JULIAN Trebarwen was in the bath when the doorbell rang. He decided, since it was eleven o'clock, that he would not answer but the caller was persistent. Knocking again and again and again.

'All right, all right! I'm coming,' Julian shouted, having no idea whether anyone on the front step would be able to hear him. 'Keep your hair on.'

He rose reluctantly from the warm bath and groped in the direction of the towel rail. He had one slightly damp leg in his jeans when the front door quite simply popped open.

'What the . . .' Julian looked over the banister in horror.

'Oh,' said his visitor. 'You're in.'

'Yes, I'm bloody well in. And who the hell are you? I've got my mobile in my hand. I'll dial the police.'

'I wouldn't bother if I were you. You'll only get us both into trouble. Finish putting your clothes on. I'll make myself at home.' The stranger waved Julian away as though he were an old friend who had turned up slightly too early for supper.

Julian hurriedly pulled his jeans up. This was no time to be pernickety about the fact that he wasn't quite dry and there's nothing worse than stiff denim on damp skin. A complete stranger had just broken into his house! Well, that would have been bad enough, but as Julian tugged a shirt over his head (he hadn't bothered to undo the buttons previously) it dawned on him that the man now 'making himself at home' wasn't a complete stranger at all. His face had been somewhat recognisable. Which meant that this was more than a mere burglar. It had to be worse.

Julian toyed with his mobile phone. The sensible thing to do would have been to call the police right away but the sensible option wasn't something that immediately appealed to someone with a past like Julian Trebarwen's. Instead, he tucked the phone into his pocket and headed downstairs. He'd risk it.

Julian's visitor was in the sitting room, standing at the mantelpiece. He had a silver-framed photograph in his hand. 'Your children?' he asked.

'My brother's,' said Julian. 'They live in Singapore.'

'Lucky.'

'Do I know you?' Julian asked.

'Anyone as active as you are in the art world should know me. Yasha Suscenko.' He extended his hand.

'Ah,' said Julian. The name gave him no further clue.

'I was lucky enough to buy one of your paintings through Ludbrook's nineteenth-century Victorian auction.'

Julian tried not to betray any concern.

'And more recently, I bought another of your paintings at the Old Masters sale.'

Julian's mouth dropped open and his lips worked silently as he tried to think of a response to that bombshell.

'Nat Wilde didn't tell me, if that's what you're thinking. I worked it out myself.'

'Which one?' asked Julian.

'The Madonna and Child.'

'Shit,' said Julian involuntarily.

'Not at all,' said Yasha. 'It had Nat Wilde fooled. And me, for a while. As did the Victorian portrait. Though when you see them side by side, it's obvious. You might have thought the artists used the same model.'

'What do you want me to do about it?'

'Perhaps we should have a drink and talk about that?' Yasha suggested.

He settled himself in the leather chair by the fireplace. Julian's favourite chair. One of the few things he had salvaged from Trebarwen before everything else went under the hammer.

'I'll have a whisky if you have any.'

Julian uncorked the decanter with shaking hands and poured out a measure.

'You could take the painting back to Ludbrook's,' said Julian. 'They're insured against this kind of thing.'

'And make it a victimless crime?'

'I didn't know they were fakes.'

'But you did. That much was clear by your initial reaction. However, while we've established that you knew the paintings were fake when you sold them, what I really want to know is whether you knew the painting was a fake when you bought them. Where did you get them? Are there others?'

Julian's mind flitted to Serena's sun-filled studio. He could see her standing at her easel in the paint-spattered man's shirt (her father's) that he found so peculiarly alluring.

'Because if there are, then I would like to see them. And if they're good, then perhaps you and I could do a deal.'

'There are no others,' said Julian.

'You're lying,' said Yasha. 'I can tell from the way your eyes flicked to the left when you said that. You were thinking about the person who paints these pictures for you. I know it isn't you. You don't have an artistic bone in your body.'

Julian swallowed. Was this Russian bloke bluffing?

'Look. You really don't have a choice. You are going to tell me who painted those pictures or I will go to the police. You haven't long been out of jail, I understand. I imagine a judge would view such well-organised attempts to defraud quite unfavourably.'

Julian felt his bowels shift at the mention of the time he had spent at her Majesty's pleasure. As a fraudster, he knew he'd had an easy time of it in the British prison system but it hadn't been *that* easy. The general public thought it was all colour TVs and day trips. They'd never shared a room with a seven-foot tall homosexual with a taste for public schoolboys. The mere thought of going back there was as effective as a knife at his throat.

'That's the choice. And if you do tell me who your artist is, I might make it worth your while. How much have you been making on these things? A few thousand a time? I'm offering you the opportunity to go big-time.'

'How much?'

'More than you could possibly imagine.'

Yasha had said the magic words. Julian buckled.

'The picture was painted by a woman down in Cornwall.'

'That's better,' Yasha nodded. 'I think we should visit her. We'll take my car.'

'It'll be the middle of the night by the time we get there.'

'This is a very urgent commission.'

Chapter Thirty-Four

WITH his hair still damp from the shower, Julian joined Yasha in the back of the Bentley. The car was driven by a man the size of a prop forward. His neck was as thick as one of Julian's thighs. Yasha spoke to the driver in rapid-fire Russian. The Russian grunted a response and soon they were on the A3.

The drive was a long one. Even at that time of night, with hardly any traffic once you got outside the M25, London to Cornwall was a four-hour trip. And despite the luxury of the Bentley, Julian was growing increasingly uncomfortable. This Yasha Suscenko seemed to know more about Julian's past- and current-misdemeanours than his probation officer did. Obviously, Suscenko knew people in some very low places.

All the way down to Trebarwen, Julian tried to think of a way to keep Serena out of this business. He tried to negotiate with Yasha, with the optimistic thought that perhaps he might even be able to make money out of this mess flickering at the back of his brain.

'How about I don't take you to meet her but you tell me what you want and I deliver it to you?'

'You want to be her agent?' Yasha smiled.

'I suppose I could be something like that.'

'Let's see how she feels about it first.'

They arrived at the gates of Trebarwen at three in the morning. Julian considered suggesting this Yasha man and his goon stay at the big house for the night. They could see Serena first thing in the morning. But Yasha was insistent.

'I have to fly to Moscow tomorrow morning. We need to conclude this business of ours right now.'

With what seemed like a casual gesture, the Russian driver hooked his thumbs in his waistband, lifting up his jacket and revealing a gun as he did so.

Still, it took a while to get Serena up. Julian had tried to phone but she'd obviously turned off her mobile before going to bed. He didn't have the number for her landline. Who used landlines these days?

Yasha's goon went to hammer on the door.

'Gently,' said Julian. 'She has a kid. We don't want to wake her daughter up.'

Julian tossed pebbles at Serena's window until her face appeared at the pane, confused and creased with sleep. She smiled at the sight of her lover but the smile quickly faded when the two other men stepped into the light of the porch.

'Julian,' said Serena as she opened the door to him and brought him inside. His companions hung back, sitting on the bonnet of the car. 'What are you doing here? What is this about? Who are they?'

'He's some Russian art dealer. He wants you to do a painting for him.'

'What?'

'He needs something copied. Something Renaissance. He bought the Madonna and the milkmaid. He knows they're fakes.'

'How the fuck?'

'I guess he knows his art,' Julian shrugged. 'He got my name from Ludbrook's. He turned up on my doorstep. He was quite insistent that I tell him who my artist was.'

'And so you told him? For Christ's sake. You promised me that you would keep me out of it! You said that no one would ever be able make a link between us and now you turn up in the middle of the night with some Russian Mafioso!'

'But you could do it. You know you could. You're the best artist I've ever met, Serena.'

'Flattery will get you nowhere. I don't want to do it. How dare he come round here at three o'clock in the morning? How dare you let him? Tell him to fuck off and find himself another artist.'

'It's not that simple. He could go back to Ludbrook's. Make a big fuss. It could get us both into a lot of trouble. If, however, you do this one painting for him, he'll see you right. There's money in it. I'm sure you could name your price.'

'No way. I have a daughter to think about. I got mixed up in your crazy scheme because I wanted better things for her. It was just going to be you and me. Now this is getting out of control.

'Don't try to tell me that there isn't a tiny part of you that would quite like to take up the challenge . . .'

'No, there isn't.'

'I was hoping you wouldn't say that.'

'We have no idea who that man is! You read about Russian oligarchs having each other assassinated all the time. You don't think he'd quite happily get rid of us the moment I finished his painting?'

'Now that would be killing the golden goose.'

Serena and Julian froze. Yasha was leaning against the doorframe.

'Don't worry, Miss Macdonald. I really am not in the business of having people assassinated. I would have thought that it would be enough of an incentive to you to know that if you work with me, I will keep you out of jail.'

Serena clutched at her forehead. Her eyes pierced Julian's, leaving him in no doubt whatsoever that she thought he was a complete and utter bastard for bringing this trouble to her door.

Chapter Thirty-Five

WITH great reluctance, Serena admitted Yasha and his driver into the kitchen. She leaned against the sink with her arms crossed tightly across her chest while Yasha explained the plan to her again, reiterating in a very soft voice the hard fate that could befall her and Julian if she disagreed.

'I will arrange for you to have everything you need,' he told her. 'I will also arrange for you to be taken somewhere quiet in the Italian countryside where you can work on the painting in peace. You'll need to be there by the end of this week.'

'That's ridiculous. I can't. I have a daughter. The school holidays are about to start.'

'Her father could look after her?'

'You've got to be joking,' said Serena.

'Then I'm sure she will enjoy a few weeks in Italy. The weather is far better than here. Think of it as a paid vacation. You'll be doing what you love in beautiful surroundings. And you'll be very well remunerated.'

'What about me?' asked Julian.

'We don't need you anymore,' said Yasha. 'I thank you for introducing me to this most talented lady and suggest that you choose a more honest profession for your future life.'

'I can't do it,' said Serena. 'I won't.'

Leonid the goon stretched so that the butt of his gun showed clear above his belt.

Serena noticed at once. As she was supposed to.

'He's got a bloody gun,' she shrieked, pointing at the thing as though the man might not have realised what he had tucked into the waistband of his trousers. 'You brought a gun into my house.' Serena levelled this accusation more at Julian than anyone else. 'Get him out of here. Get him out.'

She backed up against the kitchen units.

'Who's got a gun, Mummy?'

The four adults turned to see Katie standing in the doorway, barefoot and dressed in her pyjamas. She was holding her favourite toy bunny, twisting his ears as she looked from her mother to Julian to the two strange men for an answer.

Leonid, to his credit, immediately dropped his jacket so that it covered the pistol entirely. He raised his hands in Katie's direction. 'I haven't got a gun,' he said, his accent thick with the exotic cadences of his homeland. Yasha had the decency to look slightly shame-faced. Julian shrugged.

'Katie, darling.' Serena rushed forward to wrap her precious daughter in her arms. She smoothed her hair away from her face and looked full into her eyes as though to try and hypnotise Katie into forgetting what was in front of her. 'What are you doing up so late? You've got school in the morning.'

'I heard you shouting,' she said. 'You woke me up, Mummy. And who are these people?'

Katie looked from Yasha to his driver, as though she were a duchess finding gatecrashers at her ball.

'They're friends of Julian,' said Serena, loading the words with sarcasm.

'And we're just leaving,' said Yasha. 'Julian, I take it you can make your own way back to London?'

Julian nodded. The last thing he wanted was to spend four hours in a car with those two men again.

'Goodnight, Serena. I look forward to seeing you again very soon.'

He gave her a courtly bow. Leonid merely nodded, but was very careful not to let the door slam as he followed Yasha back out to the car.

Serena's eyes burned into Julian, over the top of Katie's head, giving him the distinct impression that only Katie's presence in the room had saved him from a knee in the nuts.

With Katie safely back in bed, Julian and Serena sat at the kitchen table nursing a matching pair of brandies.

'Jesus, Julian,' said Serena for the hundredth time. 'You told me that you would keep me out of this kind of shit.'

'I don't know how he tracked us down,' Julian said again.

'It seems pretty obvious to me. You are the weakest link.'

'It's going to be OK,' said Julian softly. 'I'll talk to him again tomorrow and try to come to a proper arrangement.'

'You heard him. You're no longer part of the equation. It's my painting talent he wants. Not your oh-so discreet ability to distribute the work. Four paintings through the same auction house. I should have known that was stupid.'

Julian set his jaw.

'You didn't say so when I brought you the money. You were absolutely fine with that. You can't seriously be thinking about doing as he asks without me. You need a middleman.'

'What are you thinking, Julian? Do you want to protect me? Or do you still want your cut?'

'You know the answer to that.'

'I think I do. And I suspect it's not the answer I want.'

'I want to protect you, darling.'

'Well, you haven't done a very good job of that so far.'

Julian reached across the table for her hand. He picked it up and kissed her fingers. She slapped him away. Tears were gathering in her eyes.

'Don't even start,' she said.

Serena went to bed alone that night, sending Julian back to the draughty big house next door on his own.

It had been like something out of a film. That Russian guy turning up in his suit and his Bentley with the driver built like a pit-bull. And a gun! In her home and in front of her daughter. It could only go badly from here on in. She berated herself over and over for having allowed Julian Trebarwen into her life, into her daughter's life, for getting involved with him because she was so lonely down there in Cornwall and she needed someone to make her feel desirable again after the end of her marriage. It just wasn't fair that it should have come to this.

What could she do? Call the police and tell them she had been a victim of blackmail? But then she would have to explain what she had to be blackmailed about and who knew what trouble that might bring to her door. It was impossible. Serena sensed that this particular nightmare was only just beginning.

Chapter Thirty-Six

$\mathcal{L}$IZZY was having a bad week. The hangover she earned on her night out with Yasha Suscenko stayed with her for a full forty-eight hours. She knew she had made a fool of herself by drinking so much and thinking that he might make a pass at her. She had called his office to thank him for the dinner and he had been short with her, claiming he had a long business trip to make and would talk to her later. She had a feeling that Yasha would be dealing with Sarah Jane from now on.

Bloody Sarah Jane. Though she had laughed out loud at the idea that Nat might try something on while they were in France, Sarah Jane had, nonetheless, gone to a huge amount of effort to prepare for the business trip. A suspiciously huge amount. One lunchtime, Lizzy walked into the office to find Sarah Jane showing Olivia a bagful of purchases from Fenwick. Two bright new bikinis and a pair of matching pareos. She stuffed them hurriedly back into the bag when Lizzy walked in.

Lizzy tried to be cool about it. 'Come on. I want to see them!' she said, all full of girly enthusiasm. 'Oh, aren't they lovely!' She could only imagine how fabulous Sarah Jane was going to look as she lounged by the pool and it didn't cheer her up at all. But Lizzy's luck was about to change.

Later that day, Lizzy was at her desk, checking for typos in a catalogue proof, when she heard the scream. The blood-curdling noise was followed by very audible panic. There were 'oh-my-God's as other people reached the scene of the disaster; even some more screaming. By the time Lizzy got to the gallery, it seemed that the entire staff of the auction house had gathered there in shock and awe.

'Is that Sarah Jane?' someone asked.

All you could see of Sarah Jane was her feet in their fishnet stockings and pointy black heels. It was like that scene in the wizard of Oz where the Wicked Witch of the East is flattened beneath Dorothy's house, except that Sarah Jane had not been flattened by a house.

'Oh my God!' Nat shouted. 'Not the Reynolds!'

Sarah Jane was pinned to the floor beneath a life-sized painting of a society lady that the Old Masters department had dubbed 'horse-face'.

An investigation would have to be made as to why the painting fell off the wall. Thankfully, the damage to the portrait was minimal. Horse-face was a tough old bird, just a few more cracks in the paint. But the damage to Sarah Jane would not be so easily repaired. The edge of the heavy frame had caught her right on the forehead, causing a concussion that meant she would have to be in hospital overnight at the very least. She'd also jolted her spine, having fallen straight backwards under the weight of the canvas. The long-term repercussions of her adventure were unclear and possibly serious.

The short-term repercussions were a cause of great delight for at least one girl in Ludbrook's fine art department.

'Don't you worry for one moment,' said Lizzy, holding Sarah Jane's hand as she was wheeled out to the ambulance by two paramedics who had been trying and failing to conceal their amusement at the circumstance of the call-out. 'I will step into your place on the Randon presentation and make sure it goes just as well as if you were there yourself.'

Sarah Jane frowned up at her. Her head was held still by a neck brace. 'Thanks,' she said. 'Thanks a lot.'

Well, it's an ill wind that blows nobody any good, as they say. Lizzy was in heaven. There was really no danger that Nat would choose to go to France on his own. He was far too lazy for that. He needed someone with him who could take calls and send faxes and make last-minute changes to presentations on PowerPoint. Nat was woefully hopeless at Power-Point. Olivia or Marcus could have done the job but of course he chose Lizzy.

The moment work ended that evening, Lizzy hit the lingerie department of Fenwick and stocked up. She blew the best part of a month's rent on French knickers and balconette bras, on lacy thongs and a white bikini with gold trim that would not have looked out of place in a Bond movie.

Back at home that evening she lay out her purchases on the bed and regarded them with adoration. The fact that she was only Nat's second choice of companion for the trip was long since forgotten. She was going to the Cap D'Antibes with the man she loved.

Chapter Thirty-Seven

CARRIE Klein had more important things to think about than what she would be wearing by the pool. Mathieu Randon was the most significant potential client Carrie had been asked to pitch to since arriving in London. The night before she flew to France to meet him, she got just four hours' sleep, working on her presentation until late and getting up early to run through it one more time.

Arriving in Nice around lunchtime, it was as though Carrie had travelled across seasons rather than simply across Europe. She left a grey London for the startling blue sea and sky of the Côte d'Azur. She had swapped the eternal gloom of the United Kingdom for a real summer. If only she were there on holiday.

Randon's assistant had arranged for a car to meet Carrie at the airport. The driver took the scenic route, following the coast, busy with holidaymakers though the real start of the season was still a couple of weeks away. Already there was barely room to put an ice-lolly stick between the brightly coloured beach umbrellas that shaded large sun-bathers and small dogs alike. The sea itself was just as busy with swimmers, water-skiers and yachts, getting sleeker and more extravagant the closer they were to the horizon.

Carrie looked out enviously, wishing she was feeling the sea breeze on her face on the deck of one of those rather than in the back-seat of a car with the air conditioner on full blast.

After an hour in snail-slow traffic, the car reached the road that curved up around the Cap. Nice's gaudy Promenade des Anglais with its roller bladers and ice-cream sellers and overheated tourists suddenly seemed a million miles away as the driver whisked Carrie on through Antibes. Here was tranquillity and exclusivity. Tall pines hid more and more impressive homes from view. The road wound higher and higher until finally the car turned through the big gates of the hotel itself. A uniformed guard touched the brim of his cap and beckoned them inside.

This beautiful hotel, built in the nineteenth century, was one of the world's most exclusive destinations. As the bellboy dealt with her bags and Carrie checked in for the weekend, she thought about the other guests who had stood on this spot in the past. From Rudolph Valentino to Johnny Depp. Scott and Zelda Fitzgerald. George Bush. It was quite something to be there on business.

Carrie could not suppress her delight as the bellboy showed her to her room. After more than a year of living in a hopelessly bare apartment, this hotel room was such a visual treat, finished as it was with chintzy fabrics and well-chosen ornaments. But this room itself was nothing compared to the aspect. Carrie had a beautiful view of the hotel's manicured park and, in the distance, the sea, azure blue and dotted with beautiful sailboats. She wondered which of the silhouettes on the horizon was Mathieu Randon's boat.

She threw open the window and breathed in the salty tang of the waves, feeling her heart lift automatically as she filled her lungs. Such a beautiful place. No wonder it was such a popular spot for honeymooners. Carrie watched with not a little envy in her heart as a couple strolled across the lawn.

Her mind wandered to another hotel room in another town. She saw Jed's tousled blond hair on the pillow at the Trump Tower. His brown shoulders rising up out of the white sheets. The very thought of it made Carrie's hand drift to her neck as though to comfort herself for the lack of him. She'd been surprised when she hadn't heard from him after their night together. He'd seemed so happy to be with her and yet . . . It obviously didn't mean as much to him as she had thought. For a moment, something like sadness overwhelmed her.

But there was no time for that. There was work to be done.

Mathieu Randon had, of course, booked two rooms for Nat Wilde and his assistant. But Lizzy didn't spend long in the room that had been allocated to her. As she was unpacking her suitcase, Nat called.

'I've got a fabulous ocean view,' he said. 'Like to see it?'

'I've got a sea view too,' said Lizzy.

'I'm sure it's not as big as mine,' said Nat. 'Come on over.'

It was so delicious. So far away from the office, there was no need to hold back or practise discretion. Lizzy abandoned her unpacking and went straight to Nat's side. He had not unpacked his suitcase either but he had organised himself enough to order a bottle of champagne from room service.

'Maison Randon, of course. I'm sure the old man won't mind.'

He handed Lizzy a flute. She giggled girlishly as she took a sip and the bubbles tickled her nose.

'To a very successful presentation,' said Nat. 'And a fabulous dirty weekend.'

Lizzy was delighted. She put her glass down on a table, kicked off her shoes and bounced on the bed.

'That's what I like to see in my employees,' said Nat, as he unbuttoned his soft white shirt. 'Enthusiasm and initiative. I think I might just have to give you an appraisal.'

'Whatever do you mean?' Lizzy's eyes were wide with disingenuity.

'Well.' Nat let his shirt drop to the floor. 'I need to evaluate your performance. Under the most testing of circumstances.'

'Will the test be very hard?' asked Lizzy, playing along.

'Oh yes,' said Nat. 'Very hard indeed.'

By now he was standing up by the side of the bed. He dropped his linen trousers and his white cotton boxer shorts (well-pressed ones) at the same time. Lizzy feigned awe as she came face to face – or rather, nose to tip – with Nat's erection. Nat put his hands on his hips and pushed his pelvis forwards.

'You can start whenever you like, Ms Duffy,' he intoned.

'Just a moment,' said Lizzy.

With one hand already wrapped around Nat's cock, Lizzy took a swig from her champagne glass. She looked up at Nat with naughty eyes.

Then, without swallowing the champagne, Lizzy took Nat's penis into her mouth in an expert manner that saw not a single drop was spilled. Nat's mouth formed an astonished 'O' as the bubbles fizzed against the swollen head of his member, ice cold and effervescent to the point of being prickly. He made a noise that was halfway between shock and delight.

Lizzy let Nat's cock slide from her mouth as she swallowed the Maison Randon vintage. When she next wrapped her lips around him, her mouth was warm again, moist and luscious.

'You absolute swine,' Nat breathed. But the champagne shock was soon forgotten as Lizzy worked her magic and brought Nat close to coming within a couple of minutes. Just as he was about to lose control he took over, pushing Lizzy backwards onto the bed and taking her without even bothering to undress her first. There wasn't time. He just pulled her knickers to one side and got stuck in.

'How did I do?' Lizzy asked when the 'evaluation' was over. 'I want to hear your appraisal.'

'You were very good,' Nat told her breathlessly. 'In fact, you were so good, you've been promoted. Next time, you're on top.'

Nat and Lizzy spent the rest of the day in bed, not even emerging from the room for dinner. They ate club sandwiches in their dressing gowns instead. Which was a very good thing for Carrie Klein, who ate a delicious three-course meal in the Restaurant Eden Roc overlooking the ocean. Knowing that she would be sharing her much anticipated cruise on *The Grand Cru* with Nat Wilde would definitely have given Carrie indigestion.

Chapter Thirty-Eight

THE next morning, Carrie was awake bright and early. She ate a small bowl of muesli in bed and prepared for the day ahead with a long cool shower. Then she got ready to meet *The Grand Cru*'s tender, which would arrive at the Hotel Du Cap's jetty at eleven thirty precisely. She had no doubt it would be on time.

Carrie dressed in a cream trouser suit, with a peach silk blouse beneath. She wore flat shoes – Chanel souliers in soft gold leather – knowing that while heels may have given her more authority on land, it was unlikely they would be welcome on the doubtless highly polished wooden decks of Randon's yacht. *The Grand Cru* was legendary. Just that morning, Carrie had found a photograph of Grace Kelly on board the yacht in a coffee table book about the Riviera. She imagined herself in the princess's place and dressed her hair accordingly. A boat as beautiful as *The Grand Cru* required that one made an effort.

She got to the jetty at twenty-five minutes past, full of delicious anticipation. The tender for Randon's yacht arrived exactly on time. It was a beautiful vintage Riva. There were two crew members aboard, both dressed in dazzling white livery with the legend 'Grand Cru' embroidered above their hearts and on the bands of their peaked caps. Trust a man like Mathieu Randon to do everything with such style.

In Nat Wilde's room, the morning scene was altogether less organised. Nat and Lizzy had also had breakfast in bed. Lizzy had two pieces of toast and a delicious mixture of yoghurt and fruit compote licked from the end of her boss's cock. After that, they both fell asleep again, waking with just minutes to go before they were supposed to be at sea.

'Old Randon will have to wait for us,' said Nat as Lizzy dashed around the room, gathering together her laptop, brochures and a sheaf of notes that she had made the previous evening, using Nat's broad back as a writing desk.

'We can't be late for this one, Nat,' she told him. 'Mathieu Randon's not one of your mates from your club. He's a serious businessman. Even more serious since he got that bump on the head.' She pulled a suit from Nat's case and shook it out so that it looked a bit presentable. Still, Nat looked like he'd had a hard night when he finally arrived on the jetty. Five minutes late.

'You?'

'You!'

Nat and Carrie echoed each other's horror exactly.

'What are you doing here?'

'What are *you* doing here?'

'I'm on my way to pitch to Mathieu Randon. On his yacht,' said Carrie, still foolishly hoping that Nat was just there on a dirty weekend.

'Well, what a godawful coincidence,' said Nat. 'So are we.'

Carrie was aghast.

'You're shitting me?'

'I am not, as they say in your charming country, *shitting* you,' Nat sneered. 'What the fuck is going on?'

'We need to get going,' said the young man who would be sailing them out to *The Grand Cru*.

Nat and Lizzy remained on the jetty.

'Did you know about this?' Nat asked his rival.

'You think I would be here if I did? I'm not happy about this at all.'

'I'm not surprised. Going to be a bit humiliating for you to have to pitch against me and lose.'

'Oh, I have no intention of losing,' said Carrie. 'So perhaps you should stay right there on the jetty to spare your blushes. I mean, I would have thought that Ludbrook's would send their top man for a pitch like this. Not a mere head of department.'

'My department turns over more than your entire auction house. You're a big fish in a puddle, Klein, and you know it.'

'Then take your chances against me. Prove you're so much better.'

'Watch me.'

Nat immediately stepped on board, with as much grace as he could muster. Which wasn't much. He sat down quickly, before he fell down. He left Lizzy on the jetty with all of Ludbrook's presentation equipment. *The Grand Cru* staff helped her. Lizzy had to sit beside Carrie.

'Sleep well?' Carrie asked her politely.

'We were up all night,' said Nat with a leer.

Carrie refused to rise to that. She knew from Lizzy's secret smile exactly what he was getting at. Did he think she would be jealous? 'I'm sorry to hear it,' she said. The thought of Nat in her hotel room all those months ago gave her reason for a secret smile of her own. She should have let the line of conversation drop but suddenly she was unable to resist telling the smug old boy, 'Apparently, making sure your feet are warm is the key to a really good night's sleep. You should try keeping your socks on in bed.'

Nat's mouth dropped open. He knew exactly what she was referring to.

'Are we ready?' one of Randon's crew asked.

'I'm ready for anything,' said Carrie.

Soon the Riva was zipping over the waves like a giant flying fish. Carrie and Lizzy faced forward, relishing the sea-spray in their faces.

At the back of the boat, clinging on until his knuckles ached from it, Nat Wilde was soon looking sea-green.

Chapter Thirty-Nine

MATTHIEU Randon greeted his guests on the foredeck. He was dressed immaculately. All in white. His patrician grey hair was slightly longer than in the *Vanity Fair* pics and was swept back from his forehead in a very flattering fashion. There was no doubt about it, he was a very attractive man. Within moments of having met Mathieu Randon, both Carrie and Lizzy could understand how he had managed to bed so many supermodels and beautiful actresses. He was, in a word, magnetic.

He kissed Carrie's hand. 'I'm so glad you could make it.'

Then he kissed Lizzy's hand. Nat made a comic scene of backing away when it was his turn to be introduced.

'None of that French kissing for me,' he said. 'I'm an Englishman.'

Randon managed a feeble chuckle.

'Ladies and . . .' he hesitated. 'Gentleman. I do hope you're not too offended to find yourselves sharing this little trip on

The Grand Cru, coming as you do from houses I understand to be sworn enemies on the London auction scene.'

Carrie and Nat both made as if to protest that Randon was wrong.

'I know that it's a little unusual for you to be asked to visit a potential client together but I hope you will appreciate that I am a very busy man. Since I got out of the hospital in San Francisco, it seems there has been little time in my life for anything but work. Trust me, I had no idea how much of a perfectionist I am until I spent eighteen months in a coma and emerged to find my empire in such a state of disarray.'

Nat, Carrie and Lizzy all nodded in understanding.

'But we'll come to business later. I'm being a bad host. Let me offer you a little something to eat and drink.'

Eat? The very thought of it made Nat want to hurl.

Randon invited his guests to seat themselves at a table on the deck. Two stewardesses were on hand to serve lunch, cooked by a chef who had been poached from a Michelin-starred restaurant for the season. There was a whole salmon and salads spiked with fruit and garnished with flowers. Carrie and Lizzy were eager to tuck into the beautiful food set before them. Nat was less enthusiastic. He hoped that a sip of wine might settle his stomach, but there was none to be had.

In any case, no one was going to be putting anything in their mouth until Randon had blessed the bounty that lay before them. He invited the three auctioneers to hold hands around the table and to bow their heads. The blessing began simply.

'We thank you, oh Lord, for your generosity manifest today in the food on this table before us.'

But it didn't stop there. Randon launched into a real sermon, asking not only God's blessing on the food but his support and protection in the trials to come. He asked for clear-headedness and a way to know the righteous path when it appeared before him. After ten minutes, Carrie's hand in Nat's was feeling uncomfortably hot. Lizzy was feeling uncomfortable at the thought of Nat holding Carrie's hand, for whatever reason. And Nat just wanted both his hands free so that he could cover his mouth in the event that he was unable to keep his breakfast down. As soon as Randon said 'Amen' the three auctioneers dropped hands as though an electric charge magnetising them and keeping them together had suddenly been switched off.

At Randon's signal a stewardess reappeared with what looked like a carafe of white wine. Nat's hopes soared and then dived when he discovered it was elderflower cordial. Nat would sooner have drunk his own urine. But he politely accepted a glass of the vile stuff, just as he forced down most of his meal. He could not be seen to pass on anything if Carrie wasn't going to. He matched everything she did. Nat wasn't convinced that Randon still had all his marbles. This deal could come down to who had eaten the most roquette.

After lunch, Randon announced that it was time to go back inside. The visitors followed him. Nat lagged behind. He had hoped that being on the bigger boat would somewhat attenuate the symptoms of nausea but, alas, that didn't seem to be the case. Lunch had not helped. But he couldn't stay on deck until the feelings passed, so he took a deep breath and followed the others into the former smoking room, now Randon's office, which thankfully had the modern addition of air conditioning.

'I think it's time for a tour,' said Randon.

*   *   *

A tour of *The Grand Cru* was a real history lesson. Every room had a story to tell.

The boat was built in the late 1920s for an American steel millionaire called Arthur Crew, who was also, as would delight Mathieu Randon more than fifty years on, a big fan of fine wines and quite the Francophile. When *The Grand Cru* was finished, she was the largest yacht in the world at that time. A veritable floating mansion house at almost 270 feet long, with staterooms for twenty guests who were waited on by sixty crew. Her state-of-the-art steam engines could propel her at a speed of fifteen knots over a range of 7000 miles.

In the heady days between the wars, *The Grand Cru* saw high jinks galore as the most popular party venue on the Seven Seas. Her owner was a very well-connected man, who invested some of his great wealth in film. As a result, all the big movie stars of the day had walked up the gangplank and danced on the deck beneath the stars.

The party came to an abrupt end, however, at the start of the Second World War. Like many other private yachts, *The Grand Cru* was requisitioned by the United States Navy. She was painted in camouflage colours and became SS *Regardless*.

After the war came many years of ignominy, several of which she spent in dry dock. Until the 1980s when Mathieu Randon bought her on a whim. Her name marked her out as his, he told his bankers. He had to have her.

Randon had restored the boat to its original glory, updated the engine room and made it the envy of the Côte d'Azur once more. There was something so elegant about *The Grand Cru*, compared to the enormous gin palaces that the newly minted billionaires of Russia and China were buying by the dozen. Its classical lines spoke of a taste and style that new money simply could not buy. And history too. *The Grand Cru* had plenty of that.

'After the Second World War, Eisenhower held a meeting of his great admirals in this room,' Randon told them.

He spoke enthusiastically also of the lengths to which he had gone to return the boat to its original state.

'Are there still sixty staff on board?' Lizzy asked.

'Fifty-five,' said Randon.

But no guests, Carrie thought. Not any more. All the young men and women in uniform who went about their work so silently were there for the convenience and comfort of only one man.

Carrie admired the decoration. 'So many yachts have interiors like trailers,' she said.

'I tried to remain true to the spirit of the boat as she was,' said Randon. 'But you must have been wondering exactly what it is I would like you to sell for me.'

Carrie and Nat both hoped that he was hoping to off-load some of the paintings that adorned the walls of the yacht's 'staterooms'. Lizzy couldn't help but gawp when she saw a Van Gogh that had recently sold at Christie's for fifty million. It couldn't be the same painting, surely. It had to be a reproduction. I mean, thought Lizzy, it can't possibly be a good idea to keep a Van Gogh on a boat, no matter how beautiful and well-finished the boat was.

'You're admiring my Van Gogh,' said Randon. 'Quite a little beauty, isn't it?'

Lizzy daren't ask the question that was hovering on her lips.

'It is the real thing, in case you're wondering. I can't think of a safer place to keep it, can you? But this, ladies and gentleman, is the work that I want to consign to you.' He paused outside a door that was in itself a work of art, inlaid with delicate veneers. 'I should warn you that the collection I have in this room is not for the narrow-minded. I spent many years gathering the items that I have here. There is more of a similar nature at my villa in Capri. Should we come to any kind of agreement today, then the items at Capri would have to be sold as well.'

Carrie and Lizzy glanced at one another, wondering what on earth they would find beyond the door. Nat was getting impatient for other reasons. Truthfully, he wanted to be off the boat as soon as possible. He was not getting those sea legs.

'It's time,' said Randon. 'Apart from my assistant Bellette, you are the first people to see inside this room in a decade. For many years this has been my private domain. Absolutely for my eyes only. It's the only place you'll ever find me doing the cleaning,' he added. The flash of humour relaxed his visitors, but only a little.

Randon pressed a code into the keypad on the wall. There was the sound of an extremely complicated locking mechanism grinding and opening with a clunk. Then, after a pause as if to allow everyone to take a deep breath, the door slid back.

'My one-time pride and joy,' said Randon, ushering them into the room. 'Now my greatest shame.'

The first thing the visitors laid eyes on was a six-foot-tall marble penis.

Chapter Forty

THE girls both gasped. Nat gave a small cough to prevent himself from saying something stupid in a knee-jerk reaction to the astonishing sight. The marble penis was truly something to behold. Absurdly outsized it may have been, but it had been skilfully rendered in astonishing anatomical detail. Though they were carved from cold stone, the veins that ran the entire length of the enormous phallus seemed to be pulsing with life. Carrie put her hand over her mouth and hoped that no one would ask her to touch it. She felt quite ill.

'Now that is what I call a big boy,' Nat whispered to Lizzy as Randon invited them further into the room. Lizzy couldn't even look at Nat, so frightened was she that if she met anyone's eye – especially Nat's – she would immediately burst out laughing.

'I can see you're all shocked,' said Randon.

Carrie nodded, lips pressed tightly together to stifle a shriek of hilarity.

Randon waved a hand towards the cock.

'This particular piece was rescued from the sea just west of the island of Ischia,' he said. 'It's thought that it may have belonged to a statue commissioned by Caligula himself, God forgive him.'

So that was the end of the mystery. The auctioneers' hopes that they had been invited to the South of France to see a lost Leonardo sketch too fragile to face the light of day had been thoroughly and quite incredibly dashed.

Mathieu Randon's one-time pride and joy was a collection of erotic art and manuscripts dating back to the Roman Empire and beyond. All Carrie and Lizzy's preparation for this moment had been way off the mark. Both had imagined that they would be viewing a couple of Caravaggios or a Raphael. A dick the size of a man and a selection of antique dildos was not what either of them had envisaged. The walls were covered in sketches and etchings that were little more than porn.

Still, the room was amazing. The insight it gave the auctioneers into Randon's personality prior to the earthquake that left him in a coma was quite something. This was a collection that had taken many years to amass. It had taken dedication. It wasn't just tat. Every item in the room had merit. Lizzy drew Nat's attention to a particularly lurid Picasso sketch, from the period towards the end of the artist's life, when he seemed to become obsessed with pudenda.

'I must apologise,' said Randon. 'For submitting you to the evidence of my former depravity, but needs must. While this collection is vile, I have good reason to believe that it is probably worth millions. And millions are required to bring to fruition my dream of a religious retreat.'

'Oh, it's not that bad,' said Nat, as he got closer to one particular painting and saw that it was not in fact a butterfly after all but a carefully drawn collection of vaginas. 'Good God,' he muttered as the details became clear. 'I think I know that girl.'

Carrie found herself drawn to a small ivory box.

'You know what that is?' asked Randon.

'Of course,' said Carrie, thanking her lucky stars that just the previous year, Ehrenpreis New York had run an Asian sale and several similar items had been consigned to it. 'This is an inro,' she said with confidence.

She bent over at the waist to look at it more closely. She didn't dare pick it up. Inro were relatively common so the fact that this particular example was in Mathieu Randon's collection, alongside items she estimated to be worth six figures, suggested that it was rare and precious indeed.

'Pick it up, if you like,' Randon told her. 'Tell me what you think of it.'

'It looks like one box,' Carrie continued. 'But it's actually a series of little nested boxes. They were originally designed to carry things like tobacco or document seals. The Japanese hung them from the obi they wore around the waist because their garments didn't have pockets. They were made out of all sorts of materials. Wood, tin, precious metals. But this one looks like real ivory. Eighteenth century, I would guess.'

'Well done, Ms Klein. Exactly right.'

Nat, irritated that Carrie had scored a point he could have got himself – who didn't know about inro? – threw in his own comment. 'So it's basically a Japanese handbag. Or a man-bag, if it belonged to a samurai.'

Lizzy managed a little laugh. Randon and Carrie ignored him.

Carrie marvelled at the intricacy of the design. As with everything else in the collection, the subject was fairly explicit. It showed a man and a woman engaged in a variety of sexual positions. Some pretty commonplace. Some quite painful-looking. But it was so delicately carved. The joins between the nesting boxes were almost entirely disguised by careful arrangement of the overlapping pieces. That someone had managed to create something so complicated out of what seemed to be a single piece of ivory was quite remarkable. Carrie would call Ehrenpreis's Asian expert as soon as she got off the boat to see if her hunch was right. Someone would pay hundreds of thousands for this.

'It's beautiful,' said Carrie, replacing the inro on its pedestal and straightening up.

'And infuriating,' said Randon. 'It's a puzzle box to me. I haven't been able to get it open since I bought it back in the 1970s. It was the very first piece in my collection. I bought it while I was in Japan to promote my champagne. It was a reward to myself.'

'Well deserved, I'm sure,' said Nat.

'Wrongheaded,' said Randon, 'As was my purchase of the centrepiece to this collection. Though I think you will understand what I was thinking at the time. I have no doubt you'll agree that it is very special indeed. Step this way.'

They followed Randon into another interconnecting room.

'You mean, the penis isn't the centrepiece?' Lizzy murmured to Nat.

'Please don't let it be a giant fanny,' Nat quipped back.

It was not a gigantic vagina. Randon took the party to a case that was covered by a velvet cloth of the kind you often see on cabinets in museums, protecting particularly delicate items from sunlight. Randon removed the cloth carefully if not reverently. He had long given up holding any of these particular artworks in reverence. Inside the cabinet was a very dusty-looking manuscript. As Randon beckoned them forward, Nat, Lizzy and Carrie crowded over it, jostling for the very best view.

'Oh my God,' said Nat, receiving a sharp dig in the ribs from Lizzy, who had worked out that this wasn't the place for blasphemy, despite the nature of the things they were seeing. But the tone of Nat's voice was different this time. Not just shock now, but awe.

'You've guessed what it is?'

Nat nodded. 'But I can hardly believe it.'

All three auctioneers were astounded. And all three of them set to work translating the words they saw before them in their heads. Carrie was so surprised by what she read, she decided she must have got some words wrong, despite her fluent French.

But this wasn't just a piece of erotica. It was a piece of history.

'These are pages from an early draft of *Justine*,' Randon told them. 'In the Marquis de Sade's own hand. Saved by a prison guard.'

De Sade, the French nobleman born in the eighteenth century, had spent much of his life in prison for his own peculiar brand of erotic philosophy which gave 'sadism' its name. Justine was one of his most infamous works, charting as it did the life of an innocent young woman who falls prey to all sorts of sexual depravity. The work's subtitle was *Les Infortunes De La Vertu*.

'Good conduct, well chastised,' Nat translated. 'A great book. I must reread it.' He earned himself another dig in the ribs from Lizzy.

'It's the work of a monumental pervert,' said Randon. 'Someone whose words should never have been published. The vile spewings of a diseased and dangerous reprobate. Allowing this kind of filth out into the public domain can only cause damage to the hearts and minds of the people who read it.'

'You could burn it,' suggested Nat.

'But it's important from a sociological point of view,' Carrie jumped in, filled with horror at the thought of such a rare and precious manuscript going up in flames in the smoking room of *The Grand Cru.*

'I won't burn it. I understand it has its worth. But the sooner it is not in my possession the better,' said Randon. 'I only hope that de Sade's soul will benefit in some way from the good I am able to do with the money I raise with the sale of this, this . . . horror . . .'

Randon dropped the velvet cover back on the cabinet as though the sight of the Marquis de Sade's feverish handwriting were actually hurting his eyes.

'Well. I think that's enough for now, don't you? I don't want to subject you to this a moment longer than I have to. Let's go back into the boardroom and discuss the business of having this collection dispersed.'

It was time at last for the auctioneers to make their presentations. Nat flipped a coin and Carrie found herself having to go first. It wasn't ideal. Especially when she realised that Randon really was going to have her present her case in front of Nat and Lizzy. She opened her laptop and connected it up so that her slides would appear on the enormous digital screen that hung where a movie screen had hung in *The Grand Cru*'s years as a party ship. It went without a hitch but

Carrie was infuriated by Nat's patronising nods when she described the service that Ehrenpreis could provide a man like Randon.

'Our London office is small,' she concluded. 'Just the size of the Old Masters department at Ludbrook's, as I'm sure Mr Wilde will tell you. But I believe that a very personal level of service is what is required here. Though, of course, if we need to, we are able to call on experts all over the world to help create the exact strategy needed for each individual item in the collection.'

It was Lizzy, not Nat, who set up Ludbrook's IT arrangement but Nat delivered the spiel. He focused heavily on the history of the house. Ludbrook's had been in existence for many hundreds of years. They had disposed of property belonging to some of the most famous people in world history. When people thought of an auction house, Ludbrook's was the name that sprang to their lips. They had an international reach. They were trusted. Nat reeled off some of their recent sales results as Lizzy flashed up graphs showing prices expected and prices achieved.

Carrie was both impressed and depressed by the expertise with which Nat made Ludbrook's case.

He finished by letting Randon know, 'You can be sure that your collection will have my personal attention, of course. I would be delighted to be a *hands-on* part of the team that takes care of this project.'

Randon laughed gamely at the reference to 'hands on'.

'Any questions?' Nat asked.

'I don't think so. Thank you all,' said Randon. 'You have given me plenty to think about. Now, if you'll excuse me, I have work to do this afternoon. I will instruct my captain to arrange for your return to the mainland forthwith.'

Without shaking anybody's hand, Randon left the room.

That was it. The end of the audience with the great man. Carrie, Lizzy and Nat remained. Not knowing what they were supposed to do next.

Nat studied the glass of fizzing water handed to him by a stewardess as they waited for the tender to be prepared. 'The man owns a champagne house. You'd think he could do better than this. Get me a slice of lemon, would you, Lizzy?' said Nat. 'I'd get up for it myself but this boat is moving way too much for me.'

Lizzy jumped at his command.

Carrie rolled her eyes.

Chapter Forty-One

NAT did not get his sea legs even by the time Randon was ready to send his visitors back to the Cap D'Antibes in the Riva. If anything, the return journey was harder. The sea was choppier than it had been when the party ventured out in the morning. Despite his conviction that he and Lizzy had swung the deal for Ludbrook's, Nat was grey-faced as he climbed into the small boat and positively green again by the time they had been at sea for five minutes.

'Look at the horizon,' Lizzy advised again, while rubbing his back.

Nat pushed her hand away.

Carrie, sitting on the other side of the deck and rather enjoying the sea breeze, couldn't disguise a smile. Seeing Nat Wilde laid so low was the only high point of her day so far. She gazed out on the approaching land, grateful also that Nat was too busy puking over the side to gloat over how much more positively Randon seemed to react to the Ludbrook's presentation. Carrie still couldn't quite believe that Randon had made them pitch head to head.

At last the boat arrived at the jetty for the Hotel Du Cap. Randon's man jumped out and offered Carrie his hand. She rested her own hand lightly upon it and stepped down onto the jetty with the grace that suggested a lifetime of sailing holidays in Nantucket (in reality, there had been just three since she moved to Manhattan and reinvented herself). Then she slipped on her little Chanel ballet flats and sashayed up the jetty to the steps, as though she were on a catwalk. She might as well have been. She knew that the people in the restaurant above would be watching eagerly to see who was arriving. She didn't want to disappoint.

Lizzy followed Carrie on-shore. She was equally self-assured. She really *had* spent much of her childhood on boating holidays, though in the chilly Solent rather than the Med. But Lizzy was absolutely unconscious about how good she looked right then. All her thoughts were with Nat who, having made the crossing without actually dying, despite all his protestations that the end was nigh, was now groaning that he couldn't possibly be expected to stand up while the boat was still rocking.

'But it won't ever stop rocking,' Lizzy explained to him as Randon's man looked on in amusement. 'It's on the sea. Come on, Nat. The sooner you're out of there, the sooner you'll start to feel better again. We'll sit by the pool and have a cocktail! How about that?'

Nat did not look tempted. Randon's man got back onto the boat and tried to help him to his feet.

'For fuck's sake,' Nat shook him off. 'I'm not a fucking invalid.'

'I'm sorry, sir, but I really need you to disembark. My captain has radioed to say that he requires all his crew back on deck within the hour. Weekly briefing. There's really nothing to it, sir. I'll help you along the passarelle. It's completely solid. It isn't going anywhere.'

'I know,' Nat exploded. He stood up and rushed for the passarelle. And Lizzy and Randon's crew member watched in shock and surprise as he stumbled while getting onto the gangplank in a hurry and ended up in the drink.

'Oh God,' Lizzy covered her mouth to hide her smile.

From the sea-view restaurant came a round of applause. Carrie paused in her ascent to add her own congratulations to Nat who came up spluttering, a thin strand of seaweed dangling from his elegant nose.

Nat's graceless disembarkation did nothing for his mood. He went straight to the bedroom, ignoring the hotel staff who tried to give him a towel as he passed through the lobby. Once in the room, he turned his fury on Lizzy as she tried to help him out of his wet jacket.

'Should I get this cleaned?' she asked. 'I'll call room service now.'

'Don't call anyone,' said Nat. 'And don't do anything. Just go and sit by the pool or something.'

'What? And leave you here like this?'

'Yes,' said Nat. 'Go. I want to be on my own.'

Reluctantly, Lizzy did as she was told. She knew from a hundred self-help books read on those long lonely nights when Nat couldn't see her, that there was absolutely no point trying to persuade him that things really weren't so bad. Not right then. Nat had gone into his cave. The only thing Lizzy could do was sit and wait for him to come back out again. And she may as well do that by the hotel's fabulous pool.

*   *   *

It was a busy weekend at the Hotel Du Cap. All day long helicopters had been landing on the lawn in front of the main house as movie stars and their minders arrived in preparation for the Cannes Film Festival, which was to take place the following week. It made the fact that Randon had somehow managed to secure three rooms at the hotel at such short notice even more impressive. Lizzy wondered who had been bumped.

But it also meant that the area around the swimming pool was absolutely packed. Seeing the sun-loungers covered by so much famously fabulous flesh, Lizzy almost turned on her heel and went straight back inside. She would just read her book in her room while Nat slept off his bad mood in his. She had no desire to stretch out in her white and gold two-piece next to a bona fide Bond girl. Suddenly she felt very untoned and much too pale.

It was too late to run, however, for among the perfect Hollywood bodies was an unusually perfect body from the world of the auction houses. Carrie Klein pulled her sun-glasses down her nose and looked over them at Lizzy. She smiled and nodded.

Damn.

There was no pretending that she hadn't spotted Carrie's greeting. Even worse, Carrie was sitting next to the one and only unoccupied sun-bed on the bright white pool terrace. One of the pool-boys was already advancing towards the sun-bed with a towel, preparing it for Lizzy's arrival.

'Deep breath,' Lizzy told herself. She would have to sit next to Carrie Klein. If she didn't she would look rude or frightened or both.

'That was some boat trip,' said Carrie when Lizzy sat down.

'Yes,' said Lizzy. 'And what a collection.'

'Indeed. But he's quite the perfectionist, old Mathieu Randon. Whichever one of our houses gets the job is going to have its work cut out.'

Lizzy nodded.

'How's your boss?'

'He's making some calls,' Lizzy lied.

'Really? It's the weekend now, isn't it?'

'I know. But when you're working on something this important, weekends don't really count, do they?'

'Good point,' said Carrie. 'But I am making use of this rare moment of down time to enjoy this pool. Isn't that a Bond girl over there?'

Lizzy pulled a face. 'Makes me wish I'd spent three months in a gym before I came out here.'

'Nonsense,' said Carrie, looking her up and down. 'You've got a lovely body. I'm sure Nat thinks so.'

Lizzy blushed to her roots. If Carrie didn't know that Lizzy was shagging her boss before she made that crack, she certainly would now. Carrie confirmed that she knew exactly what was going on with a little snort of amusement.

'He's not . . . It's not . . .' Lizzy began.

'It's not like that? Trust me,' said Carrie. 'It is. I have two things to say to you. The first is that if you're sleeping with Nat Wilde to advance your career, then you're wasting your time. The second is that if you're sleeping with Nat Wilde because you've fallen in love with him and you're hoping that you'll somehow fuck him into loving you too, then you're absolutely wasting your time. This means nothing to him. You know that. You're not the first and you won't be the last.'

Lizzy was left gasping. Carrie handed her a glass of water.

'You look like you need this.'

'But . . . but . . .' Lizzy struggled to form her rebuttal.

'I watched you very closely today. I took a sneak peak at your notes. I know that you did the bulk of the work for that presentation. Nat Wilde is cute but he's lazy. Always has been. He wouldn't wipe his own ass if he could delegate the job to you.'

Lizzy's mouth dropped open.

'I apologise for being so blunt,' said Carrie. She pulled out a compact and examined her lipstick as if her outburst of crudeness might have skewed her lip-liner. She reapplied a slick of gloss then turned towards Lizzy and fixed her with a serious look.

'What I'm saying is, you're good enough without him. You've got the knowledge and the talent to make it in our business without having to fuck the boss. And what you have to remember is that if you fuck one boss, it will be noted by your next boss and almost certainly used against you. These things never stay secret for long. Far better not to fuck any of them. Once you capitulate, you lose all your power. Use your beauty – and you are beautiful – properly. Dangle it as a bait by all means. But keep your career out of the bedroom. And make sure that your work is always without fault. And that when you do a good job, you get credit for it. I can see it now. If Randon gives Ludbrook's the consignment, Nat will be the one who gets the laurel crown. You'll be relegated to typist. Cocktail?'

Carrie raised her hand and a waiter appeared. She ordered two glasses of Champagne Arsenault.

'It's much better than Maison Randon. We'll put them on Nat's room,' she said wickedly.

Lizzy shook her head. 'I really don't know if I . . .'

'Your loyalty to your boss is impressive but also heart-breaking. I'm not saying this to you because I want to spoil whatever you might have going on, Lizzy. If what you guys have is true love, then I'll raise a toast to that. I just hate to see any bright young woman being misled. I know what it's like. You see all the prettier girls getting ahead. They're invited out to lunch. On trips like this. I did hear that Sarah Jane Kirby was going to be here before her unfortunate accident. Head through a Reynolds. That must hurt in more ways than one. Anyway, I know how it seems. You think that nobody cares about your ability to actually do the job, so when your handsome boss beckons . . . Nothing will come of it.'

'Then tell me how *you* did it. Tell me how you managed to get where you are today.'

'By working very hard and making myself extremely unpopular,' she smiled. 'Do you have sun block on?' she asked suddenly. 'Only you're very pale and I can see you're already getting a little pink on your shoulders.'

It wasn't long before Nat was fed up of sulking in his room. So much for wanting to be alone in his cave. He hadn't really wanted to be left alone. As far as Nat Wilde was concerned, it wasn't worth sulking if there was nobody there to be impressed by it. Lizzy hadn't gone back to her room, as he had expected she would. He had tried summoning her by mobile but realised after he heard the buzzing in the corner of the room that she had left it behind. That meant he had to go and fetch her if he fancied a shag. He thought he did. He certainly felt like he did while he was lying diagonally across the sumptuous California King sized bed. Much too good a mattress to waste on sleeping. When he got to his feet however, he discovered that having conquered his seasickness, he now had its corollary. The solid ground lurched as violently as any wave. It really wasn't funny. Lizzy should be there to look after him. What on earth was the girl doing? She'd never struck him as the kind that actually liked to laze around by the pool. Damn it. He was going to have to get out there and find her.

Catching sight of Nat arriving at the poolside, Carrie pushed her sunglasses back up her nose and pulled her sun hat down a little lower, as if she could fool him with such a rudimentary disguise. Her actions drew Lizzy's attention to his presence.

'I better go,' said Lizzy, jumping up at once. 'It's been nice talking to you.'

'I've enjoyed talking to you too,' said Carrie. 'Now run along. And remember what I told you . . .'

Lizzy paused. 'What?' she asked.

'Don't get burnt!'

'What were you talking about?' Nat asked.

'Nothing,' said Lizzy.

'Then why were you sitting next to that old cow?'

'It's just that it was the only sun-bed available.'

'Right,' he said. He didn't sound convinced. 'Never mind. It's too hot out here. Let's go back inside.'

Once he had Lizzy back in his room, Nat started to feel better at once. He didn't even have to make much of an effort to undress her. She just let her sarong fall to the floor.

'Here,' he said, taking off his shorts to reveal he already had a hard-on. 'Tell me this isn't every bit as impressive as that marble cock on Randon's boat.'

'You would think that cock was actually modelled on yours,' Lizzy assured him.

'It's just as hard,' Nat promised her, giving it a little waggle in her direction.

Lizzy giggled. Without being asked she got down in front of him and opened her mouth.

It was an odd thing. Lizzy was almost grateful for the chance to get on her knees for Nat right then. It suddenly seemed really important to do exactly what Nat wanted. Her conversation with Carrie had left Lizzy feeling rather rattled, more than usually insecure about Nat's feelings for her. While she had his dick in his mouth, however, she could be certain that she had his full, undivided attention. If only she could find out how to keep it.

This relationship was driving her slightly nuts. It was so different to anything Lizzy had experienced before. David, the college boyfriend, had been so steady. It wasn't very exciting to be with him but at least Lizzy never felt as though he was slipping away. They would probably still be together if he hadn't taken that missionary job in Senegal. Lizzy was, as Carrie had pointed out, not best suited to the heat.

She wanted to be in London and she wanted to be with Nat. And so, where once she had worked on her baking skills to garner David's approval, now Lizzy tried other tactics. She had gone from being a complete novice in the bedroom to a goddess, trying every trick in the book.

Right then, she swirled her tongue around the tip of Nat's penis as though she were licking a Solero. At the same time, she wrapped one hand around his shaft and cupped Nat's balls with the other. The intention was to make him feel as fully surrounded by her as if he were lying on top of her, thrusting deep inside. It certainly seemed to be working. Lizzy glanced up to where Nat's head lay on the pillows, face turned to one side. His long dark lashes fluttered on his cheeks. His short hair, greying so attractively, stuck to his dampened temples. His perfect mouth opened in silent surprise as Lizzy licked faster and faster. Seeing Nat so transported Lizzy was torn between relief and self-hatred that it seemed sometimes this was the only thing he valued about having her in his life. The sex.

It wasn't long before he told her he wanted to fuck her. 'But you'll have to go on top,' he said. 'I've got a bad knee.'

Chapter Forty-Two

CARRIE was set for another evening of room service when she got the call from Randon's assistant requesting her company at dinner.

'Really?' Carrie was surprised. 'On the boat?'

'Yes,' said Bellette. 'The tender will pick you up at eight.'

Carrie was ready five minutes early. The tender arrived exactly on time. She wondered how Randon did it. It was as though he could control the tides.

As the Riva pulled away from the jetty, Carrie felt as though she were embarking upon some secret mission. Rather than looking forward, towards the boat, as she had done that morning, Carrie turned instead to watch the hotel receding. She glanced up at the rail around the restaurant terrace, hoping to see Nat Wilde. She knew it would have spoiled his evening to see her on Randon's tender. But Nat wasn't there. No doubt he had Lizzy going through some figures in his bedroom, so for now Carrie had to hug the thought that she had been invited back to *The Grand Cru* to herself.

Randon was waiting on deck when the Riva arrived. He helped Carrie climb on board himself. She knew she looked good. She was wearing a white cotton sundress by Fendi. Around her middle was a wide tan leather belt that emphasised her narrow waist. On her feet she wore her flat gold ballet shoes. Her hair was piled into a chignon. She imagined herself as Princess Grace. Randon kissed her hand and, as he did so, she could see in his eyes that he approved.

'Thank you for agreeing to have dinner with me this evening,' he said.

'Oh,' said Carrie. 'The pleasure is all mine.'

As Randon guided her towards the dining room, Carrie wondered if that evening would be a pleasure or whether she would have to spend the meal going over what Ehrenpreis could offer a man like Randon. Or, worse, listening to a sermon. What did he want, Carrie wondered.

In the dining room, the enormous table was laid for two with pristine white linen and sparkling silverware. There were wine glasses, Carrie noticed with some surprise. At least, there were wine glasses in the place setting in front of the chair one of Randon's crew pulled out for her.

'An aperitif,' Randon suggested. 'As you know, I have given up drinking but I understand that it's not much fun to have dinner with no wine if you haven't made the decision to abstain yourself.'

Carrie accepted a glass of the champagne that kept Randon's empire afloat, but she drank only a quarter of the glass, conscious that this might be some kind of test and she didn't want to fail it. She would have to treat this evening as a business meeting.

The first course of the meal arrived. Carrie was delighted by the fresh tasting ceviche.

'I caught the fish this afternoon,' Randon told her. 'From the back of the boat.'

'Did you really?' Carrie found it hard to imagine.

'I did. Our Lord was a fisherman,' said Randon. Carrie settled in for a lecture. But none came. Instead, Randon was the charming raconteur that Carrie had heard about when she was first working in the auction world. He talked about the summers he had spent on the Côte d'Azur as a child. He spoke about seeing *The Grand Cru* in a dry dock while visiting the States on business.

'I fell in love at first sight,' he said, fixing Carrie with such a suddenly predatory look that it made her look down into her plate to hide her blushes.

'So,' Carrie thought it might be a good idea to change the subject. 'I'm sure you must have asked me to join you this evening because you had some questions about Ehrenpreis's business. We're a relatively new house in London but you have had dealings with our New York office before, I know, and . . .'

Randon held his hand up to stop her.

'I know all about Ehrenpreis the auction house. I wanted the chance to get to know *you* a little better,' he said. 'It was quite difficult to get a sense of what you're really like with that Englishman around. I understand he is very good at his job but I wonder if he wouldn't benefit from being still and quiet from time to time.'

Carrie relished hearing Randon's criticisms of Nat but she didn't rise to them. She had a feeling that would leave her looking bad in Randon's eyes.

'I have learned a great deal through being still,' said Randon. 'It's a skill I didn't have before the earthquake in San Francisco. Back then, a moment of stillness and quiet was a moment wasted.'

'I understand that feeling,' said Carrie.

Randon picked up his water glass to take a sip, keeping his eyes on her all the while. When he replaced the glass, Carrie noticed that it was on her side of the table. If she didn't know better, she might have thought he was subconsciously making a move.

And then dinner was over. What next?

'It's too late to send you back to the hotel,' said Randon.

Carrie said nothing. She couldn't quite believe it. Mathieu Randon the evangelist had brought her out to *The Grand Cru* to seduce her after all. Carrie might have known that despite all his insistence that his months in a coma had made him see the world anew, Mathieu Randon would remain a dyed-in-the-wool misogynist who thought that women were either mothers, whores or nuns. Nuns! She shook her head as she imagined Mathieu Randon's religious order. What would they have to wear? A wimple and hot pants? No, Carrie wasn't convinced by his religious conversion one bit.

'If your crew haven't been stood down for the night,' said Carrie, 'I think I would like to take the tender back to the Cap now.'

Randon summoned the first mate who told him regretfully that the Riva had already been despatched shoreward so that one of Randon's Parisian associates could catch a flight from Nice to the capital. The other boat was unfortunately unavailable for use right then.

'It's being varnished,' the young man explained.

'It would be a shame to risk your dress,' said Randon.

Carrie opened her mouth.

'Michelle,' Randon motioned to the girl who had been waiting on them. 'Please arrange for one of the guest suites to be prepared for Miss Klein. One of the rooms on the same deck as my bedroom would be best.'

'I'm happy to wait for the Riva to return . . .'

'It could take a while,' said Randon, reaching across the table to take her hand. 'And I really want to go to bed.'

'Monsieur Randon,' said Carrie. 'I don't know what kind of woman you think I am but I can assure you . . .'

'You're not that kind of girl? I know. None of you ever are. But don't worry. That's why I've had a guest room prepared. Good night. When Michelle returns she will tell you where you are to sleep.'

Randon left Carrie sitting alone at the dining table, feeling rather stupid. She had the sense that she had been ticked off. But the things he'd said to her. The innuendo. What was she supposed to think? And now she was stuck on the boat. There was nothing to be done.

Michelle reappeared presently and took Carrie through to the state room where she would be spending the night. Under any other circumstances, it would have been a delight. The room was beautiful. Like the dining room, it was entirely panelled in teak. The linen was crisp and white. A fluffy dressing gown embroidered 'Grand Cru' awaited her.

'There are toiletries in the bathroom,' Michelle explained. 'I put three kinds of toothpaste out but if you want something that isn't there, just let me know.'

'I'm sure it will be fine,' said Carrie. 'Thank you.'

Michelle left, closing the perfectly fitted door quietly behind her.

Carrie sat down on the bed and kicked off her shoes. Might as well try to get a decent night's sleep.

Mathieu Randon slept less well. He had felt the episode approaching towards the end of dinner. That was partly why he had sent Carrie away so quickly. That and his fear that if he stayed close to her for too much longer, he might say or do something inappropriate. Carrie Klein was a very lovely woman. Her slightly frosty exterior belied a vulnerability, Randon knew. It was the type of vulnerability he had once preyed upon.

Carrie was exactly the sort of woman Randon had a weakness for. He liked the angular lines of her body. Her intelligent face. Her high small breasts. Her narrow waist. He liked the fashion in which she was dressed. She had class, unlike many of the women on the Côte d'Azur who hung around the bars and clubs, waiting for a lift on a yacht, nothing Carrie wore was too brief and yet it was fitting in such a way as to reveal as much as it concealed. A woman who covered her body so well had to know that she was inviting fantasies about taking it all off. He'd wanted to reach across and put his hands up her skirt.

Randon berated himself for even thinking about it. Safely back in his own state room, he undressed and put on his nightshirt. He sat on the edge of the bed and took out the rosary in the top drawer of the bedside table that held nothing other than a Bible and a glass of water. He tried not to think about what he had found in that drawer when he first left the hospital and returned to France.

'We've left everything in your private rooms exactly as it was when you went to California,' Peter Maree, the captain of *The Grand Cru* had told him.

Where now lived a rosary, Randon found a pair of handcuffs and a bottle of lube. He also found a spherical object he didn't recognise at all but later guessed to be a sex toy. He'd wrapped them all in a towel, and, when he was sure that no one was looking, he tossed them out to sea.

He told his staff that he didn't want to hear from any of the women he had entertained prior to going into his coma. He had dropped several men from his circle of friends too, finding them far less interesting now they didn't have drinking and whoring in common.

Randon quickly began to feel calmer as the rosary beads slipped between his fingers. He muttered the words that went along with the actions. Click, click, click. Hail Mary. Forgiveness cooled his fevered brow. He must have said the rosary fifty times before he lay down to sleep. But sweet dreams were not to be his reward that night.

The harbingers of the episode were the same as they always were. First came the narrowing of his vision, then the sparks, then the blank unconsciousness that heralded a great opening of his mind.

And then she was there again. The dark-haired woman with the smooth skin and the smile that made him believe she must be straight from heaven. She reached out to him. She was asking him something. Begging. Pleading. He couldn't quite make out the words.

'Tell me what you want of me,' he implored, but she did not respond. Instead she turned away and started running along the path that led to the river.

An uglier thought came to him now. A flash of writhing bodies. Female flesh, dark pink and wet. It was brief but so very vivid. Randon could almost smell it. He felt the jolt of arousal dash throughout his body. His penis stiffened. Randon touched himself automatically. The urge was so strong. He wanted to feel that woman's flesh all around him. And then he saw the face again. The girl. This time her hands were grasping at the air, frantically, as though she were trying to catch something to keep her from falling.

'Oh, God, no,' she cried out and then she fell away from him, dragged backwards by something stronger than either of them. Her smiling mouth became an astonished 'O'. A hole in her face. Black and empty.

When Randon came round, his pen and paper were not by his side. He called for help. It arrived, quickly, in the shape of a fresh-faced girl he hadn't seen before.

'Are you OK?' she asked with an Australian accent. 'Were you having a fit?'

'Paper and a pencil,' said Randon. 'At once.'

'Shall I get a medic?'

'Just paper!' Randon ordered.

He scribbled everything down. As fast as he could. As though God were guiding his pencil. All apart from the last bit. The girl's face in what was obviously sexual ecstasy. That part of the vision couldn't possibly be divine.

Chapter Forty-Three

First thing in the morning, Carrie boarded *The Grand Cru*'s tender and headed back to the Hotel Du Cap. Randon did not appear in time to bid her farewell.

'He sends his apologies,' said the Australian stewardess. Catching Carrie's frown, she added, 'He hopes you're not offended. It's just that since he was unwell, he still suffers the occasional episode.'

Carrie knew better than to ask just what such an 'episode' involved. She reassured Michelle than she did understand, though privately she couldn't help feeling angry. Mostly angry with herself for having lectured Lizzy Duffy about the dangers of mixing business with pleasure and, hours later, allowing herself to get into such a humiliating position.

Nat Wilde and Lizzy were having breakfast on the terrace when *The Grand Cru*'s tender pulled up at the jetty once more. This time Nat did see Carrie on Randon's Riva. But he could hardly believe his eyes. He spat a mouthful of orange juice out over the white tablecloth.

'What is it?' Lizzy asked, putting on her glasses so that she could see what the fuss was about. As soon as Lizzy could focus on the person getting out of the Riva, she knew why Nat was unhappy.

'The slut!' Nat spluttered. 'I should have guessed! If bloody Randon's given her the consignment just because she slept with him! She's not that good.'

Lizzy gave Nat a curious look.

'At her job!' he clarified, understanding at once that Lizzy knew he was referring to Carrie's performance in bed. 'At her job. This is the bloody limit. There must be some kind of commission I can report this to.'

Nat was waiting at the top of the path when Carrie got there.

'Good night?' he asked.

'Great. Thank you.' Carrie tried to walk on by him but Nat blocked her way quite bodily.

'Hey,' Carrie protested. 'Get off me.'

Nat dropped back. 'So? Is there any point in Lizzy and I hanging around?'

'I don't know,' said Carrie irritably. 'Have you exhausted all the possibilities for that lovely suite you're in? Though I don't suppose it would take you all that long to run through your entire repertoire.'

'Don't play silly buggers with me,' said Nat. 'Just tell me straight. Has he given you the job?'

'I don't know,' said Carrie.

'But you spent the night on the boat.'

'Indeed I did,' Carrie confirmed. 'And nothing happened. Please, would you excuse me? I have work to do.'

*　　*　　*

In fact Randon announced his decision later that morning, before Carrie, Nat and Lizzy had time to check out of the hotel. Both teams received the exact same letter. When a bellboy delivered the envelope with the familiar crest, Carrie was barely polite, so eager was she to get rid of him so that she could read Randon's note.

Nat sent Lizzy to the door, wrapped in his bathrobe and with her hair all over the place. She was looking as though she had been 'ridden hard and put away wet', as Nat liked to tell her. She handed him the envelope and got back into bed.

'What? The daft old fucker!' Nat exclaimed.

'What did he say? Did we get it?' asked Lizzy.

'Yes,' said Nat. 'And no. The stupid old fool has decided that he wants Ludbrook's to sell half his collection and Ehrenpreis to do the rest. The house that nets the most from its sale will have the opportunity to sell the artwork from his other homes. For fuck's sake. Who does he think he's dealing with? Thinking he can put us in direct competition with another house like that? As if it weren't bad enough that he brought us out here to pitch at the same time! I have never heard anything so ridiculous in my entire life.'

Nat threw the letter to the floor. Lizzy picked it up and read it for herself.

'Oh,' she said. 'That is strange.'

'Idiot man,' said Nat. 'He must realise that the true value in a collection like this lies in the fact that it is a *collection*! Halving it merely dilutes the impact. Get him on the phone.'

Lizzy tried, but Randon was not accepting phone calls that morning. Instead she spoke to his assistant Bellette, who told Lizzy that she had her instructions, which were to tell Nat that there would be no more negotiation. Randon's decision was final. Nat could accept the challenge or leave it. In which case, Ehrenpreis would get to sell the lot.

'Damn,' said Nat. 'Tell her we'll take it. And we'll just have to hope that Carrie Klein doesn't.'

Carrie was equally disappointed when she read Randon's letter. As soon as it was a reasonable hour in New York, she called her boss, anxious to know how he would have handled the matter.

'What would you do?' she asked him. 'Should I tell him to stick it? I mean, this letter.' She read out the passage which said, 'Both presentations were equally competent.' 'Competent! I could spit. Talk about damning with faint praise. Oh, Frank,' Carrie sighed. 'I thought I had it. He invited me to join him for dinner on his boat.'

'Did you sleep with him?' Frank asked bluntly.

'I did not!' said Carrie.

'Then there you have it,' Frank laughed. 'I would take the consignment,' he said. 'Sure, you didn't get everything you went out there for, but Randon is a big fish. Half a collection is better than none. Just make sure you get the better half.'

Chapter Forty-Four

AFTER the late night visit, Serena had hoped that she had heard the last of Julian's dodgy Russian 'friend'. But it wasn't to be. First thing the next morning, Julian was back again, pleading with Serena to do as the man asked and fly out to Italy to take his commission.

'You must think I'm insane,' said Serena.

'I am begging you,' said Julian.

'What's he got on you?' Serena asked. She was surprised to hear Julian reply.

'Nothing but the paintings he got through Ludbrook's. But if he chooses to blow the whistle about the fakes I've sold him so far, I would imagine it's enough to be considered a violation of my parole.'

'Parole?' Serena echoed.

'He could send me back to prison.'

'Back to prison? *Back*? Since where were you in prison?'

'I meant to tell you,' said Julian. 'I swear I was going to. But it never seemed like the right time. I knew you would jump to all the wrong conclusions.'

'What am I supposed to do? Prison, Julian. There are no good conclusions as to what you were doing there.'

'It was an insurance fraud. That's all. No one was hurt. No one suffered.'

'Don't you dare say the words "victimless crime",' Serena warned him. 'I can't believe you didn't tell me. I've been sleeping with a bloody con.'

'Since when did you get to be the paragon of virtue?' Julian asked. 'You don't think what we've been doing for the past year is fraud? You don't think that what we've been doing is criminal? Serena, this isn't just about saving my neck. Yasha Suscenko knows enough to send us *both* to jail. Just one more picture, Serena, and then you need never pick up a paintbrush again.'

Julian looked so old right then and so tired that Serena almost felt sorry for him. She wanted to be able to reach out to him and give him a hug. She'd known before she even met him that he was unreliable and dishonest. His own mother had told Serena that. And yet she had come to love him. Despite his faults, she had been sure that deep down he was a kind man who was doing his best. What she wanted to tell him then was 'I'm scared.' But she just couldn't do it. She still blamed him absolutely for this mess that they found themselves in and her anger stood between them like a wall. Julian didn't have the energy to climb over it or push it down. But he had frightened Serena and while he knew that she wouldn't be doing it because she loved him, he knew that she would paint Suscenko's masterpiece.

'Tell him I'll do it,' she said. 'But when this is over, I never want to see you again.'

Serena called Tom later that day.

'I have to go away next week. For a fortnight or so. Can you take Katie?'

Tom sighed. 'You know we're going to Saint Tropez. You've known that for ages.'

'Yes. But a job has just come up.'

'A job? Since when did you have a job?'

'Since I realised that the amount of maintenance you're prepared to pay for your only daughter won't keep her in Petits Filous.'

'I'm sending as much as I can,' Tom growled.

'Why don't you ask your girlfriend to send me a cheque for the amount she's paying to take you to France?'

'It's all about money with you, isn't it?' Tom fired one below the belt.

'Fine. Forget it. I will take your daughter with me.'

'Where exactly are you going?'

'To Italy. Tuscany,' Serena added. It was sort of true, though she knew nothing of her travel plans once she had touched down in Pisa.

'To do what?'

'I'm painting some rich guy's family.'

'Who? Which rich guy? Are they the kind of people Katie should be around?'

'What does it matter to you? If I don't take her with me, what then? You don't want her to interrupt your romantic trip to France. Would you have me drop her off with social services for a couple of weeks instead?'

Serena slammed the phone down.

Conversations with her ex-husband were never an un-mitigated joy but his last question: are they the kind of people Katie should be around, had unnerved her. Of course they weren't the kind of people Katie should be around. They were the kind of people who turned up at your house in the middle of the night and offered you the choice of a life of crime or a bullet in the back of the head.

Yasha Suscenko was very pleased that Serena had seen sense. He was a great deal more professional than Julian had been when it came to ensuring that the link between Serena and his painting was invisible. She had to buy her own ticket to Pisa, from where she and Katie would take a train to Empoli. Then and only then would they meet one of Yasha's Italian associates who would drive them to the villa where the original painting awaited, alongside the reclaimed canvas that Serena would transform into its exact likeness.

As she watched the Italian countryside roll past and Katie slept on her knee, Serena considered that perhaps this was some kind of dream. It was unreal. Who travelled to Italy to paint a fake? She would get to Empoli and find no one waiting for her. But there was someone on the platform. Serena knew at once that this had to be Yasha's associate. The man held his cigarette pinched between thumb and forefinger in the manner of every small time crook in every gangster movie she'd ever seen. She caught his eye. He gave a flick of his head that she took to mean 'follow me'.

'Are we going in a car with that man, Mummy?' Katie asked.

'Yes. I think so.'

'Then why doesn't he help us with our bags?'

Serena forced herself to smile.

'Perhaps that's not what they do over here,' she said.

The car matched the gangster image. A sleek black Lexus that was distinctly out of place among the battered old Fiat Pandas that made up the rest of the car park.

'Is it far?' Serena asked. The driver didn't respond. She tried again, in Italian.

'*No*,' grunted the driver.

'Good,' said Katie. 'I'm hungry.'

But the driver was wrong. He was taking them a very long way from Empoli. Serena was working hard to keep the anxiety out of her voice now. They had been driving for half an hour. The last ten minutes of that half hour on a track that looked as though it hadn't been used in weeks. The further they went, the narrower it became, as the surrounding forest seemed determined to take back the land.

But finally there it was. The road widened up again and in front of them was the warm red and yellow brick of a traditional farmhouse.

From the outside it was picture postcard perfect. On the inside, where animals had once slept there was now a state-of-the-art kitchen, complete with the kind of oven that even Gordon Ramsay would be pleased with. The oven was one of the things that Serena had explained she would need – though not for cooking lasagne.

Katie immediately set about choosing her bedroom. There was a small room at the top of the house with bunk beds. Katie proclaimed it hers and installed her toy rabbit on the top bunk. Meanwhile, Serena couldn't help but give a little snort of delight and amusement when she was alone for a moment in what was to be her room – far bigger and grander than the room she and Tom had shared on their last trip to Tuscany, their honeymoon.

This was the strangest situation Serena had ever found herself in. She wasn't sure what she had expected when the Russian summoned her to Italy. A hotel room, bare and cheap. She'd expected to have to share the space with her daughter. But here they were in an enormous farmhouse with an infinity pool to themselves.

'It's brilliant,' Katie shouted as she stripped to her vest and pants and jumped in. 'Come on, Mummy.'

'All right,' Serena joined her daughter in the water.

To an observer, it looked idyllic. And on the surface it was. The house on the hill was the stuff of middle-class holiday dreams: a mother and daughter – grey from an English winter – splashing around in a pool under the Tuscan sun. But when she'd put her daughter to bed for the night, Serena's face reflected an altogether different reality. She sat on the step, smoking her first cigarette in years, and stared blindly into the trees that surrounded this gilded prison. The only sound was the curious bark of a deer. Miles away from anywhere with no lights in view to reassure her that help was within reach if she needed it, Serena felt a hot tear run down her cheek.

What would the morning bring?

Chapter Forty-Five

YASHA spent the night on the road with Leonid. Their brief time in Moscow had been far from pleasant. They were met at Domodedovo airport by more of Belanov's men, including one of his pet bankers, and driven straight to Vasilyev's veritable fortress on Rublevka Avenue. There were no niceties. No welcoming tea or vodka. Belanov's party were simply led down into the basement where the painting was kept pending sale.

The portrait, just fifteen inches high, was revealed to Yasha and his new colleagues without ceremony. It lay, unframed, on Vasilyev's desk, with a half-finished cup of coffee perilously close by. The only sign that the painting was valuable at all was the number of men who packed into the remarkably small office, with their guns on show.

'Mr Suscenko,' Vasilyev motioned for Yasha to step forward. 'Your opinion, please.'

Yasha's first instinct was that this was the real thing. He had explained to Belanov that it would take a barrage of scientific tests to be one hundred per cent sure of the painting's age and provenance but with a simple 'black light' that would highlight any recent touch-ups and a well-trained eye, Yasha felt he could give Belanov an assurance ninety-nine per cent accurate.

The room was silent as the main lights were extinguished and Yasha ran the black light over the canvas. You could have cut the tension in the air. After all, who wants to be in a dark room with fifteen armed gangsters? The whole party seemed to sigh in relief when Yasha requested that the main lights go back on again. Then he nodded towards Leonid and the nervous rat-faced banker who had joined them at the airport.

'It's what he said it was,' Yasha confirmed.

The banker stepped forward with a bag containing thirty million sterling. Vasilyev handed Yasha the painting.

'I can buy something nice and new now,' Vasilyev said.

Moron, thought Yasha as he nodded at the joke. Belanov had just got himself a bargain. Thirty million dollars for a painting that should have been priceless. Quickly, he fitted the painting into the special case he'd had especially made for the occasion. He offered Vasilyev his hand. The rich man merely looked at him.

Then it was time to get out of the house with Leonid and Basil, another of Belanov's favourite goons, close behind. The challenge ahead was to get the painting from Moscow to Portofino, where Yasha would deliver it to Belanov's yacht, without falling foul of border controls. The first leg of the journey would take them from Moscow to a private airport in Slovenia. Leonid, Basil and Yasha would be driving from there.

There was time for Yasha to visit just one of his old haunts before the private jet was due to fly: his brother's nightclub, Diamond Life. Leonid and Basil waited in the car with the painting while Yasha went up to the door. It was shut. A notice saying that the club would be closed until further notice fluttered from the door. There was little point leaving a message for his brother there. Yasha just wanted to know that Belanov hadn't been bluffing. Here was the proof. God only knew where Pavel was being kept this time.

When Yasha got back into the car, Leonid was going through the pockets of Basil, who was unconscious, soon to be dead, in the passenger seat.

'What happened?' Yasha asked.

'Heroin,' said Leonid matter-of-factly. 'Too pure for his black heart.' Leonid gazed forlornly at the syringe sticking out of his former colleague's forearm. The syringe that he had prepared himself.

'Thanks,' said Yasha.

'We'll leave him by the back of the club,' said Leonid, driving around so that he could simply roll the corpse out of the door. 'There are always druggies here. I'll tell Belanov he overdosed.'

Yasha nodded. He knew that even someone so vile as Basil had a mother to mourn him but he consoled himself with the thought that this guy had probably been part of the squad who got hold of his brother. He looked away as Leonid arranged Basil's lifeless limbs in the gutter.

'So the mission is going ahead as planned,' said Leonid, as he got back into the car.

'Yes. Yes it is.'

'Good,' Leonid nodded, then he turned to Yasha with a wicked smile that Yasha found oddly comforting.

Chapter Forty-Six

*Y*ASHA and Leonid's car – an SUV with blacked out windows – pulled into the driveway as Serena and Katie were having breakfast on the terrace. Serena, who had been awaiting this moment with dread, immediately began clearing the plates and sent Katie inside.

'What for?' Katie asked.

'Because I want you to.'

'Why?'

'You left Bunny upstairs,' said Serena, grasping for an excuse. 'I'm sure he must be lonely.'

'I'll bring him down,' said Katie, nodding.

Katie wouldn't be long but her searching for the fluffy rabbit would give Serena just enough time to have a moment alone with their visitor. Or visitors. The sight of the enormous, anonymous car was worrying and, sure enough, Yasha wasn't alone. Serena felt panic surge through her body, followed by a fresh wave of fear when Yasha reached into the passenger seat of the car and pulled out a big black case. What did that hold? A shotgun?

'Hey!' he waved to Serena and smiled cheerily, as though they were old friends. She gave an unenthusiastic wave back to let him know from the start that she was there because she had to be. She wasn't doing him any favours. Leonid waved too, before he settled himself on the bonnet of the car and rolled a cigarette.

'What do you think?' Yasha asked her. 'How are the working conditions? Will you be able to paint here? Is the oven good enough? Is it big enough?'

'The whole place is incredible,' Serena said honestly.

'I like the swimming pool,' said Katie. She was back downstairs already, having dressed Bunny in a pair of her own underpants.

'He doesn't have a pair of swimming trunks,' she explained.

Yasha beamed at her and ruffled her hair. Then he withdrew his hand quickly however when Serena glared at him. They weren't a happy family on holiday.

'Katie,' said Serena. 'Why don't you give Bunny a tour of the garden? But no swimming until I'm there to watch you.'

Katie pulled a face. 'No swimming? In that case,' she said, 'we're going to watch *High School Musical*.'

For once Serena didn't argue. Whatever it took to get Katie out of the way.

'Well,' said Yasha, suddenly businesslike. 'I suppose we should get started right away. You'll need what's in here.'

He tapped the case and they went inside, upstairs to the room that would be Serena's studio. Once the door was safely closed (and locked) behind them, Yasha clicked the case open. It contained an accordion. Yasha lifted the accordion out and played a few melancholy bars.

'Russian folk tune,' he said. 'It's the only thing I can play. I learned especially for this trip.'

'Why?'

'So that when a custom officer wants to know why I'm carrying an accordion to Italy, I can explain to him that it's because I love to play.'

Next Yasha reached into his jacket pocket and brought out a knife. 'But, of course, I don't love my accordion anywhere near as much as I love my art.' He began to slit open the velvet lining of the music case. Serena held her breath for what seemed like an age as Yasha made a neat incision all the way round. She had guessed what was beneath it and the idea of a knife in such close proximity to a priceless work of art made her feel quite queasy. At last he finished. Almost gingerly he picked up the edges of the velvet and peeled it back. And there was the pearl in the oyster.

'Oh my God,' said Serena as she finally laid eyes on the painting he expected her to copy. It was Ricasoli's painting of the Virgin Mary in a moment of contemplation before the annunciation. Property of the Wasowski family of Warsaw. Looted by the Nazis in 1944 and hidden away, until now.

Carefully, reverently, Yasha laid the painting out on the table. Serena, with her hand at her throat as though to stifle a gasp, kept her distance from it as she took her first look.

'It can't be real.'

'Of course it's real,' said Yasha.

Serena made a silent inventory of the details. The picture was so familiar. She had first set eyes on the composition as a child, seeing it in the pages of an encyclopaedia. She had fallen in love with this depiction of the Virgin Mary that brought her to life in a way that only a young girl could really appreciate. She looked so carefree, sitting by an open window with a ripe black fig in her hand. And so beautiful. Her golden hair swept back from a high forehead. Her nose, straight and elegant. Her lips were full and seemed always to be on the verge of a smile.

Never had she expected to see the original. Her father had broken the news to her that its whereabouts were unknown when once she expressed a desire to see it. The encyclopaedia that attributed the painting to the Wasowski family collection was woefully out of date. *The Virgin* had been stolen before Serena was even born.

'It has a little swastika on the back,' Yasha confirmed.

'I can't believe it,' Serena murmured.

'It's OK,' said Yasha. 'It won't disintegrate if you breathe on it! Step forward. Have a proper look. You're going to need to know it inside out.'

'It's . . .' Serena struggled to find the words. 'It's just so beautiful!'

'It is,' said Yasha.

Serena took a tentative step forward and gazed at the picture.

'I'm going to ask the obvious question.'

'And I can't tell you the answer,' said Yasha. 'So please don't ask.'

'I understand.' For the moment, Serena was content just to look at this painting, which had been lost for more than half a century. She would ask how Yasha came upon it later.

'You look a little worried.'

'I'm just wondering whether I can possibly do it justice!' she said. 'Really, Yasha. This isn't just any Old Master. It's a masterpiece. It's impossible to recreate. Impossible.'

'I don't like that word, impossible.'

'I'm afraid I would be wasting your time,' said Serena. 'I'm sorry. You need someone much better than me.'

'I can't think of any one better than you. If there were someone better than you, he or she would be here instead. I know you can do it and I didn't have you down as someone so defeatist,' said Yasha. 'You haven't even picked up your paintbrush.'

'I don't think I should. I don't think I can.'

'I need you to try,' Yasha insisted. 'You have to.'

Yasha's soft tone made Serena think that perhaps it was possible. Perhaps she could recreate the painting to such a standard that an expert might be fooled. But beneath the softness there was a determination that she would do what he required of her. And she was reminded when he said, 'I didn't bring you out here to have you make excuses,' that she had taken the commission not for the challenge of it or the incredible fifty thousand-pound fee they had negotiated but because he had made it clear to her that the alternative was far less appealing.

As she stood over the painting, studying its beauty and nibbling at one of her cuticles, the sound of Katie's singing drifted up to the open window. Serena glanced out to see her daughter serenading Bunny, who was propped up on one of the garden chairs. Leonid watched too from his seat on the bonnet of the car.

'I'll do my best,' she said.

'I know you will.'

After Yasha went back downstairs, Serena remained alone in the attic with the painting. This was by far the strangest moment of her life. She was reminded of the story of the farmer's daughter whose father told the king that she was able to spin straw into gold. She remembered a drawing in the book of fairy tales that now had a place on the shelf in Katie's bedroom. The girl all alone. The dust motes dancing in the shaft of sunlight from the single high window. The enormous pile of straw. Well, here was her enormous pile of straw: one Renaissance masterpiece and a worthless old canvas upon which to recreate it. But where was her Rumpelstiltskin?

Serena ran her fingers over the young girl's face, trying to imagine the moment when the paint was still wet and the girl sat living and breathing in front of the artist. It was as though she hoped that by touching the painting some magic might happen. Sensing a woman in distress, perhaps the artist himself might slip in spirit from the painting into the ends of her fingers. Nothing happened. And when she tried to conjure her spirit artist to her she could only see Colin Firth in that movie about Vermeer. Perhaps not even in the right movie. Was Vermeer ever wet-shirted?

She could just steal the painting. It was almost certainly in the wrong hands. There would be some kind of reward, surely, for returning it to its rightful owner? It would be enough to keep her and Katie going for a while. But glancing out of the window again, she saw Leonid, smoking in his studied casual way. She had no doubt that he did more for Yasha than park the cars and that he would be very happy to get his hands dirty. And if she did manage to get away from the farmhouse with her daughter and the picture, if she managed to get the picture to Interpol, she would have to spend her whole life on the run.

There was no way out. Only through.

So Serena decided she would give this craziest of commissions a shot. She could only hope that when Yasha saw how foolish it was to think that he could ever pass off her work as that of Ricasoli, he would not be too angry and let her and Katie go back to London without a fuss. To that end, she set up her working materials at once, so that Yasha would believe she was in earnest.

'Leonid and I are going to stay here until you're finished,' Yasha announced over lunch. 'I'm sure you understand that I don't want to leave you alone in the house with a priceless Renaissance masterpiece and it's hard to get the security staff you can trust. I mean, I don't think Luca, the guy who brought you here, knows an Old Master from his arsehole, but there have been a lot of burglaries around here lately and I don't want my painting to end up in some Sienese flea market.'

Serena nodded. Katie was less upset at the thought that they would not be alone in the house.

'Good,' she said. 'Leonid can be the lifeguard so I can go swimming.'

Chapter Forty-Seven

Just before coming to Italy, Serena had sent Yasha a shopping list. It contained not only the food she would need to keep Katie happy, but also a variety of far more rare items. Since painting the Renaissance Madonna for Julian, Serena had become quite the expert on the tools of the Renaissance artists. Yasha had sourced every one. He had understood that Serena was not going to be able to pull off this piece of alchemy with a few tubes of paint from Winsor and Newton. He'd found the raw ingredients. Here were mercury and lead oxide, resin from the Garcinia tree for gamboges, yellow ochre and lead tin. A piece of old ivory to burn for bone black. A jar of cochineal beetles to make carmine. And for the ultramarine she would need for the Virgin's robe, a piece of lapis lazuli worth thousands of pounds. From Afghanistan, Yasha promised. That was important, as at the time Ricasoli was painting, it would have been his only source. Lapis from anywhere else would give the painting away in a second when someone to sample a sliver of paint, as they inevitably would at some point. To that effect, the lead oxide to make white also gave Serena pause. 'It could give us away,' she warned Yasha over dinner.

'Ah,' said Yasha. 'I have good news. The painting was restored in the nineteenth century. That's well documented. They'll be expecting slightly later whites.'

Serena shrugged. She hoped it wouldn't be her problem by then. But her attention to detail extended even to the brushes she used. The Renaissance masters had used badger hair and thus among the haul of goodies Yasha had acquired for her were several old-fashioned gentleman's shaving brushes, which she would chop into smaller bunches of bristles.

Yasha listened in awe as she explained her methods over dinner on their first night together in the house. She told him why she wanted noxious-smelling formaldehyde. 'Traditional oil paints take half a century to dry out. Anyone could find out how recently a canvas had been painted by holding a rag dipped in alcohol over the paint and watching for a reaction.'

'I know,' said Yasha, recalling Serena's earlier attempt at faking a Renaissance painting.

'The formaldehyde will solve that problem by speeding the process up,' she promised. It would have the added advantage, Serena hoped, of discouraging Yasha from visiting her studio too often.

'Will you join me in an after-dinner drink?' he asked. 'It would be nice to get to know each other better, don't you think? Since we're going to be together for the next three weeks.'

Serena shook her head. 'I've got work to do.'

She intended to paint around the clock to ensure that she

and Katie were out of this situation as quickly as humanly possible.

So while Yasha sipped a contemplative brandy and watched the stars with Leonid, Serena set to work cleaning the worthless canvas she was hoping to transform into a priceless Old Master. Yasha had provided a rather ugly daub of a man counting money. He'd bought it in a junk shop two years before, thinking it might have potential, but never found it another home. It was the exact right period, of course, but it had another advantage. In a funny way, the pose of the man echoed the pose of the Madonna, meaning that should Serena be unable to remove the original painting absolutely, she should be able to incorporate what remained.

To remove the paint was a painstaking process. Serena was grateful for the efforts of so many forgers before her who had refined the methods she was using. Many had tried to remove old paint quickly using harsh solvents, with disastrous results. There was no substitute for plain old elbow grease. With a pumice stone and a bowl of soapy water, Serena lifted the old man from the canvas a micrometre at a time.

It took her the best part of two days just to remove the old painting and the artist's sketch beneath. She was left with the original primer layer. That layer she needed to leave intact, as a vitally important part of the process ahead.

Yasha looked in from time to time. 'Just checking you haven't climbed out of the window.'

'You think I'd leave my daughter?'

Yasha nodded at the canvas, which was now blank and rather shabby-looking.

'It's coming on,' he said.

*   *   *

Alone again in the attic, Serena put her hands on her hips and surveyed her work so far. This was a daunting moment. She had her blank canvas. Now she must find the magic. She picked up a red crayon to begin her own underdrawing. But before she started, she decided it might be a good idea to make a little record of this most important commission.

Though he seemed to have thought of everything else, Yasha had not thought to take Serena's mobile phone away. The house was extremely remote. To get a signal required an hour-long hike to the nearest high point and so he had determined that Serena would not be calling for back up. What he had failed to consider was that the camera function on her phone still worked.

'Click.'

In a second, Serena captured the Ricasoli and the blank canvas that would become its twin. Here was her insurance. Proof that a copy had been made. She would take several more pictures in the days ahead as she completed her underdrawing and at last began work on the painting.

Chapter Forty-Eight

JUST as the old portrait of the money-lender had been removed layer by layer, the new Ricasoli was built up in the same way. After each layer, the painting was put into the oven and Serena spent an anxious few hours waiting for the process to complete. A moment too long and her work could come out discoloured, over-cooked. But the ruse worked perfectly, both as a way of drying the paint and of ageing it. After each firing, the craquelure, the fine network of cracks that appear in a painting over time, would reappear exactly as they appeared in the primer layer, like a memory. A wash of Indian ink filled the new cracks to give the impression of centuries of dust. Over the course of three weeks, Serena would age her painting by almost four hundred years.

It wasn't all work. Due to the nature of the process, there were moments when Serena had nothing to do but sit on the Tuscan terrace and watch Katie playing in the sun. Katie seemed to be having a wonderful time. She had made quite a friend of Leonid, whose size and frighteningly scarred face belied a gentle nature.

'It's funny,' said Yasha, as he joined Serena on the terrace with two glasses of wine. 'How children see straight through to the essence of people. They can easily tell good from bad.'

Serena knew at once that he was talking about Leonid, who, to fulfil a role in one of Katie's complicated games, was submitting to wear a straw hat that was far too small for his enormous square head.

'He misses his children,' Yasha continued. 'He has two. A girl your daughter's age and a son, who just turned nine. His ex-wife won't let him see them.'

'That's sad. Well, he's been great at keeping Katie amused,' Serena admitted. 'As have you,' she added grudgingly. 'What was that story you told her yesterday? The one about the witch in the pestle and mortar?'

'Baba Yaga,' said Yasha. 'She lived in a house that moved around on chicken's legs and ate small children for breakfast. It was my favourite story as a child. I hope I didn't frighten Katie.'

'No,' said Serena. 'Not at all. She said it was much better than boring old Charlie and Lola.'

'A drink?' Yasha offered her the glass of wine. Serena took it cautiously. She had been careful not to drink too much, mindful that she might need to scoop up her daughter and get out of there at any moment.

'I've got much more to do tonight,' she said. 'So you can have your painting ready on time.'

There was just a week left to go before *The Virgin* had to join its new owner on a yacht in Portofino.

'I'm very grateful for your hard work,' said Yasha. 'I know you feel you didn't have a choice.'

'Did I *have* a choice? You didn't make it seem that way.'

Yasha shrugged.

'I understand why you must hate me,' he said then. 'Trust me, I hate myself for bringing you out here against your will. I wish I could have left you in peace down there in Cornwall. I'm sorry. But when I found out about your talent for imitation, it provided a solution to a very sticky problem in my life.'

Serena decided to let him talk.

'You see, *The Virgin* is about to be "found" in the attic of an old manor house in the Ukraine, stashed there by a Russian soldier who picked the painting up in Berlin and didn't have a clue what he'd got. Of course, as property looted by the Nazis, it should be returned to its original owners. But the Polish family who were the last legitimate owners of the painting are all dead. Most of them went to Auschwitz.'

Serena shivered.

'And there really are no descendants? Some of them must have survived.'

'Trust me,' said Yasha. 'There is no one left now. And so, the painting will in all probability be allowed to remain in the hands of the person on whose property it was found. My client. And he will be able to show off his new acquisition to his friends. However, should that not be the case, he doesn't want to lose it to some museum, and so, if that looks likely, your painting will be the one that is given away. It's an insurance policy.'

'That's disgusting,' Serena said.

'I don't expect you to agree with it. I don't agree with it myself, but my client is a very persuasive man. And unfortunately I owed him a favour . . .'

Yasha looked into his glass contemplatively. He thought about his brother Pavel and the mess that had been made of his face. Belanov had helpfully provided a Polaroid photograph of Pavel's injuries to help focus Yasha on his mission. If he told Serena about that, Yasha knew he would seem like less of an arsehole, but it was unlikely to make her feel any more comfortable about being there in Italy with him and Leonid, knowing the kind of people they were dealing with. He decided not to elaborate.

'So, tell me more about yourself,' he said instead, all jollity. 'What are you doing? Living down there in the middle of nowhere with no one to keep you company but an idiot like Julian Trebarwen.'

Serena gave a strained smile. 'I'm getting a divorce,' she explained. 'My husband lost his job because the woman he ran off with was his boss's wife. As he couldn't afford to keep the house in Fulham, we had to sell it and I couldn't find anything else where I wouldn't get mugged on the way to the Tube and that is how I ended up in Cornwall. It's my brother's house,' she added. 'In case you were planning to torch it when the painting's finished.'

'You're very funny.' Yasha delivered that line in such a deadpan way that Serena shuddered before she realised that he was teasing.

'Well, either your husband's mistress is an incredible woman, or, much more likely, he is a stupid man who didn't know what he had. I am sure that he will regret having walked away from you. And from your daughter.'

'Oh, I don't know about that,' said Serena.

'Well, he should regret it,' said Yasha. 'Only an idiot allows his child to be raised by another man.'

'Julian and I . . . we're not . . . he's not . . .'

'Good,' said Yasha. 'He's an idiot too.'

'I wish I could disagree.'

'Now tell me how you came to be such a great painter.'

'A great painter?' Serena shook her head.

'You are a great painter,' Yasha reiterated. 'And I want to know all about you. Where did you study? Who were your influences? What is your favourite painting in the world?'

'That's easy. Vermeer. *Girl With a Pearl Earring*,' Serena told him.

'Sentimental,' said Yasha.

'Sentimental? It's exquisite,' Serena bristled. 'Tell me yours.'

'Nicolas de Staël. *Piano Rouge*.'

'You surprise me. That's very abstract. I thought you had a thing for pretty portraits.'

'I have a thing for whatever I can sell to my clients. But I love de Staël.'

'He had an unhappy life,' Serena observed.

'Perhaps I can relate to the melancholy. It's a Russian thing,' Yasha grinned. 'All that biting wind across the steppes. The constant snow around the Kremlin. The howling wolves. The vodka.'

'It all sounds rather romantic.'

'Nothing romantic about where I grew up.'

'Where did you grow up?' Serena asked but before Yasha could begin to answer, Leonid, coming to tell them that the timer had sounded on the oven, interrupted them.

'I turned it off,' he said.

'Thanks.'

Almost missing the table as she put her glass down, Serena raced into the house like a cook worrying about a soufflé. Using oven gloves she carefully lifted her Virgin from the top shelf and placed it on a wire mesh tray. She examined the surface minutely. Yasha watched from the kitchen door.

'Everything OK?' he asked.

'I think so,' said Serena. 'Good job Leonid was in here. Would be too much to lose her at this stage.'

Yasha nodded.

'I got distracted. I'll get back to work,' Serena told him. 'Thanks for the wine.'

'My pleasure,' said Yasha.

Chapter Forty-Nine

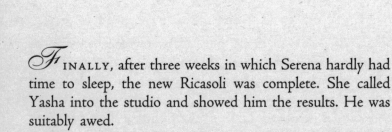

FINALLY, after three weeks in which Serena hardly had time to sleep, the new Ricasoli was complete. She called Yasha into the studio and showed him the results. He was suitably awed.

The original Ricasoli and Serena's copy stood side-by-side on their easels. To the untrained eye, there was no difference.

'The painting is perfect. My client will be delighted. Are you pleased with it?'

'I did my best,' said Serena. 'But I very much doubt you could get it past a real expert.'

Like the mother of identical twins, Serena could only see the differences.

'I sometimes think the great Renaissance painters must have been working with an angel on their shoulder . . .' she said.

There was just one more thing to add. The mark of the devil.

Yasha handed Serena a stamp.

'The real thing,' he admitted. 'Don't ask me where I got it.'

Serena held the little swastika gingerly.

'The position of the stamp on the original hasn't been recorded,' said Yasha. 'Change it slightly. It'll help us tell the paintings apart. You and I.'

The original bore its mark on the top-right corner. Serena took a deep breath and stamped her painting in the exact same place but turned the swastika very slightly anti-clockwise. It felt like putting a scar on someone she cared for.

Yasha squeezed her shoulder.

'I've got quite attached to them both,' Serena told him,

That night, for the first time since their arrival in Italy, Serena allowed herself more than a single glass of wine in celebration. Changing out of her overalls for dinner – Yasha insisted he would cook – she regarded herself in the mirror. She looked thin and tired, the very opposite of how a woman who had spent three weeks in a beautiful Tuscan farmhouse should look.

Katie, thank goodness, had thrived. Her bright blonde hair was almost white from the sun. Her chunky little legs – she had Tom's legs, poor girl – were brown despite the slathering of sun-block Serena forced on her throughout the day. It wasn't just that she looked healthy, she seemed very happy. While her mother had viewed Yasha and Leonid as their jailors, Katie had come to see them as friends.

As she walked downstairs on the evening that she finished the painting, Serena could hear her daughter chatting away as happily as she had once chatted to Julian. Katie and the Russians had forged quite a bond during their days by the pool. Yasha had even taught Katie to play that snatch of folk tune he'd learned to fool the border guards.

'Mummy!' Katie jumped up excitedly when Serena came into the kitchen. 'Leonid has taught me Russian dancing. Watch this!' She managed a brief parody of a Cossack before landing on her bottom in a fit of giggles.

'Very good,' said Serena.

'Dinner is served,' said Yasha, bringing a pot to the table. 'Leonid,' he complained to his colleague. 'Did no one ever teach you to lay a table?'

The knives and forks were the wrong way round.

Leonid shrugged like an overgrown boy.

'I'll teach you,' said Katie.

This would be the first time they had all sat together at a table since that first day. While Katie was with them the conversation jumped effortlessly from one lot of nonsense to the next but soon it was time for her to go to bed. Leonid went upstairs shortly afterwards, leaving Yasha and Serena alone.

'I need you to arrange for us to go home as soon as possible,' said Serena, as she helped him carry plates to the dishwasher.

'Of course,' Yasha replied. 'As quickly as I can. That was my promise to you.'

'And the money?'

'Already in place.'

Serena nodded. 'Good.'

The table was all but cleared.

'Thank you for sorting the cash out. I'm pretty tired now so I'll see you in the morning.'

'Won't you stay and finish this bottle of wine?' Yasha asked. 'To celebrate a job well done?'

'OK.'

They sat back down at the table. Yasha poured them both a glass. 'I'd like to raise a toast,' he said. 'To your talent.'

'I'm just a copyist.'

'You're a genius. And I'd like to thank you. Thank you for working so hard but also thank you for these past few evenings. The conversations we've had. Even the arguments,' he added with a smile at the thought of Serena's vociferous defence of Tracey Emin. 'I've enjoyed having such an interesting companion with whom to share my thoughts.'

Serena nodded in agreement. 'Me too,' she said. 'Me too.'

It was true. Once the ice between them was broken, Serena had looked forward to those moments when the painting was being fired and she had time for conversation. Talking to Yasha had made Serena aware of another part of her life that had been sadly lacking of late. She had missed having someone to talk to about art. Not that Tom had ever fulfilled that need. Serena had realised, as she grieved for her marriage, that there were some areas in which she and Tom had never had much in common. Sure, when they were first going out he was only too happy to trail around galleries on a Sunday afternoon, but only because there was a chance that she might let him cop a quick feel while they were studying a Canaletto or a Rubens. To Tom, galleries were just foreplay. And pretty soon after they got engaged, he made it clear that he just wasn't that interested. Likewise, Julian Trebarwen's interest in art was far from sincere.

Yasha was different. Serena hadn't met someone with such an encyclopaedic knowledge of painting since she left art school. Yasha had something interesting to say about everything. Had they met in different circumstances, perhaps they would have been friends.

'You're a very special woman,' said Yasha.

For a moment after he said that, they just looked into each other's eyes. It was Yasha who looked away first, leaving Serena looking at the thick dark hair that she suddenly felt a very strong urge to touch. She looked down at Yasha's hands, which rested on the table. The table was bare but for their wine glasses and a bottle of Chianti with just half an inch of wine left in the bottom. Serena put her own hands on the table, her long fingers still dotted with paint that wouldn't come off with soap and water no matter how hard she scrubbed. Her pose echoed Yasha's exactly. Her fingertips pointed towards his square fingers with their neat pink nails. She gazed at the veins on the back of his hands, which looked so masculine compared to her own. As though they were engaged in some childen's game, Serena and Yasha regarded each other and the small space that remained between them. Would either one reach out?

Serena's heart leapt as Yasha moved. But it wasn't to touch her. Instead he picked up the wine bottle and divided the very last of the Chianti between them. It was gone in two mouthfuls and then there was no reason to stay up any longer.

'I should go,' said Serena, finding as she said it that she wanted to be challenged.

But Yasha didn't challenge her this time.

'I'll tidy up,' he said, getting up from the table and taking the empty bottle with him.

'OK,' said Serena. She stood too and there was just a second or so more of potential between them before she bid Yasha goodnight. He set straight to work, carrying the glasses to the sink. Serena paused at the top of the stairs and looked down on him, missing the kiss that hadn't happened.

The following afternoon Yasha put the original Ricasoli and Serena's copy into the accordion case. Serena felt something akin to a visceral pain as she watched him close the matching Virgins away.

'Well,' said Yasha. 'I have no reason to detain you here a moment longer. I'm sure you are anxious to get back to your life in Cornwall.'

Serena nodded.

Luca arrived within the hour to drive her and Katie back to the station.

Yasha saw them off.

'I'm sure you won't ever want to see me again but rest assured I will be there if you ever need me.'

Serena shook his hand.

'Goodbye.'

As they crested the hill, Serena's mobile phone buzzed into life with the text and voicemail messages she had been unable to receive at the house. It reminded her of the one thing she had to do. She sent a very important picture message to Julian. Her insurance policy. Because as strangely fulfilling as the experience had turned out to be, she should not forget that Yasha had blackmailed her into forging a painting for him. She had to remember that she had come to Italy because she felt that she and her daughter would be in danger if she didn't. A cloud passed over her face as she thought back to that night in her kitchen back in Cornwall.

But back in the UK the following evening, she couldn't help but feel a little nostalgic as she lay in bed and listened to the night sounds outside. She imagined the house in Tuscany. Was Yasha still there or was it dark and silent again, with nobody but the deer to appreciate its tranquillity and beauty? She missed the work. She missed the house. She thought perhaps she missed Yasha.

Chapter Fifty

$\mathcal{B}$ ACK in London, Lizzy Duffy was hard at work on the Randon sale. Once he got over the indignity of it, Nat had decided he was excited by the element of direct competition with Ehrenpreis and he had transferred his enthusiasm to his staff. Lizzy was nervous. She had to come up with something very special to ensure that Ludbrook's romped home with the best results.

Her concentration on the Randon sale was interrupted about two weeks after she got back from the Côte d'Azur. It was to be an embarrassing morning. Moments after she arrived at the office she had a call from the reception desk, telling her that someone who had bought a painting at the most recent nineteenth sale was very anxious to see her.

'Very anxious,' said the receptionist, in a way that implied a 'scene' would occur if Lizzy didn't come downstairs pronto.

So, Lizzy knew even before she walked into the reception, with her best client-greeting smile on, that this was going to be a difficult encounter. Sure enough it was.

The middle-aged woman at the desk looked as though she didn't smile very often anyway, but right then she was frowning so hard, she could have easily held a two-pence piece in the crevice between her eyebrows.

'You have sold me a fake,' said the woman without preamble.

'That's quite an accusation, Mrs . . .'

'Whittaker. Denise Whittaker. You have sold me a forged painting and I want to know what you're going to do about it.'

There were a few members of the public milling about in the lobby that morning and it was obvious that they were all tuning in to what was going on. Lizzy knew that her first action should be to contain Mrs Whittaker before any more accusations were voiced out loud.

'Mrs Whittaker,' she said, steering the middle aged woman by the elbow. 'I wonder if you might come into this meeting room and explain to me why you think this misunderstanding might have occurred.'

Unfortunately, it was no misunderstanding.

Lizzy had one of the porters relieve Mrs Whittaker of the painting in question and bring it through into the private room. With the door shut so that no passers-by could hear Mrs Whittaker's rantings, Lizzy had the porter unwrap the piece and set it on an easel. She took a deep breath. It was important to remain in control of the situation no matter how nervous she felt. She remembered Nat's teaching. You must never, ever seem apologetic. Concerned. Yes. Serious. Of course. But never apologetic. It gives them reason to think you have something to apologise for.

Once the painting was uncovered, Lizzy dismissed the porter. She peered closely at the picture, which she remembered only vaguely. She brought out the eyeglass that hung around her neck at all times.

'There's no point doing that,' said Mrs Whittaker. 'You're not going to convince me I'm wrong.'

'If you'll just give me a moment,' said Lizzy, as she ran the loupe over every inch of the painting, as much to buy her time to think as to investigate its authenticity.

'I bought this painting believing it to be a genuine watercolour of the Clifton Suspension Bridge by Richard Delapole,' said Mrs Whittaker.

'Well,' said Lizzy patiently. 'It has all the hallmarks of that painter. The signature, here, is just like every example of his signature I've ever seen. And the brushstrokes representing the leaves of the trees. You see? Right there. That looseness of form is typical of Delapole's later work and . . .'

'I know,' said Mrs Whittaker. 'That's exactly what I thought. But here's the thing. My son pointed it out to me as soon as he saw the painting when he came home from school on exeat. This artist died in 1832 and the suspension bridge wasn't completed until 1864.'

There was no point arguing with Mrs Whittaker; she was absolutely right. The suspension bridge was not completed until thirty-two years after the painter's death. It took two minutes on Wikipedia to find that much out. Lizzy was mortified. It was such an easy thing to have checked up on. She immediately took the blame upon herself. She called Nat down from his office to explain the nature and extent of the debacle.

'It's a complete cock-up,' said Nat. 'Who took this picture in?'

Lizzy wasn't sure. It wasn't until much later, when Mrs Whittaker had been sent away with a full refund and firm assurances that such a matter would be properly investigated at the very highest level, that Lizzy became certain that she hadn't taken the picture in herself. It was a big ticket item. It had been sold for forty grand. She wouldn't have dared take on such an important consignment without consulting Nat first. Never. That knowledge helped her feel a little better as she went over and over her confrontation with Mrs Whittaker that afternoon. But there were other things on her mind now. Things that didn't quite seem to add up. She waited until the end of the working day to talk to Nat about the matter in private.

'Nat,' she said. 'I need to talk to you about that painting.'

'It's OK, darling. It happens to the best of us. I must have fallen for thousands of fakes during the early years of my career. You will get better at spotting them.'

'Actually,' said Lizzy. 'I didn't have the chance to spot that one. I didn't even see it until the day of the auction. You put it up for sale.'

'Did I?' Nat looked surprised. 'Gosh. Wow. I must have been having an off-day.' He shrugged. 'Still, can't be expected to know the dates of all these bloody painters, can I? I'm not a walking encyclopaedia.'

'Nat,' Lizzy ventured. 'The thing is, I don't think this is the only fake we've had in lately. I went out for dinner with Yasha Suscenko a few months ago and he was asking some very strange questions.'

'Why on earth were you having dinner with Yasha Suscenko? More to the point, why didn't you tell me?'

Lizzy shrugged. Any other time she would have been

gratified that Nat showed a little healthy jealousy but there were more important matters to discuss.

'I think he was suspicious about one of the works he bought. The milkmaid portrait. He asked a lot of questions,' she reiterated.

'Such as?'

Lizzy relayed the conversation.

'You're reading too much into that. If Yasha Suscenko thought we had sold him a moody painting, he would have come straight to me.'

'But he *did* come to you. Don't you remember? And he asked for the name of the painting's owner.'

'That wasn't about faking. He was just trying to cut out the middleman. He wanted to be able to go straight to Trebarwen and offer the brothers a deal for whatever was left in the house. That's what that was about.'

'But there was nothing left in the house. Everything of any value went into the sale. You know that. I still find it hard to believe that I would have missed that painting of the suspension bridge when I was down there organising the house for the big sale. It strikes me that one possible reason why I didn't find the painting was because when I went to the house last April, the painting *really wasn't there*. Because it didn't exist. I think it's possible that Julian Trebarwen commissioned that painting, Nat.'

'That's a crazy accusation.'

'At the very least, I think we should consider the possibility that he found it in a junk shop and thought he could get a better value for it if he said it came from his mother's estate. The idea that it came from Trebarwen certainly would have made me more likely to consider it was the real thing. I can understand what you might have thought . . .'

'Are you implying that I would have taken that painting on just because Julian Trebarwen brought it in?'

'I understand how it is. We get busy. We have our trusted sources . . .'

'Now, Lizzy,' said Nat, suddenly coming over like the boss he really was. 'As far as I am concerned the matter has been settled. Mrs Whittaker is happy with her refund and our assurances. I don't see any benefit to delving any deeper. We have received no other official complaints.'

'But don't you think it would be a good idea to pre-empt them by taking a closer look at the consignments we've had from Julian Trebarwen since the house sale?'

'No,' said Nat. 'I don't. Read the small print in the back of any one of our catalogues. We are absolutely indemnified.'

'All the same, Nat, Ludbrook's reputation is at stake. And your personal reputation too,' she added, thinking that might swing it. He would know, she was sure, that she was serious about this because she cared about him. Loved him.

'You know what, I don't think it would be a good idea to start investigating Trebarwen but I do think it would be a good idea to go out to dinner. You are free this evening, I hope? I have a table at Scott's.'

Scott's. Lizzy knew he thought it would impress her.

'I know you've always wanted to go there,' he said.

She didn't tell him that Yasha had already taken her there.

'That'd be great,' she said.

'Eight o'clock. Dress up.' Nat patted her bottom to dismiss her.

Back at her desk, Lizzy tried hard not to worry about the conversation she'd just had. She had expected Nat to take her more seriously when she raised her concerns. It was what she was supposed to do, wasn't it, as his second in command? And yet he had been dismissive. She decided she would talk to him about it later that night. When he'd had a few glasses of wine, he might be more amenable to listening to her worries. It was appropriate that they take some more time to discuss the issues between themselves, because Lizzy was going to raise them at the big interdepartmental quarterly meeting that would take place the next day and she didn't want Nat to be blindsided. She told him that much while they were drinking an aperitif.

'Let's not let work interfere with a damn good dinner,' he said. 'Come on, Lizzy. I just want to have a bit of fun this evening. I want to relax and enjoy your company.'

And how could she disagree? She still wanted him so badly. She was every bit in love with him as ever and still he showed no sign of moving her properly into his life. But perhaps the best way to have him fully for herself was to separate the two Lizzys – work Lizzy and love Lizzy – more thoroughly. Perhaps he was right. If Yasha Suscenko had made a formal complaint they would have investigated Julian Trebarwen. But he hadn't. So Lizzy had to accept that Julian had consigned the suspension bridge painting in good faith. Insurance would deal with it.

In any case, Lizzy's desire to be with Nat soon took over from her desire to know the truth behind the paintings. He was making an enormous amount of effort to make her happy that evening, it seemed. From the moment they met at the restaurant he pressed her to have the best of everything. To enjoy herself *properly*. And that meant a whole bottle of vintage champagne rather than a couple of glasses. The champagne was followed by a bottle of burgundy with the meal and brandy afterwards, which Lizzy accepted though she had never really liked the stuff. The amount of wine she had drunk made her forget that she couldn't handle spirits.

By half past ten, Lizzy was rolling. She could no more have questioned Nat coherently about the paintings than she could have driven home.

'Let's go to Annabel's,' Nat suggested.

It seemed like a very good idea at the time.

Though it was a Tuesday evening, the little club in Berkeley Square was jumping. Lizzy felt a buzz of excitement as she stepped beneath the awning that led down into the club. Like Scott's, this was a place she had always wanted to go to but never had the opportunity. Sarah Jane was always talking about the place. She had dated a string of investment bankers who were all members. Sarah Jane went to Annabel's like most of the girls at Ludbrook's went to the Pitcher and Piano. Lizzy had imagined something entirely different from the place that greeted her as they walked through the tunnel-like entrance hall.

To the right of the first bar was a salon that looked like the sitting room of a Chelsea grandmother. Beyond that was a dining room so dark, you couldn't tell if you were eating steak or chicken and a dance floor straight out of the seventies, glittering with tiny lights that were echoed in the canopy above.

The clientele were fairly homogeneous. The men were all straight from the City or Mayfair in their well-cut grey suits, the lighting doing wonders for their half-cut grey faces. The girls were a gaudier bunch. Tall, with model figures and hairdos that looked as though they incorporated the tails of a whole family of recently culled New Forest ponies. The girls all wore Versace and Cavalli, and spoke with Eastern

European accents. An alien anthropologist landing at Annabel's might assume that the female of the species was a foot taller than the male. Standing in the ladies' room, admiring the Amazon reapplying lipstick in the mirror beside her, Lizzy slicked on a little lip gloss in an attempt to keep up, though she still looked like she had come to do an audit rather than to dance.

Nat had already ordered two glasses of champagne. He patted a space on the sofa beside him and she duly sat down. He covered her with compliments as that first glass and half of his slipped down her throat. Meanwhile, the DJ played a selection of the cheesiest hits known to mankind. It was the soundtrack of a Home Counties wedding disco. The dance floor was beginning to fill up. A chap who got too hot and took his jacket off was swiftly reminded that stripping down to one's shirtsleeves simply wasn't done.

'You know what I'd really like,' Lizzy said when the DJ put on some Earth, Wind and Fire. 'I'd like to dance.'

'Your wish is my command,' said Nat, standing up and taking her hand.

Lizzy stood up too and the room whirled around her for a moment. As she swayed towards him, Nat reached out ineffectually to catch her arm. Seconds later she was on the floor. Not the dance floor, as she had hoped, but flat on her back on the carpet. Unconscious.

Nat somehow got Lizzy back to her place. He woke up her flatmate, Jools, and ensured that she was put to bed.

'Tell her I won't expect her to come in for the interdepartmental meeting in the morning,' he said as he parted. 'I'll explain to everyone that she's been taken ill.'

Lizzy didn't even wake up until the interdepartmental meeting was long finished. Her hangover definitely disproved the theory that good wine doesn't affect you so badly.

Lizzy finally made it to the office that afternoon. Sarah Jane smiled knowingly.

'First time at Annabel's, eh?' she chuckled.

'How do you know?'

'How do you think I know?'

Nat had been about as discreet as a Scouse girl's Aintree ladies' day outfit. How many people knew? Now that Sarah Jane did, probably most of Bond Street. Lizzy groaned anew. It was so unprofessional. Out with her boss, getting too drunk to come into work in time for the interdepartmental meeting.

Later that day Nat took her to one side and told her, 'Now, about last night. First things first, I don't want you to worry about this business of forgeries at all. I've had a word with old Ludbrook himself about it. And secondly, I put in a good word for you at the same time. He was quite upset that you didn't make the meeting but I told him that it was a one-off. You're not the kind of girl who can't control her drinking so far as I know.'

Lizzy was devastated. How on earth was anyone supposed to take her seriously, let alone listen to her concerns about the fakes, now it was common knowledge that she'd missed an interdepartmental meeting thanks to over-consumption of alcohol? If she raised her worries now, people would assume she was trying to deflect the heat from her drunkenness. Exactly as Nat had planned.

Chapter Fifty-One

FORTUNATELY, Lizzy was able to keep her head down. There was much to be done in preparation for the sale of Randon's collection of antique erotica. Randon himself divided his collection into what he believed was two equal halves, based on previous insurance valuations. Neither auction house was allowed to cherry pick lots. They received news of their consignments as they had received their instructions at the Hotel Du Cap, simultaneously via courier, to ensure that neither house had the advantage. Randon was obviously enjoying his little game.

Carrie clutched her forehead when she found that she had been assigned the enormous marble cock. Nat, meanwhile, was very disappointed when he discovered that the fabulous cock was not on his list.

'Damn,' he said. 'I was going to have that photographed for the cover of the catalogue.'

'Do you think that would have been such a good idea?' asked Lizzy. 'I mean, isn't it a little bit . . .'

'Magnificent,' Nat murmured, remembering it with fondness.

That was the difference between men and women, Lizzy thought. What Nat called 'magnificent' was just plain scary in Lizzy's eyes.

Carrie despatched her team to inspect and photograph the items for her auction at once. Jessica, who had listened to Carrie's description of her trip to the South of France in slack-jawed disbelief, was stunned once more when she received the picture files of the items that Carrie had described and saw them for herself.

'What in God's name is happening in that photograph?' she asked her boss. 'Is that legal? Carrie, you know I think we need to be super careful about our catalogue for this sale. I'm sure you and I could be jailed if some of these pictures get into the hands of a minor in Texas.'

'You're right,' said Carrie. 'Got to make it subtle.'

Carrie sorted through the photographs for the least offensive one to make the catalogue's cover. She chose a female nude. A simple headless and armless bust that had once adorned a Roman temple. Or brothel. Randon had claimed he couldn't remember which.

The end result from Ehrenpreis was rather lovely and sophisticated. For the cover of his catalogue, Nat chose the lithograph of vagina butterflies, which was also abstract enough to appear tasteful at first sight.

Randon insisted that he be allowed to add a foreword to the catalogue. It would be the same for the sales at Ludbrook and Ehrenpreis. Both Carrie and Nat had the same reaction when they read it.

'Oh God.'

'I have come to realise that no good can come from having this collection in my life,' Randon wrote. 'These so called "works of art" are nothing but the spewings of diseased and dirty minds that spread nothing but hatred and unhappiness to whomsoever they touch.'

Both Carrie and Nat independently came to the same decision about how they would handle Randon's words.

'I'll tell him there was a mix-up and the catalogue went to print before we got his letter,' Carrie told Jessica.

'We'll print it on a separate piece of paper to add as an inclusion,' said Nat to his team. 'Though since I know how much you people love collating mail-outs, I have no doubt that some of those inclusions will go *awry*.'

Both were of the opinion that they were saving Randon from himself. His sermon would hardly encourage buyers. And whatever Randon thought of his collection, he did seem to want to make a lot of money from it.

Carrie was very pleased with the way her catalogue turned out. It was as beautiful and tasteful as any other catalogue and might, at first glance, have looked as though it was for any ordinary sale of ancient antiquities rather than a world-class haul of filth.

It was sent out. There were a few complaints, which Carrie dealt with personally. She explained to disgruntled and disgusted customers that Randon's collection was of vast importance.

'Many of the lots are museum quality,' she said. 'In fact, we fully expect that several museums will bid on that statue of Venus and the pages from the Marquis de Sade manuscript.'

The extraordinary number of people who requested a copy of an auction house catalogue for the very first time more than equalled the complaints. It quickly became Ehrenpreis's biggest-selling catalogue ever. Copies that cost twenty pounds if you bought them from the front desk on New Bond Street were soon changing hands on eBay for five times that amount.

And Randon had given both houses an absolute gift when it came to generating PR. Ordinarily the women who staffed the PR department at Ludbrook's had an uphill struggle trying to convince the magazines that auctions could be interesting. This time was completely different. They sent out press packs to everyone. All the papers clamoured for an exclusive interview with Randon or a photograph of the giant marble phallus with one of the girls standing next to it for scale (not that any of them would have dared to actually print that).

Randon's conversion from the hedonistic head of an international lifestyle brand to the pious born-again Christian bent on creating his own religious colony was the stuff of a feature writer's dreams. The *Sunday Times* magazine ran an eight-page profile on the man and his rise to power. The photographs that accompanied the piece were marvellous. Randon had bedded dozens of fabulously beautiful and famous women. Several of the lucky ladies had posed for snapshots that now resurfaced all over the news.

But all that was behind him, Randon's staff insisted to anyone who asked. And so the public were able to access a collection that would otherwise have remained utterly private until Mathieu Randon's death.

In all his years in the auction world, Nat Wilde had never seen such a large number of people turn up to view the lots in Ludbrook's galleries. Never before. Not even when they were selling jewels that had belonged to Liz Taylor or Christina

Onassis, or the biggest crowd-pleaser of them all, the late sainted Princess Diana.

'Sex really does sell,' he commented to Lizzy.

Lizzy was kept extremely busy arranging for certain lots to be presented in private to her most highly favoured clients. The ones who required her utmost discretion. She had a number of extremely tense moments as she unveiled a particular print in front of various male clients and found that they automatically glanced straight from the painting to her, as if to ask 'Can you do that too?'

Lizzy discussed the issue with Sarah Jane, whose response was that she wasn't bothered by it at all. In fact she had managed to parley several such intimate moments into dinner invitations. She wouldn't have to cook for the following fortnight . . . From time to time, Lizzy wished she had Sarah Jane's chutzpah but for the most part she was just pleased that her rival was too busy dating to flirt with Nat. Though the collection seemed to have infused the entire auction house with the scent of lust. Lizzy found herself beneath Nat's desk many times while Randon's collection was on display downstairs.

Perhaps Randon was right about the corrupting influence of his terrible artworks. Nat seemed to be obsessed by the rock-hard model members all around him while they awaited the Randon sale. While researching the collection in order to be better able to explain many of the lots to clients, he had come across a book relating to the ancient Egyptian gods, who were widely represented. He told Lizzy the myth of Hathor, wife of Ra, who was the goddess of dance and sexuality. She was give the epithet 'Hand of God', referring to the act of masturbation, a trick she employed to keep her husband happy and the sun in the sky. In fact, some Egyptian priests devoted to Ra believed that the sun wouldn't rise unless they too greeted the dawn with an ejaculation. They employed priestesses, whose role was modelled on that of Hathor, to help ensure the world kept turning.

'Can you imagine the pressure,' said Nat wistfully. 'A few too many beers the night before and the world might end. I think perhaps that you should be contractually obliged to be my Hathor and toss me off before every auction,' he added to Lizzy.

Chapter Fifty-Two

$\mathscr{A}$ PART from the security guards Carrie was, as usual, the very last person in the Ehrenpreis offices that night. She did her customary tour of the building to ensure that everything was in its place and that the cleaners had done their job properly. More than once she'd had to let cleaners go because they couldn't seem to work to her standards. Yet when she found a good team, it seemed inevitable that she would lose them for some other reason. Pregnancy, visa problems, a partner who just wanted them to stay home. It was hard to find the right staff and harder still to get them to stay. Carrie had actually ended up scrubbing toilets herself on occasion. She wasn't too grand for that.

The Mathieu Randon collection had been on display for almost a week, during which time Ehrenpreis had seen an unprecedented number of interested parties come through the door. Most of them weren't going to be buying, of course, but no one could ever be turned away, just in case. No matter if they turned up in trainers rather than Turnbull and Asser. Even the bloke who gave Jessica 'the creeps' when she saw him standing in front of one painting with his hands in his pockets had to be treated with politeness and care.

'Most of the world's richest people are creeps,' Carrie reminded her.

But now all the punters were gone.

This was the moment in her daily routine that Carrie loved the best. With no one around but security, she was transported back to her childhood fantasies. In those she was locked into the Natural History Museum off Central Park after everyone had gone home. With no one to stop her, she could touch whatever she liked. That movie, *Night At the Museum*, could have been written just for her.

The galleries at Ehrenpreis weren't a museum, but they were almost as good. Better in some ways, since the items on display were constantly changing. A few months before, Carrie had spent three hours amusing herself with the lots for the fine jewellery sale, trying on some of the finer pieces, admiring herself in a pair of Jackie Kennedy's earrings. She decided that were a little too big and square for her heart-shaped face.

That night, Carrie wanted to take a last good look at Randon's collection. By the end of the following day, with the auction done and dusted, this amazing group of pieces would already be dispersing to the four corners of the earth. The Ehrenpreis team were preparing to take phone bids from clients in the US, Russia, China and Japan.

Even as Carrie looked at Randon's collection, it was hard to imagine the man as he had been before he was caught by a falling wine barrel in the San Francisco earthquake and fell into a coma. She'd heard the stories but they were difficult to square with the pious (often pompously so) man who ended every call with the words 'bless you'. Was it really possible that he had held orgies at his château just outside Paris, attended by supermodels, racing drivers and Hollywood movie stars? Was there any truth in the rumour that he had close friends in both the Italian and Russian mafias? The one thing that Carrie knew to be true was that Randon had once employed a serial killer. The former managing director of Maison Randon was serving a life sentence in a French prison for the murder of two prostitutes. One was a British girl, found floating face down in the Seine, wearing nothing but a shoe.

There was something very odd about Mathieu Randon. Carrie wasn't quite convinced that he wouldn't miss the paintings she studied now. But he wanted to be rid of them, he said time and time again, perhaps trying to convince himself, too. It was the best way he could imagine to raise the funds he needed for God's work, he told Carrie. He had already earmarked the plot of land on which he intended to build his church and his monastery. He had to make amends for a life of hedonism and sin. The way he spoke freaked Carrie out, especially when she remembered how oddly he had behaved on board *The Grand Cru*, but she wasn't there to worry about his sincerity. Carrie was simply there to sell Randon's shame to the highest bidder.

After donning a pair of white gloves, Carrie picked up the little Japanese inro box, made to hang from a warrior's obi, to look more closely at the intricate carving. As she did so, she heard the sound of something sliding around inside. It took her by surprise. The catalogue hadn't mentioned any moving parts. Her first thought was that some idiot must have manhandled the little box while cleaning or showing it and a piece had broken off and was now making the inro rattle.

'Damn,' she muttered. She signalled to the night watch-man that she was going to remove the piece and take it to her office to save him the bother of turning on all the gallery lights, which were on their red setting, like the nightlights in most great museums, to minimise the amount of light exposure the paintings had while they were in her care.

Back in her office, Carrie cleared a space on her blotter and placed the little box down upon it. The box was such a beautiful thing. The hours of patience it must have taken to carve the scene on the lid had been well rewarded by the quality of the results. Carrie had seen lots of inro and netsuke during her career but this was by far the best example. Ordinarily, the inro box would be held shut by a string of beads that operated like the string on a blind, but this box was held shut by a complicated mechanism. So complicated that Carrie didn't have a clue where to start.

Neither had Randon. There was a note in the file relating to this particular piece that informed Carrie that her expert on such objects had asked Randon for the combination but he was unable to supply it. The catalogue duly stated that the box would be sold as locked.

But no one had ever mentioned that there might be something inside it. Carrie had to find out what it was. There was no way she could let this box go to auction broken or, far worse, with something even more valuable than the box itself hidden inside. She determined to get the damn thing open.

The white gloves made the task especially difficult. Though they were particularly fine, they still made it hard for Carrie to know when she might have twisted the right piece into place. But after a determined hour of experimentation she found the right combination. She pressed on the exposed breast of one of the women carved on the inro and, at last, the lid and the box slid smoothly apart. Holding her breath, Carrie tipped the contents out onto the table.

'Oh God,' she recoiled as she saw what the box held. Was that *hair*?

It was hair. Three locks of dark brown hair, each one bound with a sliver of thin black ribbon. And there was more. The hair must have been what had kept the other contents of the box from rattling against the sides. Using a pencil to separate the curious items from the hair, which made her want to heave, Carrie counted out three pieces of jewellery. A heart-shaped pendant. A thin silver bracelet. And a ring, one of those friendship rings that girls give each other in high school. Clasped hands. A Claddagh, she thought it was called.

Carrie was confused. Randon claimed he'd had this box since the 1970s – it was one of the first pieces in his collection – and that he had never been able to open it, and yet the contents of this box looked to have been added to the inro more recently than that.

It was all worthless. Carrie could tell that the moment she laid eyes on the stuff. The locket, the bracelet and the ring would each have cost around twenty quid new. Second hand, it was the kind of stuff you gave to little girls for their dressing-up box. Using her tweezers, Carrie picked up the ring and held it under her desk light while she looked at it through a magnifying glass. The hallmark, which was almost rubbed away, suggested that the ring was made in 1985. Likewise, the gold locket looked to be far newer than the 1970s, though it was difficult to tell for sure because the hallmark on this piece had been entirely rubbed away. Carrie imagined a young girl smoothing the surface with nervous fingers, using the locket like worry beads.

As for the hair . . . Carrie had no idea how old that was. She'd seen Victorian mourning jewellery plenty of times. It was horrible stuff that always gave Carrie the shivers when she had to handle it. Mourning rings and lockets from that period often contain a piece of the loved one's hair and Carrie had been surprised to see how fresh it could look after almost two hundred years. So the hair might always have been inside the inro. And yet . . .

Using a pencil and her tweezers once again, Carrie separated out the three locks so that they were side by side on a piece of white paper. Under her strong desk light, Carrie could see that they weren't all from the same head. There was quite a difference in colour from one lock to the next. One was almost red in tone. Another had strands of shimmering golden blonde. None seemed particularly Japanese. A forensic scientist would be able to tell at once.

How odd. The items inside the inro box had left Carrie feeling strangely disturbed, as though she had seen something that should have been hidden for ever. But it was all such crap! Cheap mass-produced jewellery of the kind that ended up in charity shops and car boot sales. Regardless, she knew she had to tell Randon what she had found.

She pulled out a zip-lock bag from the box she had in a desk drawer, and dropped the hair and the jewellery inside, planning to give Randon a call first thing and ask whether he wanted the stuff back or whether she should just throw it away.

She didn't have to wait until morning. Her mobile phone started to vibrate in her jacket pocket.

'Monsieur Randon, *ça va?*' she greeted him.

'*Ça va bien,*' he confirmed. 'I hope you don't mind me calling you a little late in the day.'

'Not at all,' said Carrie, which is what she would have said whether she really minded or not.

'Good. I wanted to talk to you before the sale and give you my best wishes. I want to tell you how grateful I am for all your hard work so far.'

'Thank you. I hope we'll get the kind of results you're looking for.'

'I have no doubt that you will,' said Randon.

'The sale begins at ten o'clock. Will you be with us?'

'I think not,' he said. 'It wouldn't give me any pleasure to see the faces of the stupid people who want to let such filth into their lives. This is just a means to an end. I'm only interested in the good works I will be able to do with the proceeds.'

'I understand.'

'Though I am in London. I have taken a suite at Claridge's, and I would appreciate it if you could come and see me to talk through the results when you have a moment.'

'Of course,' said Carrie. 'I hope we'll be able to crack open the champagne.'

'Not for me,' said Randon. 'Not anymore.'

'I'm sorry.' Carrie berated herself for having forgotten, yet again, that the head of one of the world's finest champagne houses was now teetotal. 'Monsieur Randon, I was planning to call you first thing in the morning. I wanted to talk to you about one of the lots.'

'Yes,' said Randon. 'Go on.'

'It's the inro. The Japanese ivory box with the carving of the man and woman on the lid. The one you said you couldn't open.'

'Ah yes. The box I bought in 1973.'

'That's it. Well, I've got some news for you. I was making a final inspection of the lots earlier this evening and, when I picked the inro up, I heard something rattle inside. Believe it or not, I actually managed to get it open. I wanted to be sure that it didn't contain some rare jewel and . . .'

'What did it contain?' Randon asked.

'Not much of interest. At least, not to me as an auctioneer. But perhaps for you . . . It contained some pieces of jewellery. Inexpensive stuff. The kind you can get on any high street. I'd say it was from the 1970s or 80s. It also contained three locks of hair, which must have cushioned the jewellery, hence we didn't realise there was anything inside until now. I assumed that you wouldn't want me to sell the inro with these items still in there so I removed them. I've got them right here on my desk. Would you like them or shall I dispose of them myself?'

There was a long pause.

'They're really very cheap,' Carrie said to fill the silence and immediately wished she hadn't. Sentimental value, she knew, was often immeasurably great.

'I'd like you to send the items over to me at my hotel,' said Randon at last.

'OK. I'll do that at once.'

Carrie wanted to ask more. She wanted to ask if Randon had any idea whatsoever why the inro was stuffed with such crap. But he offered nothing and she got no sense of whether he recalled having put those things in the box – as he must surely have done. Who else could have gained access to the collection?

'Is there anything more?' asked Randon.

'No,' said Carrie. 'Everything else is ready for the sale. We're very excited.'

'Good,' said Randon. 'Make sure you send those other things over right away.'

Carrie promised she would.

Claridge's was not far from the Ehrenpreis offices so Carrie delivered the contents of the inro box to Randon's hotel by hand, passing the jiffy bag to the concierge and insisting on staying until she received confirmation that it had been handed on to Randon himself.

What a strange thing. She couldn't help thinking about those little mementoes as she sat in the back of her taxi home. Where had Randon come across them? Old girlfriends, Carrie decided. His first, second and third loves, perhaps. Though the dates were slightly off. How old was Randon? He must be in his mid-fifties. In which case he would have had his first love affair way before 1984. Surely. Perhaps later in the week, when she met Randon to discuss the results of the sale, he would throw some light on the matter. If he could.

In the privacy of his suite, Randon opened Carrie's envelope.

Her news had confused him. Randon's brain still failed him from time to time and it took a while for him to remember the inro box. Why it should have had anything inside it that wasn't from the period when the box was made was a total mystery to him. He hoped that seeing the items would jog his memory. He tipped them out onto the blotter on his desk, eager to know more.

Such a strange little collection. That tacky jewellery. Like nothing any woman he knew would have owned. And hair? Why hair? He picked up the heart-shaped locket and opened it, hoping for a further clue inside, but it was empty. Nothing but a little sliver of clear plastic that was supposed to protect a photograph. Had there ever been a photograph? He put the Claddagh ring on his pinkie finger and turned it this way and that. Had he seen it before? He didn't recall it. The bracelet equally drew a blank.

He touched one of the three locks of hair. Like Carrie, he found the very idea of it somewhat repellent. Why on earth would he have this? Who did it belong to? Randon toyed with the idea that perhaps it was his own hair. His mother was a sentimental woman who liked to save a curl from the heads of each of her children. As a child, Randon had dark brown hair. His sisters too. But that didn't explain how Randon would have ended up with *their* hair in a box.

He stared at the little collection on the blotter for quite some time, willing the memories to come back to him. The doctors had offered no hope for the recovery of some of his memory but Randon was determined that one day he would be able to remember everything that had happened prior to the earthquake in San Francisco. To that end he filled notebooks with scribbled fragments and spent hours and hours poring over photographs in the hope that it would hurry the process along.

'Come back to me,' he muttered, staring until his eyes started to hurt. Then, without knowing why, he took up one of the locks of hair, held it to his nose and inhaled deeply. Nothing. Nothing at all. But it must mean something. The action of smelling the hair had been so instinctual it must have been something he'd done before. Randon was sure now that these things had once been precious to him, but why? He put them back into the envelope. Then Randon put the envelope under his pillow and tried to sleep.

When his dreams at last came, they were far from sweet.

'Let me go. I won't tell anybody! I swear! I swear!' a woman's voice called out across the years.

Chapter Fifty-Three

$\mathcal{N}$AT Wilde started the next day in a leisurely fashion. He was very pleased that he'd managed to wangle the afternoon slot for that day's Randon auctions.

His suit for the sale was already laid out, along with a clean shirt and his lucky tie, frayed but ever faithful.

'Don't let me down today,' he said, as he tied the Hermès bunnies around his neck in a double Windsor.

This sale would go down in history, Nat knew. If not as one of the biggest then definitely as one of the most amusing. He could hardly wait to get up there with his gavel and set the crowd roaring with laughter as he described the lots.

It was going to be great fun, he was sure.

And it was. Knowing that the occasion was more than likely to end up in the papers, the girls in the department had pulled out all the stops, individualising the formal black suit, white shirt combo they were supposed to wear on auction days in a variety of entertaining ways.

Sarah Jane arrived at the office wearing an obscenely short skirt with no stockings and a gold ankle chain setting off her leopard-print shoes.

'Shouldn't you be wearing flats?' Lizzy asked her.

'Why?' asked Sarah Jane. 'What's wrong with these shoes? They're Louboutins.' She flashed a red sole.

Where to start, thought Lizzy.

'I'm only thinking of your poor back,' was what she said out loud.

Sarah Jane scowled, knowing that in putting on her leopard-print Louboutins, she had blown her chances of ever using backache caused by the Reynolds accident as an excuse for being bone idle again.

However, Lizzy was not to be outdone. Just before the sale was due to begin, Lizzy changed into a skirt that made Sarah Jane's look positively modest. Lizzy's skirt was a crotch grazer, as Harry Brown would say. Nat was delighted. There was nothing he liked more than seeing the girls in the office competing with their hemlines. It made him feel like an old lion, surrounded by a pride full of strong young lionesses, all glossy coated and eminently strokeable. Even Olivia played up to Nat's fantasy that day, swapping her A-line for something that was tight, if not short. And once they had their porters' gloves on . . .

Oh God. Just the thought of those gloves gave Nat a raging hard-on. He'd found them impossibly erotic ever since his first week as a porter at Christie's, when one of the older girls working there had taken him into the porters' lift, stopped it between floors and given him a hand-job without taking her gloves off first. Those white gloves never failed to brighten his day, as Lizzy knew only too well.

*   *   *

Unlike Nat, Carrie was dreading her sale. There would be no embellishment in her descriptions.

'Lot number thirty-six. Carved ornamental phallus. Alabaster. Eleven inches. Believed to be from Egypt, 300 BC. Who will start the bidding at thirty thousand pounds . . .'

But it was hard to retain any semblance of dignity when the dealers were shouting things like, 'You're holding that cock all wrong, love,' from the back of the room. Sometimes they were no better than the crowd you got at a second-hand car sale, thought Carrie, as she brought down her gavel like a judge to bring order to the room. When the auction was over, she retreated to her office and collapsed into her chair. It had been the toughest auction in her life.

Nat, meanwhile, had a ball. He presented his half of Randon's collection like a magician performing a well-rehearsed show, relishing every opportunity to make a joke, drawing attention to his lovely assistants as they trotted and twirled across the stage with the smaller lots. Sarah Jane wiggled and pouted so much that Nat was prompted to say, 'Hold still, Sarah Jane. The quicker I get this lithograph sold, the sooner you can go to the bathroom.' He made the crowd roar when he informed them that they would have to negotiate James and Marcus's services separately as the hapless young lads carried on a pair of enormous ceremonial dildos carved out of rosewood.

Lizzy watched from the wings. This was Nat at his very best. He made the whole process a pleasure. If anyone in the room had a spare tenner, Nat would have it added to their bid in no time and yet everyone went home happy, feeling that they had paid a fair price, or at least enjoyed a colourful performance if they lost out.

As Nat sold, Lizzy annotated the lots in her copy of the catalogue, keeping a running total on the calculator on her phone. She knew exactly what Ehrenpreis had managed to raise that morning. It was an impressive number to have to beat. By the halfway point, Lizzy was starting to be cautiously confident that victory would be theirs.

The very last item was the original Marquis de Sade manuscript. Half the room wanted to bid for that scrappy collection of papers. Nat brought the hammer down at one and a half million pounds.

'Wa-hey!' knowing that they had bust the Ehrenpreis figure, Sarah Jane jumped up in the air with glee. She landed a little awkwardly, twisting her ankle badly enough to bring tears to her eyes.

'You should stick to flats,' said Lizzy but inside she was jumping too.

The news that the Ludbrook's sale had earned so much more than her own was with Carrie seconds after it reached Nat. Jessica had been at the back of the Ludbrook's' auction room, keeping her own running total.

'Shit.'

She stared at the numbers.

'He got *how much* for that?'

Jessica tried to be positive.

'It doesn't necessarily mean that Randon will let Ludbrook's have the rest of his collection. I'm sure that when you meet with him you'll be able to explain the difference between the sales. There's no way he can believe that he assigned the two houses goods of exactly equal value.'

Carrie shrugged.

'If I were you I would tell him that he's acting like a jerk. I mean, splitting the collection and putting us into direct competition with Ludbrook's was a jerkish move in the first place. We're professionals. This is not an episode of *The Apprentice!*'

'I know. It's stupid. But you can bet that if we had won, I would absolutely be holding Randon to his word. As Nat Wilde will. I took the challenge. We have to stick to the rules.'

'It's so unfair!' Jessica cried out.

It was unfair. Not least because, in the end, Carrie had *not* had exactly half of Randon's collection to sell. At the very last minute, his assistant had called and informed Carrie that Randon no longer wished to sell the Japanese inro. It was to be withdrawn from the sale and returned to him at the hotel. Carrie had to do as she was instructed. It was deeply frustrating. She had talked to several buyers that week who were interested in purchasing the piece. Had the two heaviest hitters gone head to head over the inro in the auction room, who knows what it might have fetched? Enough to put her way ahead of Nat Wilde, she was sure. Carrie hoped that Randon would take that into consideration when looking at the results.

But it got worse. In the press reports of the sales, Carrie found herself described as a 'dominatrix'. She was not happy about that at all.

When she passed Nat in the lobby at Claridge's, he congratulated her on the photograph that had already hit the *Evening Standard* website.

'Great shoes. You could always find work in a Mayfair dungeon,' he suggested.

'Shut it, Wilde.'

Nat mimed a zip across his lips.

'It's OK,' he said. 'I won't stay here and torment you. Got some celebrating to do with my team. Do drop in and join us if you like.'

'Fuck you,' Carrie mouthed.

When she was finally admitted to his suite, Randon shook Carrie by the hand. 'You did a wonderful job and I am very grateful. I hope I didn't cause you too much inconvenience by withdrawing the inro at the last moment.'

'Of course not,' Carrie lied. What else could she say? Her eyes travelled to the other side of the room. She had noticed the inro sitting on the desk the moment she walked into the room. Randon followed her eyes towards it.

'I'm afraid I weakened,' he said. 'That inro doesn't just represent the beginning of my erotic collection. It's the first piece I bought to celebrate my success in business. The sentimental reasons for keeping it are myriad.'

Carrie nodded. Was he going to explain the items inside the box now?

He didn't. Instead he made it clear that the audience was drawing to a close.

Carrie took a taxi home and ordered a takeaway.

With Carrie gone, Randon went to his desk. He had emails to read from his lawyers and the real estate agent who had found him several suitable properties to consider for his retreat. Randon looked at the details with the same care he would once have applied to a search for a new bachelor pad, but the criteria were different now. He needed privacy. Remoteness. He no longer needed to be within ten minutes of Le Club 55 in Saint Tropez or even within half an hour of an airport. In fact, he decided, the harder it was to get to his new retreat, the better. A difficult journey to his utopia would help the supplicants arriving there to truly appreciate what they were there to learn. The road to his retreat should be like Christ's road to Calgary, beset with difficulties but with glory at the end of it.

It was to be an early night. At seven o'clock exactly, Randon turned out the light. In the darkness, his fingers played with the rosary, counting off beads and prayers.

It wasn't long before the woman was back. This time more clearly than ever. He could see that she was younger than he had thought. Only just out of her teens. And she was wearing clothes from the eighties. She was walking across a field, towards the river. She looked back towards him several times, beckoning him to follow. Getting closer at last, he saw the heart on the chain around her neck.

Chapter Fifty-Four

$\mathcal{O}$ VER at Ludbrook's, the atmosphere was altogether more exuberant. Spirits were always high after a good sale, but that afternoon had been incredible. Nat had played the crowd like a violin. Not a lot left unsold and every single one went for more than the high estimate. Seconds after the last punter left, the champagne corks and self-congratulation started flying.

Lizzy still had work to do. A small dispute was taking place at the front desk between two dealers who both claimed they had made the highest bid on a small bronze penis. It would be easy enough to resolve. Lizzy sat down with the video recording of that night's auction and reeled through the items until she found the sequence of Nat selling the disputed item. The two dealers watched the film with her and the louder of the two had to admit that he'd been mistaken. His rival got 'the dick', as he called it.

Lizzy waved them away and happily turned off her laptop for the night. Now she could join the party. Her team were in one of the boardrooms upstairs, toasting their own success. Nat had returned from his post-sale meeting with Randon and so the party could begin in earnest. Lizzy bounded up the grand central stairway two at a time, eager to be with them. She couldn't bear to wait for the passenger lift, which was notoriously erratic. Earlier that week it had been out of action for two whole days, after an episode in which a dowager duchess was treated to a yo-yo ride, ricocheting between the ground and fifth floors seven times before someone noticed what was happening and pressed the stop button. Lizzy definitely didn't want to be stuck in the lift that night. She wanted to be with her all-conquering hero. Her Nat.

'Where's Nat Wilde?'

James Ludbrook, the great-great-grandson of Ludbrook's founder and father of its current MD John, was eager to pay his respects to his star auctioneer so that he could leave the party and get home to bed. James was almost eighty-seven after all.

It suddenly struck the assembled guests that none of them had seen Nat for a while.

'Maybe he went home,' suggested Olivia.

'What?' said Harry Brown. 'After tonight's performance? No way. He never misses an opportunity to hear praises sung to him.'

'He was definitely coming to the party,' said James. 'I saw him getting into the lift with Sarah Jane. They were on their way up. But that was hours ago.'

'Where's Sarah Jane?' asked someone else.

'Oh my God,' said Marcus. 'You don't suppose . . .'

Almost everyone at the party had complained about having to walk up the stairs to the boardroom that night because the lift was taking for ever to reach the ground floor. Maybe that was because it was broken.

A search party set out at once to discover whether Nat and Sarah Jane had met the same fate as the poor dowager duchess. And it was soon confirmed that the lift was indeed stuck between floors.

Together with Harry Brown, Marcus and Olivia, Lizzy went to the maintenance room to let Nat and Sarah Jane know that their predicament had been noted and help was on its way. There was some kind of speakerphone that would allow them to send their encouragement.

Lizzy felt terrible that she had allowed herself to get swept up in the excitement of the party while poor Nat languished in the elevator. She hoped he would see the funny side.

The building's caretaker switched the CCTV camera so that they were able to see inside the lift. And there was Nat with Sarah Jane. Though they didn't look particularly bothered about having been stuck for at least a couple of hours.

Lizzy felt the blood drain from her face as, behind her, Marcus started humming Aerosmith's 'Love In An Elevator'.

'Good God. Don't they know there's a camera in there?' asked Olivia, with distaste.

Inside the elevator, Nat had Sarah Jane up against a mirrored wall. Her tight white cotton shirt was undone, revealing the magnificent creamy white breasts, perfect E-cups, that every man at Ludbrook's dreamed of getting his hands on. Sarah Jane seemed to have forgotten all about the back injury that made it impossible for her to do any of the donkey work around the department as she wrapped her long strong legs around Nat's waist and threw her head back in ecstasy while Nat ground into her, his face buried in her neck, his trousers round his ankles. It was an X-rated extravaganza.

'Nice arse,' said one of the girls from fine wines.

'I think I'm going to be sick,' said Lizzy, covering her mouth.

'Too much champagne?' suggested Harry.

'God, Harry,' said Olivia, as she followed Lizzy out, leaving the boys to their viewing. 'Are you really so bloody oblivious?'

Though the image of the man she loved screwing another woman in a lift would be with her for quite some time, Lizzy's tears dried surprisingly quickly. She agreed with Olivia that Nat was an absolute bastard but she refused to condemn Sarah Jane too badly. Lizzy knew how persuasive Nat could be and she also knew that Sarah Jane would probably have to contend with the footage from that CCTV camera turning up on YouTube (in fact, Marcus would make sure of it). It would be faintly embarrassing for Nat too, of course, but nothing like as bad as it would be for his companion. The imbalance in the world's view of male/female sexuality persisted. Nat would be a stud while Sarah Jane . . . There were still no good words for a woman who enjoyed sex as thoroughly as Sarah Jane seemed to.

'You could make a complaint about sexual harassment,' said Olivia, when her suspicion that Lizzy had been subject to Nat's charms too was at last confirmed. Olivia was keen to see Ludbrook's golden boy fall from grace. Not least because he had resisted her so thoroughly. She'd had not so much as a wink in her five years at the house

'No,' said Lizzy. 'I was a willing accomplice in my own heartbreak. Nat never promised me anything.'

'God. If I were you I would have been waiting at the bottom of the lift-shaft to claw his eyes out. And hers.'

There was no love lost between Olivia and Sarah Jane. Lizzy decided that her revenge would be much more subtle.

Chapter Fifty-Five

THE following morning, neither Sarah Jane nor Nat was in the office when Lizzy arrived. It was a good thing. Seeing either of them might have made it harder to do what she knew she had to. Lizzy called John Ludbrook's office and requested a meeting. His personal assistant, Genevieve, was unusually helpful for once and suggested that Lizzy come upstairs right away.

Lizzy knew, as she climbed the staircase, that Genevieve's eagerness to help was more out of prurience than anything else. Genevieve had doubtless heard about the incident in the lift and wanted to know more. All the *really* gory details.

But Lizzy hadn't requested a meeting to talk about Nat and Sarah Jane. She had already decided that there was little point trying to gain sympathy from the man at the top of Ludbrook's. The old-school-tie network was alive and kicking. Affairs were rife. She had heard that John Ludbrook himself was cheating on his wife with the woman who headed up the textiles department. But much more important to any of these men than their marriages was the reputation of the house. That was taken very seriously indeed. And Lizzy was sure that she had information that would compromise it.

'And all these paintings were consigned by the same person?'

'Yes. Julian Trebarwen. Nat Wilde was at school with his brother.'

John buzzed Nat's office direct. Nat was there in less than three minutes, red-faced and out of breath from having bounded up the stairs two at a time. His agitation was compounded because he'd tripped in his hurry and had banged his knee – his 'bad knee', the one that had made it 'impossible' for him to shag Lizzy of late – hard on the stairs. And when he walked into the office and saw Lizzy there, Nat was pretty sure he knew what was coming. It was inevitable.

He shook his head ever so slightly. Though he couldn't deny that in some ways he deserved it. Harry Brown had warned him a thousand times that girls today weren't like the girls who used to come to Ludbrook's by the dozen. This new breed were serious about their careers and if you fucked them and dumped them and left them thinking that you might promote someone else over their heads, they would think nothing about crying harassment.

'It's not like it used to be,' said Harry. 'Life is more complicated now. They won't think twice about dropping you in it the moment you want to fuck someone else.'

But Lizzy? Nat would never have imagined that Lizzy would go crying to the big boss. What had he really done wrong? He'd never pretended their relationship was anything more than a pleasant diversion for him. He'd assumed that she understood what he was like and when the time came and it was over, she would move aside without causing too much fuss. She should have known that he would have done his best to help her move ahead in Ludbrook's, not least because now he wanted her out of his department.

'Come on,' said Nat as he stood in front of Lizzy and his boss. 'This is madness. I think I can safely say that it was mutual.'

'What was?' asked John Ludbrook.

'It happens all the time. You yourself . . .'

Nat was ready to bring up the affair the managing director was having with the head of the textiles department when he realised, in the nick of time, that the man who held Nat's career in his hand genuinely didn't know what he was talking about.

'This isn't about you and me,' Lizzy confirmed in a low voice. 'You didn't matter *that* much.'

Nat glared.

'Miss Duffy has been sharing her concerns about some possible forgeries sold through your department.'

'The suspension bridge painting,' sighed Nat. He'd already been through this. He'd already sat in this very office and apologised until he was blue in the face that the damn thing had slipped through on his watch. 'I know, I know . . . I can't believe I didn't spot the discrepancy.'

'Not just the suspension bridge,' said Lizzy.

Nat bristled.

'John,' he appealed to his boss. 'How long have we known each other? Thirty years? How long have we worked together? How many times has a fake got past me before? I don't remember all of the paintings that Lizzy is talking about and I don't suppose she remembers them all that clearly herself. You know how seriously I take my job, John. I would not let anything I had the slightest doubts about pass. I'd send it over the road to Ehrenpreis,' he added in an attempt at levity.

But levity was not working that morning.

John Ludbrook looked through a pile of papers on his desk. Things that Lizzy had printed out to support her case.

'Miss Duffy has told me that she raised her concerns about these other paintings with you not so long ago. She said that you told her you would deal with the matter yourself. But I don't recall having been informed, nor does it seem that the proper investigations were undertaken. I don't need to tell you that these allegations of forgery are very serious indeed and should have been investigated with commensurate gravity.'

'I didn't think it was worth bothering,' Nat told him. 'There was one documented incident. Just one. Lizzy's suspicions are pure conjecture. She's very conscientious but she doesn't have my experience.

'Regardless, she should have been taken more seriously.'

'I resent being told how to do my job,' said Nat.

'I never thought I would have to tell you how to do it,' said John Ludbrook.

As he walked out of the room, Nat shot Lizzy such a look you might have thought she had just condemned him to death.

So, Lizzy had her small victory but it didn't feel half so good as she had imagined. Instead she was left reeling from the coldness in Nat's eyes. Such a look of disdain. Of hatred even. Was it really possible they had ever held each other as tenderly as they did? Was it really possible that she had ever thought Nat Wilde might love her?

Chapter Fifty-Six

THE sale of so many possible fakes through Ludbrook's had the potential to bring the house down if Lizzy's suspicions were not acted on swiftly. The very next day the police were called in and everyone in the art department was formally questioned (despite Nat's protests). Of course Julian Trebarwen was wanted for questioning. A police car was soon outside his little house in Fulham, but it was empty and a neighbour said that he hadn't seen Julian in a couple of days. His car was nowhere to be found.

A deputation was sent down to Cornwall. They arrived at Trebarwen House that night.

The grey stone house was cold and empty. No cars in the driveway. No lights on. One of the officers peered through the long narrow windows that flanked the grand door. A pile of post suggested that no one had been there for quite some time.

'He's not here,' said the constable decisively.

'There's a light on in the house over there,' his partner pointed out. 'Isn't that place part of the estate?'

Serena had just put Katie to bed when the officers knocked on her door.

'We're sorry to disturb you, Mrs Macdonald.'

She wondered for a moment how they knew her name. Then she remembered that these guys probably knew a great deal more about her than that.

'What is it?' she asked.

Please don't let it be Tom, she prayed silently. Though she had wished him dead a thousand times since he left to live with Donna the idea that something might actually have happened to him made her legs feel unsteady. But so far they hadn't asked her to sit down. They hadn't even asked to come in. They always came in and told you to sit down if there had been a death in the family, didn't they?

'Are you familiar with the people in the big house?' asked the younger guy. 'The Trebarwen house?'

'Yes,' said Serena. 'I was friendly with Louisa.'

'And her sons?'

Serena stiffened. Already she was reacting to the changing complexion of the thing. There was no reason why the police would turn up to tell her that one of the Trebarwen brothers had been killed, was there?

'Which one?' she answered, stalling for time.

'Julian.'

'I met him, yes. At his mother's funeral.'

'My name is Detective Constable James from the Arts and Antiques Unit of the Metropolitan Police. And this is DC

Havelock. You wouldn't happen to know where we could find him?'

Arts and antiques. Serena felt her cheeks flush as she heard the words. What should she do? She and Julian had agreed when they first started their little business, that they would act dumb if ever questioned. Even on their relationship with each other. They'd deny everything to save each other's skin. Art and antiques. It was obvious what this was about.

'Doesn't he have a house in London?' Serena asked, continuing to play down her acquaintance with her former lover.

'He's not there. And he's not at the big house. We thought he might have come over here, you being his nearest neighbour, and told you if he was going to leave the house empty for any length of time. Perhaps he might have left a number you could call him on if you saw anything suspicious at the big house.'

'No,' said Serena. 'I haven't seen him in weeks.' That much at least was true. The business with Yasha and the fake Ricasoli had driven them apart. Julian had tried endlessly to make amends but despite having come to no harm and made fifty grand in the process, Serena couldn't entirely forgive him and Julian grew tired of being the bad guy.

'Then we're sorry to have disturbed you,' said DC James. 'Enjoy the rest of your evening. Goodnight.'

DC Havelock actually gave a small bow as he made to leave.

The policemen gone, Serena closed the door behind them and, for the first time since she had moved down to Cornwall, turned the dead bolt. She picked up her phone. Julian's number was still in it. She wanted to call him right then and find out what on earth was going on. Serena could feel her throat tightening. She wanted to cry. She wanted Julian to tell her that everything was OK and this wasn't about their paintings . . . But she couldn't just call him. If the worst had happened and this was about their joint venture, then the last thing Serena wanted was to make a call from her mobile, one that could be traced straight back to her. She'd just told the police officers that she and Julian had met only once, at his mother's funeral.

But she needed to talk to him.

There was a pay phone in the village. Serena had often marvelled that it still existed. She'd never seen anyone use it. She wasn't sure it was still operational, but she had to find out right then.

Creeping upstairs so as not to wake her daughter, Serena looked in on Katie. She was sleeping soundly. Serena considered for a moment waking her up. She had never before left Katie alone in the house. The potentially horrifying consequences made it impossible even to think about taking such a risk. But that was before two police officers had come by looking for Julian. Katie looked so peaceful. Serena calculated that if she took the car she could get to the call box and back in less than ten minutes. If Julian picked up, she would tell him to go out and find a call box and call her on her landline at home to tell her what on earth was going on.

Uttering a small prayer for Katie's safety in her absence, Serena tugged on her denim jacket and got into the car. She was shaking all the way as she drove into the village and located the box, which unlike every box she'd ever been in before had not been vandalised and didn't smell of piss.

The call box didn't take cash. She put her credit card into the slot and dialled Julian's number.

'Please pick up,' she begged him,

Julian's phone rang and rang and finally went to voicemail.

Serena put the phone down and bowed her head. She knew she shouldn't leave a message. Where was he? What had he done to have a pair of policemen looking for him?

She had to keep reminding herself that they weren't looking for her.

But if Julian had promised that he would keep her out of any trouble, he'd already failed in that promise by bringing Yasha to her door.

Serena tried his number one more time. Maybe he wasn't picking up because he didn't recognise the number. If she persisted however, surely he would recognise the regional code and put two and two together.

No joy.

It was starting to rain. And Serena had to get back to the house. She had left Katie alone for almost fifteen minutes already and every minute longer raised the risk that Katie would wake up and wander downstairs and fly into a panic. That was when things could go wrong.

The house was dark when she arrived home. That was a good sign, she decided, since Katie was well able to turn all the lights on and would have done had she been worried. Still, Serena ran from the driveway to the front door. Inside, all was silent. She crept up the stairs and hovered by Katie's door. The soft, snuffly in-out of her breathing was the most comforting sound Serena had ever heard.

'I'll never leave you alone like that again,' she promised.

After checking on her daughter, Serena carried on up the stairs to the top of the house and her studio. Opening the door she couldn't help but imagine how it would look to a policeman investigating an accusation of forgery and fraud. All Serena's practice pieces tacked to the walls. Her experiments with pigment and producing craquelure. The pile of Victorian end papers waiting to be transformed into paintings. And on the easel the painting she had been working on most recently – a little pastiche of Ricasoli for herself, for her own pleasure – with a book about the work of the artist open for reference right beside it.

It would have to go. All of it.

Serena started by taking down the sketches and paintings she'd pinned to the wall. She made a pile with the large painting from the easel on the bottom to make it easier to carry the whole lot downstairs.

She would have to burn it. She lit a fire in the sitting room and fed the pictures into it one by one. It was hard to see her work going up in flames. There were little pieces there that she had been very proud of. But she couldn't think of it like that anymore. More than anything else, the paintings and sketches could one day turn out to be evidence in a court of law.

Only one little sketch remained. She couldn't bear to burn this one. It was a sketch she had made of Katie while they were staying in Italy for the painting of *The Virgin*. It captured her daughter at her angelic best. Her head was bent over a book. Her profile was the perfect representation of childish beauty: tiny nose, the soft contours of her round cheeks.

Serena could not burn this one. Not her own daughter's pretty face. Instead she tucked it into the family Bible.

*　　*　　*

Next morning Katie found her mother emptying the studio of the easel and paints.

'What are you doing, mummy?' she asked.

'I thought we would make this into a playroom,' she said. 'What do you think?' Katie was only too happy to go along with that. And with a dolls' house where her easel had once been, Serena felt much safer.

Chapter Fifty-Seven

$\mathscr{F}$ORTUNATELY for Nat Wilde, the potential embarrassment of the matter of the fakes that had been sold via his department was diluted by the dramatic news that a long-lost Ricasoli had suddenly resurfaced in London. The painting, known as *The Virgin Before the Annunciation*, had been revealed to the world by an anonymous Russian industrialist, who claimed to have found the picture in the attic of one of his houses in the Ukraine. Believing it to be a clever pastiche and worthless, he had brought it from his holiday home to hang on the wall in his London office. Upon discovering that it was a genuine Ricasoli, however, verified by tests at the most respectable laboratories, the industrialist set about tracking down the family who had owned the painting before it was looted by the Nazis. He had found just two surviving members of the family, an elderly brother and sister in Warsaw. But the poor Wasowskis were never to know of the change in their fortunes. They died in a house fire just twenty-four hours after the industrialist found out where they were living.

And so, at last, the authorities agreed that the lucky Russian would have the benefit of this incredible windfall. The painting was his. It was a real Ricasoli. He could tell the world. And he was free to sell it . . .

Belanov turned to Yasha Suscenko for advice on how to get the best price for *The Virgin*. An auction seemed the best idea, said Yasha. Indeed, as soon as the news of the painting's existence broke, every auction house in the world went into a frenzy as they tried to work out in whose hands the Ricasoli lay and how they could persuade him to consign his precious painting to them. Sotheby's or Christie's seemed like the obvious choice. Their Old Masters departments eagerly awaited the call. But Yasha had other ideas.

'Forget the big boys,' he told his client. 'Try Ludbrook's or Ehrenpreis. These little guys will give you a better deal on the seller's premium. Could save you millions.' Yasha knew that in reality, the big boys would cut Belanov a very good deal indeed but Belanov didn't question Yasha's wisdom on that point.

'What about the prestige?' asked Belanov. 'Marketing?'

'Nat Wilde and Carrie Klein are both pretty hot on that.'

'Are you sure? How will people know about the sale?'

'You don't need to worry about that,' Yasha told him. 'You're selling a Ricasoli. Serious collectors don't care about the auction house's name.'

Belanov nodded. He decided that Yasha was right. There was no danger that the painting wouldn't attract attention and he could drive a much harder bargain on fees if he decided to sell through a smaller house. Plus, if he was honest, there were other, more emotional reasons for wanting to avoid the traditional channels.

Though he was considered to be one of the most frightening men of his generation both in the boardroom and the back alley, the über-rich Russian had never quite shaken the insecurity of his upbringing. The eldest of six children, he had been raised by a single mother in conditions for which the word 'slum' was a little too generous. There had been no money for anything but the basics, and sometimes, not even for those. He left school as soon as he could and set to work to help provide for his youngest siblings. Fear of starvation had driven Belanov to take the first steps on the dodgy road that would eventually lead to his fortune.

However, though he would never say it to anyone, not even to his beloved wife, Belanov was intimidated by the cultured, over-educated people who thronged the European world of fine art. When he turned up to buy at auction, he often felt they were patronising him and his choices. That was why he now sent Yasha Suscenko to do his shopping for him. As they discussed the future of the Ricasoli, Belanov couldn't help remembering a woman he had met at one of the big houses and her condescending smile when he told her that he had recently purchased a painting by Jack Vettriano. 'Biscuit tin art,' was how she had referred to the picture of a dancing couple on a beach he liked so much. It didn't matter to him then that he could have bought the entire auction house and had change for an Aston Martin, her comment had left Belanov feeling humiliated. He knew he could never buy the sophistication and confidence that came from a childhood of privilege.

And so, by going with a smaller house, he would be giving the likes of that woman the finger. Belanov didn't have to follow tradition. He was part of the new order and he was going to do things his way. He decided he liked the way that Yasha was thinking.

'Try Ehrenpreis first,' he said. 'The Americans are less arrogant than the English.'

'I'll arrange for Carrie Klein to come and see the painting,' Yasha said.

Carrie Klein was not expecting to be asked to pitch to sell the Ricasoli. Like everyone else in the art world, she expected to next see it in a Sotheby's catalogue. So when the call came to visit the bank vault where the picture now lay in state, she was almost lost for words. She moved an afternoon full of meetings to be there at the earliest possible opportunity.

As she sat in the back of a taxi, wishing the traffic away, Carrie considered the momentous impact this painting could have on her career. She knew that despite her efforts, Ehrenpreis London was still at best the fifth house people thought of when they considered buying or selling at auction. This painting, lost for so many years, could change all that in a second. Like everyone else in her business, she had pored over the pictures in the papers. She had read the laboratory reports that had been circulated covertly between interested parties. She had read about the painting's history and seen copies of the documentation that confirmed its provenance, including the entry in an inventory of art claimed by the Nazis during the Second World War. As the taxi drew up outside the exclusive private bank, Carrie was almost breathless with anticipation. If she was asked to put a figure on how much she could sell it for, what could she say except, 'It's priceless.'

*   *   *

The owner's associate met Carrie in the plush waiting room. They exchanged few words while they waited to be escorted into the vault itself. They were frisked for weapons. Carrie's mobile phone and even her fountain pen were confiscated before they were allowed anywhere near the painting.

'In case you try to damage it,' said the Russian as Carrie handed over her Mont Blanc.

Carrie snorted. 'Sir, asking me to damage a Ricasoli would be like asking me to put a bullet in someone's head.'

The blank look she got in return suggested that her companion didn't think putting a bullet in someone's head was such a big deal.

At last, the painting was ready for them. The lights were harsh in the tiny room, which had walls thick enough to withstand nuclear Armageddon. There was nothing inside but the painting on an easel. It had been framed since its sojourn in Tuscany. That was frustrating to Carrie, who would have liked to have examined the edges of the canvas herself. But that could be done later if she decided to proceed.

'What do you think?' asked the owner's associate.

'It's wonderful,' Carrie confirmed. She didn't need to be an art expert to appreciate the first, visceral impact of the picture. The photographs she had seen did not do the painting justice. Even in the harsh artificial light of the vault, there was a luminous quality to the colours. They looked as fresh as if they had been painted that morning. And the subject had been rendered so exquisitely. Carrie could see the influence of Caravaggio in the Virgin's sumptuous gown and the expertly drawn fruit she held in her hand. Carrie held her loupe to her eye and leaned forward so that she could see the individual pips in the flesh of the fig. The individual hairs on the Virgin's head. Her lashes. The detail was exquisite. On the sea glimpsed through the window behind the Virgin's head, a small boat sailed. Its two sailors were clearly visible as they hauled in a net. With her magnifying glass, Carrie could even see the fish they caught.

'You think you can sell it?' the Russian interrupted Carrie's reverie.

'There's no doubt I know people who would like to buy it,' she replied.

'So, you going to tell me why my boss should let you be the one to put his Virgin up for auction.'

Carrie straightened up. She tapped the loupe against her bottom lip as she regarded the painting from a slight distance once more, taking in the overall effect, trying to tune in to something more important than her 'expert opinion' which took into account the paperwork and the lab results. She tried to tune in to her intuition.

Though it was almost two and a half years since she had unwittingly consigned that fake Constable, Carrie thought of the incident every time she looked at another painting she hoped to sell. Carrie had analysed her big mistake a thousand times and had come to the conclusion that she *had* known something was awry. She had suspected that the painting which ended up in her auction was not entirely what it should be but she had allowed herself to be convinced by the documents that accompanied it and, she finally admitted, become greedy to have such a big ticket item on her hands. The idea of the prestige associated with selling such a painting had drowned out Carrie's instinct that it wasn't the real thing. Since then, since the humiliation of being wrong, she had vowed never to distrust her instincts again.

This painting, this 'Ricasoli' was so beautiful. Its beauty alone would have made it worth consigning. But the attribution to such an important artist meant it was impossible for Carrie to take a risk. There was no way she could suggest to this particular owner that they presented the picture as 'from the studio of'. Something deep inside her was telling her that all was not right here. She couldn't put her finger on the problem. The provenance seemed to add up. The subject matter. The style. The lab results said it was old enough. And yet . . .

Carrie studied the face of the Virgin one more time. It had been painted with such care and love. Clearly, whoever captured that face had known it well but . . .

'I'm afraid I can't take this painting,' Carrie told the owner's representative.

The Russian was incredulous.

'Are you crazy?' he said. 'It's a Ricasoli. This could make your career.'

'I know,' said Carrie.

'So what's with your arrogance?'

'Not arrogance,' said Carrie. 'On the contrary, seeing this painting makes me feel rather humble.' She was grateful that she was able to couch her answer in business terms, rather than have to voice her rather nebulous doubts about the painting itself. 'The thing is, your boss wants consignment terms that are impossible for me to offer. I'm sure that the bigger houses like Christie's or Sotheby's would actually be happy to sell this painting at no cost to your employer at all, making all their money on the buyer's premium, but Ehren- preis is a very small house and we're unable to make such concessions. The cost of insuring such a painting while it is in our possession would be prohibitive. We don't have the necessary security infrastructure. I'm sure you understand.'

'I don't,' said the Russian.

'I'm sorry,' said Carrie. 'I apologise for having wasted your time.' She left the bank vault with her heart in her mouth, praying that she wasn't wrong.

Next it was the turn of Ludbrook's. Nat took Lizzy, of course. He didn't want to, but she was his deputy and something like this required a trustworthy second opinion.

Nat joked with the owner's representative in the private bank's waiting room.

'Trying to make sure she stays a virgin until the big day,' he commented on the decision to have the painting in a vault.

The Russian nodded.

'Right bundle of laughs,' Nat muttered as he and Lizzy followed the man into the vault.

The painting was back on its easel, all the more stunning for its rather plain surroundings.

Nat made a lot of fuss with his black-light and his loupe, though the black-light was pretty useless since security in the bank vault meant that the main lights could not be turned off. Lizzy smiled tightly as Nat ran through the spiel he had learned just that morning. He talked about Ricasoli as though he had known the man himself. Lizzy knew that Nat's encyclopaedic knowledge came from a page of notes typed up by Sarah Jane.

'Utterly typical of the man,' Nat pontificated. 'Figs were a popular motif. Of course they represent female sexuality of which Ricasoli was a great connoisseur.'

Lizzy frowned. She couldn't think of a single Ricasoli fig painting. But she let Nat rattle on. 'The artist was a veritable Casanova,' he continued. 'It's said that he left behind more children than paintings . . .'

'Can you sell it?' was the only question the Russian had to ask.

Nat leapt straight in with Ludbrook's terms and conditions. He had practically shaken hands on the deal when Lizzy drew him aside.

'Nat,' she said. 'I'm not quite sure about this. I want to go upstairs and talk about it.'

'What's your issue? The owner is a renowned collector.'

'What? We don't know who he is,' Lizzy pointed out.

'OK. But the provenance checks out. And it looks like one of Ricasoli's paintings to me. What exactly is your problem?'

'It's just a feeling,' whispered Lizzy. 'An instinct.'

'Ah, you girls and your instincts. I appreciate your integrity, my dear,' he said, with nothing 'dear' in his tone as he said it. 'But I do not want to lose the consignment of a century just because you've got your period. I say it's the real thing.'

'I'm not sure. I'm not willing to consign this painting.'

'Overruled,' said Nat.

'OK,' said Lizzy at last. There was little point arguing. And in any case, Nat's certainty made Lizzy's own convictions feel just a little unsteady. If she had prevented Nat from consigning a genuine painting by Giancarlo Ricasoli then she would never recover from the ignominy. If, on the other hand, the painting was eventually deemed to be a fake, it was off her conscience. Lizzy surprised herself with the Machiavellian nature of her calculation. Perhaps Nat's influence had rubbed off on her in more ways than one.

'OK. Let's tell him we'll take it,' Lizzy sighed. 'It could be the high point of your career.'

Having made the decision that the painting was real, Nat wasted no time. Guessing what concessions Christie's and

Sotheby's might have offered, not knowing that they hadn't even been asked to pitch, he offered at once to waive any consignment fee.

'We'll more than make up for it with the buyer's premium,' he said conspiratorially.

The deal was soon done.

Nat walked back into the Ludbrook's office with the swagger of a general returning from a successful campaign. The news that he had bagged the Ricasoli was around the building within minutes. Harry Brown stopped by Nat's office to congratulate him and suggest that they nip out for a quick glass of something to celebrate. Nat didn't refuse, though there was plenty of work to be done. He left that to the girls and boys in his office. Lizzy prepared a brief for the PR department who set to work alerting all the daily newspapers to the upcoming sale. Ordinarily, the PR department targeted the broadsheets, since their readership was most likely to be interested in something like fine art or sculpture, but the news that the painting would almost certainly fetch more than fifty million made it something that all the papers would write about. Even if the *Express*, the *Sun* and the *Daily Mail* accompanied the news with headlines like, 'Is this painting really worth fifty mill?' or 'Old painting that costs more than a hospital. Has the world gone mad?'

'Yes,' thought Lizzy. The world has gone mad. But it had been mad for a long time. She was increasingly aware of the difference in the lives between those people who consigned or bought items worth millions of dollars through her auction house and the lives of the average Londoner. During the day, Lizzy routinely tucked paintings worth a couple of hundred grand under her arm and walked around the building with them as though they were just pieces of canvas and wood. Which in a way they were, if you thought about it. In the evenings she scoured the property pages of the *Evening Standard* and wondered how easy it would be to commute from Scotland to Mayfair on a daily basis. Because that's what she expected to have to do if she ever wanted to have her own place.

Lizzy wanted more. The time had come for her to step out of Nat's shadow. She knew that. But how was she going to be able to do it? She didn't think Nat would write her a glowing reference if she tried to move to another house. Since Lizzy blew the whistle about the fake Victorian paintings, Nat had been remarkably civil. To all intents and purposes, they seemed to have reached a détente. But she had a feeling that underneath the pretence that everything was as it should be – they just weren't sleeping together any more – Nat must be planning some kind of payback.

At the end of the day, one of the girls from PR dropped by Lizzy's office and handed her a sheet outlining her plans for promoting *The Virgin*.

'I've sent you a copy via email,' the girl explained. 'But I thought I better print one out for Nat.' She rolled her eyes. Nat was a dinosaur when it came to in-house correspondence. He liked to have everything printed out. It made Lizzy wonder for a second whether he had printed out the cheeky emails she sent him back when he was still interested in seeing her out of hours.

'This is going to be super-easy,' the PR continued. 'The *Telegraph* and *The Times* have already confirmed that they'd like to run the piece. They were wondering if it would be possible to get a better picture, though.'

'I'll get on to that,' said Lizzy. 'I think our photographer is going to take pictures for the catalogue tomorrow morning.'

'Cool,' said the PR. 'This is going to be one hell of a sale.'

While the hard work was going on without him, Nat spent the afternoon at his club with Harry. They had both been members there for many years and loudly appreciated the fact that it was still possible to find a place that wasn't overrun with women. Much as they both appreciated women, they were incredibly reactionary when it came to what they thought women could and should do. Or be seen doing. Drinking the afternoon away was not on Nat and Harry's list of ladylike activities.

'Congratulations, old chum,' said Harry again. Considering he spent so much of his life raising glasses in a toast, he didn't have much of a repertoire. Congratulations. Cheers. Bottoms up. That was about the extent of it. Still Nat was very happy to be toasted, however inexpertly.

'They went to Ehrenpreis before us? Can you believe that? Still, she obviously didn't do much of a job of it,' said Nat. 'She' being Carrie Klein. 'They were about ready to bite my hand off when I started to offer them terms. They know a real expert when they see one.'

'They certainly do,' said Harry. 'What do you think of this claret? A little musty, I believe. I think we should upgrade. Is this on your account or mine?'

Harry called over the nearest waiter and requested a bottle of something twice as expensive as the one they were working their way through. This was how afternoons with Nat and Harry always proceeded. They started out fairly modestly. Sometimes even the house claret. But with each bottle they upped the ante, until they were drinking the kind of wines that most people save for eightieth birthday parties and wedding anniversaries, not for a Tuesday evening after work.

'So,' said Harry. 'How has it been going with that Lizzy girl? I must say, Nat, after your candid camera moment in the lift, I thought you were toast. I thought, he's done it now. He's stuck his pecker in the wrong pie. Lizzy Duffy is going to take him down. But she didn't . . .' Harry added with a slightly puzzled look on his face.

'She tried,' said Nat. 'You don't really think it was any coincidence that I got called into John's office about those stupid Victorian watercolours again? I'm sure that won't be the last time she pulls a stunt like that. I've got to get her out of my hair.'

'How are you going to do that? It's bloody hard to sack someone these days, Nat. She could be here till she dies.'

'If that's what it takes,' said Nat, grimly.

Harry straightened up in his armchair. It wasn't easy. The chair had cradled many distinguished bottoms over the years and had the consistency of blancmange. Once someone settled into it, they were generally there until one of the club staff tipped them out of it at home time.

'Nat, you're not . . .'

'Of course I'm not,' said Nat. 'It was a figure of speech. But trust me, I am keeping a close eye on Lizzy Duffy and I predict it won't be long before she makes a mistake . . .'

Relieved that Nat wasn't really considering murder as an answer to the Lizzy problem, Harry sank back into the warm and welcoming cushions of his wing chair and took another glug of wine.

'This is OK,' he said.

'Bloody should be,' said Nat. 'It's seven hundred pounds a bottle.'

'Yes,' said Harry. 'But imagine how much you would have to pay for this retail!'

They contemplated the horror for a second or two. Harry never paid retail for wine.

'So,' said Harry. 'About those fake Victorians. Do you think you've heard the last of that?'

Nat nodded. 'Oh yes,' he said. 'I don't think there will be any more developments on that front. I'll soon have everything sorted out.'

Chapter Fifty-Eight

A WEEK after her late night visit from the police, Serena still jumped out of her skin every time the doorbell rang or her mobile chirruped to let her know she had a message. She tried to convince herself that the fact that Julian hadn't been in touch was good news. It meant either that nothing was wrong after all or that the police had tracked him down but their enquiries had not led them back in Serena's direction. But it was tough to stay optimistic and when she received a call from a landline she didn't recognise – a London number – she immediately assumed the worst.

'You sound terrible,' said her old friend Jane. 'Are you expecting bad news? Well, if you want some, I've got some. My bloody husband has been having an affair. I found three orders from Moyses Stevens on his credit card bill. I'm at the Berkeley Hotel. I need you here at once.'

Fortunately for Jane, it was one of those rare weekends when Tom was actually doing his fatherly duty and Serena could get away. The following day Serena travelled up to London with Katie on the train and did the handover at Paddington Station. Katie had spent much of the journey up complaining that she didn't want to spend time with her father and his new girlfriend so Serena was glad to see that she was in the end easily distracted by promises of a trip on the London Eye and lots of ice cream.

Serena took the Tube to the hotel, where she found Jane lounging by the pool, a bottle of champagne chilling in a bucket beside her. She was sparing no expense on her emergency therapy and thankfully it seemed to be working.

'Is there no hope you two can patch things up?' Serena asked.

'Of course there is,' said Jane. In truth, Jane had little evidence of an affair but the appearance of that florist on his Amex bill and she had yet to give him a chance to explain that away. 'He's been calling every three minutes. I'll go home tomorrow night but I want this little mini-break of mine to be a shot across his bows and remind him how painful it's going to be if I ask for a divorce.'

Serena was glad to see her friend on relatively good form. She had expected a twenty-four-hour nightmare of sobbing but Jane wasn't having that. She didn't want to talk about it. There was nothing to do except be pampered and read the papers. That was how Serena discovered the terrible news . . .

'Oh my God,' she couldn't help but exclaim.

'What's up?' Jane looked up from behind a copy of *Vogue*. 'Someone you know die?'

It was far worse than that but Serena couldn't possibly explain so to Jane right at that moment. Instead, she winged it.

'I was just looking at this picture of Cate Blanchett in Cannes. She's thin as a rake. Can't believe she ever had a baby.'

Jane tutted. 'Perhaps she didn't. I heard about one Hollywood star who went around with a strap on bump while a surrogate carried her child. Baby's born. A week later the star's tum is flat as an ironing-board – of course – and she's promoting a post-baby diet book. It's an absolute scandal. Then our bloody husbands expect us to keep up.'

Serena was glad to let Jane rant on about the unfairness of it all while she let the news sink in.

'I've come to take you for your massage,' a fresh-faced beautician interrupted.

'See you later,' Jane said and left Serena alone by the pool. Serena picked up the colour supplement again and read the article more closely this time. It wasn't possible. Yasha had promised this would never happen. At least not in her lifetime. But there it was in full colour.

'Ludbrook's the auctioneer have consigned a previously lost work by Ricasoli for their forthcoming Old Masters sale.'

Serena stared at the tiny photograph. It was too small to be one hundred per cent certain but something inside her, almost a parental instinct, told her that the painting in that photo was not a Ricasoli original.

Jane emerged from her treatment looking pink and slightly breathless.

'I've got to go,' Serena told her. 'Something urgent.'

'What? Now? What's happened? Has something happened to Katie?'

Serena crossed her fingers behind her back as she told her big lie. 'Yes. Tom's bloody cow of a girlfriend has come down with shingles and he doesn't think Katie should be around her.'

'Katie's had chicken pox, hasn't she?' said Jane.

'Yes. I know. But I suppose that stupid bitch doesn't want Tom's attention to be diverted in any way. I'm going to pick Katie up and take her home. I don't want her to be where she's not welcome.'

Jane bristled. 'Tom's her father, Serena. You've got to tell him to step up and take his responsibility towards his daughter seriously. He can't keep off-loading her like this. I swear, Serena, if I were you I would have told him you're staying here all week. This is the first time he's had Katie to stay in months.'

'I know,' said Serena, looking at the floor, fearing that if she looked up, Jane would see she was lying. She almost felt wicked for maligning Tom when, for once, he didn't deserve it. But she had to get away and she didn't want Jane to come with her.

'I'll come with you,' said Jane. 'You and Katie can stay with me for a couple of days then, when Madam is feeling a little better, you can send Katie back to Tom and we'll finish this spa break.'

'No,' said Serena. 'You'll lose what you spent on this weekend.'

'It's not my money,' Jane reminded her with a grin.

'I really don't want you to cut short your weekend for me.'

Jane narrowed her eyes. 'You know,' she said. 'If I didn't know you better, I might think that you were hiding something from me.'

Oh God, thought Serena. Here we go. It was all going to come out. But Serena couldn't let it come out. Much as she loved Jane, she knew that her friend was an impossibly awful gossip. She had never before managed to keep a secret on

Serena's behalf for anything longer than five minutes. And this was a secret that just could not be allowed to escape. Serena's stomach lurched as she thought of the painting she had created in an attic in Italy being pored over by world-renowned art experts and put up for sale with an estimated price in the tens of millions. If it got out that the painting was a fake, then heads would roll. Literally, she had no doubt.

'OK. I was lying about the shingles.'

'Whatever for?'

'I can't tell you.'

'Why are you being so weird. Come on,' Jane gave her a friendly prod in the stomach. 'You can tell me. It's a man, isn't it? You're sneaking off to see a man.'

Serena found herself nodding. This was the path of least resistance. She would let Jane make all the inferences.

'You've been seeing someone, you sneaky cow. Why didn't you tell me? I'm supposed to be your friend.' Jane looked thoughtful for a moment. 'Oh God. It can only mean one thing. He's married, isn't he? Serena, tell me you're not the girl who's been fucking my husband?'

'Christ, no,' Serena jumped in. 'Jane, I would *never* do that to you. But yes, it is a man. And yes, the situation is very complicated.'

'Complicated!' Jane spat. 'I can't believe you would do that to some other girl after what you and I have been through.'

Serena hung her head. Jane should have known that Serena would never, never sleep with another woman's husband. Especially after what she had been through with Tom and bloody Donna. But right then all she needed was to get away and if the only means of achieving that without having to tell Jane the whole story was to leave Jane thinking the worst of her, then Serena would do it.

'God, Serena,' Jane continued. 'I would have thought you had more sense. And compassion. What did he tell you? That their marriage is dead except on paper? That they haven't slept together in years? I hope you're listening well because that's exactly what Tom said to Donna and it's what your new man will be saying to the next sucker about you in a few short months, if not weeks.'

'Jane,' Serena interrupted. 'I can't talk about it now. I will explain everything one day, I promise. You have to believe that I'm the person I always was and I would never do anything to betray our friendship.'

Jane harrumphed. 'Whatever,' she said, dismissing Serena with a flick of her wrist.

Leaving the Berkeley Hotel spa without even drying her hair, Serena jumped into a taxi and headed for Mayfair. She had to find Yasha.

Yasha wasn't at his gallery and the girl on the front desk was understandably reluctant to let a very wild-looking Serena know where he might be. But Serena didn't have to look far. As she walked back out of the gallery she caught sight of him sitting outside a café a little further down, reading the very supplement in which she had discovered his betrayal.

'My driver needs paying,' she said, slapping down her copy of the newspaper on the table in front of him.

'Serena?' Yasha was surprised. 'This is an unexpected pleasure.'

'This is not a pleasure trip,' said Serena. 'I'm out of cash. I would be grateful if you could pay the cabbie and then you and I can get out of here and have a conversation.'

Yasha did as he was told.

'What is this about?'

'Middle pages.'

Yasha opened the paper. 'Ah yes.'

'Is that all you're going to say?'

'Let's go for a walk,' he suggested, leaving a little pile of change on the table for the waitress. 'I don't think we want to be overheard, do you?'

Chapter Fifty-Nine

T HEY walked from the café to Hyde Park. It was a beautiful afternoon and the park was full of people eager to enjoy the sunshine. This was London after all. Any sunny day might be the last till the next year.

Yasha and Serena walked close, talking quietly so as not to be overheard. From a distance, they might have looked like lovers, but their conversation had no loving tone.

'You knew about this?'

'Of course I did,' said Yasha. 'I set up the auction. And in due time I was going to let you know. I didn't realise that Ludbrook's would let the news slip quite so early. But why are you so worried?'

'Come on,' Serena frowned. 'Because this is not the real painting.'

'Of course it is.'

'Yasha, I know. It isn't. I just know.'

'What? You think that Ludbrook's would consign a fake?'

'I know that Ludbrook's would consign a fake!'

'Not at this level. Or do you think my client would try to pull the wool over everyone's eyes by giving Ludbrook's the fake once they'd consigned it?'

'That's what it looks like to me. You can't let it happen,' said Serena.

'So what if it isn't the real thing? What am I supposed to do?'

'Tell someone. If you don't, I'm going to go to the police.'

'Why would you do that?'

'Because they'll find out. And it will get back to me. I'll tell them that I was coerced.'

'But how would it ever be traced back to you?' Yasha asked. 'I promised you I would keep you safe from any repercussions and I will. Don't go to the police. You have no idea who you're up against and everyone says they were coerced. You'll go to jail, my darling.'

'Don't call me darling.'

'You'll go to jail and you'll lose your daughter. And where will she go? You've already told me that it's hard to persuade your ex-husband to have her for a whole weekend. Do you think his new girlfriend is going to want Katie in their lives on a permanent basis? She'll end up in foster care. Maybe a children's home. It's no place for a young girl. For any young child.'

'That wouldn't happen,' said Serena. But she thought about the options. If Tom really didn't step up then where could Katie go? Serena's mother was months away from needing to go into a care home. Would her brother be willing to offer a home to his niece?

Serena began to cry. Yasha stopped walking and pulled her to sit down on the grass beside him.

'I'm sorry. I'm sorry,' he said. 'I didn't mean to sound so harsh. Look. So what if the painting is yours? There's no reason why you should worry at all. In fact, I think you should be very pleased with yourself. You convinced some of the world's most highly respected art experts. Apparently any one of the big auction houses would have been happy to take it on. I told you it's a great painting, Serena. Here's your proof.'

'It won't last,' said Serena. 'Someone will question it's authenticity again at some point and then . . .'

'It won't happen,' said Yasha. 'No one wants to hear it. Too many people would end up red-faced. The painting will sell. Probably for way more than its estimate. And then we won't hear of it again for years. Paintings like this don't keep turning up at auction. And even if it did, every time it is sold, it gets that little bit harder to trace it back to us.'

'Yasha, the thing is, I think someone is on to Julian and me. The police came looking for him at my place. And well . . .'

'It could have been about anything.'

'No. I don't think so. They were from the Met's department of art and antiques. I tried to raise Julian afterwards but he didn't return my calls.'

'But they haven't come back for you? Then it's fine.'

Serena bit her lip. She was on the point of telling Yasha about the pictures she had taken on her phone and sent to her former lover. If Julian was wanted in connection with their forgeries then wasn't it likely that someone would seize his phone and see the evidence?

'I'm just so worried,' she said without elaborating.

'Serena,' Yasha promised. 'I will deal with this. You are safe, I swear to you. I will keep you safe. No one will ever find out that you painted *The Virgin*. As for Julian Trebarwen, the only thing you can do is keep your mouth shut. I very much doubt that this is about the paintings you did for him. He's not an honest man, Serena. I can think of a thousand reasons why the police might want to question him.'

Serena's brow wrinkled.

'I promise you,' said Yasha. 'That so long as you let me handle this, and follow my instructions, everything will be fine. Now, I want you to carry on as normal. Forget about Julian Trebarwen. Whatever you do, don't call him. You haven't called him, have you?'

Serena shook her head. That call from the box in the centre of Trelawney village didn't count, did it? She hadn't got through.

'Good,' said Yasha. 'Keep up the radio silence. The less ways there are for anyone to link you to that loser the better.'

Serena shook her head. She had to tell him about the photographs she had taken and forwarded. Then he would realise how serious the situation could be. If Julian was fingered by Ludbrook's for the other paintings then Serena couldn't be sure that he wouldn't use those photos of the Ricasoli to get himself out of a hole. But she didn't have a chance. Suddenly, Yasha gathered her into his arms. Being held like this, she felt for a moment that Yasha really might be able to protect her. She had missed the feeling of a man's arms around her like this. She couldn't remember when Tom had stopped trying to comfort her physically whenever she was worried. She breathed in the warm scent of Yasha's chest. His clean blue shirt.

Yasha kissed her gently on the top of her head. Serena found herself turning her face towards him quite instinctively. Their eyes met. A smile softened the corners of his.

'I'm glad you came to find me,' he said. 'I'm sorry it was only because you were scared. I have thought about you often.'

Slowly, but inevitably, their mouths moved closer and soon they were kissing.

'Come on,' said Yasha, finishing the kiss and holding her hand. 'I'll look after you. Come with me.'

They went back to his house. Yasha led Serena by the hand up the stairs to his bedroom. She didn't resist. This was the culmination of a long-held desire for both of them.

It was the last thing Serena had expected and yet it felt so natural. This was what should have happened that night in Italy, when, with a glass of wine inside and an empty kitchen table between them, she almost felt brave enough to touch him.

The smell of Yasha's skin was so delicious to her. Absolutely right. She fingered his face tenderly and smiled as he returned the gesture. She loved the way he almost hummed with pleasure when she touched him as he wanted to be touched. His approval both reassured her and turned her on.

'I'm so sorry,' said Serena. 'I came straight from the spa. I must look a mess.'

'You look beautiful,' Yasha told her. The way he gazed at her told her he was telling his truth and as a result she started to feel beautiful, not worrying about what Yasha would find beneath the shirt and jeans she had pulled on that morning in the darkness of her farmhouse in Cornwall as she hurried to catch the early train.

Under Yasha's gaze, Serena glowed. As he unbuttoned her shirt, she swayed towards him as though entranced. His hands roamed her neck and her shoulders. When she was naked from the waist up, he lay one palm flat on her breastbone as though feeling for her heart. It was racing.

Serena pressed her own hands against Yasha's broad chest. He was wearing a silky soft blue shirt that she remembered from Italy. Closing her eyes she could picture him back there, standing in the garden as she watched from the window.

'I watched you take this shirt off and dive into the pool and do twenty laps,' she said.

Yasha blushed. 'I watched you swimming too. Early in the morning when everyone else was still asleep.'

The memory of the way they had circled each other for those three weeks only intensified what Serena was feeling now. She could recall how he had looked so well and now she was touching him. The hair on his chest felt rough beneath her fingers. Comfortingly masculine like the taut muscles beneath.

Pulling Yasha close, so that their naked torsos were pressed together, Serena slid her hands around to his back. She smoothed her palms across his shoulder blades and down towards his waist. Then she followed the curve of his belt around to the buckle and started to work it free.

Yasha helped her out of her own jeans and once she was completely undressed, lifted her off her feet and placed her gently in the centre of the bed.

If sleeping with Julian had reminded Serena what it felt like to lust after someone, then going to bed with Yasha reminded her of the real meaning of 'making love'. Yasha didn't take his eyes off hers, ensuring Serena that it wasn't just her body he wanted to connect with.

Yasha's hands were warm and soft as they followed the contours of her body. He murmured his approval of her smooth skin. He placed a kiss on each of her nipples and a whole line of them connecting the notch at her throat to her belly button. He rested for a moment with his head on her stomach.

'I want you,' she said.

'I want you too.'

But he wouldn't let her have him. Not quite yet. Instead he teased her with more fluttering kisses across her body and down to the place where her hips met her pubic bone. Feeling his hot breath on her pubis, she sighed at the exquisite agony of wanting what he wouldn't yet give her. She felt herself arch towards his mouth.

When finally he entered her, his long hard shaft encountering no resistance from her waiting body, Serena wanted to cry. She held his head in her hands as he moved inside her. She kissed his face. He kept his eyes on hers.

When he came he begged her to hold him. She wrapped her arms tightly around him, holding him so close.

Afterwards, they slept for what seemed like hours. Serena felt safe in his arms. When they woke, the sky outside was dark. They turned to face each other and murmured their happiness.

They were interrupted by Yasha's phone.

'I have to go out,' said Yasha as he frowned at a text.

Serena put her arm across his body. 'Are you sure?'

'I'm sorry.' He got out of the bed and began searching for the clothes he had discarded.

'Shall I wait here?' Serena asked hopefully.

'Look. The more I think about it, the more I think you're right. We need to be more careful. You need to stay away from me. At least until all this is concluded. You should leave now. Go back to Cornwall. Keep your head down and don't answer questions. Never talk about the Ricasoli. Never mention my name. If anything should go wrong, I don't want you to be connected to me in any way. It's safest like that.'

'But . . .' Serena didn't want to be disconnected from Yasha. Not now.

'It's the safest way,' Yasha insisted. 'You have no idea how vengeful my client can be.'

Yasha picked up Serena's jeans from the floor and handed them to her. 'I have to meet someone in my office. You need to go now.'

'You're serious.'

'I'm afraid so.'

Later that night, Serena found herself in a hotel in Earls Court. There was no point going back to Cornwall when she had to pick Katie up the following day. She didn't want to go back to the Berkeley and face Jane's questions. So she booked into the kind of hotel that made backpackers wonder why they ever left Bondi, and cried. Much as she wanted to believe Yasha's insistence that they had to stay apart for her safety, she couldn't help wondering if he simply didn't want her to stay the night.

Chapter Sixty

$\mathcal{S}$ ERENA wasn't the only person surprised by the news that *The Virgin* was up for auction. Yasha hadn't seen Julian Trebarwen face to face since that night in Cornwall. But as soon as the sale of *The Virgin* was announced, Trebarwen was on Yasha's doorstep, large as life and twice as ugly. He looked as though he hadn't slept in a week. He was sporting a scruffy beard and exuded alcohol fumes as though he had been marinating in whisky.

'You look tired,' said Yasha. 'So I suppose you ought to sit down. Now what is this about?'

'As if you don't know. I see you're selling *The Virgin* through Ludbrook's.'

'Not me,' said Yasha. 'It's not my picture.'

'But you commissioned it. You know it's a fake.'

'Don't be ridiculous. You think Ludbrook's would consign a fake?'

Julian snorted.

'It's real,' said Yasha. He assumed that Julian was bluffing. How could he know that the painting Ludbrook's would be selling wasn't genuine? Nat Wilde hadn't been able to tell.

'Prove it.'

'And if I can't? What are you going to do about it?'

'That depends on what you can do for me. Tell your client I need a million. I've got to get away.'

'A million in exchange for what?'

'My silence. And these.' He brought an envelope out of his pocket. It contained a series of grainy print-outs, pictures of Serena working on the painting. 'She sent them to my mobile phone, which is currently in a bank vault.'

'Is this blackmail?' asked Yasha.

'If that's what you want to call it. One million for my old phone's SIM card and you'll never see me again.'

Yasha shook his head. 'Trust me, Julian. It's really not a good idea to talk to anyone about this. There is no question of you making any money out of this situation. It's simply not going to happen. But should you choose to make things difficult, then the cost to you could be far greater than you could ever imagine.'

The two men stared at each other across the desk. Julian's hard-man act was let down by the shakes that were a symptom of alcohol withdrawal.

'I need the money.'

'You need to take a bath and go to bed.'

'I'll tell the police everything about you and Serena and Italy.'

'What is it with you people, thinking that's the worst you can threaten me with? You need to keep your mouth shut, Mr Trebarwen.'

'Get me a plane ticket. Five hundred grand.'

'You're dreaming.'

'You need to make sure I keep the fake a secret. That's worth at least a hundred.'

'Take me to the vault.' Yasha sighed.

Chapter Sixty-One

ONTRARY to Yasha's predictions the police were back, and very quickly. Less than a week after she left Yasha's bed, they were on Serena's doorstep again. Different officers. In Uniform. And this time they did ask to come in.

'Is your daughter here?' asked DC Arnold.

'She's with her father in London,' said Serena.

'That's a good thing,' he nodded. 'Mrs Macdonald, I'm afraid we're going to have to ask you to come with us into Truro. For questioning.'

It was worse than Serena could ever have imagined. Julian Trebarwen had been found at last. But he was dead. He'd been discovered floating face down in the Thames. Of course, the circumstances were suspicious, given the fact that the police were already keen to question him in connection with a series of fakes. Suicide was what they thought at first. It was a possibility but not much of one. He'd been found with a bloody nose that the forensic scientists soon decided was not due to the impact of a fall from a bridge. He'd almost certainly been punched in the face before he took his dive.

A yellow police board was placed on Hammersmith Bridge, asking members of the public whether they had seen anything suspicious on the night Julian went into the drink. So far no one had called the hotline.

'I don't understand,' said Serena, feeling her body temperature rise quite uncomfortably. 'What has all this got to do with me? I told you I met him once, at his mother's funeral. Oh, and he came round for some milk one night after that but that's all. Why have you brought me in here?'

The older policeman gave her a wan smile. 'Because shortly after two officers paid you a visit to enquire about his whereabouts – that very night, in fact – you used your credit card to place a call to Julian Trebarwen's mobile from the call box in Old Trelawney.'

Oh God. She was finished. Julian Trebarwen had been murdered and the police knew for certain that she had been closer to the dead man than she claimed. There was no way to save her skin but to tell the truth about the paintings and hope that they would believe she had been coerced into collaborating with him. She just had to make them believe that she would not have murdered him. Surely, she thought, they couldn't consider her a murder suspect? Julian was a good five stone heavier than she was. She could never have pitched him over the side of Hammersmith Bridge and into the Thames. Though she knew someone who did have the strength. She thought of Yasha and Leonid with his arms as big as thighs.

'We need to know everything about your involvement with Julian Trebarwen. We need to know everything he ever told you. You might hold the key to the mystery of who killed him.'

Thank God Katie was with her father that weekend, Serena thought as she watched the countryside stream by en route to the main station in Truro.

'I think I'd like to have a solicitor present,' she said to the officer sitting in the back of the car with her.

And so a solicitor was called and Serena found herself in the type of room she had only ever seen on television. It was a dark room, painted a shade of green that had probably been proven to calm the criminal mind. No decoration. Just a table and four chairs. One for her, one for her lawyer and one each for the two police officers conducting the interview. DC Arnold placed a recording machine in front of Serena and adjusted the microphone.

She was brought hot tea and biscuits. She didn't touch them. How could she eat right them? Every minute that passed intensified the horror. Julian was dead and Serena was going to have to put her own head in the noose to absolve herself of any suspicion.

She weighed a fast way out of the interview room against the possible cost of implicating Yasha. If she sent the police to his door, would she be the next to die? His promise to "take care" of her took on a sinister tone.

At last the solicitor, a woman, arrived. She seemed terribly young but was reassuringly matter of fact. She assured Serena that there was nothing to fear. All she had to do was explain where she'd been when Julian Trebarwen died.

'Julian and I were lovers,' Serena confirmed as the tape began to roll.

*　　*　　*

Despite her worst fears, Serena was back at home in her own bed that night. The interview had not gone as she expected. The first question DC Arnold asked was whether Serena was aware that Julian had also been seeing a girl called Annabel? It was clear that DC Arnold hoped for an explanation as simple as a woman scorned. The paintings did not come up. And Serena decided against offering the information. Julian was dead. She couldn't bring him back with a confession of fraud. She was released without charge, though told to keep the police appraised of her whereabouts. But the landscape of her world had been irrevocably changed. She knew that much. She would have to tell Tom, because, if she didn't and her being questioned under caution came to the attention of his lawyer at a later time, it could present problems with the divorce. Serena had to get her side of the story to Tom first and make sure he knew that Katie had never been in any danger. Serena could almost convince herself that was true. But it wasn't how she really felt.

Someone had taken Julian's life. Someone had got angry enough to beat Julian to a pulp and then throw him into the river. Was he unconscious when it happened? Serena wondered. Did he try to swim to the shore? Was he already dead when he hit the water? Serena hoped so. The mythology of death said that drowning was a nice way to go but Serena had never believed that. Just thinking about it made her heart begin to pound. She imagined the muddy water of the Thames in her own nostrils, filling her lungs. She could almost feel that burning sensation that comes with inhaling liquid. How could breathing in water make you feel like you were on fire?

There was only one explanation. Apart from Yasha and his associates, Julian was the only person who knew that

Priceless

Serena was the artist behind a painting that was about to go on sale for millions. What more motive did anyone need to get rid of him? Was this what Yasha had meant when he promised to 'sort things out'?

Chapter Sixty-Two

MATHIEU Randon was in his apartment in the 16th arondissement of Paris. He'd just finished a very simple dinner. Plainly cooked lamb chops and boiled potatoes, water instead of wine, of course. And now he had retired for a moment of quiet contemplation. He chose his library, as he always had done when he wanted a moment to himself, though these days the only book he read was the Bible. Many of the others in his collection had been burned in the huge stone fireplace flanked by his favourite reading chair and another chair that was always empty.

That night, however, Randon was not reading. Instead he sat in his chair and stared into the empty grate. It was too warm for a fire. And yet he thought he could see some kind of light there. He stared without focusing.

What was real and what was not? Since Randon had awoken from his coma the dark-eyed girl had been trying to tell

Randon something important. He'd assumed she was a messenger sent from God. Now he realised with sickening clarity that the woman he thought was an angel was merely a shard of the shattered glass globe that was his memory.

Getting up, he crossed the room to his desk and opened a locked drawer. He brought out the jiffy bag of items that Carrie had brought to him at Claridge's. Looking at the three locks of hair he remembered everything. Worse still, as the memories became clearer he reacted in the way he used to. That anguished look still excited him. It made him hard.

Oh God. He slammed shut the drawer and turned to his rosary. He needed to know what to do next. He prayed for God to give him guidance.

He had his driver take him to the Domaine Randon office on the Champs-Elysées. The building was empty but for a security guard. Randon locked himself into his office and spent the night reading and rereading all the press cuttings on Domaine Randon from the period he spent in a coma. There was a lot about one man in particular: Axel Delaflote. The young man was one of the people Randon didn't remember so well but Bellette had explained that Delaflote had risen very suddenly through the ranks to head up Maison Randon. His fall was equally sudden, unexpected and dramatic, resulting as it did not from a professional mistake but from a murder charge.

'Is this the face of a serial killer?' asked the newspapers. Axel Delaflote looked out, wide eyes and white cheeks, stricken. He had claimed that he had nothing to do with the murders of two young prostitutes but his card had been found in the handbag of one of them. He had been seen leaving a hotel with the other on the night of her death. His DNA was found on her body. That was more than enough for the jury.

Randon knew what he would see when he turned the page. It was the face of his angel. Gina Busiri. A prostitute from London. Twenty-two years old when she died. Beside her a French girl, Odette. Dark-haired, dark-eyed. Could have been Gina's sister. In the photograph she was wearing a heart-shaped locket.

For a short while, Randon tried to convince himself that it was coincidence. He must have heard about the murder of these girls before he went into his coma. His doctor had warned him that real memories could and would get mixed up with things he had seen on television or read. It happened often. Sometimes people recovering from a head injury would start to talk about past lives in incredibly convincing detail, only to discover that their former life as an Egyptian princess was actually based on a diorama they'd seen on a childhood visit to a museum. But the mementos from the inro suggested that Randon's memories were very real. It was practically impossible that Axel Delaflote could have gained access to Randon's erotic collection and hidden the jewellery and hair in the little Japanese box himself. There really was only one good explanation.

And lately, in the past few days, the 'visions' had been getting clearer. And now he knew that the house by the river was not where he should set his retreat but a place he had once hired for the weekend to host a grand party for the launch of a new clothing line. The girl had been at the party. Randon had asked Axel Delaflote to arrange for several girls to be brought out to the country from Paris. And this was the one that Randon had chosen for himself. He had fucked her in a boathouse at the bottom of the house's sweeping lawn, taking her from behind so that he didn't have to look at her eyes. And then he had ended her life. He'd rolled her body into the water and said nothing more about it. No one asked. The party was full of people who shouldn't have been there doing things that could send them to jail. Randon had learned early in his career that encouraging people to act upon their basest desires could buy their complicity. Providing a busload of prostitutes and enough drugs to kill a horse guaranteed it.

Randon shuddered as he thought of that girl. Her family. He had taken her life as easily as he had given Bellette a job. He had assumed she didn't matter but she must have mattered to someone. It had all been a game to him. A compulsion he gave into like some people gave in to an extra cookie. He must have known that no one would come looking for him. They didn't dare. Even if he had been a suspect, Randon held too many secrets for powerful men.

It crossed Randon's mind that he himself might have set Axel up to take his fall. Whatever the real story was, an innocent man was in prison and Randon held the key to his escape.

But God's instructions were not forthcoming in anything like as clear a fashion as Randon had hoped for.

Obviously, no one was looking for him with regard to the deaths of those women. The police had long since put their suspect in jail. As far as they were concerned the case was closed. They wouldn't be in any hurry to reopen it. Apart from Carrie Klein, no one knew about the mementos inside the inro. There was no reason why Carrie should start to question their origin. Gina and Odette were long dead and so was their story.

And Randon knew what would happen if he gave himself up. With two murders, possibly three, to confess to, he would go straight into custody. That was OK. It was right and proper. His due. His penance. But Randon had so much work to do before he could let that happen. If he went to prison now, his dream of building a church fit to glorify his god would be over. His property would be impounded. His bank accounts frozen. He had to find the land he needed and hand the money over to a serious group of believers who could complete his mission first.

'I am sorry, Monsieur Delaflote,' he said to the young man in the photograph. 'It seems you must have been in the wrong place at the wrong time. I will get you out of your predicament, but first, God's work is to be done.'

Randon took the file containing cuttings regarding Axel Delaflote with him back to his apartment. There he put the file inside the safety box with Gina's glossy hair and Odette's necklace and locked it with the combination that only he knew. He crossed himself as he heard the bolts slide into place.

'Forgive me,' he prayed. To his god. To the girls.

Chapter Sixty-Three

$\mathcal{I}$N the run-up to the sale of *The Virgin*, the staff in the Old Masters department at Ludbrook's were working flat out, liaising with potential buyers and arranging last-minute private viewings for the kind of people who had shopping lists that read: Chelsea mansion, football team, priceless Renaissance painting. People flew in from all over the world to look at the most extraordinary painting to be offered for sale in a century. One Russian tried to stop the painting from going to auction at all, by offering a million over the high estimate if he could take the picture away with him right then.

The day before the sale, Carrie Klein decided she had to see *The Virgin* one more time. She slipped into the Ludbrook's gallery unnoticed, wearing a pair of big dark glasses and a Ferragamo scarf over her hair. It was a rudimentary but very effective disguise.

The painting was torturing her. It haunted her waking hours and her dreams. Nat Wilde was gaining so much publicity for its upcoming sale. It drove her nuts to see him quoted in all the papers. Especially since the attention could all have been on her. She wanted to reassure herself that she had made the right choice, in telling its owner that she couldn't agree with its attribution. There was something not quite right about it.

If the painting were real, however, that would be equally tragic. The estimated price for this painting would almost certainly mean that it would end up in the hands of a private collector and be lost from public view for decades. A number of museum curators had expressed their interest, but none had the means to save the painting for their nation. None at all. The annual acquisition budget of all the museums combined would not stretch to the amount of money Ludbrook's hoped to bring in with this single sale.

Carrie positioned herself in front of the painting. It was late in the day and she found herself alone. Free to take a really good look, and she did. That little voice was with her again. Instinct.

There was something very modern about the way the woman looked. Knowing. An artist who understood the female heart had executed this painting, Carrie decided. Ricasoli was not known for his well-developed feminine side. She wondered why she hadn't noticed it when she first saw the photographs of the newly rediscovered work. It seemed so obvious now. It was almost as though this was a different painting from the one she'd seen on the news a couple of months before.

'What's your secret?' Carrie asked the girl in the picture. 'Who are you? What are you doing here?'

'Good question,' said a voice behind her. 'What are you doing here?'

Carrie turned to find Nat Wilde behind her.

'I'm looking at your painting. It's on public view, isn't it?'

'Not for much longer,' said Nat, echoing Carrie's earlier thoughts. He too knew that this painting would disappear into a private collection. They were quiet for a moment, both contemplating this work of art.

'Anyway, congratulations,' said Carrie. 'It's quite an honour to be asked to sell something so amazing.'

Nat shrugged as though it were an everyday occasion at Ludbrook's.

'I do hope you're not too disappointed to have missed out,' he said. 'The owner wanted experience, I suppose.'

Carrie looked down so that he wouldn't see her smile. He obviously didn't know she'd had first refusal.

'You know,' he said then. 'I do believe that this is the first time you and I have found ourselves properly alone since that rather lovely evening at Claridge's.'

Carrie pursed her lips. 'Is it really?'

'I think of it often,' he told her. 'I suppose I should feel honoured that you chose to sleep with me one more time before you set about trying to muscle in on my patch.'

Carrie shook her head. 'I don't particularly want to think about it,' she said.

'I have wanted to tell you ever since how amazed and delighted I was to discover that the mousy little Carrie Klein who worked for me all those years ago turned into such a beauty.'

'Save your flattery,' said Carrie.

'Why? I'm feeling particularly generous tonight.'

'That's a first.'

'Well, I have reason. You have to admit that it's going to be a long time before you're able to match tomorrow's sale. Maybe you never will. Maybe you will just have to give up and head back to NYC with your tail between your legs. Leave London to the big boys . . .'

Carrie snorted.

'But while we're alone I have to ask the obvious question. Why did you do it, Carrie? Until that night, I thought that I must be your sworn enemy for having taken your virginity under false pretences. Though I still maintain that had you asked if I was married I would have told you.'

'That's kind.'

'Why, after all those years, did you come back to give me a second bite at the cherry, as it were?'

Carrie knew what Nat wanted to hear. He wanted to hear that he had been on her mind constantly since that dreadful day back in 1990 and that she had spent many sleepless nights since then dreaming of what might have been. She tilted her head to one side and let her eyes drift lazily over his face. The grey eyes, the well-shaped lips, the square jaw. In two decades he had hardly changed at all. He would be considered attractive in any age, in any part of the world. She decided she could be forgiven for having wanted to taste that mouth just one more time. To have wanted to prove to herself that he wanted her too.

Bored of her hesitation, even if she had filled it with a long admiring look at him, Nat raised his hand. 'It's OK. You don't have to tell me if you'd find it embarrassing.'

'Not at all,' said Carrie. 'I'm more than happy to let you know what was going through my mind. Why don't you let me whisper it? I'd hate for your security guards to be eavesdropping on my big admission.'

With his hands in his pockets, Nat leaned forward obligingly. Such intimacy. She would say something flattering, of course.

Carrie whispered, 'I think I wanted to know if my first fuck with you was my worst fuck ever because I was a virgin, or simply because you're a selfish, clumsy lover. And I'm afraid to report that it's the latter.'

Nat's mouth dropped open.

'Goodnight.'

Carrie turned and left, leaving Nat gaping after her. She knew she'd struck a low blow and it was a small victory, but it felt like a good one.

Chapter Sixty-Four

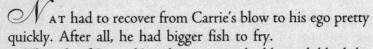

$\mathcal{N}$ AT had to recover from Carrie's blow to his ego pretty quickly. After all, he had bigger fish to fry.

The sale of Ricasoli's unknown saint had been dubbed the 'sale of the century'. Nat Wilde was interviewed about the painting for several news channels. 'Undoubtedly,' he told the pretty blonde from *Sky News*, 'this is one of the most important paintings to be sold through Ludbrook's since the auction house held its very first sale in 1708.'

The painting had drawn huge crowds (though not quite as big as the crowds that had been drawn by Mathieu Randon's museum-quality smut). Soon the other paintings in the sale started to seem like nothing more than a garnish to the main dish, though there were at least five other works that should break though the ten-million barrier if they had been priced correctly.

Adrenalin was high throughout the building as the day of reckoning drew near. Nat Wilde felt like a rock star as his colleagues buzzed around him, all of them sure that he was going to turn in the performance of his life.

Two days before the sale, Nat had handed his lucky tie to Sarah Jane and instructed her to try to do something about the gravy stains upon it.

'Should I take it to the dry cleaner?' she asked.

'Absolutely not,' Nat was horrified. 'They might lose it. Just dab something on it. Make it look reasonable. You know what to do. You're a clever girl.'

Sarah Jane said she would do her best. Then she went straight to Lizzy to ask what she thought should be done.

'I don't know,' Lizzy shrugged and was glad that since she was no longer Nat's office concubine she no longer had to care.

Sarah Jane walked away from Lizzy's desk looking so nervous, you might have thought she had been asked to sponge clean a Caravaggio (a request that was made of most new recruits to the department as a joke).

'Don't worry about it,' Lizzy called after her. 'Though your entire future at Ludbrook's depends on it.'

Of course Sarah Jane's attempts to clean Nat's lucky tie ended in disaster. Having spent the best part of the afternoon online, googling stain removal solutions, she had finally plumped on a mixture of hand-wash liquid and cold water. In theory, it should have been fine. In practice, though Sarah Jane applied the solution with a gentle hand and dried the tie flat between two sheets of plain white blotting paper pinched from Nat's desk, it didn't work at all. The stains were gone but in their place were several lightened patches that were somehow more noticeable and looked far worse than the original marks.

'It's a disaster,' Sarah Jane was crying as she brought the tie back into the fine art office.

'It's only a tie,' said Marcus.

'Only a tie?' echoed Lizzy, hamming things up. 'That is the tie that Nat has worn for every single auction he's conducted since 1989. Without that tie, Nat is like a warrior going into battle without his armour.'

'He's like Luke Skywalker without his light sabre,' suggested Olivia.

'He's like Harry Potter without a wand,' Lizzy continued. 'He's . . . he's . . . he's nothing.'

'You're not helping,' said Sarah Jane.

'I'm not trying to,' Lizzy assured her. It felt good. Though Lizzy felt less good when she realised that Nat was 'comforting' Sarah Jane in the way he used to 'discipline' her behind the closed door of his office when he thought that no one was listening. Sarah Jane emerged after fifteen minutes looking flushed and happy. 'He says he'll wear it anyway,' she smiled. 'He knows I did my best.'

But Nat did not wear the tie. For the first time ever he looked at the Hermès bunny rabbits and felt something approaching revulsion. At last the scales had fallen from his eyes. His beautiful tie had become nothing but a ratty piece of cloth. It was so horribly frayed and filthy, it ought to have been consigned to the dustbin a long, long time before. The tie was twenty-eight years old. There were staff in his department who had not been born when Nat first wore those bloody rabbits. Nat was keeping the damn thing for sentimental reasons only and there was absolutely no reason why he should be so sentimental. He was a grown man. He was one of the best auctioneers in the business – in the *history* of the business – because he had worked hard and had a natural talent. His success did not reside in his bloody tie and that night Nat was determined to prove it.

In the top drawer of Nat's desk was another tie. Like his lucky tie, it was from Hermès. It had been a birthday gift from Sarah Jane. It was red with a pattern of pale blue monkeys, which really shouldn't have worked. However, as with all Hermès ties, it did. Nat had yet to wear it though Sarah Jane had worn it, and nothing else, in the Polaroid picture which she slipped into the box as a birthday card.

With the very happy image of Sarah Jane in that photo in mind, Nat tied his new tie around the collar of a blue and white striped shirt. It was the perfect combination. He slipped on his beautifully cut jacket and stepped out into the main office of the fine art department. A hush fell over his team as they regarded him. They knew at once that something was wrong though it took a couple of seconds for them to work out exactly what. Sarah Jane was the first to realise because, of course, she recognised her gift around her beloved's neck.

'You're wearing . . .' she began.

'You're not wearing your lucky tie!' Marcus interrupted. He looked panicked. Almost distraught. 'Where is it? What's going on? For heaven's sake, Nat! This is the most important night of the year!'

'Calm down,' said Nat. 'It's really no big deal. The success of this department can't really be down to a scrap of silk, can it?'

The boys in particular looked unsure. James had been using the same pair of lucky boxer shorts every time he played an important amateur football match since his late teens.

'Of course it can't,' Nat continued. 'The amazing success of this department is all down to the talent and dedication of its individual team members. I promise you that just because I am not wearing the bunny rabbits, I will not forget how to do my job. I will get up on that stage and sell the hell out of our paintings. And who knows,' he added with a wink at Sarah Jane, 'this tie may turn out to be even luckier than the old one.'

Sarah Jane led the others in a round of applause. Lizzy joined in half-heartedly.

Nat calmed them down by raising his hands like a priest blessing his flock.

'Come on then, girls and boy. Let's sell the fuck out of that painting.'

Chapter Sixty-Five

$\mathscr{A}$ ND then it was time for the show to begin. Downstairs, the lobby and the auction room were already filling up with people keen to know how far Nat Wilde could take *The Virgin*. This wasn't just an auction. It was an occasion. The punters had really made an effort and dressed up to be there. There was a full contingent from the press.

Photographers lined the road outside the Ludbrook's building, hoping to catch a snap of someone notable heading for the sale. Soon the scene on New Bond Street was more like the run-up to a film premiere than an art auction. Limousines and gleaming classic cars disgorged famous faces by the dozen. Oligarchs with their entourages. Actors and politicians eager to prove they were in the cultural loop, even if they didn't have a hope in hell of affording what was on sale that night.

Glancing from her office window, Lizzy watched for a moment in disbelief as a particularly fame-hungry starlet, famous more for her string of high-profile married lovers than her acting, twirled on the carpet at the entrance as though she were the main attraction. Certainly, her dress was a spectacle – a body-contoured mesh of fine gold wire and crystals that turned her into a walking jewel. Still, despite the glitter, the starlet was outdone moments later by the arrival of the former beauty-queen girlfriend of a Siberian media magnate. Though the night was particularly mild, she wore an enormous fur. Real, without doubt. And as she stepped in front of the photographers, she simply let the fur drop to the floor to reveal a red dress with a back that scooped as low as the top of her diamond-studded thong. She posed for a good ten minutes with her puddle of mink around her feet, her expression never changing from a mask of beautiful disdain or, perhaps, pity for those people whose boyfriends would not be in the running for a multimillion-pound painting that night.

But Nat Wilde's team did not have time to watch the spectacle. Lizzy and the others set to work telephoning absent bidders to make sure that they were ready to bid when the moment came. More junior members of the Ludbrook's events team circulated with trays of the very best vintage champagne, following Nat's instructions to make sure that no potential buyer was ever seen with an empty glass. They did their job so well that the starlet in the gold mesh dress was soon sitting on the lap of the head of a large retail chain, eyes glazed from drinking too much fizz on an empty stomach.

Lizzy worked the room, chatting to clients that she knew well. She answered questions for journalists and ensured that her team were ready to spring into action the moment it was required. She was nervous too. It wasn't just Nat who needed to be on the ball that night. If Nat was like a shepherd then his crew were like sheepdogs, ensuring that he didn't miss a single crucial member of the flock. Lizzy, Sarah Jane and the others would draw his attention to the buyers he should be watching out for as each lot came up. As the crowd started to take their places, Lizzy made a mental map of where the really big hitters or their agents were sitting. She briefed Nat in the moments before the auction so that he could be sure to address his funniest remarks at the right people. It was an important way to build trust and maintain relationships with those buyers who might leave that auction disappointed. It was all about ensuring they came back.

By ten to seven all the seats in the auction room had been filled. It was a case of standing room only. Lizzy scanned the people who had arrived late and had to remain on their feet nervously, praying that no one who might bid on *The Virgin* had suffered such an indignity. Satisfied that all was well, she took her place at one of the phones.

Yasha Suscenko slipped in at the very last moment and leaned against the back wall. Though he wasn't buying that night, he wouldn't have missed it for the world. This was going to be a very interesting sale indeed.

It started relatively sedately. A series of three small altarpieces attributed to the studio of a minor Renaissance artist achieved a little over their estimate. Lizzy wasn't surprised. They were very pretty. Had she had the price of a studio flat in Chelsea to spare, she would have liked them for herself. Just a little later in the sale, a similar lot went for even more. Already Lizzy could feel a crackle of energy in the room. It boded well for the big ticket items yet to come.

A portrait of a washerwoman attributed to one of the Caravaggisti was the first lot to go for seven figures. After that the numbers just mushroomed. A million here, a million there. Nat took the big bids without blinking; he could have been selling second-hand cars. The running total for the sale soon equalled the GNP of a small African nation. And then it was time.

'Lot number 147. *The Virgin Before The Annunciation*. A painting by Giancarlo Ricasoli.'

Nat read out the particulars of the lot just as he had read the details of all the others, as if he considered it to be no more remarkable a painting than all those that had gone before. But then he paused and smiled at the crowd, who looked up at him like excited children at a pantomime. They too knew that the real action was about to kick off.

'Who will start the bidding at sixty-five million pounds? Anyone? Sixty-five million pounds?'

Sixty-five million pounds! There was a moment of palpable shock in the room as the assembled people realised that Nat had started the bidding with a figure *above* the high estimate. A cool ten million above. It was a huge surprise. A risky strategy that could end up back-firing. Ordinarily, bidders saw the high estimate as the maximum they would have to pay, *not* the starting point. Lizzy and her colleagues shared worried glances as they waiting for Nat to continue.

'Sixty-five million pounds,' he said again.

'Oh God,' said Olivia. 'He's lost it.'

If nobody answered Nat's call, he would have to lower the starting bid. It would be an enormous humiliation.

But Nat's gamble worked. After a few seconds when it seemed as though the sale had stalled at the first bid, three paddles shot up at once. Two on the floor and one at the back of the room. Sarah Jane's phone bidder. Nat pointed at the person he considered to have been first.

'Sixty-five million, five hundred . . .'

The other bidder on the floor nodded quickly, eager to be the one with the bid in his hand.

'Sixty-six million.'

Sarah Jane had it now.

Nat was his usual unruffled self as the bids crept up in increments of half a million. Soon it seemed silly that anyone might have thought he had over-reached himself by jumping straight in over the estimate. Sarah Jane looked faintly sick as she continued to bid for her client.

'Seventy-five million. Seventy-five million, five hundred thousand . . . seventy-nine million. Seventy-nine million five hundred . . .'

'Oh God,' breathed Lizzy. 'He's going to do it.'

'Eighty million pounds,' said Nat.

The room erupted. Half shock, half awe. It was twice the highest price that had ever been achieved at Ludbrook's. And yet Nat wasn't finished. One bidder remained on the floor. Sarah Jane was still in the game too, taking another bid on the phone, looking perhaps faintly disturbed that every nod of her head sent the numbers up by the price of a small house in Clapham.

Lizzy was open-mouthed as she watched the figures scrolling across the monitor above Nat's head. She tried to count the noughts but could hardly keep up with the pace.

'Ninety million, five hundred thousand.'

These were hardly the kind of increments you'd find on eBay, thought Lizzy. She was deeply envious of Sarah Jane at that moment in time. Lizzy's own phone buyer had folded his cards before bidding even began. He'd banked on the painting not reaching its estimate. Now Sarah Jane and the mysterious man at the centre of the room were engaged in the most exciting bid-off Lizzy had ever seen.

'Ninety-five million,' said Nat. Sarah Jane relayed the news to her bidder and returned Nat's look with a shake of her head. The gavel was poised to come down. In the centre of the room, the other bidder's shoulders relaxed, though not much. The punters sitting around the leading bidder stared openly. What did a man who was about to spend ninety-five million pounds look like?

'Ninety-five million pounds for this painting of *The Virgin Before* . . .'

At the back of the room, one of the unmanned telephones started to ring. It was a loud, ugly sound.

Nat paused. He looked a little irritated. He did not appreciate this interruption to his moment of glory.

'I'll get it,' said Lizzy, who was nearest. 'Lizzy Duffy, Ludbrook's,' she said. The room held its breath. 'Right,' she nodded as the caller identified himself. 'Are you sure? Well, I think I can. Hold on. I'll just find out.'

Lizzy turned back towards the room and raised a finger to Nat, asking him to hang on just a little longer. There was a flurry of activity as she sent Marcus to confirm what was being said. Her caller was indeed registered to bid. There was no reason why he shouldn't.

'But it's at ninety-five million,' Lizzy warned him. 'That's nine five. Six zeros.'

At last, Lizzy took the phone away from her mouth and shouted, 'Ninety-six million,' at Nat.

The bidder in the room, who had been so sure that he had it, let out an expletive. The bidding was at ninety-nine million within a minute.

Lizzy's heart was pounding as she relayed every second in the auction room to her bidder. On the other end of the line, his voice remained perfectly modulated and calm, and then Lizzy too began to relax into her role. She didn't have to worry whether this particular buyer would be good for the cash. Of that there was no doubt.

Finally the man at the centre of the room shook his head and shrugged his shoulders. He was dropping out. Nat brought down the gavel . . .

'Sold at ninety-nine million, five hundred thousand pounds.'

'You've got it,' Lizzy told her bidder. 'The painting is yours. Ninety-nine million five hundred thou.'

'Good,' said her bidder, as though she had just told him that he had won ten pounds on the lottery. 'Thank you very much. I'll be in touch to tell you where the painting should be sent.'

Lizzy was left holding a silent phone while the room went crazy. Everyone knew that records had been broken, smashed like so much glass. Marcus offered Olivia a high five and for once, amazingly, she shrugged off her uptight demeanour and reciprocated. James planted a kiss on Lizzy's cheek.

'You're amazing,' he told her.

'I didn't do anything,' said Lizzy. 'I just kept calm. Nat did it all.' She gazed towards the podium in something approaching admiration. Much as she hated him, he'd done a stunning job. Nat was accepting congratulations from people on either side of him but at last he brought down his gavel and asked for silence.

'Ladies and gentlemen,' he said. 'Much as I would like to crack open the champagne right this minute, we have another seven lots to go. Up next, this sketch by Rembrandt. Going cheap at a mere one million five hundred thousand. Who'll give me one million five hundred thousand to start?'

The comparison with *The Virgin* must have made the Rembrandt seem like a bargain indeed. Eight hands shot into the air.

At the back of the room, Yasha Suscenko nodded in satisfaction. The matter was concluded for him now. But as he left the Ludbrook's building and walked home through Mayfair, Yasha was surprised to see a police car pulling up outside his own gallery.

'Mr Suscenko, may we have a word?'

Chapter Sixty-Six

THE success of the auction had created an air of extremely high energy at Ludbrook's. Even those buyers who were disappointed when they saw the paintings they had come to bid for go to other people at such high prices, were buoyed up by the knowledge that there was still money out there. The recession had not come to the art world. There would still be super-yachts in Monaco and jam for tea.

When all the members of the general public had been safely shuffled from the building, the Ludbrook's team went upstairs to the boardroom, where, as usual, John Ludbrook had laid on champagne to celebrate their great success. He believed in congratulating his staff at every opportunity. Even the fact that the last time the fine art department had a party had ended in scandal with Sarah Jane and Nat's elevator tryst had not changed his policy.

This time, everybody took the stairs. Harry Brown had

stuck a hand-made sign saying 'out of order except for Nat Wilde' on the lift door. Even Lizzy had to smile.

'Congratulations,' she said to Nat when she caught up with him. 'The tie must have worked.'

Nat flipped up the end and studied the monkeys. 'I sincerely hope it wasn't the tie,' he said. 'Can't bloody stand it. Red with blue monkeys. Can't think why Sarah Jane thought I would like the damn thing.'

Lizzy knew exactly why. Because you call her 'monkey', she thought to herself. Just like you used to call me your little monkey too.

Sarah Jane slipped her arm through Nat's proprietarily. 'Come over here. Harry has a little surprise for you.'

Lizzy let them wander off. She took just three more sips of her champagne before she placed her glass down on the boardroom table and headed for home. There was nothing more for her there.

Harry's surprise for Nat was a bottle of the finest vintage champagne, Clos De Larmes by Champagne Arsenault.

'Look,' he said, pointing out the vintage. 'I even managed to get one from your date of birth.'

'1958?' Sarah Jane goggled, realising for the first time that Nat really was the same age as her father. '1958? Are you sure?'

'Sarah Jane,' said Nat. 'You're as old as the woman you feel.'

The revelation of his age didn't unduly bother Nat. There was no sense in which anyone could accuse him of being past it. That night he was at the very top of his game. He had reaffirmed his position in the pantheon of legendary auctioneers. Right up there with the best of them. Under Nat's gentle coercion, the Emir of Qatar would have bought back his own oil at one and a half times the high estimate. Nat could sell anything to anyone.

Right then, his adrenalin and testosterone levels were through the roof. He held court, feeling like Alexander the Great, like Napoleon and Genghis Khan, all wrapped up in one body. Everyone in the room wanted to talk to him and ask how it felt to preside over such a spectacular sale. The morning's papers would be full of it. Nat had already made sure that the PR department sent out the right photograph of him standing on his podium to all the picture desks. It was ten years old but it would give people a rough idea of what he looked like in action.

But much as he liked the adulation, after a couple of hours, Nat was starting to get a little bored of the questions of younger guys who hoped to emulate him. Glancing across the room while some little twerp from the wine department expounded on the price he hoped to achieve for a bottle of Château Mouton Rothschild from the late Queen Mother's personal cellar, Nat caught Sarah Jane's eye. She made a subtle gesture with her head. Nat understood immediately. Moments later he excused himself to follow Sarah Jane to his office.

When Nat walked into his office, he found Sarah Jane sitting on the desk. She was already half undressed. She had unbuttoned her sober white blouse to the waist, revealing the hot pink underwear beneath. The thought of that underwear had been tantalising Nat all day, since the pink bra had showed quite clearly through the thin white cotton.

'Is this my reward?' he asked, reaching inside her blouse and cupping both her breasts in his hands.

'You certainly deserve one,' she told him. 'I don't think I've ever seen anything so impressive as you were today. You were magnificent.'

Nat grinned. 'You say all the right things,' he said, dipping his head to place a kiss on the curved flesh of her bosom held so proudly upright by her bra. Sarah Jane sighed and tipped her head back so that Nat could kiss her throat. As he moved lower again she loosened her long brown hair from its restrained bun and let it tumble over her bare shoulders. Nat plunged his hands into the cascading curls and pulled her wet-lipped mouth towards his.

'God, Nat,' she breathed when he let her come up for air. 'I couldn't take my eyes off you all night. You're making me crazy.'

It was exactly what he wanted to hear. 'How crazy?'

'I just want you to take me right now. On your desk. So I think you should take this off for me.' She started to undo his tie. 'Aren't you glad you've got a new lucky tie?' she asked as she did so.

'I certainly am. I can think of only one thing that would make this evening better.'

'What's that?'

'Will you model it for me? Like you did in that special birthday photograph.'

Sarah Jane gave her lover a slow, dirty smile. 'With pleasure,' she whispered huskily.

Sarah Jane stripped off in a second. Then she took the long sliver of red silk, patterned with those silly little monkeys and quickly transformed it into a prop worthy of the dancers at The Crazy Horse in Paris. Wearing nothing else but her leopardskin Louboutins (which she'd decided were her lucky shoes), she strutted around Nat's office, stopping every now and then to grind her pelvis against a book case or the back of a chair. Remembering everything she had been taught in rhythmic gymnastics classes at her exclusive girls' – only boarding school, she made the tie dance through the air. Then she let it loop lazily around her body. It encircled her waist, caressed her breasts. She gave a little shiver as it trailed across her rosy pink nipples. She let it slide between her legs, moaning as she pulled the silk taut against her carefully coiffed mons pubis.

'Oh yes,' said Nat. 'Now that is what I call a lucky tie.'

Chapter Sixty-Seven

WHILE Nat was busy indulging in his reward for a very good day at the office, the party in the boardroom upstairs was interrupted by the arrival of three police officers, two uniformed and one in plain clothes. They stood at the end of the beautiful panelled room that had been a dining room back when Ludbrook's offices had been a private house like the ghosts of Christmasses past, present and future. At first, only Harry Brown noticed they were there at all. The officers refused a glass of champagne from an overly attentive waiter. Instead they asked the waiter a couple of questions and the waiter shrugged and pointed straight at Harry.

'Nat Wilde?' the detective asked.

'Not guilty,' said Harry reflexively.

'Could you tell me where he is?'

'Who wants to know?' said Harry.

'Detective Sergeant Simpson, CID. And this is Detective Constable James and Detective French. We need to speak to

Mr Wilde as a matter of some urgency. I wonder if we might step out into the corridor.'

'Excuse me,' Harry said to his companions. 'Save some of that Arsenault for me.'

Outside in the corridor, Harry could only give the same response. 'I don't know where he is,' Harry said, though he had noticed even in his drunken haze that Sarah Jane was missing from the party too. He immediately put two and two together and figured the worst. 'He might be in his office?' Harry suggested. 'Doing some paperwork?' he added feebly. 'I'll try calling his mobile.' If Sarah Jane was with him, as Harry strongly suspected she would be, Nat would almost certainly need a moment to compose himself.

'No need. Let's just go straight to his office,' said Detective Simpson.

Harry had no choice but to lead the policemen down the stairs. He felt like a Judas, though he wasn't sure why. It wasn't as though he could have refused to take the policemen to Nat's office. And, in any case, perhaps they just wanted to see Nat on a routine matter. Though what on earth could that 'routine matter' be? It had to have something to do with the Trebarwen fakes.

'This is it,' said Harry, pausing outside the big wooden door with its highly polished brass name-plate. Nathaniel Wilde. Such proud letters. Without knocking, Detective Simpson pushed the door open. And froze . . .

'And this is what they call a Double Windsor,' Sarah Jane was saying. She was standing on Nat's desk, in nothing but her red-soled shoes and his tie. Nat was sitting in his chair, leaning back as far as he could to get the best view of Sarah Jane's Brazilian.

'Oh my God,' said Detective French, the female detective. She immediately turned away. The two male detectives and Harry Brown were transfixed as Sarah Jane gyrated to Barry White's 'Sho' You Right', which was belting out of the CD player in the corner of the room. Nat too, was completely absorbed. The song had finished before he or Sarah Jane noticed that they had visitors.

'A-hem,' Detective Simpson coughed before Barry White could launch into 'Can't Get Enough of Your Love.'

The police allowed Nat and Sarah Jane a few moments of privacy to compose themselves before they got down to their official business. When Sarah Jane emerged looking as red as the soles of her Louboutins, she was sent back to the party.

'I'll be there in a moment or two,' said Nat. 'Save me some champagne.'

But Nat would not be back at the party that night. Closing the door so that he would be less likely to be overheard, Detective Simpson delivered the speech that Nat had hitherto only heard in television dramas.

'You do not have to say anything . . .'

'There's been some kind of mistake,' said Nat, although deep down he knew that there hadn't.

Chapter Sixty-Eight

$\mathcal{B}$LOODY Trebarwen. Nat should have known that idiot Julian would cock things up for the pair of them.

The moment Nat saw the painting of the suspension bridge, he had known that something wasn't quite right. But his desire to make a quick buck had overridden his professional faculties. Once he had Julian over a barrel and made him agree to share the profits, Nat forgot to ask himself whether the fake would get past everybody else. Of course the subject was wrong. He knew that now.

And then Lizzy, bloody Lizzy, was on to the case. Maybe he could have kept her quiet. Perhaps he should have brought Lizzy in on the secret and held off fucking Sarah Jane until Lizzy found herself someone else to take her mind off him. For it was undoubtedly her going to John Ludbrook that had made this moment inevitable.

Nat hadn't intended to go so far as murder. He had used Sarah Jane's mobile phone to call Julian and request a meeting. They met at The Dove, a quiet pub on the riverbank in Hammersmith. Nat wanted to hammer out a new deal. Julian needed to say that he had been working alone. Nat was facing the end of a thirty-year career over this.

'Come on, Ju,' he said. 'Neither of us has to go down. You just finger the forger. I can collaborate with you and explain that it's easy to see why you were fooled. I've got thirty years' experience and I didn't spot the fakes. You brought the paintings to me in good faith. But you have to say where you got them.'

'I can't do that,' said Julian.

'What do you mean you can't? You have to. If you hand in the forger then neither of us has committed an offence. There's no crime in being duped. Where did you get them, Julian? Did you actually have them painted to order?'

A micro-expression on Julian's fat face told Nat that Julian had indeed instructed the creation of the works. In that knowledge, Nat saw a way out. A way of making it seem that he and Julian were the victims of this whole mess.

'I can't tell you where I got the paintings,' said Julian. 'I promised.'

'You promised? Fuck's sake. You're going to go to prison.'

'Or maybe you are. I'm not an art expert,' said Julian. 'I brought them to you for evaluation. You should have told me they were moody and refused to take them on.'

'My judgement failed me.'

'Three times?'

'You fucker, Trebarwen. If you think I'm going to lose my job and possibly my liberty to save your mystery painter . . . Tell me the fucking name.'

The pub was about to close. One of the bar staff was moving around the floor, collecting glasses. She edged nearer to Nat and Julian, keen to retrieve their empty glasses but put off by their heated tones. Nat caught her eye and gestured to Julian that they should pause for a moment.

'We're closing up now, guys,' she said.

'Let's go,' Nat said to Julian. 'We'll continue this discussion outside.'

They walked along the embankment. The conversation continued in the same vein, with Nat insisting that the only way to save both their skins was to place the blame firmly with the forger and Julian resisting the idea like he was some Second World War hero facing the Gestapo.

'Fuck all this bloody honour shit, Trebarwen. Who the hell is it?'

'I'll never give you her name.'

'Ah,' said Nat. 'A woman. You must be fucking her.'

Julian winced. 'She didn't want to get into this. It was an accident. She painted that picture for my mother. The one of the two dogs. You attributed it to Delapole and it went for twenty-five grand.'

Now Nat winced to think he had genuinely thought that painting to be the real thing. They stepped on to Hammersmith Bridge, still arguing.

'She's got a kid, Nat. She's on her own. I talked her into it and I swore I would keep her out of trouble.'

'Just tell me her fucking name. Tell me her fucking name!'

'I will not.' Julian grabbed Nat by the collar and spat the words into his face. 'You absolute shit.'

'Me a shit? You're the one who got her into this.'

'And I want to keep her out of it.'

'Too late. Should have thought of that before you got me involved. Now, would you do me the favour of taking your hands off my lapels? You are creasing them.'

Julian let go of Nat's lapels but he wasn't about to let go of the fight. He swung at Nat's head, connecting with his cheekbone.

'I wouldn't start that if I were you,' said Nat. 'I boxed for Oxford.'

'Fuck off.'

Julian chanced another slug in Nat's direction. Though he hadn't put on the gloves thirty years, Nat was pleased to discover that he still knew what he was doing. He avoided Julian's flailing punches effortlessly, while delivering several of his own that went straight to the mark.

Pretty soon Julian, who had not been making much effort to keep himself in shape, was panting. Nat pummelled him until Julian barely had enough breath to beg for mercy.

'You had enough?' Nat asked.

'Yes,' said Julian. 'Ye-sssss.' The word came out like the hiss of a punctured bicycle tyre. His bottom lip was badly split. Julian put his hand to his nose. It was pointing in a different direction from usual.

'You see,' said Nat proudly. 'No one messes with Nat Wilde.'

'Oh shut the fuck up, you old Etonian arse-wipe.'

Seconds later, Julian was sailing backwards over the side of the bridge and into the river.

Nat hadn't expected Julian to drown. He'd thrown him into the river to teach him a lesson. No one took the name of Nat's alma mater in vain. Nat thought that Julian would pop up spluttering and contrite and head for the bank and that would be it. He'd watched over the side of the bridge for a while. He hadn't seen Julian come up but he didn't worry. It was dark. The water was black. Julian was out there some-where, doing the doggy paddle.

'I didn't know he couldn't swim,' said Nat to the officer who interviewed him. 'I mean, everybody can swim, can't they?'

'Regardless of whether or not he was able to swim, Mr Trebarwen was in no fit state to get himself out of the Thames at high tide. He had several broken ribs.'

There was no point in Nat pretending he hadn't been there. The girl who worked at The Dove had called the police when she saw a photograph of Julian Trebarwen in the paper. She said she had seen him earlier that night, in a heated row with another man. She later identified Nat from a photo in press coverage of the Ricasoli sale.

'I remember him,' she said. 'Because he tried to chat me up while he was waiting for the dead guy to arrive. I thought he was a right old sleaze.'

The best Nat could hope for was that a jury would accept that Julian's death was an accident. Sure Nat had trained as a boxer but he wasn't given to violence unless provoked. Julian had been more than a match for him in size and weight.

'I didn't know he couldn't swim,' Nat said again and again. Though gradually it came to make sense. Like his brother Mark 'Chubby' Trebarwen, Julian had been a fat kid back when fat kids were far less common. He hadn't wanted to go swimming with the rest of the boys because they teased him so mercilessly about the rolls of blubber around the waistband of his shorts. His mother, Louisa, had collaborated, telling the PE teacher that Julian had a weak chest and mustn't sit around in the cold and the wet. So while the rest of his classmates grew up knowing how to keep afloat at the very least, Julian never learned how.

Nat looked at his long-fingered hands, which were clutching a white plastic cup full of undrinkable coffee. There was no hint that those hands had been able to kill.

'Am I going to be charged with his murder?' Nat asked his solicitor.

'I'll go for manslaughter,' the solicitor said.

Chapter Sixty-Nine

$\mathscr{N}$AT'S arrest and subsequent charge of manslaughter turned the fine art department at Ludbrook's upside-down, totally overshadowing the Ricasoli sale. About a month after the arrest, John Ludbrook himself asked to see Lizzy.

'I feel I owe you an apology, Lizzy,' said John. 'It's clear that I underestimated you. With someone as brash as Nat Wilde heading up the department, it wasn't always easy to see who was actually doing the work. I've been talking to the directors. It's time you realised your potential. We'd like to make you acting head of department with a view to taking the position on on a permanent basis once we have discovered what our obligations are with regard to Nat.'

Lizzy said she would be delighted to give the position her consideration. But it wasn't the only position she had to choose from right then.

* * *

That evening, Lizzy had a dinner date at Scott's. She took great care with her appearance. Even more than she had done when she had first started her affair with Nat. She was rewarded for her efforts.

'That is a fantastic dress,' said Carrie Klein. 'Where did you get it?'

Lizzy beamed. 'Oh, this is just some old thing,' she lied. She'd bought it from Amanda Wakeley earlier that afternoon. It was more than she had ever spent on a single piece of clothing but Lizzy had decided that it was time to change her image. To sharpen up with style. The fact that Carrie Klein had approved was a very good sign.

'As you know,' said Carrie. 'I have been watching you very closely since I came to London. And everything I've seen or heard about you – with the exception of the obvious . . .'

Lizzy rolled her eyes at this coded mention of Nat.

'Everything has left me very impressed.'

'Thank you.'

'You know what you're doing and you care about getting things right. I can see why Ludbrook's want you at the helm of their fine art department.'

'How did you know . . . ?' The offer was supposed to be top secret.

'Nothing escapes my notice for very long. Have you accepted the offer?'

'Not yet,' said Lizzy.

'Good. Because I would like to make you a better one. Forget Ludbrook's, Lizzy. It's a dinosaur. Come to Ehrenpreis and work with me. I'll match any offer they've made you to be my head of fine art.'

*   *   *

432

For the first time, Lizzy found herself lying awake because of a lovely dilemma. Ludbrook's or Ehrenpreis. Where would she go? Carrie's offer had been astonishing. But how should she choose? Ludbrook's was the bigger house. Being head of the fine art department there was a position of bigger responsibility. But Ehrenpreis was growing fast and Lizzy wondered if she might not have more freedom to do things her own way with Carrie Klein.

The following morning, she called Carrie as she walked into Ludbrook's for her last day as second in command of the fine art department.

'You made your mind up quickly,' said Carrie. 'I knew you would. When can you start?'

'I start tomorrow,' said Lizzy. 'But not at Ehrenpreis.'

'What?' Carrie exclaimed. 'I must have offered you twice as much money.'

'I appreciate that,' said Lizzy. 'But you know yourself that the money isn't really what matters to me right now. I want to make my mark on this world and I'm not sure that I could do it in your shadow. Because the thing is, I don't think I could be entirely in your shadow. I believe I could go head to head with you sooner than you think.'

Carrie was shocked but impressed.

'Brave words,' she said. 'And I'll let you take them back if you want to.'

'That won't be necessary,' said Lizzy.

'Well,' Carrie sighed. 'What can I say? I hope you won't blame me for making my offer.'

'I'm flattered. And I hope you aren't too offended by my refusal.'

Carrie assured Lizzy that she wasn't. Perhaps she had patronised the girl by expecting her to take a second-in-

433

command position at Ehrenpreis rather than the top job at Ludbrook's, with the chance to learn from Carrie as the bait.

'I'm sure we'll see plenty of each other over the coming years as we compete over sales,' said Carrie.

'Yes,' said Lizzy. 'And may the best woman win.'

That afternoon, Lizzy conducted her first sale since the Trebarwen debacle. The bi-monthly Ludbrook's Old Masters sale. Moments before the sale was auction to start, Olivia asked her whether she truly felt she was ready.

'We'll all do our best to support you,' she said. 'But none of us knows how to read a room like Nat did.'

'I might,' Lizzy smiled.

Where once she would have panicked to know that Nat wasn't there in the background, ready to prompt her, now she was glad to look out over that room and not have to see his face. She was on her own and it felt great.

She didn't need Nat. In actual fact she had never really needed him but somehow her confidence had become wrapped up in his approval of her, his desire. His influence had started to wane the day she saw him fucking Sarah Jane but it was only as she stood at the block in the auction room and addressed the crowd that Lizzy knew for sure he no longer had any hold on her at all. A good job, she thought to herself. She had no desire to go visiting a mentor in prison.

'Ladies and gentlemen,' she welcomed the crowd. 'My name is Lizzy Duffy and I am head of Ludbrook's Department of Old Masters and Nineteenth-Century Art.'

It was to be a very special afternoon.

'Lot twenty four. A small painting of a horse by George Stubbs. Do I have one million pounds?'

Lizzy did.

'One million pounds.'

As she said the words, she couldn't keep the smile from her face. It was her first seven-figure sale.

John Ludbrook was there to congratulate her in person when she stepped down from the block.

'How did it feel?' he asked.

'Like losing my virginity,' she said. 'But much, much, much more satisfying.'

As she undressed to get into bed that evening, Lizzy still had a smile on her face. Taking off her earrings, she pondered for a moment making the tiny diamond chips her auction mascots. Her lucky earrings . . . But no, she decided finally. She didn't need luck. Lizzy Duffy had something more enduring and much, much better. Lizzy Duffy knew she had talent.

Chapter Seventy

OLD Ehrenpreis came to London to celebrate the third anniversary of the opening of the London office. There was another party, of course, expertly arranged by Jessica, who had recently announced her intention to become a Brit by marrying one.

'So you don't want a transfer back to New York?' Carrie asked her.

'I'll kill you if you pull that one on me now,' Jessica assured her. 'But how about you? Are you happy here in London?' she asked.

Old Ehrenpreis had asked the exact same question just that afternoon, while he and Carrie were lunching at Gordon Ramsay on Royal Hospital Road. Carrie's old boss and opposite number in New York was close to retirement. If Carrie wanted to apply for it the position would almost certainly be hers.

Am I happy in London? Carrie asked herself. She was certainly proud of what she had achieved over the past few years. The London office was performing well in excess of the targets that had been set for her when she took the job. Walking around the building, she was certain that her staff were happy. Her clients were happy. But was she?

Carrie thought about the question again that night when she was alone in her flat, taking off her make-up. Later, standing with her hands on her hips in the living room, she surveyed the place she called 'home'. More than three years since she had arrived in London she was still in the same rental flat. She hadn't had time to look for somewhere more permanent. But this was ridiculous. In the corner of the living room were five huge boxes of her personal effects; unopened since the day they were delivered. Though she was surrounded by art all day long and loved to be able to rest her eyes on a beautiful painting, the walls of Carrie's home were completely bare. As she looked at the boxes it struck her that if Ehrenpreis demanded that she move back to Manhattan tomorrow, she wouldn't even have to pack.

Suddenly Carrie felt very homesick indeed. London was wonderful but her family, her friends, even her favourite junk food, was all on the other side of the Atlantic. Along with the best job offer she had ever had.

The following morning, she told Jessica that she would be going back to New York.

'I can't go with you,' Jessica said in a panic. The exact mirror image reaction of the panic she'd had three years before, when Carrie announced the move to London.

'You don't have to,' Carrie promised. 'I'll make sure that you keep your job.'

Old Ehrenpreis was delighted. 'My best girl at the helm of my best office,' he said. 'When are you coming?'

It all happened very quickly. Just two months later, Carrie handed over the reins to her successor, a man from Boston who had been snapping at her heels from day one.

'Good luck with the Brits,' Carrie told him within earshot of Jessica. 'They are weird.'

'No, they're not,' her assistant leapt to the defence of her adopted nation.

Arriving back in her old apartment, Carrie felt at last that she was in the right place. This time she didn't hesitate to unpack. When her furniture was released from storage she replaced each piece exactly as it had been when she got the call to London. With a whole blissfully empty week to go before she took over the role of CEO of Ehrenpreis New York, Carrie spent her time going down to see her family, catching up with old friends and eating in her favourite restaurants. It was as though nothing had changed.

On the Friday evening, she was having dinner on the terrace at Barbuto in the meatpacking district when he walked past.

'Who is it?' noticing Carrie's stricken expression, her friend Georgie swivelled around.

It was Jed. But he wasn't alone. On his arm was a blonde, about Carrie's height. She had a heart-shaped face and a body to die for, shown off to perfection by a simple white cotton dress, perfect for the warm summer evening. She had her arm linked through Jed's and was laughing at something he'd told her.

Something had changed. Carrie didn't know why she felt so awful. It was inevitable. She was the one who had told Jed they couldn't be together. She had no right to be upset that he had found someone new. Someone so young and beautiful and who was clearly crazy about him. Someone so much younger and more beautiful than Carrie felt right then.

'Isn't that . . . ?' Georgie asked.

'Yes,' said Carrie in a whisper. 'It's Jed.'

There was nowhere to escape to. Jed was going to walk right by their table. If she stood up on the pretence of going to the loo, he would spot her at once. The only thing to do was suck it up and say hello. Act pleased to see him. And whoever she was.

She hadn't wanted him, had she? She'd sent him away because he wasn't right for her. It didn't matter, she told herself over and over, steeling herself for the moment when he finally saw her by taking a big swig of her wine.

'Jed,' she said.

He looked pleased to see her. He broke away from the girl and leaned over the fence that surrounded the terrace to plant a kiss on each of Carrie's cheeks.

'You look amazing,' he said. 'What are you doing back here? Flying visit?'

'I'm back for good,' she told him. 'I got the top job at Ehrenpreis New York.'

'Wow, good for you. I always knew you would end up running that place.'

'Thank you. And you?'

'There's been a lot of change on the job front for me too. I gave up modelling. I'm working as a commercials director.'

'Just like that?'

'Not just like that. I was taking classes when I last saw you, remember? I did a promo video for a friend and it took off from there.'

'Wow. Congratulations.'

Carrie wished she could look into Jed's eyes for longer but she was acutely aware that standing just behind him was the girl. She shifted uneasily from foot to foot as Jed was talking. It was obvious that she wanted to be somewhere else. Even Carrie started to feel that Jed was being a little inconsiderate. Eventually, the girl actually tugged at Jed's arm.

'Jed,' she said. 'Don't you think you should introduce me?'

Carrie arranged her face to look friendly, neutral, as Jed apologised for not having introduce her to . . .

'My little sister, Tiffany.'

'Your sister,' Carrie couldn't help sounding relieved.

'Yes. She's fresh in from the country today. She's decided, of all the stupid things, to move to New York and try her hand as a model.'

'I've got an interview at Elite Model Management tomorrow.'

'Then you better have an early night,' said Jed. 'You do not want to turn up with bloodshot eyes.'

'I can have one cocktail,' she said. 'You promised!'

'I promised our mother I would keep you out of trouble. Will you excuse me,' Jed said to Carrie as he took his sister in a playful headlock. 'She's out of control,' he explained.

'No, I am not!' Tiffany protested when he let her go. 'You have totally ruined my hair.'

Carrie was reminded exactly what she had liked about Jed. He was playful. But she could also see how much he cared about his little sister. Family and friends were very important to him.

'We should leave you ladies to have dinner,' he said then. 'But I hope I'll see you soon,' he added for Carrie's benefit.

'Tomorrow night?' she blurted.

'I'll have to check my diary,' said Jed.

Tiffany pulled a face at him, as if to say 'you jerk'.

Jed broke in a grin. 'I would love that. Where will I find you?'

'Same apartment, same phone number,' said Carrie.

'I'll think of something good to do.'

'I wouldn't leave anything to him if I were you,' said Tiffany. 'He'll come up with something totally lame.'

'See you tomorrow,' said Jed. He kissed her goodbye.

'Carrie Klein,' said Georgie. 'You are a totally jammy cow.'

Carrie spent the next day in a state of nervous excitement. Jed called at lunchtime to tell her that he'd made a reservation in one of her favourite restaurants. They didn't ever get there. As soon as Jed planted a kiss on Carrie's mouth when she opened the door to him, she knew they had more important things to do than share a bowl of pasta.

It wasn't long before they were taking each other's clothes off. Carrie ran her hands over Jed's fine, broad chest, honed by hours in the gym. He lowered his head and kissed each of her nipples in turn, tenderly, as if he were greeting old friends.

'I've missed you,' he said, addressing her breasts.

Carrie gave him a mock frown, but she realised as she kissed Jed how much she had missed his body too. Each kiss was like a step along a familiar path to a place that felt like home. She touched her lips to the stubble on his cheek like a traveller kissing the ground after a long, lonely flight.

Naked at last, she pressed her body hard against him and held him tight, wanting to feel connected along their entire lengths. Their lips just touching, they murmured sweet nothings to each other. Apologies and promises. As Jed told her that he loved her, Carrie thought that she might cry.

'I love you too,' she admitted at last. What's more, she realised that she trusted him. He was a good man.

Meanwhile, she felt his penis grow hard against her and her own body cried out for a total reunion that would heal the pain of the years apart. Carrie wrapped her legs around her lover so that was nowhere for him to go but into her.

Carried cried out in joy as Jed made his first thrust with his face buried in her neck as though to hide the strength of the emotion on his face. Later, when he raised himself above her, their eyes met and a thousand secrets passed between them. As they came in perfect unison, Carrie knew she would not leave him again.

Chapter Seventy-One

$\mathcal{S}$ERENA waited to hear that she would be expected to give evidence at Nat's trial but the request didn't come. As DC Arnold outlined the counselling and support that might be available to her in the light of her connection to Julian, Serena realised that Julian must have kept his promise. It seemed that no one but Yasha had worked out her connection to the fakes.

Serena read about the record-breaking sale of *The Virgin* on the Internet just a few hours after the auction finished. She couldn't believe it. At first she thought that the figures must be wrong. A stray zero had got in there somewhere. But news site after site gave the same story. The tiny painting that Serena had created in an attic room in Tuscany not so long ago had achieved the highest price ever for a painting of its type and age. The *Daily Mail* ran an article that compared what the painting's new owner might have got for his money had he spent it elsewhere. A fifty-five metre yacht. Fifteen years full board in the best hotel in the world. It was staggering.

But not so staggering as the news that Nat Wilde had been arrested and charged with the death of Julian Trebarwen.

'He's admitted it,' said DC Arnold. 'We thought you would want to know.'

Serena went out into the garden of her house, sat down beneath the tree where she and Julian had shared many glasses of wine while Katie was sleeping, and cried. Having felt so angry with Julian, she now felt sorry for him, dying so suddenly and violently. She wondered who was making arrangements for his funeral. Would his brother care to celebrate his life? Would Serena be able to go along to say goodbye? Serena felt sad and angry and guiltily relieved. Most importantly, she knew that Yasha had not been involved.

The weekend after the auction and Nat's arrest for murder, Serena's ex-husband Tom drove down to Cornwall. He had rented a cottage in the village where he would stay with Katie for the week. It was the arrangement that Katie liked best. She said that she didn't like going to London because there weren't many toys in Donna's house, though Serena hoped Donna's coldness wasn't the real reason. Katie loved to be at the cottage in the village because she could make her father drive her back home if she needed a different outfit for a Barbie doll.

Tom arrived just two hours late. He looked frazzled.

'Traffic bad?' Serena asked.

'Everything's bad,' said Tom.

'Ah,' said Serena. 'Cup of tea?'

*   *   *

Somehow, Tom ended up staying for supper. Katie was being unusually difficult. She threw such an almighty tantrum when Serena asked her to get Bunny ready for the trip to the cottage, that Serena uncharacteristically backed down and said that Katie could go to the cottage in the morning if she preferred. She put the tantrum down to the fact that Tom had been late and that had made Katie anxious.

Tom ate the pasta gratefully.

'Never allowed pasta anymore,' he said. 'Donna's got me on a diet.'

Serena, who had her back to her ex-husband, allowed herself a little smile but stopped short of telling Tom that Donna was right. He was looking a little soft around the midriff. And grey. As she passed him a wine bottle so that he could open it, she thought she saw liver spots on the back of his hands.

The wine soon loosened his tongue.

'It's not working out,' he said. 'It was fine before her divorce came through but as soon as she got the settlement things started to change. I know what it is, Serena. She doesn't think I'm a big enough success for her. She dumped the boss for the office junior is how she sees it.'

Serena nodded, thinking: and now the sex has started to seem less interesting, other issues are rearing their heads.

'And now I've been laid off.' Tom was referring to a job he had at an investment bank run by the husband of one of Donna's friends.

'You have?'

'Yes. Last in, first out. Don't worry,' he added quickly. 'You'll still get money for Katie.'

'Actually,' Serena said truthfully. 'That wasn't the first thing that came to my mind. What are you going to do?'

'I'm going to set up on my own, of course.'

'It's what you always hoped to do eventually,' Serena reminded him. 'You're just doing it a little earlier that you thought. That's all.'

'Donna isn't happy. She thinks I should just get another job. But it's not so easy. The market is flooded with guys ten years younger than me. All the guys my age are being laid off.'

'And setting up on their own,' Serena murmured. She imagined Donna's horror at the thought that she had accidentally traded down. Perhaps she thought that Tom would one day eclipse her husband, and now she realised that he wouldn't. Who was going to keep Donna in Pilates lessons for the rest of her life? Perhaps she was thinking, God forbid, that she might even have to get a job. No wonder she was making Tom's life a misery.

'I've been thinking about calling my company Phoenix. It speaks of rebirth and success, don't you think?'

'I think it speaks of middle-aged, unemployed banker taking a last shot at owning an Aston Martin.'

Tom managed a smile. 'You're right.' He downed half a glass of wine. 'I have fucked up, Serena. Everything I touched has turned to shit. Sitting here in this kitchen talking to you, with our daughter playing upstairs, feels so right. It's so comfortable. You understand me.'

I just don't expect anything of you, Serena thought.

'You wouldn't be barking at me every morning, asking me to produce a fucking spreadsheet showing how my job search is progressing. I swear when I signed on for Jobseeker's Allowance after college the woman at the job centre didn't ride my arse about it like Donna does.'

'The woman at the job centre probably didn't have a Pilates habit,' Serena smiled.

'I don't know what I'm doing with my life. I'm nudging fifty. I'm unemployed. I'm living with a woman who only ever looks at me now with disappointment in her eyes. What did I do, Serena? Why did I leave you? You were the best thing in my life.'

Serena shook her head ever so slightly.

'Why didn't you try harder to stop me?'

'Why didn't you try harder to stay?'

'I don't know. Because . . . because it was all getting so stifling,' he said. 'It was the same thing every day. I'd come home and find you covered in baby sick.'

'From *our* baby,' Serena pointed out.

'Come on,' said Tom. 'You have to admit that you weren't the woman I married.'

Serena reeled. But managed not to fight back. There was no point. She had long since let go of Tom Macdonald. And he was deep in his cups. He was slurring his words.

'Donna was so different,' he recalled. 'She paid attention to me.'

'Because she didn't have to pay attention to anything else. She paid people to do the worrying for her,' Serena said.

'Suddenly, it seemed like there was fun to be had again. You can't blame me. I was doing eleven hours a day at work. I was under incredible stress . . . But I got it wrong. I should have told you what was going through my head. I can see that now. Can you ever forgive me? Sit here, Serena. Sit next to me. I want to hold you. I want to come back to you. I want to work on our marriage.'

It had taken a long time, but now Serena knew that she was over Tom Macdonald. People had told her that this moment would come. That one day he would tell her that he had made a mistake and beg to be allowed to come back. Night after night she had dreamed of it. Longed to hear him say that he loved her. She imagined that she would hesitate for just a moment, to give him pause, before she threw herself into his arms and told him, yes, yes, he must never go away again.

But now the moment had arrived she felt quite differently.

'Tom,' she said. 'We don't have a marriage to work on anymore. We're divorced.'

Serena put him to bed in the spare room. Her ex-husband. She didn't want him any more. It was over. As was her career as a forger. She'd survived the end of her marriage and her involvement with Julian. She had a wonderful daughter, she had her health and her talent. She would work on original paintings. Make a name for herself in her own right. She would raise a happy daughter. It was time to move forward with no regrets, she told herself as Tom began snoring next door. No regrets. Especially not about Yasha . . .

Chapter Seventy-Two

ㄚASHA had been deadly serious when he said that he thought he and Serena should remain apart for her safety. But that didn't mean he didn't think about her. He thought about her often. He could picture her smiling face as she played with her daughter on the terrace in Italy. He could hear the soft sighs that escaped her mouth when they made love in his apartment in London.

He tried to put her out of his mind but eventually he knew that he had to see her. The Ricasoli was old news. Belanov had cashed his cheque. The new owner professed himself delighted. Perhaps it was safe for Yasha to make his move now. With the SIM card from Julian Trebarwen's phone safely in his possession, Yasha knew that there was no danger of any revelations unless Serena herself chose to make them. And Yasha longed to see her. He had something he desperately wanted to show her. He had a task ahead that would require her help.

He arrived on her doorstep just after Tom left with Katie for their holiday. He was carrying the accordion case in which he had secreted *The Virgin* for its trip to Italy all those months before.

Serena had been right. The painting of Ricasoli's *The Virgin Before The Annunciation* that sold through Ludbrook's was not the original but her own clever fake. However, the painting that had been submitted to a barrage of carbon dating tests was the original. Evgeny Belanov knew nothing of the switch. The oligarch had never even known that there was a painting to switch with his priceless chattel. As far as Belanov was concerned, Yasha and Leonid had spent the three weeks between the Virgin's purchase and her arrival on his yacht taking the scenic route across Europe. He knew nothing at all of the house in Tuscany and Serena.

'But you commissioned the painting for Belanov.' Serena was confused.

'I'm afraid I lied to you about that,' said Yasha. 'Your painting was always for me.'

'And Leonid? He was Belanov's man.'

'Leonid's nobody's man. And everybody's. The money I gave him to help me out was enough to convince his wife to give him one more chance.'

'And you trusted him to keep quiet?'

'After I saw the way he was around your daughter, yes. Besides, he has as much to lose as I do now.'

And so Yasha explained to Serena how he had bided his time, keeping her painting hidden away until the right moment came. He said he had always known that Belanov would not want to keep the Ricasoli for himself. Yasha's own upbringing made it easy for him to understand the richer man. It didn't matter that the Ricasoli Virgin was unique, one of a kind, priceless. Yasha knew that Belanov would eventually look at the painting, just fifteen inches square, and think he wanted more for his money. No matter how precious, one small painting would start to look like a very bad deal when Belanov could have a super-yacht or a dozen houses in its place.

'I knew he would sell it. So I made sure I advised him on the sale. For security and his privacy, I told him that the Ricasoli should be viewed in a bank vault. I took the original into the bank vault in my faithful accordion case, but it was your painting that went into the safe.'

'But why did you take the risk? Why were you involved in the first place?'

'Belanov was the only person standing between my brother and jail. The night the painting was sold, my brother was discovered in the animal hold of a 747 from Moscow. Hardly the safe first-class passage for him that my client promised as part of my commission for *The Virgin's* sale. Still, my brother lived. When the police turned up at my gallery that night, I was certain they would have far worse news.'

Serena listened in disbelief.

'So now the saga is almost complete. Belanov has exchanged what he thought was a real Ricasoli for nearly a hundred million pounds, which is what he really wanted in the first place. My brother is no longer in danger of spending the rest of his life in a Russian jail. And I still have the real Virgin.'

He tapped the accordion case.

'Would you care to come on a musical tour of Europe with me?' he asked Serena.

*   *   *

A week later, they were back in Italy, at a tiny church in a village near Naples.

The priest welcomed them warmly. Yasha had called ahead to let him know that they would be arriving, with a gift for the priest and his congregation. Like Robin Hood, Yasha had decided it was time to redistribute some wealth.

In the welcome coolness of the sacristy, Yasha opened the accordion case once more.

'It is a very good copy,' the priest nodded when he saw the painting. 'Thank you for offering it to us. I am very glad to accept. When I heard that *The Virgin* had been rediscovered, I prayed with all my heart that she might find her way back to us. This church has never quite forgiven itself for letting her go when times got hard in the eighteenth century. But times are still hard and not even the Vatican could have paid the price they wanted for her this time. A hundred million, you say?'

'Ninety-nine five hundred.'

'Silly money.'

Yasha and Serena murmured sympathetically.

'Still, there is something of the original's spirit here in your copy,' the priest continued. 'And I know that she will make people very happy indeed. Shall we put her back in her place?'

Yasha and Serena followed the priest to the tiny chapel off the main body of the church, where *The Virgin* had spent her early years. Yasha smiled to himself as the priest told them that the original had been slightly bigger. He really did have no idea that what he was holding was the real thing.

At last Serena saw how *The Virgin* was supposed to have looked. In the quiet light of the candles, the gold leaf that surrounded her head seemed to glow with an inner light of its own. There was a magic here that was lost when you saw the painting under the bright lights of a gallery.

'Thank you,' said the priest. 'For bringing our lady back to us. Would you like to stay for lunch, perhaps? There is enough for all.'

Yasha answered for them. 'That's very kind,' he said. 'But we have a plane to catch.'

Serena gave him a quizzical look. He explained once they were outside.

'I do not want to waste a single moment of my time with you with a priest sitting between us. There's a good restaurant in the village if you're hungry.'

'Not really,' said Serena.

'Then what shall we do?' Yasha asked.

'I'm sure we'll think of something. Do you think they'll let us into the hotel room yet?'

The room was plain but perfect, with its dark wood furniture and crisp white linen. Two single beds, placed decently far apart (Yasha had forgotten to ask for a 'letto matrimoniale'). Voile curtains fluttered at the windows. There was a small terrace that overlooked the sea, which was where Yasha joined Serena now. He put his arms around her waist and rested his chin on her shoulder.

'You can see Capri from here,' he told her.

'I've always wanted to go there,' said Serena.

'Scene of some very bad behaviour,' said Yasha. 'You know what Caligula did on that island? He had virgins shipped over there by the dozen to amuse himself and his friends.'

'Tell me more. What did he do with them?'

'Why don't you come inside and I'll show you?'

Serena laughed and let herself be led back into the cool dark bedroom, full of desire and delight as Yasha span stories about the erotic history of Italy from the Romans to the Renaissance. She had never known any man who could turn her on with knowledge.

But as Yasha peeled Serena's white dress from her warm and sticky body and she returned the favour and licked the salty sweat from his chest, neither of them knew just how closely they were reliving history. The narrow single bed on which they chose to express their love for one another stood in the exact spot where once there had been a screen to change behind. And as Serena cried out in her passion, giving herself up to her lover completely, her voice echoed the earlier passionate cries of an innocent village girl who had stepped behind that screen to be ruined by Giancarlo Ricasoli.

Chapter Seventy-Three

THE *Grand Cru* had another VIP on board. This one arrived quietly and in a casket.

Randon placed the little Ricasoli Virgin in the room that had once contained his erotic collection. *The Virgin* would be the perfect painting with which to begin the art collection for his new church, the construction of which would begin any day. The travertine marble was waiting to be transformed for the glory of God.

Randon crossed himself as he backed out of the room and began to operate the lock. But then he stopped. He reopened the door and went back in. The room was entirely empty but for *The Virgin* and one other familiar item. The inro . . .

Randon fingered the carved ivory. Carrie Klein had made a note of how the box opened and Randon referred to it now.

He tipped the mementos hidden inside out for one last inspection. In just a few days he would hand them over to the police. He had decided that the time had come. The builders for his masterpiece, his very own church of the rock, had been paid in advance. His lawyer was authorised to act in his absence. Randon sat very still in his sanctuary and considered the ordeals ahead. It would not be pleasant to spend the rest of his life in prison but right now an innocent man was suffering for his sins. Axel Delaflote had already spent more than five years in jail. Randon could not allow that man to continue to pay for his crimes.

Or could he?

Opening the inro one more time, he tipped Odette's heart-shaped pendant out into his palm. So shiny. Cheap as it was, he remembered how pretty it had looked as it rested in the perfect dent between her collar bones. He held a lock of hair in his other hand. This was her hair. The lightest of the three locks. The one with the bounciest curl. He pressed the hair against his mouth and relished the silkiness as it slid over his skin. And then he was back in that room, feeling her white flesh beneath his hands. His fingers closing around her throat. Deciding in the end to use her scarf to finish her off because those fingermarks might send him to jail.

'Please, please don't. I won't tell anybody,' Odette begged him across the years.

Suddenly, feeling one hundred per cent himself again for the first time since he came out of his coma, Mathieu Randon echoed her promise. 'I won't tell anybody either,' he smiled.

Poor old Axel Delaflote would have to stay in jail.

Randon instructed his Captain to sail on towards Capri.

Acknowledgements

I FEEL very lucky to be able to make my living as an author. Not only because I don't have to change out of my pyjamas to go to work but also because my job brings me into contact with so many wonderful people. For their advice and support with the business of writing *Priceless*, I'd like to thank:

John Tiller, Robert Brooks, Bella Bishop, Dillon Bryden, Adam Gahlin, Victoria Routledge, Serena Mackesy, Guy Hazel, M. Finkelkraut, Peter Dailey, Dr David Jordan, Dr Daron Burrows, James Waller, my agents Antony Harwood, Tony Gardner and James Macdonald Lockhart, copy-editor Justine Taylor, my editors Carolyn Mays and Kate Howard and the still lovely Nat Wilde, who is nothing like the character to whom he lends his name.

OLIVIA DARLING

Three women who dare to make it in a man's world.
One sparkling prize.

Madeleine Arsenault has prepared for this moment all her life. She is determined to rescue the beloved family chateau and prove she's got what it takes to run the most successful champagne house in France.

Former supermodel Christina Morgan knows she hasn't got what it takes. But she's sure as hell not going to show it. And with the help of her friends, she'll turn her ex-husband's hobby Californian vineyard into a major player.

Chambermaid Kelly Elson would rather drink vodka and coke than champagne. Then she inherits a vineyard and suddenly she's thirsty for success.

Watching over them all is Mathieu Randon. Super-rich. Seductive. And a sociopath.

Competing to produce the world's best sparkling wine, the three women are swept into a world of feuds, back-stabbing, sabotage and seduction. Have they got what it takes to survive?

Out now in Hodder paperback

HODDER